THE GARIES
AND THEIR FRIENDS

broadview editions
series editor: Martin R. Boyne

THE GARIES
AND THEIR FRIENDS

Frank J. Webb

edited by
William Huntting Howell and Megan Walsh

broadview editions

BROADVIEW PRESS – www.broadviewpress.com
Peterborough, Ontario, Canada

Founded in 1985, Broadview Press remains a wholly independent publishing house. Broadview's focus is on academic publishing; our titles are accessible to university and college students as well as scholars and general readers. With over 600 titles in print, Broadview has become a leading international publisher in the humanities, with world-wide distribution. Broadview is committed to environmentally responsible publishing and fair business practices.

The interior of this book is printed on 30% recycled paper.

© 2016 William Huntting Howell and Megan Walsh

Library and Archives Canada Cataloguing in Publication

Webb, Frank J., author
   The Garies and their friends / Frank J. Webb ; edited by William Huntting Howell and Megan Walsh.

(Broadview editions)
Includes bibliographical references.
ISBN 978-1-55481-151-9 (paperback)

   1. African American families—Fiction. 2. Racially mixed people—Fiction. 3. African Americans—Fiction. 4. Race relations—Fiction. 5. Domestic fiction. I. Walsh, Megan, editor II. Howell, William Huntting, editor III. Title. IV. Series: Broadview editions

PS3157.W62G37 2016   813'.3   C2016-900689-1

Broadview Editions
The Broadview Editions series is an effort to represent the ever-evolving canon of texts in the disciplines of literary studies, history, philosophy, and political theory. A distinguishing feature of the series is the inclusion of primary source documents contemporaneous with the work.

Advisory editor for this volume: Denis Johnston

Broadview Press handles its own distribution in North America
PO Box 1243, Peterborough, Ontario K9J 7H5, Canada
555 Riverwalk Parkway, Tonawanda, NY 14150, USA
Tel: (705) 743-8990; Fax: (705) 743-8353
email: customerservice@broadviewpress.com

Distribution is handled by Eurospan Group in the UK, Europe, Central Asia, Middle East, Africa, India, Southeast Asia, Central America, South America, and the Caribbean. Distribution is handled by Footprint Books in Australia and New Zealand.

Broadview Press acknowledges the financial support of the Government of Canada through the Canada Book Fund for our publishing activities.

Typesetting and assembly: True to Type Inc., Claremont, Canada
Cover Design: Lisa Brawn

PRINTED IN CANADA

Contents

List of Illustrations

Acknowledgements

We began working on this project because *The Garies and Their Friends* fundamentally changed the way we thought about the history of African-American writing and about the antebellum novel. Since our first encounter with the book, we have shared our enthusiasm for it with anyone who would listen; we are grateful that so many people have. We are delighted to be a part of bringing Webb's novel back into print in an edition designed to reach the greatest number of readers.

Several institutions helped to make this project possible. First, we would like to thank the McNeil Center for Early American Studies at the University of Pennsylvania for providing a space for collaborations like this one to germinate. We are also grateful to the staff at the Library Company of Philadelphia and to our colleagues and students at St. Bonaventure University and Boston University. We have received support from our home institutions in the form of a Faculty Research Grant from St. Bonaventure and funding from the Boston University Center for the Humanities. A Northeast Modern Language Association Fellowship at the American Antiquarian Society and a Lillian Gary Taylor Fellowship at the Mary and David Harrison Institute and the Small Special Collections Library at the University of Virginia afforded us critical access to materials related to *The Garies*; the immense generosity of the librarians and staff members at these institutions helped us to make the most of it.

We are also grateful to the editors of earlier editions of *The Garies* and to the anonymous readers at Broadview Press.

Introduction

Frank J. Webb's *The Garies and Their Friends* (1857) is the second published novel to have been written by an African American.[1] It tells the story of two families—one from the south, one from the north; one multi-racial, one black—as they work to establish a stable place in the complex and unequal social world of the mid-nineteenth-century United States. The narrative opens in the plantation south, near Savannah, Georgia, sometime in the 1830s. Clarence Garie, a white plantation owner, Emily Garie—a woman whom Clarence considers to be his wife but whom the state (and the majority of Clarence's relatives) holds to be his slave—and their two children host a dinner for a friend recently returned from the north. The food is delightful and the atmosphere convivial, but the "peculiar Construction" (p. 43) of the family means that there is also tension in the air. Their guest's stories about the relative freedoms, opportunities, and legal rights afforded to non-white persons in the north highlight the difficulties of the Garies' own situation in the eyes of southern law and custom. Because Emily is black and is Clarence's property as well as his partner, the Garies are excluded from the polite society that their economic situation might otherwise attract; they may have "visitors," as Emily puts it, but they can have no "friends" in Savannah.

Most pointedly, because the Garies' marriage is not recognized by the state, the Garie children have no legal standing. Little Clary and Em cannot attend school, will not inherit their father's property, and could be sold to settle debts should the need arise; they may show "no trace whatever of African origin" (p. 44), but they are nonetheless subject to the white supremacist dictates of racialized servitude. The next day, Emily reveals that she is pregnant. She begs Clarence to consider emigration to Europe, or at least to a free state: "It will kill me to have another child born here! its infant smiles would only be a reproach to me. Oh! ... it is a fearful thing to give birth to an inheritor of chains" (p. 88). After much consideration, Garie agrees to move to Pennsylvania, one of the few northern states that did not explicitly prohibit interracial marriage.

The laws of Pennsylvania may be different from those of Georgia, but racism in Webb's America is structurally pervasive: one of the most important lessons of the novel is that the north-

---

1 The first was William Wells Brown's *Clotel* (1853); see below, p. 20.

ern drawing-room can illustrate the deleterious effects of prejudice just as vividly as the fields of the plantation or the stalls of the slave market. As new residents of Philadelphia, the Garies are regularly confronted by the attitudes that they had hoped to leave behind. In one early example, their neighbor, the white Mrs. Stevens, openly discusses her contempt for black people during an evening visit to the Garies' house. When a servant brings a lamp, Mrs. Stevens is shocked and embarrassed to discover Emily's skin color and beats a hasty retreat back to her own home. The reversal is striking: Emily Garie belongs in this genteel parlor, but Mrs. Stevens does not. The latter's claims of white supremacy become evidence of her own baseness: the anger and disgust Mrs. Stevens subsequently manifests simultaneously reveal the ugly side of bourgeois politeness and mark *her* as the real outlier to gentility. Even so, there is no real victory for the Garies: young Clary happens to overhear Mrs. Stevens's disdainful report to her husband about the visit. Although his initial response is righteous indignation, Clary is soon overwhelmed by an all-consuming (and family-threatening) grief: "It was his custom ... to go and pour out his troubles on the breast of his mother; but he instinctively shrunk from confiding this to her; for, child as he was, he knew it would make her very unhappy. He therefore gently stole into the house, crept quietly up to his room, lay down, and sobbed himself to sleep" (p. 153).

Responses to the endemic problem of racism—both psychological and practical, implicit and explicit—animate the rest of the narrative. As Clary grows up, he is encouraged by adult advisers to repudiate his own racial heritage and "pass" as white. Although the trope is sometimes considered to have emerged in twentieth-century fiction, the question of passing is vital to *The Garies'* mixed-race characters: Clary's assumption of a white identity reveals the difficult choices that some black Americans made, as well as the sometimes disastrous consequences that resulted from those decisions.[1] At one point in the novel, one character advises another of

---

1 Webb never uses "passing" as a stand-alone term, instead writing "passing for white" (p. 79). Nevertheless, *The Garies* lays some of the groundwork for the twentieth-century concept of "passing," which the *OED* defines as "To be accepted as or believed to be, or to represent oneself successfully as, a member of an ethnic or religious group other than one's own, esp. one having higher social status; *spec.* (of a person of black ancestry in a racially segregated society) to be accepted as white." The term appeared famously in print as the title of African-American writer Nella Larsen's novel *Passing* (1929).

passing's dangers: "Either you must live exclusively amongst coloured people, or go to the whites and remain with them. But to do the latter, you must bear in mind that it must never be known that you have a drop of African blood in your veins, or you would be shunned as if you were a pestilence; no matter how fair in complexion or how white you may be" (p. 79). Clary spurns his black family and friends, but he is ultimately rejected by white society; he suffers terribly as a result of his decision. His sister Em, on the other hand, chooses not to pass but to identify with the black community; she grows up in prosperity and happiness. While many nineteenth-century novels represent mixed-race characters as the inevitable victims of tragic endings, *The Garies* embraces an alternative outcome in Em. In both cases, Webb's mixed-race characters are agents with complicated motives and complex responses, not simply at the mercy of fate. They have the potential to shape their own life choices, and not merely to confirm cultural truisms or to inhabit identities imposed upon them by others.

The other family in *The Garies*—the *Friends* of the novel's title—are the Ellises. Mr. Ellis is a carpenter; his wife keeps house and works as a seamstress. They have three children—daughters Esther and Caroline (nicknamed Caddy) and son Charlie—and they own a house in a relatively quiet part of Philadelphia. The novel devotes considerable space to the routines of the Ellises' black middle-class domestic life, including Mr. Ellis's carpentry business and the household tasks of Mrs. Ellis and her daughters. The girls' interactions are precisely the stuff of mid-nineteenth-century white domestic fiction, in which the preparation of meals, the cleaning of dishes, and the scouring of floors serve as occasions to express ideas and moral opinions—and in which the dignity and psychological depth of everyday labor are alternately affirmed and critiqued. Charlie's hijinks—especially with his friend Kinch—along with his attempts to go to school and to find a job that suits his personality invite readers to see *The Garies* as a *Bildungsroman*, a type of novel in which the protagonist learns life lessons on the path from childhood to young adulthood. On the whole, the Ellis experience touches every corner of the nineteenth-century novel, from heartwarming romance to workplace drama, from daring adventure to comedy of manners. That they happen to be a black family participating in the rituals of civility, domestic respectability, and everyday urban life imagined by racist ideology to be beyond the capacities of black people suggests one of Webb's central claims: the Ellises stand for the possibility of a shared humanity beyond the markers of racial difference. Or, as Samuel Otter has argued, the "novels of domesticity, sensation, and reform converge" in *The Garies*, a narrative in which "the most insulated spaces and humble particulars are shown to bear the weight of history" (244).

In offering up this portrait of urban, middle-class black domesticity, *The Garies* may be said to align with that broad category of texts that Amanda Claybaugh has identified as the Victorian "novel of purpose": it not only tells a vivid story, but also offers a clear and damning indictment of a social problem (7). In this case, the problem is American racism—the "crying vice of the free states" that correlates all too well with the horrors of Southern slavery (see Appendix A2, p. 371). The basic assumptions of *The Garies*—that black gentility exists, that slavery is a moral and legal catastrophe, and that racial identifications may themselves be fluid or mutable over time and space—extended existing arguments made by black activists. Whereas famous writers such as Frederick Douglass (1818–95) and Richard Allen (1760–1831) had agitated for the equal legal treatment of black people years before Webb was writing,[1] *The Garies* renders many of their core arguments concrete, intimate, and readily accessible in narrative form. Indeed, the novel's reformatory goals come to light precisely *because* it is a conventional narrative about middle-class culture and values: to tell a story about the complex psychological (or existential) problems that inform black experience is to refute paternalist arguments about black emotional and intellectual "simplicity" and (at least potentially) to offer an emerging black middle class a validating portrait of itself.

Black Philadelphia, Mob Violence, and the Question of History

In Philadelphia in the 1830s and 1840s, the setting for most of the novel, free black people formed an economically and cultur-

---

1   See for example Frederick Douglass, *Oration Delivered in Corinthian Hall, Rochester* (Rochester, NY: Lee, Mann, and Co., 1852); *Narrative of the Life of Frederick Douglass, an American Slave* (Boston: Anti-Slavery Office, 1845); and *My Bondage and My Freedom. Part I. Life as a Slave. Part II. Life as a Freeman* (New York: Miller, Orton & Mulligan, 1855); and Richard Allen, *The Life, Experience, and Gospel Labours of the Rt. Rev. Richard Allen. To Which is Annexed the Rise and Progress of the African Methodist Episcopal Church in the United States of America. Containing a Narrative of the Yellow Fever in the Year of Our Lord 1793: With an Address to the People of Colour in the United States* (Philadelphia: Martin & Boden, 1833).

ally diverse community that shaped nearly all aspects of the city's civic life. They lived mostly in dense neighborhoods beyond the city center, and in unincorporated areas such as Southwark, Moyamensing, Kensington, and Northern Liberties (see map, Appendix C1), but they circulated everywhere. Some were poor and tradeless, having come to the city from slavery. Even those born in the city and trained in skilled occupations often found themselves pushed to the margins in a society where black people had trouble securing permanent work. There were also, however, increasingly robust black middle and upper classes: men such as political activist Robert Purvis (1810–98), inventor and sailmaker James Forten (1766–1842), and barber and money-lender Joseph Cassey (1789–1848) wielded considerable power in the community. Like Mr. Walters in Webb's novel, who proudly displays a large portrait of the Haitian revolutionary leader Toussaint L'Ouverture[1] in full military dress, many of these black businessmen actively argued that the broader culture should acknowledge their financial and civic contributions. (Purvis, for instance, protested the loss of black male suffrage in Pennsylvania in his 1838 pamphlet, *Appeal of Forty Thousand Citizens, Threatened with Disenfranchisement*; see Appendix C3.)

The very existence of a rising black bourgeoisie and its institutional and material accompaniments affronted advocates of white supremacist ideology. As it became clear that "wealth" and "culture" were not universally or necessarily reserved for white people, detractors of the black middle classes became even more vocal. Edward Williams Clay's *Life in Philadelphia* engravings series (1828–30), for example, viciously satirized black assertions of social equality. One of these images, designed to convey the presumed absurdity of the notion of black refinement, depicts a woman in genteel dress sweating profusely on a hot summer day: "I think I aspire too much," she says (see Appendix B6, p. 391). Racist cartoons like these echoed the sentiments of white writers who cast the continuation of white dominance as fundamental to the national project. John F. Denny, for example, wrote in 1836 of

---

1   François-Dominique Toussaint L'Ouverture (1743–1803) was a key figure in the uprising of the black slaves of Saint-Domingue against their French Colonial rulers, which resulted in the end of slavery there and the creation of the Republic of Haiti. A renowned military strategist and charismatic leader, L'Ouverture was often compared to the dynamic French emperor Napoleon Bonaparte (1769–1821). After being betrayed by supporters, L'Ouverture was arrested and died in prison in France.

"repulsive notions of [racial] equality ... [that] may well be fitted to effect the purposes of foreign incendiaries, whose aim is to unsettle the principles of our social order; or to reign in the meridian of Hayti, where they are habitually realized among a mixed and licentious population; but they have nothing germane to the habitudes of the American people" (see Appendix B3, p. 386).

Inspired by economic uncertainty and widespread fears of organized black insurrections like those led by Denmark Vesey (1767–1822) and Nat Turner (1800–31)[1]—not to mention texts like Clay's and Denny's—waves of white-led violence spread through Philadelphia (and other cities) in the 1830s and 1840s (see Appendix D). Such riots ravaged black neighborhoods, where churches and other places of community assembly were often singled out for attack. The most infamous mob violence in Philadelphia was the burning of Pennsylvania Hall on 17 May 1838. Completed only three days earlier, the building was meant as a meeting place for groups such as the Pennsylvania Anti-Slavery Society. Like other assaults on the black community and the revocation of black male suffrage in Pennsylvania earlier that same year, the burning of Pennsylvania Hall was directed locally, but it was also part of a broader national backlash against the anti-slavery movement. Origin stories for these crowd actions proliferated in newspapers and in polemical tracts: abolitionists (i.e., activists favoring the abolition of slavery) speculated that the attacks had been engineered by interested southerners who had drummed up violence among the city's disaffected white population while pro-slavery writers deemed them spontaneous products of grassroots resistance. Four years later, another riot motivated by racism rocked the city. On 1 August 1842, an Irish Catholic mob attacked a large parade held by the black Young Men's Vigilant Association commemorating the eighth anniversary of the end of slavery in the British West Indies. Over the next three days, rioters looted and burned countless homes and businesses with little intervention from the Philadelphia police force.

---

1   A free carpenter and co-founder of the African Methodist Episcopal Church in Charleston, South Carolina, Vesey was tried and convicted of planning a slave revolt in the city in 1822. He was executed, even though his plans never came to fruition. By contrast, Turner led a violent uprising with somewhat more success just over a decade later. Turner and his followers killed more than 50 white people in Southampton County, Virginia, in August 1831. In retaliation, over 100 black people were killed, either executed for their role in the uprising by the state or attacked by vigilante militias.

Webb's novel focuses intensely on how black Philadelphia came to be understood through the national attention that the riots generated, yet it frames this unrest much differently than the popular press did. Where newspapers tended to attribute this violence to broad cultural antipathy between blacks and whites, *The Garies* suggests that interested, malevolent individuals might be at fault instead. In Webb's riots, the evil white lawyer Stevens ("Slippery George") exploits racist attitudes and engineers mob actions in very particular ways for his own material gain. He makes a list of targets and blackmails one of his criminal clients into putting together a band of working-class white Philadelphians to carry out the attacks. This mob destroys multiple houses to cover up the fact that they have been tasked with terrorizing and murdering specific people. When Stevens's henchman McCloskey has a change of heart at the critical moment, Stevens himself steps in to carry out the novel's most atrocious attack. In other words, though many are complicit, the abiding cause of all this horror and violence is a single malevolent actor; by focusing on his motivations, Webb's narrative puts forward a rather more optimistic view of the riots than the traditional pro- or anti-slavery parties had done. Because these murderous acts are neither organic to the culture nor generic to the white population but rather the product of one monstrous man, there is something like hope for the future on offer. The structural inequalities of America may be real and terrible, but they may also be mutable; if white-on-black violence is rooted more in the contingencies of greed than in a natural and irremediable racial hostility, things might be better down the line.

Biographical Contexts

Frank J. Webb was the last of five children born into a middle-class free black Philadelphian family in the spring of 1828. His father, Francis Webb (1788–1829), was an official in the African Episcopal Church. His mother, Louisa Burr Webb (c. 1785–1878), was the illegitimate daughter of Aaron Burr (the vice president of the United States from 1801 to 1805) and one of the Burr family servants, probably either Eugenie Beauharnais or Mary Emmons. For much of her adult life Louisa Burr Webb worked as a servant, largely as a nurse, in the household of Elizabeth Powel Francis Fisher, a member of Philadelphia's merchant elite. Neither Francis Webb's position in the church nor Louisa Burr Webb's status as servant prevented them from staking political claims: like many middling and prosperous black families in antebellum Philadelphia, the Webbs were active in various causes promoting racial uplift. From 1824 to 1826, for example, Webb's parents had been a part of a failed colonization venture for American free blacks in Haiti; after returning to the US, Francis Webb served as the Philadelphia distributor for the black abolitionist weekly newspaper *Freedom's Journal*.

Francis Webb died when Frank was a toddler. Louisa Burr Webb remarried not long after, and the family remained solvent enough to send Frank and his surviving siblings to school and to prepare them for middle-class lives. In 1845, at seventeen, Webb married a fellow person of color, Mary Espartero. About the early part of Webb's married life, we know relatively little. Philadelphia city directories for 1850 through 1854 list him alternatively as the operator of a clothing store and as a designer for the commercial printing trade.[1] Webb himself claims to have been a "failure in business."[2] He presented a speech on "The Martial Capacity of Blacks" in 1854 at the Banneker Institute, an organization and library dedicated to the intellectual growth of Philadelphia's black community, but otherwise he seems to have kept out of the public spotlight.[3] Mary, on the other hand, had begun a promising career as a performer and elocutionist. She made her debut in Philadelphia on 19 April 1855 and soon became something of a lecture-circuit celebrity. Frank assumed the role of stage manager and occasional scene-partner as Mary toured the northern United States, performing monologues from Shakespeare, short stories by E.D.E.N. Southworth (1819–99), and poems such as Henry Wadsworth Longfellow's "The Song of Hiawatha" (1855)—this last while wearing Native-American-style dress.

The Webbs left the US in 1856 for an eighteen-month trip to England. Mary toured the country giving readings; Frank, who managed the logistics of Mary's tour and periodically accompanied her on stage, began writing *The Garies*. The American novelist and abolitionist Harriet Beecher Stowe (1811–96) was an important catalyst for both of these projects. In one of the several letters of introduction that she wrote for the Webbs, Stowe claimed that she felt "the deepest interest in [Mary's] success," and added that Frank was "a gentleman of talent and cultivation" (Appendix C5, p. 400). (Mary's most noteworthy performances

---

1 See P.S. Lapsansky 35; Crockett, "*The Garies*" 18.
2 Webb, "Biographical Sketch" ii.
3 For a fuller account of Webb's biography, see Gardner, "'A Gentleman,'" and Maillard.

were of a shortened and dramatized version of Stowe's anti-slavery novel *Uncle Tom's Cabin* [1852] titled *The Christian Slave*, which Stowe had written expressly for her to deliver.) Over the course of their visit to England, the Webbs met numerous leaders in London's anti-slavery and literary circles, including Lord Henry Brougham (1778–1868) and John Cropper (1797–1876).

As the tour progressed, Mary developed respiratory problems. The Webbs spent the winter of 1857–58 in Cannes, hoping to take advantage of a change of climate, and then returned to Philadelphia briefly in March 1858. Ultimately, though, they relocated to Jamaica, where they had leveraged an acquaintance with George Campbell, 8th Duke of Argyll (Postmaster General of the UK from 1855 to 1858) into a £200-per-year appointment in the Kingston Post Office for Frank.[1] Mary continued to give performances, but her health declined precipitously. She died of tuberculosis on 17 June 1859. The pair had no children.

Frank Webb remained in Jamaica for ten years, marrying Mary Rosabelle Rodgers (b. 1845), the daughter of a Jamaican merchant, in December 1864. Webb and his second wife had six children, four born in Jamaica and another two born in the United States: Frank (1865–1901), Evangeline (1866–1945), Ruth (1867–1930), Clarice (1869–1962), Ethelynd (1874–1969), and Thomas R. (1877–1964). In 1869, Webb moved for a short time to Washington, DC; it is not clear if his second wife and their children were with him. On his return to the US, he was surprised at how much had changed during his time overseas. "The last time I was in Washington," he wrote to his friend Robert Morris, "I walked out at night in fear and trembling lest some watchful guardian of the public peace should lock me up—a black man from the north, loose in Washington, in those days, being considered a highly dangerous thing. Now, were I arrested, the chances are that I might fall into the hands of a black policeman[!]"[2]

Webb lived in Washington for a year, taking classes at Howard University Law School and working for the Freedmen's Bureau, a federal agency that aided impoverished former slaves in the decades following the Civil War. He also began contributing to *The New Era*, an African-American weekly newspaper edited by J. Sella Martin (1832–76) and, later, by Frederick Douglass. Webb's *New Era* writings include poetry ("None Spoke a Word to Me" and "Waiting"), essays ("International Exhibition," "The Mixed School Question,"

---

1   *Literary Gazette* (London), 6 May 1858.
2   Frank J. Webb to Robert Morris, 29 November 1869, *Papers of Robert Morris*, Boston Athenaeum.

and "An Old Foe with a New Face"), and two novellas.[1] Although there is some evidence that he might have written at least part of another one, no novel by Webb besides *The Garies* was ever published. After living in Washington for a short time, Webb moved with his family to southeast Texas, where he spent the remaining 23 years of his life. He continued his journalistic pursuits, founding a newspaper for the black community (the *Galveston Republican*) in late 1870. When the paper folded, he found a job clerking in the Galveston post office. In 1881, he began work as a teacher and administrator at the Barnes Institute School for African-American children. He died in Galveston on 7 May 1894.

Publication History

The Garies first appeared in the fall of 1857 in England. It was issued as part of George Routledge & Co.'s "Cheap Series," a richly varied line of inexpensively manufactured books marketed to mass audiences. (Other books in the Routledge Cheap Series appearing in 1857 included James Fenimore Cooper's *Precaution*, Alexandre Dumas's *The Vicomte de Bragelonne*, and Anna Maria Hall's *The Lucky Penny*.) Although Webb retained the US copyright, he left no evidence that he ever sought a US publisher. (Given the prejudices against black Americans in the 1850s it is not likely that one would have taken on his novel. At the time Webb was writing, William Wells Brown's *Clotel: Or, The President's Daughter* was the only other published novel by a black American in existence; it too had a London imprint.[2]) Routledge may have been suggested to Webb by Stowe or another supporter, since Webb only completed the novel once he and his wife were already in England for her oratory tour.

Like the volumes in Routledge's more famous "Railway Library," which they closely resemble, Cheap Series imprints were small (octavo; approximately 16.5 cm tall) and bound in brightly colored paper-wrapped boards. The front board of *The Garies* features an image printed with minimal coloring on a yellow ground (below, p. 31). It is both sentimental and lurid: depicting the pastoral pleasures of a family picnic in the foreground and the threat of whips and chains in the margins, the

---

1 These writings are collected in Webb's *Fiction, Essays, and Poetry*.

2 William Wells Brown, *Clotel: Or, The President's Daughter* (London: Partridge & Oakley, 1853). See the recent edition in the Broadview Editions series, edited by Geoffrey Sanborn (Peterborough, ON: Broadview, 2016).

cover frames the narrative for the widest possible readership. *The Garies* was priced like the other books in the Cheap Series, selling for a shilling and sixpence (about £6 or $10 in today's money). A few weeks later Routledge also brought forth a cloth-bound "Library" version of the text—on slightly larger and higher quality paper, differently typeset, and including a table of contents—for 3 shillings (about £12 or $20 in today's money).[1] This practice of issuing two different editions at two different price points was not especially uncommon for the firm, and it likely reflects Routledge's interest in capturing both popular and middle-brow market segments.

George Routledge (1812–88) enjoyed great success publishing American books for the London trade in the 1850s. Like other English publishers, he had done especially well with Stowe's *Uncle Tom's Cabin*, though works by Nathaniel Hawthorne (1804–64) and Washington Irving (1783–1859) were also steady sellers. That said, he was not afraid of working with first-time authors. Routledge must have thought especially highly of *The Garies*'s prospects: he paid Webb £75 (the equivalent of nearly $10,000 today) for the English copyright—considerably more than he paid most of his other authors. Routledge also included riders in the contract to the effect that his firm would pay Webb as much as an additional £50 if more than 20,000 copies of the book were printed. Routledge's further investment was considerable: the firm spent almost £300 to produce the inexpensive board-bound edition, of which 12,000 copies were printed, and nearly £200 to manufacture the clothbound edition, of which 2,000 copies were produced.

Despite breathless advertising claims about "demand having exhausted"[2] the first edition of the book, sales of Webb's novel did not match Routledge's hopes. After the initial marketing campaign died down, the firm ordered no more copies, and *The Garies* appeared in later Routledge catalogues (up through the 1870s) at discount prices. A German translation of the novel appeared as a three-volume novel in 1859, but it does not seem to have sold especially well either, since only one edition was printed.[3] The novel remained in relative obscurity until the twen-

---

1 Advertisement, *Leader and Saturday Analyst* (London), 3 October 1857.
2 Advertisement, *Athenaeum* (London), 12 September 1857.
3 Frank J. Webb, *Die Garies und ihre Freunde*, 3 vols. (Leipzig: Christian Ernst Kollmann, 1859). Kollmann published the novel as part of his *"Amerikanische Bibliotek"* series, which also included the work of pro-slavery southerner William Gilmore Simms (1806–70).

tieth century, when it was returned to print in a 1969 facsimile edition by Arno Press and the *New York Times* as part of the "American Negro: His History and Literature" paperback series. Johns Hopkins University Press printed another facsimile edition in 1997, and in 2004 Toby Press published the novel in a collection of Webb's writing. Although it is difficult to know how many readers *The Garies* had in the US in its own day, these new editions suggest that it has become far more popular among modern readers.

Critical Reception

When *The Garies* was first reviewed in British newspapers and literary journals, some critics were keen to draw connections with the most popular contemporary British fiction. The London *Daily News*, for example, argued that Webb had "evidently been a careful reader of Dickens and Thackeray" (Appendix A5, p. 375).[1] For better and for worse, however, most reviews of *The Garies* focused more pointedly on Webb's race than on the novel that he wrote. For the *Daily News*, Webb's blackness was a mark in the book's favor, as the structural inequality of the US made Webb's novelistic feat even more impressive: "we ... acknowledge that [*The Garies*] would be on the whole, good and pleasant reading, coming from any one. How much greater, then, must be its merit, as the production of one whose father would perhaps have been tarred and feathered if he had dared to take a pen in his hand, or even to learn his alphabet?" (p. 376). The London *Literary Gazette* called Webb a "very remarkable specimen of a free coloured man" but was less sanguine about the novel itself. According to this reviewer, Webb had produced "in some respects a clever book, and certainly, considering its origin and its subject, a curious book. The case is singular, almost as singular as that of Touissant [*sic*] L'Ouverture; and if it prove anything at all in reference to the race of free negroes in the northern States, it proves that, whatever capacity they may possess, literature is not one of the channels in which it works" (Appendix A2, p. 371). The London *Examiner* said more or less the same thing: the novel was "more remarkable for the earnestness and good feeling with which" it had "been written than for literary merit."[2]

---

1 See below, p. 375, note 2.
2 *Examiner* (London), 10 October 1857.

In the bulk of the British reviews, the most important literary point of comparison for *The Garies* was *Uncle Tom's Cabin*, which had been as big a hit in England as it had been in the US. Routledge's own advertising copy touted Webb's novel as an "Uncle Tom Book." Yet some readers understood *The Garies* as a much richer portrayal of black American life than Stowe had attempted. The London *Literary Gazette* noted that the "dramatic power displayed in the story is not so vivid or intense as that of 'Uncle Tom,' and the delineation of character is not so subtle. But it is truer in all essential particulars to the instincts of African blood, and the habits of the mixed African race; and taking into account the circumstances under which it was produced, it is a much more remarkable book" (Appendix A2, p. 372). More significantly, perhaps, for this reviewer, with respect to *Uncle Tom's Cabin*, *The Garies* "conveys a more just and practical moral. It is different from all other slave stories in the ground it occupies, and the lesson it enforces. Other slave stories are addressed to the evils of American slavery; this story is addressed to the most monstrous and glaring evil of American liberty. Other writers have depicted the vices of the slave states; Mr. Webb, with great reason, and more likelihood of success, exposes the crying vice of the free states" (p. 371). Northern racism, in other words, is a corollary to Southern slavery; liberty is as much under threat in the parts of the country where it theoretically exists as in those parts of the country where it does not. While Stowe may mount an indictment of the slave system, for this reviewer Webb makes clearer just how poisonous the underlying ideology of white supremacy behind it could be.

Although *The Garies* was rarely discussed in nineteenth-century periodicals after its initial publication, a year later an anonymous writer in the progressive *Edinburgh Review* turned to the novel in the context of a larger political essay about the slave trade:

> Those who have read Mr. Webbe's tale, "The Garies and their Friends," will be less surprised than others at some recent movements of the free negroes of the United States. Persons of any complexion who, like the personages in Mr. Webbe's book, are in the possession of houses, shipping, stores, funded property, and other forms of wealth, are likely to have an intelligence and a will of their own as to where and how they will live, and what they will do. A race, however depressed, which produced clergy, physicians, lawyers, professors, and artists,

will be pretty well able to hold a practical citizenship though the judges decide that men of colour cannot register coasting-vessels, or purchase a land-title; and even though the Supreme Court declares that "the black man has no rights which the white man is bound to respect." In spite of all such dispiriting influences, the free negroes are assuming a social position which points significantly to an approaching annihilation of the slave-trade, while it settles the fate of Liberia and its adjuncts. For some time past we have observed signs of a determination on the part of leading free negroes to raise their class above that doom of mere menial labour to which their countrymen have hitherto consigned them. They will not henceforth be only barbers and porters, and hotel-waiters and hack-drivers, and hangers-on, where there is dirty work to be done.[1]

Treating Webb's novel as though it were a non-fiction account of Philadelphia's black bourgeoisie, this writer cites the ownership of property and businesses as definitive proof of "intelligence" and "will," conditions necessary for "practical citizenship" even in the face of white supremacist laws. Not only are the lives of the fictional characters in *The Garies* an argument against the slave trade, but they also, and more significantly, suggest that systematic racial and economic inequality has an expiration date.

This sentiment is echoed in the only critical notice of Webb's novel to appear in America in the nineteenth century—a reprint on the front page of *Frederick Douglass' Paper* of the London *Daily News* review mentioned above. In this American context, the British reviewer's rhetorical questions become even more pressing: "are the negroes capable of freedom, self-government, and progress?" The answer, as it appeared on both sides of the Atlantic, was unequivocal: "To affect a doubt upon this matter is simply 'bosh.' Whoever heard of a dominant race that would admit of the presence of the governing faculty in those whom they oppressed?" (Appendix A5, p. 376). For this reviewer, black Americans not only deserved rights; any debate about whether they deserved those rights simply confirmed the absurd (if not unexpected) premises of white supremacy.

More recently, *The Garies* has been resurrected from obscurity as part of scholarly efforts to expand African-American literary history. Its first American edition in 1969 was part of a large-scale labor to bring forgotten black authors back into print. *The*

---

1 "The Slave-trade in 1858," *Edinburgh Review*, October 1858.

Garies's status as one of the earliest African-American novels, however, has not insulated it from criticism: initial twentieth-century responses to the novel were generally disappointed in its portrayal of black life. Many scholars insisted that Webb portrayed characters who, as James Kinney writes, would "prefer to be white" (93), while others, such as Bernard W. Bell, argued that the novel completely ignores the issue of slavery.[1] In his introduction to the 1969 edition, Arthur P. Davis not only commented on the relative invisibility of slavery in the novel, but also noted its "highly contrived plot" and "purple patches" (viii).

Since 2000, by contrast, scholars have read the novel not as a repudiation of abolitionist politics, but instead as a nuanced look at free black life that inherently condemns slavery by virtue of its topic. An enigmatic historical figure, Webb has inspired a number of critics to pursue biographical readings of his work, particularly with respect to his (and his wife's) time in England and their relationship to the transatlantic anti-slavery movement.[2] Others have extended existing discussions of nineteenth-century African-American literature by turning to Webb's portrayal of everyday life, particularly his treatment of gendered identity roles and the institution of marriage.[3] There has also been a good deal of work that positions *The Garies* as a rich response to the violence and racism that marked Webb's Philadelphia.[4] All of this recent scholarship suggests not only that *The Garies* is a remarkable book, but also that it can be remarkably helpful in terms of re-evaluating long-held assumptions about African-American writing in the nineteenth century. Indeed, by presenting the complex social worlds and intricate personal lives of black and mixed-race people in the context of their efforts to secure equality and justice in a frankly racist culture, one of *The Garies*'s most compelling arguments is that the genre of the middlebrow novel itself has an important role in the ongoing struggle against white supremacy.

---

1 Bell notes, "we do not find a direct attack on slavery anywhere" (42) in
   The Garies.
2 See Gardner, "Frank J. Webb," "'A Gentleman,'" and "'A Nobler End'";
   Korobkin; and Maillard.
3 For examples of this approach, see Chakkalakal; duCille; Duane; Reid-
   Pharr, *Conjugal Union* and "Introduction"; and Stockton.
4 On Webb's relationship to Philadelphia, see Borgstrom; Engle; Kohl;
   Levine; Nyong'o; Otter; and Rael.

Frank J. Webb: A Brief Chronology

1828	Francis (Frank) Johnson Webb born in Philadelphia on 21 March to Francis and Louisa (Burr) Webb.
1829	His father Francis Webb dies in July.
1845	Marries Mary Espartero.
1851	Frank and Mary Webb listed in *McElroy's Philadelphia Directory* as "designer" and "trimmer," respectively, in a clothing shop at 120 N. 9th Street.
1854	Presents "The Martial Capacity of Blacks" at the Banneker Institute in Philadelphia.
1856–57	Webbs live in London while Mary performs dramatic readings, including *The Christian Slave*, an adaptation of Harriet Beecher Stowe's *Uncle Tom's Cabin*.
1857	*The Garies and Their Friends* published in London by George Routledge & Co.
1857–58	Webbs make extended visit to Cannes for Mary's ailing health.
1858	In early March, Webbs return from Europe and visit Philadelphia. In late March, Webbs move to Kingston, Jamaica. Frank appointed to Kingston Post Office; Mary continues to perform dramatic readings.
1859	Mary dies on 17 June, perhaps from tuberculosis.
1864	In December, Webb marries Mary Rosabelle Rodgers in Kingston.
1869–70	Webb and his new family move to Washington, DC. Poems, articles, and two short novellas appear in *The New Era*.
1870	Webb and his family relocate to Galveston, Texas. Webb circulates prospectus and solicits subscriptions for *Galveston Republican*, a partisan newspaper aimed at Galveston's black population.
1881–94	Serves as principal of Barnes Institute, a public school for black students in Galveston.
1894	Dies in Galveston on 7 May.

A Note on the Text

The text that follows is from the "Cheap Series" edition of *The Garies and Their Friends* published by George Routledge & Co. in London in 1857. Because it was less expensive than the cloth-bound edition published a few weeks later, this text was likely the more widely read of the two nineteenth-century editions. We have preserved its original formatting as much as possible, retaining inconsistencies in spelling and punctuation. Obvious typographical errors have been silently corrected.

"Cheap Series" cover image for *The Garies and Their Friends* (1857). Courtesy the Bodleian Library, University of Oxford. (OC) 249 u. 258.

THE GARIES

AND

THEIR FRIENDS.

BY

FRANK J. WEBB.

With an Introductory Preface by

MRS. HARRIET B. STOWE,

AUTHOR OF "UNCLE TOM'S CABIN."

LONDON:
G. ROUTLEDGE & CO. FARRINGDON STREET;
NEW YORK: 18, BEEKMAN STREET.

1857.

Title page from *The Garies and Their Friends* (1857). Courtesy Albert and Shirley Small Special Collections Library, University of Virginia.

TO THE

LADY NOEL BYRON[1]

THIS BOOK

IS, BY HER KIND PERMISSION,

MOST AFFECTIONATELY INSCRIBED,

WITH PROFOUND RESPECT,

BY HER GRATEFUL FRIEND,

THE AUTHOR.

---

1   Anne Isabella Noel Byron (1792–1860), estranged wife of the poet
George Gordon, Lord Byron (1788–1824), was a prominent British
reformer and anti-slavery activist.

CONTENTS

FROM LORD BROUGHAM.[1]

***

I have been requested by one who has long known the deep interest I have ever taken in the cause of Freedom, and in the elevation of the coloured race, to supply a few lines of introduction to Mr. Webb's book.

It was the intention of Mrs. Harriet Beecher Stowe[2] to introduce this work to the British public, but I am truly sorry to learn that a severe domestic affliction,[3] since her return to America, has postponed the fulfilment of her promise.

I am, however, able to state her opinion of the book, expressed in a letter to one of her friends.

She says:—"There are points in the book of which I think very highly. The style is simple and unambitious—the characters, most of them faithfully drawn from real life, are quite fresh, and the incident, which is also much of it fact, is often deeply interesting.

"I shall do what I can with the preface. I would not do as much unless I thought the book of worth *in itself*. It shows what I long have wanted to show; what the *free people of colour do attain*, and what they can do in spite of all social obstacles."

I hope and trust that Mr. Webb's book will meet with all the success to which its own merit, and the great interest of the subject, so well entitle it. On this, Mrs. Stowe's authority is naturally of the greatest weight; and I can only lament that this prefatory notice does not come accompanied with her further remarks and illustrations.

4, GRAFTON-STREET, *July* 29, 1857.

---

1 Henry Peter Brougham (1778–1868) founded the progressive *Edinburgh Review*, sat as a member of Parliament for many years, and served as Lord High Chancellor of Great Britain from 1830 to 1834. He was an influential advocate for the British anti-slavery movement and other reformist causes.

2 Stowe (1811–96) was one of the most popular and prominent American writers of the nineteenth century. Her anti-slavery novel *Uncle Tom's Cabin* (1852) became an international best-seller, galvanizing the abolitionist movement and establishing her as a major voice in social-reform circles. Stowe became friends with Webb and his wife in the mid-1850s.

3 On 9 July 1857, Stowe's oldest son Henry Ellis Stowe drowned in a swimming accident in the Connecticut River. He was nineteen years old.

★★★

NOTE.—Since the above was written, the preface by Mrs. Stowe has been received. It was deemed best, however, to still retain the introduction so kindly given by Lord Brougham, whose deep interest in the freedom and welfare of the African race none feel more grateful for than does the author of the following pages.

PREFACE.[1]

★★★

The book which now appears before the public may be of interest in relation to a question which the late agitation of the subject of slavery has raised in many thoughtful minds; viz.—Are the race at present held as slaves capable of freedom, self-government, and progress?

The author is a coloured young man, born and reared in the city of Philadelphia.

This city, standing as it does on the frontier between free and slave territory, has accumulated naturally a large population of the mixed and African race.

Being one of the nearest free cities of any considerable size to the slave territory, it has naturally been a resort of escaping fugitives, or of emancipated slaves.

In this city they form a large class—have increased in numbers, wealth, and standing—they constitute a peculiar society of their own, presenting many social peculiarities worthy of interest and attention.

The representations of their positions as to wealth and education are reliable, the incidents related are mostly true ones, woven together by a slight web of fiction.

The scenes of the mob describe incidents of a peculiar stage of excitement, which existed in the city of Philadelphia years ago, when the first agitation of the slavery question developed an intense form of opposition to the free coloured people.

Southern influence at that time stimulated scenes of mob violence in several Northern cities where the discussion was attempted. By prompt, undaunted resistance, however, this spirit was subdued, and the right of free inquiry established; so that discussion of the question, so far from being dangerous in Free States, is now begun to be allowed in the Slave States; and there are some subjects the mere discussion of which is a half-victory.

---

1 It is not clear whether this preface was solicited by Webb or by his publisher George Routledge—who was also one of Stowe's publishers in the UK. Stowe's endorsement would have been seen as helpful in establishing Webb's credibility and thus increasing the book's sales. A number of initial reviews mention these two prefaces: see Appendix A.

The author takes pleasure in recommending this simple and truthfully-told story to the attention and interest of the friends of progress and humanity in England.

(Signed)   H. B. STOWE.

ANDOVER, U. S.,
   August 17, 1857.

THE GARIES.

CHAPTER I.

In which the Reader is introduced to a Family of peculiar Construction.

IT was at the close of an afternoon in May, that a party might have been seen gathered around a table covered with all those delicacies that, in the household of a rich Southern planter, are regarded as almost necessaries of life. In the centre stood a dish of ripe strawberries, their plump red sides peeping through the covering of white sugar that had been plentifully sprinkled over them. Geeche limes,[1] almost drowned in their own rich syrup, temptingly displayed their bronze-coloured forms just above the rim of the glass that contained them. Opposite, and as if to divert the gaze from lingering too long over their luscious beauty, was a dish of peaches preserved in brandy, a never-failing article in a Southern matron's catalogues of sweets. A silver basket filled with a variety of cakes was in close proximity to a plate of corn-flappers,[2] which were piled upon it like a mountain, and from the brown tops of which trickled tiny rivulets of butter. All these dainties, mingling their various odours with the aroma of the tea and fine old java[3] that came steaming forth from the richly-chased silver pots, could not fail to produce a very appetizing effect.

There was nothing about Mr. Garie, the gentleman who sat at the head of the table, to attract more than ordinary attention. He had the ease of manner usual with persons whose education and associations have been of a highly refined character, and his countenance, on the whole, was pleasing, and indicative of habitual good temper.

Opposite to him, and presiding at the tea-tray, sat a lady of marked beauty. The first thing that would have attracted attention on seeing her were her gloriously dark eyes. They were not

---

1   The sour, non-citrus fruit of the Ogeechee lime tree, also known as the white tupelo. Because the geeche lime is native only to the banks of the Ogeechee River in eastern Georgia, this is a delicacy more or less unique to the Savannah area.

2   Likely cornmeal pancakes or flapjacks.

3   Coffee.

entirely black, but of that seemingly changeful hue so often met with in persons of African extraction, which deepens and lightens with every varying emotion. Hers wore a subdued expression that sank into the heart and at once riveted those who saw her. Her hair, of jetty black, was arranged in braids; and through her light-brown complexion the faintest tinge of carmine was visible. As she turned to take her little girl from the arms of the servant, she displayed a fine profile and perfectly moulded form. No wonder that ten years before, when she was placed upon the auction-block at Savannah, she had brought so high a price. Mr. Garie had paid two thousand dollars for her, and was the envy of all the young bucks in the neighbourhood who had competed with him at the sale. Captivated by her beauty, he had esteemed himself fortunate in becoming her purchaser; and as time developed the goodness of her heart, and her mind enlarged through the instructions he assiduously gave her, he found the connection that might have been productive of many evils, had proved a boon to both; for whilst the astonishing progress she made in her education proved her worthy of the pains he took to instruct her, she returned threefold the tenderness and affection he lavished upon her.

The little girl in her arms, and the boy at her side, showed no trace whatever of African origin. The girl had the chestnut hair and blue eyes of her father; but the boy had inherited the black hair and dark eyes of his mother. The critically learned in such matters, knowing his parentage, might have imagined they could detect the evidence of his mother's race, by the slightly mezzo-tinto[1] expression of his eyes, and the rather African fullness of his lips; but the casual observer would have passed him by without dreaming that a drop of negro blood coursed through his veins. His face was expressive of much intelligence, and he now seemed to listen with an earnest interest to the conversation that was going on between his father and a dark-complexioned gentleman who sat beside him.

"And so you say, Winston, that they never suspected you were coloured?"

"I don't think they had the remotest idea of such a thing. At least, if they did, they must have conquered their prejudices most effectually, for they treated me with the most distinguished con-

---

1 Italian phrase meaning half-dyed or half-colored. Cf. "mezzotint," a printmaking method popular in the nineteenth century that produced subtly-shaded engravings.

sideration. Old Mr. Priestly was like a father to me; and as for his daughter Clara and her aunt, they were politeness embodied. The old gentleman was so much immersed in business, that he was unable to bestow much attention upon me; so he turned me over to Miss Clara to be shown the lions.[1] We went to the opera, the theatre, to museums, concerts, and I can't tell where all. The Sunday before I left I accompanied her to church, and after service, as we were coming out, she introduced me to Miss Van Cote and her mamma. Mrs. Van Cote was kind enough to invite me to her grand ball."

"And did you go?" interrupted Mr. Garie.

"Of course I did—and what is more, as old Mr. Priestly has given up balls, he begged me to escort Clara and her aunt."

"Well, Winston, that is too rich," exclaimed Mr. Garie, slapping his hand on the table, and laughing till he was red in the face; "too good, by Jove! Oh! I can't keep that. I must write to them, and say I forgot to mention in my note of introduction that you were a coloured gentleman. The old man will swear till everything turns blue; and as for Clara, what will become of her? A Fifth-avenue belle escorted to church and to balls by a coloured gentleman!" Here Mr. Garie indulged in another burst of laughter so side-shaking and merry, that the contagion spread even to the little girl in Mrs. Garie's arms, who almost choked herself with the tea her mother was giving her, and who had to be hustled and shaken for some time before she could be brought round again.

"It will be a great triumph for me," said Mr. Garie. "The old man prides himself on being able to detect evidences of the least drop of African blood in any one; and makes long speeches about the natural antipathy of the Anglo-Saxon to anything with a drop of negro blood in its veins. Oh, I shall write him a glorious letter expressing my pleasure at his great change of sentiment, and my admiration of the fearless manner in which he displays his contempt for public opinion. How he will stare! I fancy I see him now, with his hair almost on end with disgust. It will do him good: it will convince him, I hope, that a man can be a gentleman even though he has African blood in his veins. I have had a series of quarrels with him," continued Mr. Garie; "I think he had his eye on me for Miss Clara, and that makes him particularly fierce

---

1 I.e., shown all of the objects of interest. "To see the lions" had become proverbial for sightseeing as early as the sixteenth century (Farmer and Henley 4.205).

about my present connection. He rather presumes on his former great intimacy with my father, and undertakes to lecture me occasionally when opportunity is afforded. He was greatly scandalized at my speaking of Emily as my wife; and seemed to think me cracked because I talked of endeavouring to procure a governess for my children, or of sending them abroad to be educated. He has a holy horror of everything approaching to amalgamation;[1] and of all the men I ever met, cherishes the most unchristian prejudice against coloured people. He says, the existence of a 'gentleman' with African blood in his veins, is a moral and physical impossibility, and that by no exertion can anything be made of that description of people. He is connected with a society for the deportation of free coloured people,[2] and thinks they ought to be all sent to Africa, unless they are willing to become the property of some good master."

"Oh, yes; it is quite a hobby of his," here interposed Mr. Winston. "He makes lengthy speeches on the subject, and has published two of them in pamphlet form. Have you seen them?"

"Yes, he sent them to me. I tried to get through one of them; but it was too heavy, I had to give it up. Besides, I had no patience with them; they abounded in mis-statements respecting the free coloured people. Why even here in the Slave states—in the cities of Savannah and Charleston—they are much better situated than he describes them to be in New York; and since they can and do prosper here, where they have such tremendous difficulties to encounter, I know they cannot be in the condition he paints, in a state where they are relieved from many of the oppressions they labour under here. And, on questioning him on the subject, I found he was entirely unacquainted with coloured people; pro-

---

1 Interracial procreation. With its air of biological precision, the word "miscegenation," coined just after the Civil War, replaced "amalgamation" in the latter part of the nineteenth century.

2 The most prominent institutional advocate for the relocation of freed blacks beyond the borders of the United States was the American Colonization Society, which proved instrumental in the founding of Liberia in 1821. Philosophical justifications for deportation schemes ranged from white-supremacist claims that blacks were unfit to live in civil society to black-nationalist arguments that true freedom for people of color was impossible in the inherently racist US. Accordingly, supporters of deportation (including Thomas Jefferson [1743–1826], Harriet Beecher Stowe, Abraham Lincoln [1809–65], and the African-American writer Martin Delany [1812–85]) came from many different parts of the political spectrum.

foundly ignorant as to the real facts of their case. He had never been within a coloured church or school; did not even know that they had a literary society amongst them.[1] Positively, I, living down here in Georgia, knew more about the character and condition of the coloured people of the Northern states, than he who lived right in the midst of them. Would you believe that beyond their laundress and a drunken negro that they occasionally employed to do odd jobs for them, they were actually unacquainted with any coloured people: and how unjust was it for him to form his opinion respecting a class numbering over twenty thousand in his own state, from the two individuals I have mentioned and the negro loafers he occasionally saw in the streets."

"It is truly unfortunate," rejoined Mr. Winston; "for he covers his prejudices with such a pretended regard for the coloured people, that a person would be the more readily led to believe his statements respecting them to be correct; and he is really so positive about it, and apparently so deaf to all argument, that I did not discuss the subject with him to any extent; he was so very kind to me, that I did not want to run a tilt against his favourite opinions."

"You wrote me he gave you letters[2] to Philadelphia; was there one amongst them to the Mortons?"

"Yes. They were very civil, and invited me to a grand dinner they gave to the Belgian Chargé d'Affaires.[3] I also met there one or two scions of the first families of Virginia.[4] The Belgian minister did not seem to be aware that slavery is a tabooed subject in polite circles, and he was continually bringing it forward, until slaves, slavery, and black people in general became the principal topic of conversation, relieved by occasional discussion upon some new book or pictures, and remarks in praise of the viands before us. A very amusing thing occurred during dinner. A bright-faced little coloured boy who was assisting at the table,

---

1 There were black literary societies in a number of northern cities. Such institutions provided space and occasion for literate, middle-class blacks to accumulate and display humanistic and scientific knowledge. Here, Webb may be thinking particularly of The Philadelphia Library Company of Colored People, founded in 1833.

2 I.e., letters of introduction.

3 A diplomatic office-holder, second only in rank and importance to an ambassador.

4 Common shorthand for wealthy, culturally prominent families that traced their lineage directly back to seventeenth-century European settlers of the Virginia colony.

seemed to take uncommon interest in the conversation. An animated discussion had arisen as to the antiquity of the use of salad, one party maintaining that one of the oldest of the English poets had mentioned it in a poem, and the other as stoutly denying it. At last a reverend gentleman, whose remarks respecting the intelligence of the children of Ham[1] had been particularly disparaging, asserted that nowhere in Chaucer, Spenser, nor any of the old English poets, could anything relating to it be found. At this, the little waiter became so excited that he could no longer contain himself, and, despite the frowns and nods of our hostess, exclaimed, 'Yes it can, it's in Chaucer; here,' he continued, taking out a book from the book-case, 'here is the very volume,'[2] and turning over the leaves, he pointed out the passage, to the great chagrin of the reverend gentleman, and to the amusement of the guests. The Belgian minister enjoyed it immensely. 'Ah,' said he, 'the child of Ham know more than the child of Shem, dis time.' Whereupon Mrs. Morton rejoined that in this case it was not so wonderful, owing to the frequent and intimate relations into which ham and salad were brought, and with this joke the subject was dismissed. I can't say I was particularly sorry when the company broke up."

"Oh, George, never mind the white people," here interposed Mrs. Garie. "Never mind them; tell us about the coloured folks; they are the ones I take the most interest in. We were so delighted with your letters, and so glad that you found Mrs. Ellis. Tell us all about that."

"Oh, 'tis a long story, Em, and can't be told in a minute; it would take the whole evening to relate it all."

---

1 Genesis 9:20–27 tells the story of Noah's three sons, Ham, Shem, and Japheth. After Ham finds his father in a tent drunk on wine and sleeping naked, he tells his brothers Shem and Japheth to enter the tent backwards and cover their father's nakedness without looking at him. When Noah wakes up, he is furious: he places a curse on Ham's child, Canaan, claiming that he will be a "servant of servants ... unto his brethren." In many eighteenth- and nineteenth-century scriptural exegeses, Canaan and his brothers were thought to be the ancestors of the African nations and the curse of Canaan (or the curse of Ham) was frequently invoked as a way of providing historical and biblical justification for the contemporary enslavement of black people. See Goldenberg.

2 [Webb's note:] See Chaucer, "Flower and the Leaf." ["The Floure and the Leafe" was an anonymous fifteenth-century poem originally thought to have been written by the English poet Geoffrey Chaucer (c. 1343–1400).]

"Look at the children, my dear, they are half-asleep," said Mr. Garie. "Call nurse and see them safe into bed, and when you come back, we will have the whole story."

"Very well," replied she, rising and calling the nurse. "Now remember, George, you are not to begin until I return; for I should be quite vexed to lose a word."

"Oh, go on with the children, my dear, I'll guarantee he shall not say a word on the subject till you come back."

With this assurance Mrs. Garie left the room, playfully shaking her finger at them as she went out, exclaiming, "Not a word, remember now, not a word."

After she left them, Mr. Garie remarked, "I have not seen Em as happy as she is this afternoon for some time. I don't know what has come over her lately; she scarcely ever smiles now, and yet she used to be the most cheerful creature in the world. I wish I knew what is the matter with her; sometimes I am quite distressed about her. She goes about the house looking so lost and gloomy, and does not seem to take the least interest in anything. You saw," continued he, "how silent she has been all tea-time, and yet she has been more interested in what you have been saying than in anything that has transpired for months. Well, I suppose women will be so sometimes," he concluded, applying himself to the warm cakes that had just been set upon the table.

"Perhaps she is not well," suggested Mr. Winston; "I think she looks a little pale."

"Well, possibly you may be right; but I trust it is only a temporary lowness of spirits, or something of that kind. Maybe she will get over it in a day or two;" and with this remark the conversation dropped, and the gentlemen proceeded to the demolition of the sweetmeats[1] before them. And now, my reader, whilst they are finishing their meal, I will relate to you who Mr. Winston is, and how he came to be so familiarly seated at Mr. Garie's table.

Mr. Winston had been a slave. Yes! that fine-looking gentleman seated near Mr. Garie and losing nothing by the comparison that their proximity would suggest, had been fifteen years before sold on the auction-block in the neighbouring town of Savannah; had been made to jump, show his teeth, shout to test his lungs, and had been handled and examined by professed negro traders and amateur buyers, with less gentleness and commiseration than every humane man would feel for a horse or an ox. Now do not doubt me—I mean that very gentleman, whose polished manners

---

1 Sugary treats (the "warm cakes" above).

and irreproachable appearance might have led you to suppose him descended from a long line of illustrious ancestors. Yes—he was the offspring of a mulatto[1] field-hand by her master. He who was now clothed in fine linen, had once rejoiced in a tow[2] shirt that scarcely covered his nakedness, and had sustained life on a peck of corn[3] a week, receiving the while kicks and curses from a tyrannical overseer.

The death of his master had brought him to the auction-block, from which, both he and his mother were sold to separate owners. There they took their last embrace of each other—the mother tearless, but heart-broken—the boy with all the wildest manifestations of grief.

His purchaser was a cotton broker from New Orleans, a warm-hearted, kind old man, who took a fancy to the boy's looks, and pitied him for his unfortunate separation from his mother. After paying for his new purchase, he drew him aside, and said, in a kind tone, "Come, my little man, stop crying; my boys never cry. If you behave yourself, you shall have fine times with me. Stop crying now, and come with me; I am going to buy you a new suit of clothes."

"I don't want new clothes—I want my mammy," exclaimed the child, with a fresh burst of grief.

"Oh dear me!" said the fussy old gentleman, "why can't you stop—I don't want to hear you cry. Here," continued he, fumbling in his pocket—"here's a picayune."[4]

"Will that buy mother back?" said the child, brightening up.

"No, no, my little man, not quite—I wish it would. I'd purchase the old woman; but I can't—I'm not able to spare the money."

"Then I don't want it," cried the boy, throwing the money on the ground. "If it won't buy mammy, I don't want it. I want my mammy, and nothing else."

At length, by much kind language, and by the prospect of many fabulous events to occur hereafter, invented at the moment by the old gentleman, the boy was coaxed into a more quiescent

---

1 Mixed-race, here designating an individual with one nominally black parent and one nominally white parent.
2 A coarse fabric made from the shorter fibers of the flax plant.
3 Here likely in the general sense of "grain," although maize is also possible.
4 A five-cent piece; hence something of proverbially little value. See *OED* 1a.

state, and trudged along in the rear of Mr. Moyese—that was the name of his purchaser—to be fitted with the new suit of clothes. The next morning they started by the stage for Augusta. George, seated on the box with the driver, found much to amuse him; and the driver's merry chat and great admiration of George's new and gaily-bedizened suit, went a great way towards reconciling that young gentleman to his new situation.

In a few days they arrived in New Orleans. There, under the kind care of Mr. Moyese, he began to exhibit great signs of intelligence. The atmosphere into which he was now thrown, the kindness of which he was hourly the recipient, called into vigour abilities that would have been stifled forever beneath the blighting influences that surrounded him under his former master. The old gentleman had him taught to read and write, and his aptness was such as to highly gratify the kind old soul.

In course of time, the temporary absence of an out-door clerk caused George's services to be required at the office for a few days, as errand-boy. Here he made himself so useful as to induce Mr. Moyese to keep him there permanently. After this he went through all the grades from errand-boy up to chief clerk, which post he filled to the full satisfaction of his employer. His manners and person improved with his circumstances; and at the time he occupied the chief clerk's desk, no one would have suspected him to be a slave, and few who did not know his history would have dreamed that he had a drop of African blood in his veins. He was unremitting in his attention to the duties of his station, and gained, by his assiduity and amiable deportment, the highest regard of his employer.

A week before a certain New-year's-day, Mr. Moyese sat musing over some presents that had just been sent home, and which he was on the morrow to distribute amongst his nephews and nieces. "Why, bless me!" he suddenly exclaimed, turning them over, "why, I've entirely forgotten George! That will never do; I must get something for him. What shall it be? He has a fine watch, and I gave him a pin and ring last year. I really don't know what will be suitable;" and he sat for some time rubbing his chin, apparently in deep deliberation. "Yes, I'll do it!" he exclaimed, starting up; "I'll do it! He has been a faithful fellow, and deserves it. I'll make him a present of himself! Now, how strange it is I never thought of that before—it's just the thing;—how surprised and delighted he will be!" and the old gentleman laughed a low, gentle, happy laugh, that had in it so little of selfish pleasure, that had you only heard him, you must have loved him for it.

Having made up his mind to surprise George in this agreeable manner, Mr. Moyese immediately wrote a note, which he despatched to his lawyers, Messrs. Ketchum and Lee, desiring them to make out a set of free papers for his boy George, and to have them ready for delivery on the morrow, as it was his custom to give his presents two or three days in advance of the coming year.

The note found Mr. Ketchum deep in a disputed will case, upon the decision of which depended the freedom of some half-dozen slaves, who had been emancipated by the will of their late master; by which piece of posthumous benevolence his heirs had been greatly irritated, and were in consequence endeavouring to prove him insane.

"Look at that, Lee," said he, tossing the note to his partner; "if that old Moyese isn't the most curious specimen of humanity in all New Orleans! He is going to give away clear fifteen hundred dollars as a New-year's gift!"

"To whom?" asked Mr. Lee.

"He has sent me orders," replied Mr. Ketchum, "to make out a set of free papers for his boy George."

"Well, I can't say that I see so much in that," said Lee; "how can he expect to keep him? George is almost as white as you or I, and has the manners and appearance of a gentleman. He might walk off any day without the least fear of detection."

"Very true," rejoined Ketchum, "but I don't think he would do it. He is very much attached to the old gentleman, and no doubt would remain with him as long as the old man lives. But I rather think the heirs would have to whistle for him after Moyese was put under ground. However," concluded Mr. Ketchum, "they won't have much opportunity to dispute the matter, as he will be a free man, no doubt, before he is forty-eight hours older."

A day or two after this, Mr. Moyese entertained all his nephews and nieces at dinner, and each was gratified with some appropriate gift. The old man sat happily regarding the group that crowded round him, their faces beaming with delight. The claim for the seat of honour on Uncle Moyese's knee was clamorously disputed, and the old gentleman was endeavouring to settle it to the satisfaction of all parties, when a servant entered, and delivered a portentous-looking document, tied with red tape.[1] "Oh, the

---

1 Beginning in the seventeenth century, bundles of associated legal documents were conventionally tied together with red ribbon (tape). By the eighteenth century, "red tape" had begun to accumulate its current significance as a metaphor for bureaucratic inefficiency or intransigency.

papers—now, my dears, let uncle go. Gustave, let go your hold of my leg, or I can't get up. Amy, ring the bell, dear." This operation Mr. Moyese was obliged to lift her into the chair to effect, where she remained tugging at the bell-rope until she was lifted out again by the servant, who came running in great haste to answer a summons of such unusual vigour.

"Tell George I want him," said Mr. Moyese.

"He's gone down to the office; I hearn him say suffin bout de nordern mail as he went out—but I duno what it was"—and as he finished he vanished from the apartment,[1] and might soon after have been seen with his mouth in close contact with the drumstick of a turkey.

Mr. Moyese being now released from the children, took his way to the office, with the portentous red-tape document that was to so greatly change the condition of George Winston, in his coat pocket. The old man sat down at his desk, smiling, as he balanced the papers in his hand, at the thought of the happiness he was about to confer on his favourite. He was thus engaged when the door opened, and George entered, bearing some newly-arrived orders from European correspondents, in reference to which he sought Mr. Moyese's instructions.

"I think, sir," said he, modestly, "that we had better reply at once to Ditson, and send him the advance he requires, as he will not otherwise be able to fill these;" and as he concluded, he laid the papers on the table, and stood waiting orders respecting them.

Mr. Moyese laid down the packet, and after looking over the papers George had brought in, replied: "I think we had. Write to him to draw upon us for the amount he requires.—And, George," he continued, looking at him benevolently, "what would you like for a New-year's present?"

"Anything you please, sir," was the respectful reply.

"Well, George," resumed Mr. Moyese, "I have made up my mind to make you a present of—" here he paused and looked steadily at him for a few seconds; and then gravely handing him the papers, concluded, "of yourself, George! Now mind and don't throw my present away, my boy."

George stood for some moments looking in a bewildered manner, first at his master, then at the papers. At last the reality of his good fortune broke fully upon him, and he sank into a chair, and, unable to say more than, "God bless you, Mr. Moyese!" burst into tears.

---

1 I.e., from the room.

"Now you are a pretty fellow," said the old man, sobbing himself, "it's nothing to cry about—get home as fast as you can, you stupid cry-baby, and mind you are here early in the morning, sir, for I intend to pay you five hundred dollars a year, and I mean you to earn it;" and thus speaking he bustled out of the room, followed by George's repeated "God bless you!" That "God bless you" played about his ears at night, and soothed him to sleep; in dreams he saw it written in diamond letters on a golden crown, held towards him by a hand outstretched from the azure above. He fancied the birds sang it to him in his morning walk, and that he heard it in the ripple of the little stream that flowed at the foot of his garden. So he could afford to smile when his relatives talked about his mistaken generosity, and could take refuge in that fervent "God bless you!"

Six years after this event Mr. Moyese died, leaving George a sufficient legacy to enable him to commence business on his own account. As soon as he had arranged his affairs, he started for his old home, to endeavour to gain by personal exertions what he had been unable to learn through the agency of others—a knowledge of the fate of his mother. He ascertained that she had been sold and re-sold, and had finally died in New Orleans, not more than three miles from where he had been living. He had not even the melancholy satisfaction of finding her grave. During his search for his mother, he had become acquainted with Emily, the wife of Mr. Garie, and discovered that she was his cousin; and to this was owing the familiar footing on which we find him in the household where we first introduced him to our readers.

Mr. Winston had just returned from a tour through the Northern states, where he had been in search of a place in which to establish himself in business.

The introductions with which Mr. Garie had kindly favoured him, had enabled him to see enough of Northern society to convince him, that, amongst the whites, he could not form either social or business connections, should his identity with the African race be discovered; and whilst, on the other hand, he would have found sufficiently refined associations amongst the people of colour to satisfy his social wants, he felt that he could not bear the isolation and contumely to which they were subjected. He therefore decided on leaving the United States, and on going to some country where, if he must struggle for success in life, he might do it without the additional embarrassments that would be thrown in his way in his native land, solely because he belonged to an oppressed race.

CHAPTER II.

A Glance at the Ellis Family.

"I WISH Charlie would come with that tea," exclaimed Mrs. Ellis, who sat finishing off some work,[1] which had to go home that evening. "I wonder what can keep him so long away. He has been gone over an hour; it surely cannot take him that time to go to Watson's."

"It is a great distance, mother," said Esther Ellis, who was busily plying her needle; "and I don't think he has been quite so long as you suppose."

"Yes; he has been gone a good hour," repeated Mrs. Ellis. "It is now six o'clock, and it wanted three minutes to five when he left. I do hope he won't forget that I told him half black and half green—he is *so* forgetful!" And Mrs. Ellis rubbed her spectacles and looked peevishly out of the window as she concluded.— "Where can he be?" she resumed, looking in the direction in which he might be expected. "Oh, here he comes, and Caddy with him. They have just turned the corner—open the door and let them in."

Esther arose, and on opening the door was almost knocked down by Charlie's abrupt entrance into the apartment, he being rather forcibly shoved in by his sister Caroline, who appeared to be in a high state of indignation.

"Where do you think he was, mother? Where *do* you think I found him?"

"Well, I can't say—I really don't know; in some mischief, I'll be bound."

"He was on the lot playing marbles[2]—and I've had such a time to get him home. Just look at his knees; they are worn through. And only think, mother, the tea was lying on the ground, and might have been carried off, if I had not happened to come that way. And then he has been fighting and struggling with me all the way home. See," continued she, baring her arm, "just look how he has scratched me;" and as she spoke she held out the injured member for her mother's inspection.

---

1   I.e., needlework. Like many women of the lower and middling sorts, the women in the Ellis household take in sewing as a way to make money.

2   Any number of games could fall under Caddy's designation here, but all of them would require Charlie to be kneeling on the ground and taking much greater care with his little glass spheres than with his groceries.

"Mother," said Charlie, in his justification, "she began to beat me before all the boys, before I had said a word to her, and I wasn't going to stand that. She is always storming at me. She don't give me any peace of my life."

"Oh yes, mother," here interposed Esther; "Cad is too cross to him. I must say, that he would not be as bad as he is, if she would only let him alone."

"Esther, please hush now; you have nothing to do with their quarrels. I'll settle all their differences. You always take his part, whether he be right or wrong. I shall send him to bed without his tea, and to-morrow I will take his marbles from him; and if I see his knees showing through his pants again, I'll put a red patch on them—that's what I'll do. Now, sir, go to bed, and don't let me hear of you until morning."

Mr. and Mrs. Ellis were at the head of a highly respectable and industrious coloured family. They had three children. Esther, the eldest, was a girl of considerable beauty, and amiable temper. Caroline, the second child, was plain in person, and of rather shrewish disposition; she was a most indefatigable housewife, and was never so happy as when in possession of a dust or scrubbing-brush; she would have regarded a place where she could have lived in a perpetual state of house-cleaning, as an earthly para-dise. Between her and Master Charlie continual warfare existed, interrupted only by brief truces brought about by her necessity for his services as water-carrier. When a service of this character had been duly rewarded by a slice of bread and preserves, or some other dainty, hostilities would most probably be recom-menced by Charlie's making an inroad upon the newly-cleaned floor, and leaving the prints of his muddy boots thereon.

The fact must here be candidly stated, that Charlie was not a tidy boy. He despised mats, and seldom or never wiped his feet on entering the house; he was happiest when he could don his most dilapidated unmentionables,[1] as he could then sit down where he pleased without the fear of his mother before his eyes, and enter upon a game of marbles with his mind perfectly free from all harassing cares growing out of any possible accident to the aforesaid garments, so that he might give that attention to the game that its importance demanded.

He was a bright-faced pretty boy, clever at his lessons, and a favourite both with tutors and scholars.[2] He had withal a thor-

---

1 Trousers. See *OED* "unmentionables" B1a.
2 I.e., teachers and students.

ough boy's fondness for play, and was also characterized by all the thoughtlessness consequent thereon. He possessed a lively, affectionate disposition, and was generally at peace with all the world, his sister Caddy excepted.

Caroline had recovered her breath, and her mind being soothed by the judgment that had been pronounced on Master Charlie, she began to bustle about to prepare tea.

The shining copper teakettle was brought from the stove where it had been seething and singing for the last half-hour; then the teapot of china received its customary quantity of tea, which was set upon the stove to brew, and carefully placed behind the stove-pipe, that no accidental touch of the elbow might bring it to destruction. Plates, knives, and teacups came rattling forth from the closet; the butter was brought from the place where it had been placed to keep it cool, and a corn-cake was soon smoking on the table, and sending up its seducing odour into the room over-head to which Charlie had been recently banished, causing to that unfortunate young gentleman great physical discomfort.

"Now, mother," said the bustling Caddy, "it's all ready. Come now and sit down whilst the cake is hot—do put up the sewing, Esther, and come!"

Neither Esther nor her mother needed much pressing, and they were accordingly soon seated round the table on which their repast was spread.

"Put away a slice of this cake for father," said Mrs. Ellis, "for he won't be home until late; he is obliged to attend a vestry meeting[1] to-night."

Mrs. Ellis sat for some time sipping the fragrant and refreshing tea. When the contents of two or three cups one after another had disappeared, and sundry slices of corn-bread had been deposited where much corn-bread had been deposited before, she began to think about Charlie, and to imagine that perhaps she had been rather hasty in sending him to bed without his supper.

"What had Charlie to-day in his dinner-basket to take to school with him?" she inquired of Caddy.

"Why, mother, I put in enough for a wolf; three or four slices of bread, with as many more of corn-beef; some cheese, one of

---

1 A gathering of parishioners to discuss church business. See *OED* "vestry" 2a.

those little pies, and all that bread-pudding which was left at dinner yesterday—he must have had enough."

"But, mother, you know he always gives away the best part of his dinner," interposed Esther. "He supplies two or three boys with food. There is that dirty Kinch that he is so fond of, who never takes any dinner with him, and depends entirely upon Charlie. He must be hungry; do let him come down and get his tea, mother."

Notwithstanding the observations of Caroline that Esther was just persuading her mother to spoil the boy, that he would be worse than ever, and many other similar predictions, Esther and the tea combined won a signal triumph, and Charlie was called down from the room above, where he had been exchanging telegraphic communications with the before-mentioned Kinch, in hopes of receiving a commutation of sentence.

Charlie was soon seated at the table with an ample allowance of corn-bread and tea; and he looked so demure, and conducted himself in such an exemplary manner, that one would have scarcely thought him given to marbles and dirty company. Having eaten to his satisfaction, he quite ingratiated himself with Caddy by picking up all the crumbs he had spilled during tea, and throwing them upon the dust-heap.[1] This last act was quite a stroke of policy, as even Caddy began to regard him as capable of reformation.

The tea-things washed up and cleared away, the females busied themselves with their sewing, and Charlie immersed himself in his lessons for the morrow with a hearty goodwill and perseverance, as if he had abjured marbles for ever.

The hearty supper and persevering attention to study soon began to produce their customary effect upon Charlie. He could not get on with his lessons. Many of the state capitals positively refused to be found, and he was beginning to entertain the sage notion that probably some of the legislatures had come to the conclusion to dispense with them altogether, or had had them placed in such obscure places that they could not be found. The variously coloured states began to form a vast kaleidoscope, in which the lakes and rivers had been entirely swallowed up. Ranges of mountains disappeared, and gulfs, and bays, and islands were entirely lost. In fact, he was sleepy, and had already had two or three narrow escapes from butting over the candles; finally he fell from his chair, crushing Caddy's newly-trimmed

---

1 I.e., onto the pile of household garbage.

bonnet, to the intense grief and indignation of that young lady, who inflicted summary vengeance upon him before he was sufficiently awake to be aware of what had happened.

The work being finished, Mrs. Ellis and Caddy prepared to take it home to Mrs. Thomas, leaving Esther at home to receive her father on his return, and give him his tea.

Mrs. Ellis and Caddy wended their way towards the fashionable part of the city, looking in at the various shop-windows as they went. Numberless were the great bargains they saw there displayed, and divers[1] were the discussions they held respecting them.

"Oh, isn't that a pretty calico, mother, that with the green ground?"

"'Tis pretty, but it won't wash, child; those colours always run."

"Just look at that silk though—now that's cheap, you must acknowledge—only eighty-seven and a half cents; if I only had a dress of that, I should be fixed."

"Laws,[2] Caddy," replied Mrs. Ellis, "that stuff is as slazy[3] as a washed cotton handkerchief, and coarse enough almost to sift sand through. It wouldn't last you any time. The silks they make nowadays ain't worth anything; they don't wear well at all. Why," continued she, "when I was a girl they made silks that would stand on end—and one of them would last a lifetime."

They had now reached Chestnut-street, which was filled with gaily-dressed people, enjoying the balmy breath of a soft May evening. Mrs. Ellis and Caddy walked briskly onward, and were soon beyond the line of shops, and entered upon the aristocratic quarter into which many of its residents had retired, that they might be out of sight of the houses in which their fathers or grandfathers had made their fortunes.

"Mother," said Caddy, "this is Mr. Grant's new house—isn't it a splendid place? They say it's like a palace inside. They are great people, them Grants. I saw in the newspaper yesterday that young Mr. Augustus Grant had been appointed an attaché to the American legation at Paris; the newspapers say he is a rising man."

"Well, he ought to be," rejoined Mrs. Ellis, "for his old granddaddy made yeast enough to raise the whole family. Many a pennyworth has he sold me. Laws! how the poor old folk do get up!

---

1   Diverse; many and varied.

2   Mild dialect oath expressing surprise.

3   I.e., "sleazy": thin and flimsy. See *OED* "sleazy" 2a.

I think I can see the old man now, with his sleeves rolled up, dealing out his yeast. He wore one coat for about twenty years, and used to be always bragging about it."

As they were thus talking, a door of one of the splendid mansions they were passing opened, and a fashionably dressed young man came slowly down the steps, and walked on before them with a very measured step and peculiar gait.

"That's young Dr. Whiston, mother," whispered Caddy; "he's courting young Miss Morton."

"You don't say so!" replied the astonished Mrs. Ellis. "Why, I declare his grandfather laid her grandfather out! Old Whiston was an undertaker, and used to make the handsomest coffins of his time. And he is going to marry Miss Morton! What next, I'd like to know! He walks exactly like the old man. I used to mock him when I was a little girl. He had just that hop-and-go kind of gait, and he was the funniest man that ever lived. I've seen him at a funeral go into the parlour, and condole with the family, and talk about the dear departed until the tears rolled down his cheeks; and then he'd be down in the kitchen, eating and drinking, and laughing, and telling jokes about the corpses, before the tears were dry on his face. How he used to make money! He buried almost all the respectable people about town, and made a large fortune. He owned a burying-ground in Coates-street, and when the property in that vicinity became valuable, he turned the dead folks out, and built houses on the ground!"

"I shouldn't say it was a very pleasant place to live in, if there are such things as ghosts," said Caddy, laughing; "I for one wouldn't like to live there—but here we are at Mr. Thomas's—how short the way has seemed!"

Caroline gave a fierce rap at the door, which was opened by old Aunt Rachel, the fat cook, who had lived with the Thomases for a fabulous length of time. She was an old woman when Mrs. Ellis came as a girl into the family, and had given her many a cuff in days long past; in fact, notwithstanding Mrs. Ellis had been married many years, and had children almost as old as she herself was when she left Mr. Thomas, Aunt Rachel could never be induced to regard her otherwise than as a girl.

"Oh, it's you, is it?" said she gruffly, as she opened the door; "don't you think [you] better break de door down at once—rapping as if you was guine to tear off de knocker—is dat de way, gal, you comes to quality's houses? You lived here long nuff to larn better dan dat—and dis is twice I've been to de door in de last half-hour—if any one else comes dere they may stay outside.

Shut de door after you, and come into de kitchen, and don't keep me standin' here all night," added she, puffing and blowing as she waddled back into her sanctum.[1]

Waiting until the irate old cook had recovered her breath, Mrs. Ellis modestly inquired if Mrs. Thomas was at home. "Go up and see," was the surly response. "You've been up stars often enuff to know de way—go long wid you, gal, and don't be botherin' me, 'case I don't feel like bein' bothered—now, mind I tell yer.— Here, you Cad, set down on dis stool, and let that cat alone; I don't let any one play with my cat," continued she, "and you'll jest let him alone, if you please, or I'll make you go sit in de entry till your mother's ready to go. I don't see what she has you brats tugging after her for whenever she comes here—she might jest as well leave yer at home to darn your stockings—I 'spect dey want it."

Poor Caddy was boiling over with wrath; but deeming prudence the better part of valour, she did not venture upon any wordy contest with Aunt Rachel, but sat down upon the stool by the fire-place, in which a bright fire was blazing. Up the chimney an old smoke-jack[2] was clicking, whirling, and making the most dismal noise imaginable. This old smoke-jack was Aunt Rachel's especial *protégé*, and she obstinately and successfully defended it against all comers. She turned up her nose at all modern inventions designed for the same use, as entirely beneath her notice. She had been accustomed to hearing its rattle for the last forty years, and would as soon have thought of committing suicide as consenting to its removal.

She and her cat were admirably matched; he was as snappish and cross as she, and resented with distended claws and elevated back all attempts on the part of strangers to cultivate amicable relations with him. In fact, Tom's pugnacious disposition was clearly evidenced by his appearance; one side of his face having a very battered aspect, and the fur being torn off his back in several places.

Caddy sat for some time surveying the old woman and her cat, in evident awe of both. She regarded also with great admiration the scrupulously clean and shining kitchen tins that garnished the walls and reflected the red light of the blazing fire. The wooden

---

1   Shorthand for *sanctum sanctorum* (Latin for "holy of holies"): her inviolable private space.
2   A mechanical device that uses the power of hot air rising through a chimney to turn a roasting-spit.

dresser was a miracle of whiteness; and ranged thereon was a set of old-fashioned blue china, on which was displayed the usual number of those unearthly figures which none but the Chinese can create. Tick, tick, went the old Dutch clock in the corner, and the smoke-jack kept up its whirring noise. Old Tom and Aunt Rachel were both napping; and so Caddy, having no other resource, went to sleep also.

Mrs. Ellis found her way without any difficulty to Mrs. Thomas's room. Her gentle tap upon the door quite flurried that good lady, who (we speak it softly) was dressing her wig, a task she entrusted to no other mortal hands.[1] She peeped out, and seeing who it was, immediately opened the door without hesitation.

"Oh, it's you, is it? Come in, Ellen," said she; "I don't mind you."

"I've brought the night-dresses home," said Mrs. Ellis, laying her bundle upon the table,—"I hope they'll suit."

"Oh, no doubt they will. Did you bring the bill?" asked Mrs. Thomas.

The bill was produced, and Mrs. Ellis sat down, whilst Mrs. Thomas counted out the money. This having been duly effected, and the bill carefully placed on the file, Mrs. Thomas also sat down, and commenced her usual lamentation over the state of her nerves, and the extravagance of the younger members of the family. On the latter subject she spoke very feelingly. "Such goings on, Ellen, are enough to set me crazy—so many nurses— and then we have to keep four horses—and it's company, company from Monday morning until Saturday night; the house is kept upside-down continually—money, money for every- thing—all going out, and nothing coming in!"—and the unfortu- nate Mrs. Thomas whined and groaned as if she had not at that moment an income of clear fifteen thousand dollars a year, and a sister who might die any day and leave her half as much more.

Mrs. Thomas was the daughter of the respectable old gentle- man whom Dr. Whiston's grandfather had prepared for his final resting-place. Her daughter had married into a once wealthy, but now decayed, Carolina family. In consideration of the wealth bequeathed by her grandfather (who was a maker of leather breeches, and speculator in general), Miss Thomas had received the offer of the poverty-stricken hand of Mr. Morton, and had accepted it with evident pleasure, as he was undoubtedly a

---

1   The narrator is suggesting Mrs. Thomas's embarrassment at wearing a
    wig to conceal her baldness.

member of one of the first families of the South, and could prove a distant connection with one of the noble families of England.

They had several children, and their incessant wants had rendered it necessary that another servant should be kept. Now Mrs. Thomas had long had her eye on Charlie, with a view of incorporating him with the Thomas establishment, and thought this would be a favourable time to broach the subject to his mother: she therefore commenced by inquiring—

"How have you got through the winter, Ellen? Everything has been so dear, that even we have felt the effect of the high prices."

"Oh, tolerably well, I thank you. Husband's business, it is true, has not been as brisk as usual, but we ought not to complain; now that we have got the house paid for, and the girls do so much sewing, we get on very nicely."

"I should think three children must be something of a burthen—must be hard to provide for."

"Oh no, not at all," rejoined Mrs. Ellis, who seemed rather surprised at Mrs. Thomas's uncommon solicitude respecting them. "We have never found the children a burthen, thank God—they're rather a comfort and a pleasure than otherwise."

"I'm glad to hear you say so, Ellen—very glad, indeed; for I have been quite disturbed in mind respecting you during the winter. I really several times thought of sending to take Charlie off your hands: by the way, what is he doing now?"

"He goes to school regularly—he hasn't missed a day all winter. You should just see his writing," continued Mrs. Ellis, warming up with a mother's pride in her only son—"he won't let the girls make out any of the bills, but does it all himself—he made out yours."

Mrs. Thomas took down the file and looked at the bill again. "It's very neatly written, very neatly written, indeed; isn't it about time that he left school—don't you think he has education enough?" she inquired.

"His father don't. He intends sending him to another school, after vacation, where they teach Latin and Greek, and a number of other branches."

"Nonsense, nonsense, Ellen! If I were you, I wouldn't hear of it. There won't be a particle of good result to the child from any such acquirements. It isn't as though he was a white child. What use can Latin or Greek be to a coloured boy? None in the world—he'll have to be a common mechanic, or, perhaps, a servant, or barber, or something of that kind; and then what use would all his fine education be to him? Take my advice, Ellen, and don't have him taught things that will make him feel above the situation he, in all probability, will have to fill. Now," continued she, "I have a proposal to make to you: let him come and live with me awhile—I'll pay you well, and take good care of him; besides, he will be learning something here,—good manners, &c. Not that he is not a well-mannered child; but, you know, Ellen, there is something every one learns by coming in daily contact with refined and educated people, that cannot but be beneficial—come now, make up your mind to leave him with me, at least until the winter, when the schools again commence, and then, if his father is still resolved to send him back to school, why he can do so. Let me have him for the summer at least."

Mrs. Ellis, who had always been accustomed to regard Mrs. Thomas as a miracle of wisdom, was, of course, greatly impressed with what she had said. She had lived many years in her family, and had left it to marry Mr. Ellis, a thrifty mechanic, who came from Savannah, her native city. She had great reverence for any opinion Mrs. Thomas expressed; and, after some further conversation on the subject, made up her mind to consent to the proposal, and left her with the intention of converting her husband to her way of thinking.

On descending to the kitchen, she awoke Caddy from a delicious dream, in which she had been presented with the black silk that they had seen in the shop window marked eighty-seven and a half cents a yard. In the dream she had determined to make it up with tight sleeves and infant waist,[1] that being the most approved style at that period.

"Five breadths are not enough for the skirt, and if I take six I must skimp the waist and cape," murmured she in her sleep.

"Wake up, girl! What are you thinking about?" said her mother, giving her another shake.

"Oh!" said Caddy, with a wild and disappointed look—"I was dreaming, wasn't I? I declare I thought I had that silk frock in the window."

"The girls' heads are always running on finery—wake up, and come along, I'm going home."

Caddy followed her mother out, leaving Aunt Rachel and Tom nodding at each other as they dozed before the fire.

That night Mr. Ellis and his wife had a long conversation upon the proposal of Mrs. Thomas; and after divers objections raised by him, and set aside by her, it was decided that Charlie should

---

1 Decorative collar or placket covering the chest.

be permitted to go there for the holidays at least; after which, his father resolved he should be sent to school again.

Charlie, the next morning, looked very blank on being informed of his approaching fate. Caddy undertook with great alacrity to break the dismal tidings to him, and enlarged in a glowing manner upon what times he might expect from Aunt Rachel.

"I guess she'll keep you straight;—you'll see sights up there! She is cross as sin—she'll make you wipe your feet when you go in and out, if no one else can."

"Let him alone, Caddy," gently interposed Esther; "it is bad enough to be compelled to live in a house with that frightful old woman, without being annoyed about it beforehand. If I could help it, Charlie, you should not go."

"I know you'd keep me home if you could—but old Cad, here, she always rejoices if anything happens to me. I'll be hanged if I stay there," said he. "I won't live at service—I'd rather be a sweep, or sell apples on the dock. I'm not going to be stuck up behind their carriage, dressed up like a monkey in a tail coat—I'll cut off my own head first." And with this sanguinary threat he left the house, with his schoolbooks under his arm, intending to lay the case before his friend and adviser, the redoubtable and sympathizing Kinch.

CHAPTER III.

Charlie's Trials.

CHARLIE started for school with a heavy heart. Had it not been for his impending doom of service in Mr. Thomas's family, he would have been the happiest boy that ever carried a school-bag. It did not require a great deal to render this young gentleman happy. All that was necessary to make up a day of perfect joyfulness with him, was a dozen marbles, permission to wear his worst inexpressibles, and to be thoroughly up in his lessons. To-day he was possessed of all these requisites; but there was also in the perspective a long array of skirmishes with Aunt Rachel, who, he knew, looked on him with an evil eye, and who had frequently expressed herself regarding him, in his presence, in terms by no means complimentary or affectionate; and the manner in which she had intimated her desire, on one or two occasions, to have an opportunity of reforming his personal habits, were by no means calculated to produce a happy frame of mind, now that the opportunity was about to be afforded her.

Charlie sauntered on until he came to a lumber-yard, where he stopped and examined a corner of the fence very attentively. "Not gone by yet. I must wait for him," said he; and forthwith he commenced climbing the highest pile of boards, the top of which he reached at the imminent risk of his neck. Here he sat awaiting the advent of his friend Kinch, the absence of death's head and cross-bones from the corner of the fence being a clear indication that he had not yet passed on his way to school.

Soon, however, he was espied in the distance, and as he was quite a character in his way, we must describe him. His most prominent feature was a capacious hungry-looking mouth, within which glistened a row of perfect teeth. He had the merriest twinkling black eyes, and a nose so small and flat that it would have been a prize to any editor living, as it would have been a physical impossibility to have pulled it, no matter what outrage he had committed.[1] His complexion was of a ruddy brown, and his hair, entirely innocent of a comb, was decorated with diverse feathery tokens of his last night's rest. A cap with the front torn off, jaun-

---

1 In the nineteenth century, the pulling of the nose was considered an accusation of lying or dishonorable conduct. As purveyors of news, gossip, and innuendo, editors might have thought themselves particularly vulnerable to such accusations. See Greenberg, esp. 68–69.

tily set on one side of his head, gave him a rakish and wide-awake air; his clothes were patched and torn in several places, and his shoes were already in an advanced stage of decay. As he approached the fence, he took a piece of chalk from his pocket, and commenced to sketch the accustomed startling illustration which was to convey to Charlie the intelligence that he had already passed there on his way to school, when a quantity of sawdust came down in a shower on his head. As soon as the blinding storm had ceased, Kinch looked up and intimated to Charlie that it was quite late, and that there was a probability of their being after time at school.

This information caused Charlie to make rather a hasty descent; in doing which his dinner-basket was upset, and its contents displayed at the feet of the voracious Kinch.

"Now I'll be even with you for that sawdust," cried he, as he pocketed two boiled eggs, and bit an immense piece out of an apple-tart, which he would have demolished completely but for the prompt interposition of its owner.

"Oh! my golly! Charlie, your mother makes good pies!" he exclaimed with rapture, as soon as he could get his mouth sufficiently clear to speak. "Give us another bite,—only a nibble."

But Charlie knew by experience what Kinch's "nibbles" were, and he very wisely declined, saying sadly as he did so, "You won't get many more dinners from me, Kinch. I'm going to leave school."

"No! you ain't though, are you?" asked the astonished Kinch. "You are not going, are you, really?"

"Yes, really," replied Charlie, with a doleful look; "mother is going to put me out at service."

"And do you intend to go?" asked Kinch, looking at him incredulously.

"Why of course," was the reply. "How can I help going if father and mother say I must?"

"I tell you what I should do," said Kinch, "if it was me. I should act so bad that the people would be glad to get rid of me. They hired me out to live once, and I led the people they put me with such a dance, that they were glad enough to send me home again."

This observation brought them to the school-house, which was but a trifling distance from the residence of Mrs. Ellis.

They entered the school at the last moment of grace, and Mr. Dicker looked at them severely as they took their seats. "Just saved ourselves," whispered Kinch; "a minute later and we would have been done for;" and with this closing remark he applied himself to his grammar; a very judicious move on his part, for he had not looked at his lesson, and there were but ten minutes to elapse before the class would be called.

The lessons were droned through as lessons usually are at school. There was the average amount of flogging performed; cakes, nuts, and candy confiscated; little boys on the back seats punched one another as little boys on the back seats always will do, and were flogged in consequence. Then the boy who never knew his lessons was graced with the fool's cap, and was pointed and stared at until the arrival of the play-hour relieved him from his disagreeable situation.

"What kind of folks are these Thomases?" asked Kinch, as he sat beside Charlie in the playground munching the last of the apple-tart; "what kind of folks are they? Tell me that, and I can give you some good advice, may-be."

"Old Mrs. Thomas is a little dried-up old woman, who wears spectacles and a wig. She isn't of much account—I don't mind her. She's not the trouble; it's of old Aunt Rachel I'm thinking. Why, she has threatened to whip me when I've been there with mother, and she even talks to her sometimes as if she was a little girl. Lord only knows what she'll do to me when she has me there by myself. You should just see her and her cat. I really don't know," continued Charlie, "which is the worst-looking. I hate them both like poison," and as he concluded, he bit into a piece of bread as fiercely as if he were already engaged in a desperate battle with Aunt Rachel, and was biting her in self-defence.

"Well," said Kinch, with the air of a person of vast experience in difficult cases, "I should drown the cat—I'd do that at once—as soon as I got there; then, let me ask you, has Aunt Rachel got corns?"

"Corns! I wish you could see her shoes," replied Charlie. "Why you could sail down the river in 'em, they are so large. Yes, she has got corns, bunions, and rheumatism, and everything else."

"Ah! then," said Kinch, "your way is clear enough if she has got corns. I should confine myself to operating on them. I should give my whole attention to her feet. When she attempts to take hold of you, do you jist come down on her corns, fling your shins about kinder wild, you know, and let her have it on both feet. You see I've tried that plan, and know by experience that it works well. Don't you see, you can pass that off as an accident, and it don't look well to be scratching and biting. As for the lady of the house, old Mrs. what's-her-name, do you just manage to knock her wig off before some company, and they'll send you home at once—they'll hardly give you time to get your hat."

Charlie laid these directions aside in his mind for future application, and asked,

"What did you do, Kinch, to get away from the people you were with?"

"Don't ask me," said Kinch, laughing; "don't, boy, don't ask me—my conscience troubles me awful about it sometimes. I fell up stairs with dishes, and I fell down stairs with dishes. I spilled oil on the carpet, and broke a looking-glass; but it was all accidental—entirely accidental—they found I was too ''spensive,' and so they sent me home."

"Oh, I wouldn't do anything like that—I wouldn't destroy anything—but I've made up my mind that I won't stay there, at any rate. I don't mind work—I want to do something to assist father and mother; but I don't want to be any one's servant. I wish I was big enough to work at the shop."

"How did your mother come to think of putting you there?" asked Kinch.

"The Lord alone knows," was the reply. "I suppose old Mrs. Thomas told her it was the best thing that could be done for me, and mother thinks what she says is law and gospel. I believe old Mrs. Thomas thinks a coloured person can't get to Heaven, without first living at service a little while."

The school bell ringing, put an end to this important conversation, and the boys recommenced their lessons.

When Charlie returned from school, the first person he saw on entering the house was Robberts, Mrs. Thomas's chief functionary, and the presiding genius of the wine-cellar—when he was trusted with the key. Charlie learned, to his horror and dismay, that he had been sent by Mrs. Thomas to inquire into the possibility of obtaining his services immediately, as they were going to have a series of dinner-parties, and it was thought that he could be rendered quite useful.

"And must I go, mother?" he asked.

"Yes, my son; I've told Robberts that you shall come up in the morning," replied Mrs. Ellis. Then turning to Robberts, she inquired, "How is Aunt Rachel?"

At this question, the liveried gentleman from Mrs. Thomas's shook his head dismally, and answered: "Don't ask me, woman; don't ask me, if you please. That old sinner gets worse and worse every day she lives. These dinners we're 'spectin to have has just set her wild—she is mad as fury 'bout 'em—and she snaps me up just as if I was to blame. That is an awful old woman, now mind I tell you."

As Mr. Robberts concluded, he took his hat and departed, giving Charlie the cheering intelligence that he should expect him early next morning.

Charlie quite lost his appetite for supper in consequence of his approaching trials, and, laying aside his books with a sigh of regret, sat listlessly regarding his sisters; enlivened now and then by some cheerful remark from Caddy, such as:—

"You'll have to keep your feet cleaner up there than you do at home, or you'll have Aunt Rach in your wool[1] half a dozen times a day. And you mustn't throw your cap and coat down where you please, on the chairs or tables—she'll bring you out of all that in a short time. I expect you'll have two or three bastings before you have been there a week, for she don't put up with any nonsense. Ah, boy," she concluded, chuckling, "you'll have a time of it—I don't envy you!"

With these and similar enlivening anticipations, Caddy whiled away the time until it was the hour for Charlie to retire for the night, which he did with a heavy heart.

Early the following morning he was awakened by the indefatigable Caddy, and he found a small bundle of necessaries prepared, until his trunk of apparel could be sent to his new home. "Oh, Cad," he exclaimed, rubbing his eyes, "how I do hate to go up there! I'd rather take a good whipping than go."

"Well, it is too late now to talk about it; hurry and get your clothes on—it is quite late—you ought to have been off an hour ago."

When he came down stairs prepared to go, his mother "hoped that he was going to behave like a man," which exhortation had the effect of setting him crying at once; and then he had to be caressed by the tearful Esther, and, finally, started away with very red eyes, followed to the door by his mother and the girls, who stood looking after him for some moments.

So hurried and unexpected had been his departure, that he had been unable to communicate with his friend Kinch. This weighed very heavily on his spirits, and he occupied the time on his way to Mrs. Thomas's in devising various plans to effect that object.

On arriving, he gave a faint rap, that was responded to by Aunt Rachel, who saluted him with—

---

1 I.e., in his hair; chiding him.

"Oh, yer's come, has yer—wipe your feet, child, and come in quick. Shut the door after yer."

"What shall I do with this?" timidly asked he, holding up his package of clothes.

"Oh, dem's yer rags is dey—fling 'em anywhere, but don't bring 'em in my kitchen," said she. "Dere is enuff things in dere now—put 'em down here on this entry table, or dere, long side de knife-board—any wheres but in de kitchen."

Charlie mechanically obeyed, and then followed her into her sanctuary.

"Have you had your breakfast?" she asked, in a surly tone. "'Cause if you haven't, you must eat quick, or you won't get any. I can't keep the breakfast things standing here all day."

Charlie, to whom the long walk had given a good appetite, immediately sat down and ate a prodigious quantity of bread and butter, together with several slices of cold ham, washed down by two cups of tea; after which he rested his knife and fork, and informed Aunt Rachel that he had done.

"Well, I think it's high time," responded she. "Why, boy, you'll breed a famine in de house if you stay here long enough. You'll have to do a heap of work to earn what you'll eat, if yer breakfast is a sample of yer dinner. Come, get up, child! and shell dese 'ere pease—time you get 'em done, old Mrs. Thomas will be down stairs."

Charlie was thus engaged when Mrs. Thomas entered the kitchen. "Well, Charles—good morning," said she, in a bland voice. "I'm glad to see you here so soon. Has he had his breakfast, Aunt Rachel?"

"Yes; and he eat like a wild animal—I never see'd a child eat more in my life," was Aunt Rachel's abrupt answer.

"I'm glad he has a good appetite," said Mrs. Thomas, "it shows he has good health. Boys will eat; you can't expect them to work if they don't. But it is time I was at those custards. Charlie, put down those peas and go into the other room, and bring me a basket of eggs you will find on the table."

"And be sure to overset the milk that's 'long side of it—yer hear?" added Aunt Rachel.

Charlie thought to himself that he would like to accommodate her, but he denied himself that pleasure; on the ground that it might not be safe to do it.[1]

---

1   Charlie takes Aunt Rachel's ironic directive to spill ("overset") the milk seriously for a moment, but then realizes that she would be angry if he were to actually make such a mess.

Mrs. Thomas was a housekeeper of the old school, and had a scientific knowledge of the manner in which all sorts of pies and puddings were compounded. She was so learned in custards and preserves that even Aunt Rachel sometimes deferred to her superior judgment in these matters. Carefully breaking the eggs, she skilfully separated the whites from the yolks, and gave the latter to Charlie to beat. At first he thought it great fun, and he hummed some of the popular melodies of the day, and kept time with his foot and the spatula. But pretty soon he exhausted his stock of tunes, and then the performances did not go off so well. His arm commenced aching, and he came to the sage conclusion, before he was relieved from his task, that those who eat the custards are much better off than those who prepare them.

This task finished, he was pressed into service by Aunt Rachel, to pick and stone some raisins which she gave him, with the injunction either to sing or whistle all the time he was "at 'em;" and that if he stopped for a moment she should know he was eating them, and in that case she would visit him with condign punishment on the spot, for she didn't care a fig whose child he was.

Thus, in the performance of first one little job and then another, the day wore away; and as the hour approached at which the guests were invited, Charlie, after being taken into the dining-room by Robberts, where he was greatly amazed at the display of silver, cut glass, and elegant china, was posted at the door to relieve the guests of their coats and hats, which duty he performed to the entire satisfaction of all parties concerned.

At dinner, however, he was not so fortunate. He upset a plate of soup into a gentleman's lap, and damaged beyond repair one of the elegant china vegetable-dishes. He took rather too deep an interest in the conversation for a person in his station; and, in fact, the bright boy alluded to by Mr. Winston, as having corrected the reverend gentleman respecting the quotation from Chaucer, was no other than our friend Charlie Ellis.

In the evening, when the guests were departing, Charlie handed Mr. Winston his coat, admiring the texture and cut of it very much as he did so. Mr. Winston, amused at the boy's manner, asked—

"What is your name, my little man?"

"Charles Ellis," was the prompt reply. "I'm named after my father."

"And where did your father come from, Charlie?" he asked, looking very much interested.

"From Savannah, sir. Now tell me where you came from," replied Charles.

"I came from New Orleans," said Mr. Winston, with a smile. "Now tell me," he continued, "where do you live when you are with your parents? I should like to see your father." Charlie quickly put his interrogator in possession of the desired information, after which Mr. Winston departed, soon followed by the other guests.

Charlie lay for some time that night on his little cot before he could get to sleep; and amongst the many matters that so agitated his mind, was his wonder what one of Mrs. Thomas's guests could want with his father. Being unable, however, to arrive at any satisfactory conclusion respecting it, he turned over and went to sleep.

CHAPTER IV.

In which Mr. Winston finds an old Friend.

In the early part of Mr. Winston's career, when he worked as a boy on the plantation of his father, he had frequently received great kindness at the hands of one Charles Ellis, who was often employed as carpenter about the premises.

On one occasion, as a great favour, he had been permitted to accompany Ellis to his home in Savannah, which was but a few miles distant, where he remained during the Christmas holidays. This kindness he had never forgotten; and on his return to Georgia from New Orleans he sought for his old friend, and found he had removed to the North, but to which particular city he could not ascertain.

As he walked homewards, the strong likeness of little Charlie to his old friend forced itself upon him; and the more he reflected upon it the more likely it appeared that the boy might be his child; and the identity of name and occupation between the father of Charlie and his old friend led to the belief that he was about to make some discovery respecting him.

On his way to his hotel he passed the old State House, the bell of which was just striking ten. "It's too late to go to-night," said he, "it shall be the first thing I attend to in the morning;" and after walking on a short distance farther, he found himself at the door of his domicile.

As he passed through the little knot of waiters who were gathered about the doors, one of them turning to another, asked, "Ain't that man a Southerner, and ain't he in your rooms, Ben?"

"I think he's a Southerner," was the reply of Ben. "But why do you ask, Allen?" he inquired.

"Because it's time he had subscribed something," replied Mr. Allen. "The funds of the Vigilance Committee[1] are very low indeed; in fact, the four that we helped through last week have

---

1   Locally-controlled organization devoted to small-scale, practical resistance to slave law. Vigilance committees provided aid to fugitive slaves, promoted speakers and fund-raising events, and coordinated general social agitation; they were critical elements of the abolitionist movement, particularly in the so-called Underground Railroad. Black businessman Robert Purvis (1810–98) founded the Vigilant Committee of Philadelphia in 1837 as a clandestine adjunct to the more decorous public advocacy of the Vigilant Association; it operated, off and on, until 1852.

completely drained us. We must make a raise from some quarter, and we might as well try it on him."

Mr. Winston was waiting for a light, that he might retire to his room, and was quickly served by the individual who had been so confidentially talking with Mr. Allen.

After giving Mr. Winston the light, Ben followed him into his room and busied himself in doing little nothings about the stove and wash-stand. "Let me unbutton your straps, sir," said he, stooping down and commencing on the buttons, which he was rather long in unclosing. "I know, sir, dat you Southern gentlemen ain't used to doing dese yer things for youself. I allus makes it a pint to show Southerners more 'tention dan I does to dese yer Northern folk, 'cause yer see I knows dey'r used to it, and can't get on widout it."

"I am not one of that kind," said Winston, as Ben slowly unbuttoned the last strap. "I have been long accustomed to wait upon myself. I'll only trouble you to bring me up a glass of fresh water, and then I shall have done with you for the night."

"Better let me make you up a little fire; the nights is werry cool," continued Ben. "I know you must feel 'em; I does myself; I'm from the South, too."

"Are you?" replied Mr. Winston, with some interest; "from what part?"

"From Tuckahoe county, Virginia; nice place dat."

"Never having been there I can't say," rejoined Mr. Winston, smiling; "and how do you like the North? I suppose you are a runaway?" continued he.

"Oh, no sir! no sir!" replied Ben, "I was sot free—and I often wish," he added in a whining tone, "dat I was back agin on the old place—hain't got no kind marster to look after me here, and I has to work drefful hard sometimes. Ah," he concluded, drawing a long sigh, "if I was only back on de old place!"

"I heartily wish you were!" said Mr. Winston, indignantly, "and wish, moreover, that you were to be tied up and whipped once a day for the rest of your life. Any man that prefers slavery to freedom deserves to be a slave—you ought to be ashamed of yourself. Go out of the room, sir, as quick as possible!"

"Phew!" said the astonished and chagrined Ben, as he descended the stairs; "that was certainly a great miss," continued he, talking as correct English, and with as pure Northern an accent as any one could boast.

"We have made a great mistake this time; a very queer kind of Southerner that is. I'm afraid we took the wrong pig by the ear;"

and as he concluded, he betook himself to the group of white-aproned gentlemen before mentioned, to whom he related the incident that had just occurred.

"Quite a severe fall that, I should say," remarked Mr. Allen. "Perhaps we have made a mistake and he is not a Southerner after all. Well he is registered from New Orleans, and I thought he was a good one to try it on."

"It's a clear case we've missed it this time," exclaimed one of the party, "and I hope, Ben, when you found he was on the other side of the fence, you did not say too much."

"Laws, no!" rejoined Ben, "do you think I'm a fool? As soon as I heard him say what he did, I was glad to get off—I felt cheap enough, now mind, I tell you any one could have bought me for a shilling."

Now it must be here related that most of the waiters employed in this hotel were also connected with the Vigilance Committee of the Under-ground Railroad Company—a society formed for the assistance of fugitive slaves; by their efforts, and by the timely information it was often in their power to give, many a poor slave was enabled to escape from the clutches of his pursuers.

The house in which they were employed was the great resort of Southerners, who occasionally brought with them their slippery property;[1] and it frequently happened that these disappeared from the premises to parts unknown, aided in their flight by the very waiters who would afterwards exhibit the most profound ignorance as to their whereabouts. Such of the Southerners as brought no servants with them were made to contribute, unconsciously and most amusingly, to the escape of those of their friends.

When a gentleman presented himself at the bar wearing boots entirely too small for him, with his hat so far down upon his forehead as almost to obscure his eyes, and whose mouth was filled with oaths and tobacco, he was generally looked upon as a favourable specimen to operate upon; and if he cursed the waiters, addressed any old man amongst them as "boy," and was continually drinking cock-tails and mint-juleps,[2] they were sure of their man; and then would tell him the most astonishing and distressing tales of their destitution, expressing, almost with tears in their eyes, their deep desire to return to their former masters;

---

1 Slaves.

2 Mixed drink made with spirits (typically bourbon or brandy), mint, and simple syrup over crushed ice.

whilst perhaps the person from whose mouth this tale of woe proceeded had been born in a neighbouring street, and had never been south of Mason and Dixon's[1] line. This flattering testimony in favour of "the peculiar institution" generally had the effect of extracting a dollar or two from the purse of the sympathetic Southerner; which money went immediately into the coffers of the Vigilance Committee.

It was this course of conduct they were about to pursue with Mr. Winston; not because he exhibited in person or manners any of the before-mentioned peculiarities, but from his being registered from New Orleans.

The following morning, as soon as he had breakfasted, he started in search of Mr. Ellis. The address was 18, Little Green-street;[2] and, by diligently inquiring, he at length discovered the required place.

After climbing up a long flight of stairs on the outside of an old wooden building, he found himself before a door on which was written, "Charles Ellis, carpenter and joiner."[3] On opening it, he ushered himself into the presence of an elderly coloured man, who was busily engaged in planing off a plank. As soon as Mr. Winston saw his face fully, he recognized him as his old friend. The hair had grown grey, and the form was also a trifle bent; but he would have known him amongst a thousand. Springing forward, he grasped his hand, exclaiming, "My dear old friend, don't you know me?" Mr. Ellis shaded his eyes with his hand, and looked at him intently for a few moments, but seemed no wiser from his scrutiny. The tears started to Mr. Winston's eyes as he said, "Many a kind word I'm indebted to you for—I am George Winston—don't you remember little George that used to live on the Carter estate?"

---

1   [Webb's note:] The line dividing the Free from the Slave states.

2   Street-naming conventions were notoriously erratic in nineteenth-century Philadelphia. Some sources identify Little-Green Street as a two-block alley (now Merino Street) running East–West between Second Street and Germantown Avenue in Philadelphia's then-unincorporated Northern Liberties. Another much longer Green Street runs parallel to Little-Green Street some ten blocks south in the same neighborhood. Other contextual clues, however, place the Ellis house in South Philadelphia, likely in the Southwark or Moyamensing areas; see map of Philadelphia, Appendix C1.

3   Woodworker responsible for fine and ornamental projects, including furniture.

"Why, bless me! it can't be that you are the little fellow that used to go home with me sometimes to Savannah, and that was sold to go to New Orleans?"

"Yes, the same boy; I've been through a variety of changes since then."

"I should think you had," smilingly replied Mr. Ellis; "and, judging from appearances, very favourable ones! Why, I took you for a white man—and you are a white man, as far as complexion is concerned. Laws, child!" he continued, laying his hand familiarly on Winston's shoulders, "how you have changed—I should never have known you! The last time I saw you, you were quite a shaver, running about in a long tow shirt, and regarding a hat and shoes as articles of luxury far beyond your reach. And now," said Mr. Ellis, gazing at him with admiring eyes, "just to look at you! Why, you are as fine a looking man as one would wish to see in a day's travel. I've often thought of you. It was only the other day I was talking to my wife, and wondering what had become of you. She, although a great deal older than your cousin Emily, used to be a sort of playmate of hers. Poor Emily! we heard she was sold at public sale in Savannah—did you ever learn what became of her?"

"Oh, yes; I saw her about two months since, when on my way from New Orleans. You remember old Colonel Garie? Well, his son bought her, and is living with her. They have two children—she is very happy. I really love him; he is the most kind and affectionate fellow in the world; there is nothing he would not do to make her happy. Emily will be so delighted to know that I have seen your wife—but who is Mrs. Ellis?—any one that I know?"

"I do not know that you are acquainted with her; but you should remember her mother, old Nanny Tobert, as she was called; she kept a little confectionery—almost every one in Savannah knew her."

"I can't say I do," replied Winston, reflectively.

"She came here," continued Mr. Ellis, "some years ago, and died soon after her arrival. Her daughter went to live with the Thomases, an old Philadelphia family, and it was from their house I married her."

"Thomases?" repeated Mr. Winston; "that is where I saw your boy—he is the image of you."

"And how came you there?" asked Ellis, with a look of surprise.

"In the most natural manner possible. I was invited there to dinner yesterday—the bright face of your boy attracted my attention—so I inquired his name, and that led to the discovery of yourself."

"And do the Thomases know you are a coloured man?" asked Mr. Ellis, almost speechless with astonishment.

"I rather think not," laughingly rejoined Mr. Winston.

"It is a great risk you run to be passing for white in that way," said Mr. Ellis, with a grave look. "But how did you manage to get introduced to that set? They are our very first people."[1]

"It is a long story," was Winston's reply; and he then, as briefly as he could, related all that had occurred to himself since they last met. "And now," continued he, as he finished his recital, "I want to know all about you and your family; and I also want to see something of the coloured people. Since I've been in the North I've met none but whites. I'm not going to return to New Orleans to remain. I'm here in search of a home. I wish to find some place to settle down in for life, where I shall not labour under as many disadvantages as I must struggle against in the South."

"One thing I must tell you," rejoined Mr. Ellis; "if you should settle down here, you'll have to be either one thing or other— white or coloured. Either you must live exclusively amongst coloured people, or go to the whites and remain with them. But to do the latter, you must bear in mind that it must never be known that you have a drop of African blood in your veins, or you would be shunned as if you were a pestilence; no matter how fair in complexion or how white you may be."

"I have not as yet decided on trying the experiment, and I hardly think it probable I shall," rejoined Winston. As he said this he took out his watch, and was astonished to find how very long his visit had been. He therefore gave his hand to Mr. Ellis, and promised to return at six o'clock and accompany him home to visit his family.

As he was leaving the shop, Mr. Ellis remarked: "George, you have not said a word respecting your mother." His face flushed, and the tears started in his eyes, as he replied, in a broken voice, "She's dead! Only think, Ellis, she died within a stone's throw of me, and I searching for her all the while. I never speak of it unless compelled; it is too harrowing. It was a great trial to me; it almost broke my heart to think that she perished miserably so near me, whilst I was in the enjoyment of every luxury. Oh, if she could only have lived to see me as I am now!" continued he; "but He ordered it otherwise, and we must bow. 'Twas God's will it

---

1 I.e., of high social standing.

should be so. Good bye till evening. I shall see you again at six."

Great was the surprise of Mrs. Ellis and her daughters on learning from Mr. Ellis, when he came home to dinner, of the events of the morning; and great was the agitation caused by the announcement of the fact that his friend was to be their guest in the evening.

Mrs. Ellis proposed inviting some of their acquaintances to meet him; but to this project her husband objected, saying he wanted to have a quiet evening with him, and to talk over old times; and that persons who were entire strangers to him would only be a restraint upon them.

Caddy seemed quite put out by the announcement of the intended visit. She declared that nothing was fit to be seen, that the house was in a state of disorder shocking to behold, and that there was scarce a place in it fit to sit down in; and she forthwith began to prepare for an afternoon's vigorous scrubbing and cleaning.

"Just let things remain as they are, will you, Caddy dear," said her father. "Please be quiet until I get out of the house," he continued, as she began to make unmistakable demonstrations towards raising a dust. "In a few moments you shall have the house to yourself, only give me time to finish my dinner in peace."

Esther, her mother, and their sewing were summarily banished to an upstairs room, whilst Caddy took undivided possession of the little parlour, which she soon brought into an astonishing state of cleanliness. The ornaments were arranged at exact distances from the corners of the mantelpiece, the looking-glass was polished, until it appeared to be without spot or blemish, and its gilt frame was newly adorned with cut paper to protect it from the flies. The best china was brought out, carefully dusted, and set upon the waiter,[1] and all things within doors placed in a state of forwardness to receive their expected guest. The door-steps were, however, not as white and clean as they might be, and that circumstance pressed upon Caddy's mind. She therefore determined to give them a hasty wipe before retiring to dress for the evening.

Having done this, and dressed herself to her satisfaction, she came down stairs to prepare the refreshments for tea. In doing this, she continually found herself exposing her new silk dress to

---

1 Dumb-waiter, in the early sense of a movable stand for dishes or bottles. See *OED* "dumb-waiter" 1.

great risks. She therefore donned an old petticoat over her skirt, and tied an old silk handkerchief over her head to protect her hair from flying particles of dust; and thus arrayed she passed the time in a state of great excitement, frequently looking out of the window to see if her father and their guest were approaching.

In one of these excursions, she, to her intense indignation, found a beggar boy endeavouring to draw, with a piece of charcoal, an illustration of a horse-race upon her so recently cleaned door-steps.

"You young villain," she almost screamed, "go away from there. How dare you make those marks upon the steps? Go off at once, or I'll give you to a constable." To these behests the daring young gentleman only returned a contemptuous laugh, and put his thumb to his nose in the most provoking manner. "Ain't you going?" continued the irate Caddy, almost choked with wrath at the sight of the steps, over which she had so recently toiled, scored in every direction with black marks.

"Just wait till I come down, I'll give it to you, you audacious villain, you," she cried, as she closed the window; "I'll see if I can't move you!" Caddy hastily seized a broom, and descended the stairs with the intention of inflicting summary vengeance upon the dirty delinquent who had so rashly made himself liable to her wrath. Stealing softly down the alley beside the house, she sprang suddenly forward, and brought the broom with all her energy down upon the head of Mr. Winston, who was standing on the place just left by the beggar. She struck with such force as to completely crush his hat down over his eyes, and was about to repeat the blow, when her father caught her arm, and she became aware of the awful mistake she had made.

"Why, my child!" exclaimed her father, "what on earth is the matter with you, have you lost your senses?" and as he spoke, he held her at arm's length from him to get a better look at her. "What are you dressed up in this style for?" he continued, as he surveyed her from head to foot; and then bursting into a loud laugh at her comical appearance, he released her, and she made the quickest possible retreat into the house by the way she came out.

Rushing breathless upstairs, she exclaimed, "Oh, mother, mother, I've done it now! They've come, and I've beat him over the head with a broom!"

"Beat whom over the head with a broom?" asked Mrs. Ellis.

"Oh, mother, I'm so ashamed, I don't know what to do with myself. I struck Mr. Winston with a broom. Mr. Winston, the gentleman father has brought home."

"I really believe the child is crazy," said Mrs. Ellis, surveying the chagrined girl. "Beat Mr. Winston over the head with a broom! how came you to do it?"

"Oh, mother, I made a great mistake; I thought he was a beggar."

"He must be a very different looking person from what we have been led to expect," here interrupted Esther. "I understood father to say that he was very gentlemanlike in appearance."

"So he is," replied Caddy.

"But you just said you took him for a beggar?" replied her mother.

"Oh, don't bother me, don't bother me! my head is all turned upside down. Do, Esther, go down and let them in—hear how furiously father is knocking! Oh, go—do go!"

Esther quickly descended and opened the door for Winston and her father; and whilst the former was having the dust removed and his hat straightened, Mrs. Ellis came down and was introduced by her husband. She laughingly apologized for the ludicrous mistake Caddy had made, which afforded great amusement to all parties, and divers were the jokes perpetrated at her expense during the remainder of the evening.

Her equanimity having been restored by Winston's assurances that he rather enjoyed the joke than otherwise—and an opportunity having been afforded her to obliterate the obnoxious marks from the door-steps—she exhibited great activity in forwarding all the arrangements for tea.

They sat a long while round the table—much time that, under ordinary circumstances, would have been given to the demolition of the food before them, being occupied by the elders of the party in inquiries after mutual friends, and in relating the many incidents that had occurred since they last met.

Tea being at length finished, and the things cleared away, Mrs. Ellis gave the girls permission to go out. "Where are you going?" asked their father.

"To the library company's room—to-night is their last lecture."[1]

"I thought," said Winston, "that coloured persons were excluded from such places. I certainly have been told so several times."

"It is quite true," replied Mr. Ellis; "at the lectures of the white library societies a coloured person would no more be permitted to enter than a donkey or a rattle-snake. This association they

---

1 See above, p. 47, note 1.

speak of is entirely composed of people of colour. They have a fine library, a debating club, chemical apparatus, collections of minerals, &c. They have been having a course of lectures delivered before them this winter, and tonight is the last of the course."

"Wouldn't you like to go, Mr. Winston?" asked Mrs. Ellis, who had a mother's desire to secure so fine an escort for her daughters.

"No, no—don't, George," quickly interposed Mr. Ellis; "I am selfish enough to want you entirely to myself to-night. The girls will find beaux enough, I'll warrant you." At this request the girls did not seem greatly pleased; and Miss Caddy, who already, in imagination, had excited the envy of all her female friends by the grand *entrée* she was to make at the Lyceum, leaning on the arm of Winston, gave her father a by no means affectionate look, and tying her bonnet-strings with a hasty jerk, started out in company with her sister.

"You appear to be very comfortable here, Ellis," said Mr. Winston, looking round the apartment. "If I am not too inquisitive—what rent do you pay for this house?"

"It's mine!" replied Ellis, with an air of satisfaction; "house, ground, and all, bought and paid for since I settled here."

"Why, you are getting on well! I suppose," remarked Winston, "that you are much better off than the majority of your coloured friends. From all I can learn, the free coloured people in the Northern cities are very badly off. I've been frequently told that they suffer dreadfully from want and privations of various kinds."

"Oh, I see you have been swallowing the usual dose that is poured down Southern throats by those Northern negro-haters, who seem to think it a duty they owe the South to tell all manner of infamous lies upon us free coloured people. I really get so indignant and provoked sometimes, that I scarcely know what to do with myself. Badly off, and in want, indeed! Why, my dear sir, we not only support our own poor, but assist the whites to support theirs, and enemies are continually filling the public ear with the most distressing tales of our destitution![1] Only the other day the Colonization Society had the assurance to present a petition to the legislature of this state, asking for an appropriation to assist them in sending us all to Africa, that we might no longer remain a burthen upon the state—and they came very near

---

1 Ellis here tracks closely the arguments made by Robert Purvis in *Appeal of Forty Thousand Citizens*; see Appendix C3.

getting it, too; had it not been for the timely assistance of young Denbigh, the son of Judge Denbigh, they would have succeeded, such was the gross ignorance that prevailed respecting our real condition, amongst the members of the legislature. He moved a postponement of the vote until he could have time to bring forward facts to support the ground that he had assumed in opposition to the appropriation being made. It was granted; and, in a speech that does him honour, he brought forward facts that proved us to be in a much superior condition to that in which our imaginative enemies had described us. Ay! he did more—he proved us to be in advance of the whites in wealth and general intelligence: for whilst it was one in fifteen amongst the whites unable to read and write, it was but one in eighteen amongst the coloured (I won't pretend to be correct about the figures, but that was about the relative proportions); and also, that we paid, in the shape of taxes upon our real estate, more than our proportion for the support of paupers, insane, convicts, &c."

"Well," said the astonished Winston, "that is turning the tables completely. You must take me to visit amongst the coloured people; I want to see as much of them as possible during my stay."

"I'll do what I can for you, George. I am unable to spare you much time just at present, but I'll put you in the hands of one who has abundance of it at his disposal—I will call with you and introduce you to Walters."

"Who is Walters?" asked Mr. Winston.

"A friend of mine—a dealer in real estate."

"Oh, then he is a white man?"

"Not by any means," laughingly replied Mr. Ellis. "He is as black as a man can conveniently be. He is very wealthy; some say that he is worth half a million of dollars. He owns, to my certain knowledge, one hundred brick houses. I met him the other day in a towering rage: it appears, that he owns ten thousand dollars' worth of stock, in a railroad extending from this to a neighbouring city. Having occasion to travel in it for some little distance, he got into the first-class cars; the conductor, seeing him there, ordered him out—he refused to go, and stated that he was a shareholder. The conductor replied, that he did not care how much stock he owned, he was a nigger, and that no nigger should ride in those cars; so he called help, and after a great deal of trouble they succeeded in ejecting him."

"And he a stockholder! It was outrageous," exclaimed Winston. "And was there no redress?"

"No, none, practically. He would have been obliged to institute a suit against the company; and, as public opinion now is, it would be impossible for him to obtain a verdict in his favour."

The next day Winston was introduced to Mr. Walters, who expressed great pleasure in making his acquaintance, and spent a week in showing him everything of any interest connected with coloured people.

Winston was greatly delighted with the acquaintances he made; and the kindness and hospitality with which he was received made a most agreeable impression upon him.

It was during this period that he wrote the glowing letters to Mr. and Mrs. Garie, the effects of which will be discerned in the next chapter.

CHAPTER V.

The Garies decide on a Change.

WE must now return to the Garies, whom we left listening to Mr. Winston's description of what he saw in Philadelphia, and we need not add anything respecting it to what the reader has already gathered from the last chapter; our object being now to describe the effect his narrative produced.

On the evening succeeding the departure of Winston for New Orleans, Mr. and Mrs. Garie were seated in a little arbour at a short distance from the house, and which commanded a magnificent prospect up and down the river. It was overshadowed by tall trees, from the topmost branches of which depended large bunches of Georgian moss, swayed to and fro by the soft spring breeze that came gently sweeping down the long avenue of magnolias, laden with the sweet breath of the flowers with which the trees were covered.

A climbing rose and Cape jessamine had almost covered this arbour, and their intermingled blossoms, contrasting with the rich brown colour of the branches of which it was constructed, gave it an exceedingly beautiful and picturesque appearance.

This arbour was their favourite resort in the afternoons of summer, as they could see from it the sun go down behind the low hills opposite, casting his gleams of golden light upon the tops of the trees that crowned their summits. Northward, where the chain of hills was broken, the waters of the river would be brilliant with waves of gold long after the other parts of it were shrouded in the gloom of twilight.

Mr. and Mrs. Garie sat looking at the children, who were scampering about the garden in pursuit of a pet rabbit which had escaped, and seemed determined not to be caught upon any pretence whatever.

"Are they not beautiful?" said Mr. Garie, with pride, as they bounded past him. "There are not two prettier children in all Georgia. You don't seem half proud enough of them," he continued, looking down upon his wife affectionately.

Mrs. Garie, who was half reclining on the seat, and leaning her head upon his shoulder, replied, "Oh, yes, I am, Garie; I'm sure I love them dearly—oh, so dearly!" continued she, fervently— "and I only wish"—here she paused, as if she felt she had been going to say something that had better remain unspoken.

"You only wish what, dear? You were going to say something," rejoined her husband. "Come, out with it, and let me hear what it was."

"Oh, Garie, it was nothing of any consequence."

"Consequence or no consequence, let me hear what it was, dear."

"Well, as you insist on hearing it, I was about to say that I wish they were not little slaves."

"Oh, Em! Em!" exclaimed he, reproachfully, "how can you speak in that manner? I thought, dear, that you regarded me in any other light than that of a master. What have I done to revive the recollection that any such relation existed between us? Am I not always kind and affectionate? Did you ever have a wish ungratified for a single day, if it was in my power to compass it? or have I ever been harsh or neglectful?"

"Oh, no, dear, no—forgive me, Garie—do, pray, forgive me—you are kindness itself—believe me, I did not think to hurt your feelings by saying what I did. I know you do not treat me or them as though we were slaves. But I cannot help feeling that we are such, and it makes me very sad and unhappy sometimes. If anything should happen that you should be taken away suddenly, think what would be our fate. Heirs would spring up from somewhere, and we might be sold and separated for ever. Respecting myself I might be indifferent, but regarding the children I cannot feel so."

"Tut, tut, Em! don't talk so gloomily. Do you know of any one, now, who has been hired to put me to death?" said he, smiling.

"Don't talk so, dear; remember, 'In the midst of life we are in death.' It was only this morning I learned that Celeste—you remember Celeste, don't you?—I cannot recall her last name."

"No, dear, I really can't say that I do remember whom you refer to."

"I can bring her to your recollection, I think," continued she. "One afternoon last fall we were riding together on the Augusta-road, when you stopped to admire a very neat cottage, before the door of which two pretty children were playing."

"Oh, yes, I remember something about it—I admired the children so excessively that you became quite jealous."

"I don't remember that part of it," she continued. "But let me tell you my story. Last week the father of the children started for Washington; the cars ran off the track, and were precipitated down a high embankment, and he and some others were killed. Since his death it has been discovered that all his property was heavily mortgaged to old MacTurk, the worst man in the whole of Savannah; and he has taken possession of the place, and thrown her and the children into the slave-pen, from which they will be sold to the highest bidder at a sheriff's sale. Who can say that a similar fate may never be mine? These things press upon my spirit, and make me so gloomy and melancholy at times, that I wish it were possible to shun even myself. Lately, more than ever, have I felt disposed to beg you to break up here, and move off to some foreign country where there is no such thing as slavery. I have often thought how delightful it would be for us all to be living in that beautiful Italy you have so often described to me—or in France either. You said you liked both those places— why not live in one of them?"

"No, no, Emily; I love America too much to ever think of living anywhere else. I am much too thorough a democrat ever to swear allegiance to a king. No, no—that would never do—give me a free country."

"That is just what I say," rejoined Mrs. Garie; "that is exactly what I want; that is why I should like to get away from here, because this is *not* a free country—God knows it is not!"

"Oh! you little traitor! How severely you talk, abusing your native land in such shocking style, it's really painful to hear you," said Mr. Garie in a jocular tone.

"Oh, love," rejoined she, "don't joke, it's not a subject for jesting. It is heavier upon my heart than you dream of. Wouldn't you like to live in the Free states? There is nothing particular to keep you here, and only think how much better it would be for the children: and Garie," she continued in a lower tone, nestling close to him as she spoke, and drawing his head towards her, "I think I am going to—" and she whispered some words in his ear, and as she finished she shook her head, and her long curls fell down in clusters over her face.

Mr. Garie put the curls aside, and kissing her fondly, asked, "How long have you known it, dear?"

"Not long, not very long," she replied. "And I have such a yearning that it should be born a free child. I do want that the first air it breathes should be that of freedom. It will kill me to have another child born here! its infant smiles would only be a reproach to me. Oh!" continued she, in a tone of deep feeling, "it is a fearful thing to give birth to an inheritor of chains;" and she shuddered as she laid her head on her husband's bosom.

Mr. Garie's brow grew thoughtful, and a pause in the conversation ensued. The sun had long since gone down, and here and there the stars were beginning to show their twinkling light. The moon, which had meanwhile been creeping higher and higher in the blue expanse above, now began to shed her pale, misty beams on the river below, the tiny waves of which broke in little circlets of silver on the shore almost at their feet.

Mr. Garie was revolving in his mind the conversation he had so recently held with Mr. Winston respecting the Free states. It had been suggested by him that the children should be sent to the North to be educated, but he had dismissed the notion, well knowing that the mother would be heart-broken at the idea of parting with her darlings. Until now, the thought of going to reside in the North had never been presented for his consideration. He was a Southerner in almost all his feelings, and had never had a scruple respecting the ownership of slaves. But now the fact that he was the master as well as the father of his children, and that whilst he resided where he did it was out of his power to manumit[1] them; that in the event of his death they might be seized and sold by his heirs, whoever they might be, sent a thrill of horror through him. He had known all this before, but it had never stood out in such bold relief until now.

"What are you thinking of, Garie?" asked his wife, looking up into his face. "I hope I have not vexed you by what I've said."

"Oh, no, dear, not at all. I was only thinking whether you would be any happier if I acceded to your wishes and removed to the North. Here you live in good style—you have a luxurious home, troops of servants to wait upon you, a carriage at your disposal. In fact, everything for which you express a desire."

"I know all that, Garie; and what I am about to say may seem ungrateful; but believe me, dear, I do not mean it to be so. I had much rather live on crusts and wear the coarsest clothes, and work night and day to earn them, than live here in luxury, wearing gilded chains. Carriages and fine clothes cannot create happiness. I have every physical comfort, and yet my heart is often heavy— oh, so very heavy; I know I am envied by many for my fine establishment; yet how joyfully would I give it all up and accept the meanest living for the children's freedom—and your love."

"But, Emily, granted we should remove to the North, you would find annoyances there as well as here. There is a great deal of prejudice existing there against people of colour, which often exposes them to great inconveniences."

"Yes, dear, I know all that; I should expect that. But then, on the other hand, remember what George said respecting the

---

1 Free an enslaved person.

coloured people themselves; what a pleasant social circle they form, and how intelligent many of them are! Oh, Garie, how I have longed for friends!—we have visitors now and then, but none that I can call friends. The gentlemen who come to see you occasionally are polite to me, but, under existing circumstances, I feel that they cannot entertain for me the respect I think I deserve. I know they look down upon and despise me because I'm a coloured woman. Then there would be another advantage; I should have some female society—here I have none. The white ladies of the neighbourhood will not associate with me, although I am better educated, thanks to your care, than many of them; so it is only on rare occasions, when I can coax some of our more cultivated coloured acquaintances from Savannah to pay us a short visit, that I have any female society; and no woman can be happy without it. I have no parents, nor yet have you. We have nothing we greatly love to leave behind—no strong ties to break; and in consequence would be subjected to no great grief at leaving. If I only could persuade you to go!" said she, imploringly.

"Well, Emily," replied he, in an undecided manner, "I'll think about it. I love you so well, that I believe I should be willing to make any sacrifice for your happiness. But it is getting damp and chilly; and you know," said he, smiling, "you must be more than usually careful of yourself now."

The next evening, and many more besides, were spent in discussing the proposed change. Many objections to it were stated, weighed carefully, and finally set aside. Winston was written to and consulted, and though he expressed some surprise at the proposal, gave it his decided approval. He advised, at the same time, that the estate should not be sold, but be placed in the hands of some trustworthy person, to be managed in Mr. Garie's absence. Under the care of a first-rate overseer, it would not only yield a handsome income; but, should they be dissatisfied with their Northern home, they would have the old place still in reserve; and with the knowledge that they had this to fall back upon, they could try their experiment of living in the North with their minds less harassed than they otherwise would be respecting the result.

As Mr. Garie reflected more and more on the probable beneficial results of the project, his original disinclination to it diminished, until he finally determined on running the risk; and he felt fully rewarded for this concession to his wife's wishes when he saw her recover all her wonted serenity and sprightliness.

They were soon in all the bustle and confusion consequent on preparing for a long journey. When Mr. Garie's determination to remove became known, great consternation prevailed on the plantation, and dismal forebodings were entertained by the slaves as to the result upon themselves. Divers were the lamentations heard on all sides, when they were positively convinced that "massa was gwine away for true;" but they were somewhat pacified, when they learned that no one was to be sold, and that the place would not change hands. For Mr. Garie was a very kind master, and his slaves were as happy as slaves can be under any circumstances. Not much less was the surprise which the contemplated change excited in the neighbourhood, and it was commented on pretty freely by his acquaintances. One of them—to whom he had in conversation partially opened his mind, and explained that his intended removal grew out of anxiety respecting the children, and his own desire that they might be where they could enjoy the advantages of schools, &c.—sneered almost to his face at what he termed his crack-brained notions; and subsequently, in relating to another person the conversation he had had with Mr. Garie, spoke of him as "a soft-headed fool, led by the nose by a yaller[1] wench. Why can't he act," he said, "like other men who happen to have half-white children—breed them up for the market, and sell them?" and he might have added, "as I do," for he was well known to have so acted by two or three of his own tawny offspring.

Mr. Garie, at the suggestion of Winston, wrote to Mr. Walters, to procure them a small, but neat and comfortable house, in Philadelphia; which, when procured, he was to commit to the care of Mr. and Mrs. Ellis, who were to have it furnished and made ready to receive him and his family on their arrival, as Mr. Garie desired to save his wife, as much as possible, from the care and anxiety attendant upon the arrangement of a new residence.

One most important matter, and on which depended the comfort and happiness of his people, was the selection of a proper overseer. On its becoming known that he required such a functionary, numbers of individuals who aspired to that dignified and honourable office applied forthwith; and as it was also known that the master was to be absent, and that, in consequence, the party having it under his entire control, could cut and slash without being interfered with, the value of the situation was

---

1 I.e., yellow: a common designation for mixed-race people in the nineteenth century, here used derisively.

greatly enhanced. It had also another irresistible attraction,—the absence of the master would enable the overseer to engage in the customary picking and stealing operations, with less chance of detection.

In consequence of all these advantages, there was no want of applicants. Great bony New England men, traitors to the air they first breathed, came anxiously forward to secure the prize. Mean, weasen[1]-faced, poor white Georgians, who were able to show testimonials of their having produced large crops with a small number of hands, and who could tell to a fraction how long a slave could be worked on a given quantity of corn, also put in their claims for consideration. Short, thick-set men, with fierce faces, who gloried in the fact that they had at various times killed refractory negroes, also presented themselves to undergo the necessary examination.

Mr. Garie sickened as he contemplated the motley mass of humanity that presented itself with such eagerness for the attainment of so degrading an office; and as he listened to their vulgar boastings and brutal language, he blushed to think that such men were his countrymen.

Never until now had he had occasion for an overseer. He was not ambitious of being known to produce the largest crop to the acre, and his hands had never been driven to that shocking extent, so common with his neighbours. He had been his own manager, assisted by an old negro, called Ephraim—most generally known as Eph, and to him had been intrusted the task of immediately superintending the hands engaged in the cultivation of the estate. This old man was a great favourite with the children, and Clarence, who used to accompany him on his pony over the estate, regarded him as the most wonderful and accomplished coloured gentleman in existence.

Eph was in a state of great perturbation at the anticipated change, and he earnestly sought to be permitted to accompany them to the North. Mr. Garie was, however, obliged to refuse his request, as he said that it was impossible that the place could get on without him.

An overseer being at last procured, whose appearance and manners betokened a better heart than that of any who had yet applied for the situation, and who was also highly recommended for skill and honesty; nothing now remained to prevent Mr. Garie's early departure.

---

1 Variant spelling of "wizened"; shriveled-up.

CHAPTER VI.

Pleasant News.

ONE evening Mr. Ellis was reading the newspaper, and Mrs. Ellis and the girls were busily engaged in sewing, when who should come in but Mr. Walters, who had entered without ceremony at the front door, which had been left open, owing to the unusual heat of the weather.

"Here you all are, hard at work," exclaimed he, in his usual hearty manner, accepting at the same time the chair offered to him by Esther.

"Come, now," continued he, "lay aside your work and newspapers, for I have great news to communicate."

"Indeed, what is it?—what can it be?" cried the three females, almost in a breath; "do let us hear it!"

"Oh," said Mr. Walters, in a provokingly slow tone, "I don't think I'll tell you to-night; it may injure your rest; it will keep till to-morrow."

"Now, that is always the way with Mr. Walters," said Caddy, pettishly; "he always rouses one's curiosity, and then refuses to gratify it;—he is so tantalizing sometimes!"

"I'll tell you this much," said he, looking slily at Caddy, "it is connected with a gentleman who had the misfortune to be taken for a beggar, and who was beaten over the head in consequence by a young lady of my acquaintance."

"Now, father has been telling you that," exclaimed Caddy, looking confused, "and I don't thank him for it either; I hear of that everywhere I go—even the Burtons know of it."

Mr. Walters now looked round the room, as though he missed some one, and finally exclaimed, "Where is Charlie? I thought I missed somebody—where is my boy?"

"We have put him out to live at Mrs. Thomas's," answered Mrs. Ellis, hesitatingly, for she knew Mr. Walters' feelings respecting the common practice of sending little coloured boys to service. "It is a very good place for him," continued she—"a most excellent place."

"That is too bad," rejoined Mr. Walters—"too bad; it is a shame to make a servant of a bright clever boy like that. Why, Ellis, man, how came you to consent to his going? The boy should be at school. It really does seem to me that you people who have good and smart boys take the very course to ruin them. The worst thing you can do with a boy of his age is to put him at service.

Once get a boy into the habit of working for a stipend, and, depend upon it, when he arrives at manhood, he will think that if he can secure so much a month for the rest of his life he will be perfectly happy. How would you like him to be a subservient old numskull, like that old Robberts of theirs?"

Here Esther interrupted Mr. Walters by saying, "I am very glad to hear you express yourself in that manner, Mr. Walters—very glad. Charlie is such a bright, active little fellow; I hate to have him living there as a servant. And he dislikes it, too, as much as any one can. I do wish mother would take him away."

"Hush, Esther," said her mother, sharply; "your mother lived at service, and no one ever thought the worse of her for it."

Esther looked abashed, and did not attempt to say anything farther.

"Now, look here, Ellen," said Mr. Walters. (He called her Ellen, for he had been long intimate with the family.) "If you can't get on without the boy's earning something, why don't you do as white women and men do? Do you ever find them sending their boys out as servants? No; they rather give them a stock of matches, blacking, newspapers, or apples, and start them out to sell them. What is the result? The boy that learns to sell matches soon learns to sell other things; he learns to make bargains; he becomes a small trader, then a merchant, then a millionaire. Did you ever hear of any one who had made a fortune at service? Where would I or Ellis have been, had we been hired out all our lives at so much a month? It begets a feeling of dependence to place a boy in such a situation; and, rely upon it, if he stays there long, it will spoil him for anything better all his days."

Mrs. Ellis was here compelled to add, by way of justifying herself, that it was not their intention to let him remain there permanently; his father only having given his consent for him to serve during the vacation.

"Well, don't let him stay there longer, I pray you," continued Walters. "A great many white people think that we are only fit for servants; and I must confess we do much to strengthen the opinion by permitting our children to occupy such situations when we are not in circumstances to compel us to do so. Mrs. Thomas may tell you that they respect their old servant Robberts as much as they do your husband; but they don't, nevertheless— I don't believe a word of it. It is impossible to have the same respect for the man who cleans your boots, that you have for the man who plans and builds your house."

"Oh, well, Walters," here interposed Mr. Ellis, "I don't intend the boy to remain there, so don't get yourself into an unnecessary state of excitement about it. Let us hear what this great news is that you have brought."

"Oh, I had almost forgotten it," laughingly replied Walters, at the same time fumbling in his pocket for a letter, which he at length produced. "Here," he continued, opening it, "is a letter I have received from a Mr. Garie, inclosing another from our friend Winston. This Mr. Garie writes me that he is coming to the North to settle, and desires me to procure them a house; and he says also that he has so far presumed upon an early acquaintance of his wife with Mrs. Ellis as to request that she will attend to the furnishing of it. You are to purchase all that is necessary to make them comfortable, and I am to foot the bills."

"What, you don't mean Emily Winston's husband?" said the astonished Mrs. Ellis.

"I can't say whose husband it is; but from Winston's letter," replied Mr. Walters, "I suppose he is the person alluded to."

"That *is* news," continued Mrs. Ellis. "Only think, she was a little mite of a thing when I first knew her, and now she is a woman and the mother of two children. How time does fly. I must be getting quite old," concluded she, with a sigh.

"Nonsense, Ellen," remarked Mr. Ellis, "you look surprisingly young, you are quite a girl yet. Why, it was only the other day I was asked if you were one of my daughters."

Mrs. Ellis and the girls laughed at this sally of their father, who asked Mr. Walters if he had as yet any house in view.

"There is one of my houses in Winter-street that I think will just suit them. The former tenants moved out about a week since. If I can call for you to-morrow," he continued turning to Mrs. Ellis, "will you accompany me there to take a look at the premises?"

"It is a dreadful long walk," replied Mrs. Ellis. "How provoking it is to think, that because persons are coloured they are not permitted to ride in the omnibuses[1] or other public conveyances! I do hope I shall live to see the time when we shall be treated as civilized creatures should be."

"I suppose we shall be so treated when the Millennium[2] comes," rejoined Walters, "not before, I am afraid; and as we have

---

1 Horse-drawn mass-transit vehicles.
2 The thousand-year period of Christ's reign after the end of the world. See Revelation 20.

no reason to anticipate that it will arrive before to-morrow, we shall have to walk to Winter-street, or take a private conveyance. At any rate, I shall call for you to-morrow at ten. Good night—remember, at ten."

"Well, this is a strange piece of intelligence," exclaimed Mrs. Ellis, as the door closed upon Mr. Walters. "I wonder what on earth can induce them to move on here. Their place, I am told, is a perfect paradise. In old Colonel Garie's time it was said to be the finest in Georgia. I wonder if he really intends to live here permanently?"

"I can't say, my dear," replied Mr. Ellis; "I am as much in the dark as you are."

"Perhaps they are getting poor, Ellis, and are coming here because they can live cheaper."

"Oh, no, wife; I don't think that can be the occasion of their removal. I rather imagine he purposes emancipating his children. He cannot do it legally in Georgia; and, you know, by bringing them here, and letting them remain six months, they are free—so says the law of some of the Southern States, and I think of Georgia."[1]

The next morning Mrs. Ellis, Caddy, and Mr. Walters, started for Winter-street; it was a very long walk, and when they arrived there, they were all pretty well exhausted.

"Oh, dear," exclaimed Mrs. Ellis, after walking upstairs, "I am so tired, and there is not a chair in the house. I must rest here," said she, seating herself upon the stairs, and looking out upon the garden. "What a large yard! if ours were only as large as this, what a delightful place I could make of it! But there is no room to plant anything at our house, the garden is so very small."

After they were all somewhat rested, they walked through the house and surveyed the rooms, making some favourable commentary upon each.

"The house don't look as if it would want much cleaning," said Caddy, with a tone of regret.

"So much the better, I should say," suggested Mr. Walters.

---

1   Mr. Ellis may be referring to a law of Pennsylvania, not Georgia. In Pennsylvania, *An Act for the Gradual Abolition of Slavery*, which passed in 1780, granted enslaved people their freedom on their 28th birthday and declared that any slave who entered the state with an owner and lived there for longer than six months would automatically become free. In 1847, Pennsylvania outlawed slavery entirely.

"Not as Caddy views the matter," rejoined Mrs. Ellis. "She is so fond of house-cleaning, that I positively think she regards the cleanly state of the premises as rather a disadvantage than otherwise."

They were all, however, very well pleased with the place; and on their way home they settled which should be the best bedroom, and where the children should sleep. They also calculated how much carpet and oilcloth[1] would be necessary, and what style of furniture should be put in the parlour.

"I think the letter said plain, neat furniture, and not too expensive, did it not?" asked Mrs. Ellis.

"I think those were the very words," replied Caddy; "and, oh, mother, isn't it nice to have the buying of so many pretty things? I do so love to shop!"

"Particularly with some one else's money," rejoined her mother, with a smile.

"Yes, or one's own either, when one has it," continued Caddy; "I like to spend money under any circumstances."

Thus in conversation relative to the house and its fixtures, they beguiled the time until they reached their home. On arriving there, Mrs. Ellis found Robberts awaiting her return with a very anxious countenance. He informed her that Mrs. Thomas wished to see her immediately; that Charlie had been giving that estimable lady a world of trouble; and that her presence was necessary to set things to rights.

"What has he been doing?" asked Mrs. Ellis.

"Oh, lots of things! He and aunt Rachel don't get on together at all; and last night he came nigh having the house burned down over our heads."

"Why, Robberts, you don't tell me so! What a trial boys are," sighed Mrs. Ellis.

"He got on first rate for a week or two; but since that he has been raising Satan. He and aunt Rachel had a regular brush yesterday, and he has actually lamed the old woman to that extent she won't be able to work for a week to come."

"Dear, dear, what am I to do?" said the perplexed Mrs. Ellis; "I can't go up there immediately, I am too tired. Say to Mrs. Thomas I will come up this evening. I wonder," concluded she, "what has come over the boy."

---

1   Canvas treated with oil or resin to make it water-resistant. It was used in numerous domestic capacities, including floor-coverings and tablecloths.

"Mother, you know how cross aunt Rachel is; I expect she has been ill-treating him. He is so good-natured, that he never would behave improperly to an old person unless goaded to it by some very harsh usage."

"That's the way—go on, Esther, find some excuse for your angel," said Caddy, ironically. "Of course that lamb could not do anything wrong, and, according to your judgment, he never does; but, I tell you, he is as bad as any other boy—boys are boys. I expect he has been tracking over the floor after aunt Rachel has scrubbed it, or has been doing something equally provoking; he has been in mischief, depend upon it."

Things had gone on very well with Master Charlie for the first two weeks after his introduction into the house of the fashionable descendant of the worthy maker of leathern breeches. His intelligence, combined with the quickness and good-humour with which he performed the duties assigned him, quite won the regard of the venerable lady who presided over that establishment. It is true she had detected him in several attempts upon the peace and well-being of aunt Rachel's Tom; but with Tom she had little sympathy, he having recently made several felonious descents upon her stores of cream and custards. In fact, it was not highly probable, if any of his schemes had resulted seriously to the spiteful *protégé* of aunt Rachel, that Mrs. Thomas would have been overwhelmed with grief, or disposed to inflict any severe punishment on the author of the catastrophe.

Unfortunately for Mrs. Thomas, Charlie, whilst going on an errand, had fallen in with his ancient friend and adviser—in short, he had met no less a person than the formerly all-sufficient Kinch. Great was the delight of both parties at this unexpected meeting, and warm, indeed, was the exchange of mutual congratulations on this auspicious event.

Kinch, in the excess of his delight, threw his hat several feet in the air; nor did his feelings of pleasure undergo the least abatement when that dilapidated portion of his costume fell into a bed of newly-mixed lime,[1] from which he rescued it with great difficulty and at no little personal risk.

"Hallo! Kinch, old fellow, how are you?" cried Charlie; "I've been dying to see you—why haven't you been up?"

"Why, I did come up often, but that old witch in the kitchen wouldn't let me see you—she abused me scandalous. I wanted to pull her turban off and throw it in the gutter. Why, she called me

---

1 Mortar.

a dirty beggar, and threatened to throw cold water on me if I didn't go away. Phew! ain't she an old buster!"

"Why, I never knew you were there."

"Yes," continued Kinch; "and I saw you another time hung up behind the carriage. I declare, Charlie, you looked so like a little monkey, dressed up in that sky-blue coat and silver buttons, that I liked to have died a-laughing at you;" and Kinch was so overcome by the recollection of the event in question, that he was obliged to sit down upon a door-step to recover himself.

"Oh, I do hate to wear this confounded livery!" said Charlie, dolefully—"the boys scream 'Johnny Coat-tail' after me in the streets, and call me 'blue jay,' and 'blue nigger,' and lots of other names. I feel that all that's wanting to make a complete monkey of me, is for some one to carry me about on an organ."[1]

"What do you wear it for, then?" asked Kinch.

"Because I can't help myself, that's the reason. The boys plague me to that extent sometimes, that I feel like tearing the things into bits—but mother says I must wear it. Kinch," concluded he, significantly, "something will have to be done, I can't stand it."

"You remember what I told you about the wig, don't you?" asked Kinch; and, on receiving an affirmative reply, he continued, "Just try that on, and see how it goes—you'll find it'll work like a charm; it's a regular footman-expatriator—just try it now; you'll see if it isn't the thing to do the business for you."

"I'm determined to be as bad as I can," rejoined Charlie; "I'm tired enough of staying there: that old aunt Rach is a devil—I don't believe a saint from heaven could get on with her; I'm expecting we'll have a pitched battle every day."

Beguiling the time with this and similar conversation, they reached the house to which Charlie had been despatched with a note; after which, he turned his steps homeward, still accompanied by the redoubtable Kinch.

As ill luck would have it, they passed some boys who were engaged in a game of marbles, Charlie's favourite pastime, and, on Kinch's offering him the necessary stock to commence play, he launched into the game, regardless of the fact that the carriage was ordered for a drive within an hour, and that he was expected to fill his accustomed place in the rear of that splendid vehicle.

---

1 Here, Charlie compares his lot as a footman to a monkey kept on a leash by an organ-grinder. These street performers were especially prevalent in nineteenth-century Western Europe, but they were by no means an uncommon sight in the urban US.

Once immersed in the game, time flew rapidly on. Mrs. Thomas awaited his return until her patience was exhausted, when she started on her drive without him. As they were going through a quiet street, to her horror and surprise, prominent amidst a crowd of dirty boys, she discovered her little footman, with his elegant blue livery covered with dirt and sketches in white chalk; for, in the excitement of the game, Charlie had not observed that Kinch was engaged in drawing on the back of his coat his favourite illustration, to wit, a skull and cross-bones.

"Isn't that our Charlie?" said she to her daughter, surveying the crowd of noisy boys through her eye-glass. "I really believe it is—that is certainly our livery; pull the check-string,[1] and stop the carriage."

Now Robberts had been pressed into service in consequence of Charlie's absence, and was in no very good humour at being compelled to air his rheumatic old shins behind the family-carriage. It can therefore be readily imagined with what delight he recognized the delinquent footman amidst the crowd, and with what alacrity he descended and pounced upon him just at the most critical moment of the game. Clutching fast hold of him by the collar of his coat, he dragged him to the carriage-window, and held him before the astonished eyes of his indignant mistress, who lifted up her hands in horror at the picture he presented. "Oh! you wretched boy," said she, "just look at your clothes, all covered with chalk-marks and bespattered with lime! Your livery is totally ruined—and your knees, too—only look at them—the dirt is completely ground into them."

"But you haven't seed his back, marm," said Robberts; "he's got the pirate's flag drawn on it. That boy'll go straight to the devil—I know he will."

All this time Charlie, to his great discomfiture, was being shaken and turned about by Robberts in the most unceremonious manner. Kinch, with his usual audacity, was meanwhile industriously engaged in tracing on Robberts' coat a similar picture to that he had so skilfully drawn on Charlie's, to the great delight of a crowd of boys who stood admiring spectators of his artistic performances. The coachman, however, observing this operation, brought it to a rather hasty conclusion by a well directed cut of the whip across the fingers of the daring young artist. This so enraged Kinch, that in default of any other missile,

---

1   The check-string connects to a small bell near the driver of a carriage. A passenger pulls the string to indicate a wish to stop.

he threw his lime-covered cap at the head of the coachman; but, unfortunately for himself, the only result of his exertions was the lodgment of his cap in the topmost bough of a neighbouring tree, from whence it was rescued with great difficulty.

"What *shall* we do with him?" asked Mrs. Thomas, in a despairing tone, as she looked at Charlie.

"Put him with the coachman," suggested Mrs. Morton.

"He can't sit there, the horses are so restive, and the seat is only constructed for one, and he would be in the coachman's way. I suppose he must find room on behind with Robberts."

"I won't ride on the old carriage," cried Charlie, nerved by despair; "I won't stay here nohow. I'm going home to my mother;" and as he spoke he endeavoured to wrest himself from Robberts' grasp.

"Put him in here," said Mrs. Thomas; "it would never do to let him go, for he will run home with some distressing tale of ill-treatment; no, we must keep him until I can send for his mother—put him in here."

Much to Mrs. Morton's disgust, Charlie was bundled by Robberts into the bottom of the carriage, where he sat listening to the scolding of Mrs. Thomas and her daughter until they arrived at home. He remained in disgrace for several days after this adventure; but as Mrs. Thomas well knew that she could not readily fill his place with another, she made a virtue of necessity, and kindly looked over this first offence.

The situation was, however, growing more and more intolerable. Aunt Rachel and he had daily skirmishes, in which he was very frequently worsted. He had held several hurried consultations with Kinch through the grating of the cellar window, and was greatly cheered and stimulated in the plans he intended to pursue by the advice and sympathy of his devoted friend. Master Kinch's efforts to console Charlie were not without great risk to himself, as he had on two or three occasions narrowly escaped falling into the clutches of Robberts, who well remembered Kinch's unprecedented attempt upon the sacredness of his livery; and what the result might have been had the latter fallen into his hands, we cannot contemplate without a shudder.

These conferences between Kinch and Charlie produced their natural effect, and latterly it had been several times affirmed by aunt Rachel that, "Dat air boy was gittin' 'tirely too high—gittin' 'bove hissef 'pletely—dat he was gittin' more and more aggriwatin' every day—dat she itched to git at him—dat she 'spected nothin' else but what she'd be 'bliged to take hold o' him;" and she comported herself generally as if she was crazy for the conflict which she saw must sooner or later occur.

Charlie, unable on these occasions to reply to her remarks without precipitating a conflict for which he did not feel prepared, sought to revenge himself upon the veteran Tom; and such was the state of his feelings, that he bribed Kinch, with a large lump of sugar and the leg of a turkey, to bring up his mother's Jerry, a fierce young cat, and they had the satisfaction of shutting him up in the wood-house with the belligerent Tom, who suffered a signal defeat at Jerry's claws, and was obliged to beat a hasty retreat through the window, with a seriously damaged eye, and with the fur torn off his back in numberless places. After this Charlie had the pleasure of hearing aunt Rachel frequently bewail the condition of her favourite, whose deplorable state she was inclined to ascribe to his influence, though she was unable to bring it home to him in such a manner as to insure his conviction.

CHAPTER VII.

Mrs. Thomas has her Troubles.

MRS. THOMAS was affected, as silly women sometimes are, with an intense desire to be at the head of the *ton*.[1] For this object she gave grand dinners and large evening parties, to which were invited all who, being two or three removes from the class whose members occupy the cobbler's bench or the huckster's stall, felt themselves at liberty to look down upon the rest of the world from the pinnacle on which they imagined themselves placed. At these social gatherings the conversation never turned upon pedigree, and if any of the guests chanced by accident to allude to their ancestors, they spoke of them as members of the family, who, at an early period of their lives, were engaged in mercantile pursuits.

At such dinners Mrs. Thomas would sit for hours, mumbling[2] dishes that disagreed with her; smiling at conversations carried on in villainous French, of which language she did not understand a word; and admiring the manners of addle-headed young men (who got tipsy at her evening parties), because they had been to Europe, and were therefore considered quite men of the world. These parties and dinners she could not be induced to forego, although the late hours and fatigue consequent thereon would place her on the sick-list for several days afterwards. As soon, however, as she recovered sufficiently to resume her place at the table, she would console herself with a dinner of boiled mutton and roasted turnips, as a slight compensation for the unwholesome French dishes she had compelled herself to swallow on the occasions before mentioned.

Amongst the other modern fashions she had adopted, was that of setting apart one morning of the week for the reception of visitors; and she had mortally offended several of her oldest friends by obstinately refusing to admit them at any other time. Two or three difficulties had occurred with Robberts, in consequence of this new arrangement, as he could not be brought to see the propriety of saying to visitors that Mrs. Thomas was "not at home," when he knew she was at that very moment upstairs peeping over

---

1   At the height of fashion, here expressed in suitably fashionable French.

2   I.e., gumming; chewing tentatively, often without the benefit of teeth. See *OED* "mumble" 1a and 1b.

the banisters. His obstinacy on this point had induced her to try whether she could not train Charlie so as to fit him for the important office of uttering the fashionable and truthless "not at home" with unhesitating gravity and decorum; and, after a series of mishaps, she at last believed her object was effected, until an unlucky occurrence convinced her to the contrary.

Mrs. Thomas, during the days on which she did not receive company, would have presented, to any one who might have had the honour to see that venerable lady, an entirely different appearance to that which she assumed on gala days. A white handkerchief supplied the place of the curling wig, and the tasty French cap was replaced by a muslin one, decorated with an immense border of ruffling, that flapped up and down over her silver spectacles in the most comical manner possible. A short flannel gown and a dimity[1] petticoat of very antique pattern and scanty dimensions, completed her costume. Thus attired, and provided with a duster, she would make unexpected sallies into the various domestic departments, to see that everything was being properly conducted, and that no malpractices were perpetrated at times when it was supposed she was elsewhere. She showed an intuitive knowledge of all traps set to give intimation of her approach, and would come upon aunt Rachel so stealthily as to induce her to declare, "Dat old Mrs. Thomas put her more in mind of a ghost dan of any other libin animal."

One morning, whilst attired in the manner described, Mrs. Thomas had been particularly active in her excursions through the house, and had driven the servants to their wits' ends by her frequent descents upon them at the most unexpected times, thereby effectually depriving them of the short breathing intervals they were anxious to enjoy. Charlie in particular had been greatly harassed by her, and was sent flying from place to place until his legs were nearly run off, as he expressed it. And so, when Lord Cutanrun,[2] who was travelling in America to give his estates in England an opportunity to recuperate, presented his card, Charlie, in revenge, showed him into the drawing-room, where he knew that Mrs. Thomas was busily engaged trimming an oil-lamp. Relying on the explicit order she had given to say that she was not at home, she did not even look up when his lordship

---

1 Sturdy, typically utilitarian cotton fabric.
2 A pun on the phrase "cut and run."

entered, and as he advanced towards her, she extended to him a basin of dirty water, saying, "Here, take this." Receiving no response she looked up, and to her astonishment and horror beheld, not Charlie, but Lord Cutanrun. In the agitation consequent upon his unexpected appearance, she dropped the basin, the contents of which, splashing in all directions, sadly discoloured his lordship's light pants, and greatly damaged the elegant carpet.

"Oh! my lord," she exclaimed, "I didn't—couldn't—wouldn't—" and, unable to ejaculate further, she fairly ran out of the apartment into the entry, where she nearly fell over Charlie, who was enjoying the confusion his conduct had created. "Oh! you limb![1]—you little wretch!" said she. "You knew I was not at home!"

"Why, where are you now?" he asked, with the most provoking air of innocence. "If you ain't in the house now, you never was."

"Never mind, sir," said she, "never mind. I'll settle with you for this. Don't stand there grinning at me; go upstairs and tell Mrs. Morton to come down immediately, and then get something to wipe up that water. O dear! my beautiful carpet! And for a lord to see me in such a plight! Oh! it's abominable! I'll give it to you, you scamp! You did it on purpose," continued the indignant Mrs. Thomas. "Don't deny it—I know you did. What are you standing there for? Why don't you call Mrs. Morton!" she concluded, as Charlie, chuckling over the result of his trick, walked leisurely upstairs. "That boy will be the death of me," she afterwards said, on relating the occurrence to her daughter. "Just to think, after all the trouble I've had teaching him when to admit people and when not, that he should serve me such a trick. I'm confident he did it purposely." Alas! for poor Mrs. Thomas; this was only the first of a series of annoyances that Charlie had in store, with which to test her patience and effect his own deliverance.

A few days after, one of their grand dinners was to take place, and Charlie had been revolving in his mind the possibility of his finding some opportunity, on that occasion, to remove the old lady's wig; feeling confident that, could he accomplish that feat, he would be permitted to turn his back for ever on the mansion of Mrs. Thomas.

Never had Mrs. Thomas appeared more radiant than at this dinner. All the guests whose attendance she had most desired

---

1   Shortened version of "devil's limb": a mischievous rascal. See *OED* "limb" 3b and 3c.

were present, a new set of china had lately arrived from Paris, and she was in full anticipation of a grand triumph. Now, to Charlie had been assigned the important duty of removing the cover from the soup-tureen which was placed before his mistress, and the little rogue had settled upon that moment as the most favourable for the execution of his purpose. He therefore secretly affixed a nicely crooked pin to the elbow of his sleeve, and, as he lifted the cover, adroitly hooked it into her cap, to which he knew the wig was fastened, and in a twinkling had it off her head, and before she could recover from her astonishment and lay down the soup-ladle he had left the room. The guests stared and tittered at the grotesque figure she presented,—her head being covered with short white hair, and her face as red as a peony at the mortifying situation in which she was placed. As she rose from her chair Charlie presented himself, and handed her the wig, with an apology for the *accident*. In her haste to put it on, she turned it wrong side foremost; the laughter of the guests could now no longer be restrained, and in the midst of it Mrs. Thomas left the room. Encountering Charlie as she went, she almost demolished him in her wrath; not ceasing to belabour him till his outcries became so loud as to render her fearful that he would alarm the guests; and she then retired to her room, where she remained until the party broke up.

It was her custom, after these grand entertainments, to make nocturnal surveys of the kitchen, to assure herself that none of the delicacies had been secreted by the servants for their personal use and refreshment. Charlie, aware of this, took his measures for an ample revenge for the beating he had received at her hands. At night, when all the rest of the family had retired, he hastily descended to the kitchen, and, by some process known only to himself, imprisoned the cat in a stone jar that always stood upon the dresser, and into which he was confident Mrs. Thomas would peep. He then stationed himself upon the stairs, to watch the result. He had not long to wait, for as soon as she thought the servants were asleep, she came softly into the kitchen, and, after peering about in various places, she at last lifted up the lid of the jar. Tom, tired of his long confinement, sprang out, and, in so doing, knocked the lamp out of her hand, the fluid from which ignited and ran over the floor.

"Murder!—Fire!—Watch!" screamed the thoroughly frightened old woman. "Oh, help! help! fire!" At this terrible noise nearly every one in the household was aroused, and hurried to the spot whence it proceeded. They found Mrs. Thomas standing in the dark, with the lid of the jar in her hand, herself the per-sonification of terror. The carpet was badly burned in several places, and the fragments of the lamp were scattered about the floor.

"What has happened?" exclaimed Mr. Morton, who was the first to enter the kitchen. "What is all this frightful noise occasioned by?"

"Oh, there is a man in the house!" answered Mrs. Thomas, her teeth chattering with fright. "There was a man in here—he has just sprung out," she continued, pointing to the bread-jar.

"Pooh, pooh—that's nonsense, madam," replied the son-in-law. "Why an infant could not get in there, much less a man!"

"I tell you it was a man then" angrily responded Mrs. Thomas; "and he is in the house somewhere now."

"Such absurdity!" muttered Mr. Morton; adding, in a louder tone: "Why, my dear mamma, you've seen a mouse or something of the kind."

"Mouse, indeed!" interrupted the old lady. "Do you think I'm in my dotage, and I don't know a man from a mouse?"

Just then the cat, whose back had got severely singed in the *mêlée*, set up a most lamentable caterwauling; and, on being brought to light from the depths of a closet into which he had flown, his appearance immediately discovered the share he had had in the transaction.

"It must have been the cat," said Robberts. "Only look at his back—why here the fur is singed off him! I'll bet anything," continued he, "that air boy has had something to do with this—for it's a clear case that the cat couldn't git into the jar, and then put the lid on hissef."

Tom's inability to accomplish this feat being most readily admitted on all sides, inquiry was immediately made as to the whereabouts of Charlie; his absence from the scene being rather considered as evidence of participation, for, it was argued, if he had been unaware of what was to transpire, the noise would have drawn him to the spot at once, as he was always the first at hand in the event of any excitement. Robberts was despatched to see if he was in his bed, and returned with the intelligence that the bed had not even been opened.

Search was immediately instituted, and he was discovered in the closet at the foot of the stairs. He was dragged forth, shaken, pummelled, and sent to bed, with the assurance that his mother should be sent for in the morning, to take him home, and keep him there. This being exactly the point to which he was desirous of bringing matters, he went to bed, and passed a most agreeable night.

Aunt Rachel, being one of those sleepers that nothing short of an earthquake can rouse until their customary time for awaking, had slept soundly through the stirring events of the past night. She came down in the morning in quite a placid state of mind, expecting to enjoy a day of rest, as she had the night before sat up much beyond her usual time, to set matters to rights after the confusion consequent on the dinner party. What was her astonishment, therefore, on finding the kitchen she had left in a state of perfect order and cleanliness, in a condition that resembled the preparation for an annual house-cleaning.

"Lord, bless us!" she exclaimed, looking round; "What on yarth has happened? I raly b'lieve dere's bin a fire in dis 'ere house, and I never knowed a word of it. Why I might have bin burnt up in my own bed! Dere's de lamp broke—carpet burnt—pots and skillets hauled out of the closet—ebery ting turned upside down; why dere's bin a reg'lar 'sturbance down here," she continued, as she surveyed the apartment.

At this juncture, she espied Tom, who sat licking his paws before the fire, and presenting so altered an appearance, from the events of the night, as to have rendered him unrecognizable even by his best friend.

"Strange cat in de house! Making himself quite at home at dat," said aunt Rachel, indignantly. Her wrath, already much excited, rose to the boiling point at what she deemed a most daring invasion of her domain. She, therefore, without ceremony, raised a broom, with which she belaboured the astonished Tom, who ran frantically from under one chair to another till he ensconced himself in a small closet, from which he pertinaciously refused to be dislodged. "Won't come out of dere, won't you?" said she. "I'll see if I can't make you den;" and poor Tom dodged behind pots and kettles to avoid the blows which were aimed at him; at last, thoroughly enraged by a hard knock on the back, he sprang fiercely into the face of his tormentor, who, completely upset by the suddenness of his attack, fell sprawling on the floor, screaming loudly for help. She was raised up by Robberts, who came running to her assistance, and, on being questioned as to the cause of her outcries, replied:—

"Dere's a strange cat in de house—wild cat too, I raly b'lieve;" and spying Tom at that moment beneath the table, she made another dash at him for a renewal of hostilities.

"Why that's Tom," exclaimed Robberts; "don't you know your own cat?"

"Oh," she replied, "dat ar isn't Tom now, is it? Why, what's the matter wid him?"

Robberts then gave her a detailed account of the transactions of the previous night, in which account the share Charlie had taken was greatly enlarged and embellished; and the wrathful old woman was listening to the conclusion when Charlie entered. Hardly had he got into the room, when, without any preliminary discussion, aunt Rachel—to use her own words—pitched into him to give him particular fits. Now Charlie, not being disposed to receive "particular fits," made some efforts to return the hard compliments that were being showered upon him, and the advice of Kinch providentially occurring to him—respecting an attack upon the understanding of his venerable antagonist—he brought his hard shoes down with great force upon her pet corn, and by this *coup de pied*[1] completely demolished her. With a loud scream she let him go; and sitting down upon the floor, declared herself lamed for life, beyond the possibility of recovery. At this stage of the proceedings, Robberts came to the rescue of his aged coadjutor,[2] and seized hold of Charlie, who forthwith commenced so brisk an attack upon his rheumatic shins, as to cause him to beat a hurried retreat, leaving Charlie sole master of the field. The noise that these scuffles occasioned brought Mrs. Thomas into the kitchen, and Charlie was marched off by her into an upstairs room, where he was kept in "durance vile"[3] until the arrival of his mother.

Mrs. Thomas had a strong liking for Charlie—not as a boy, but as a footman. He was active and intelligent, and until quite recently, extremely tractable and obedient; more than all, he was a very good-looking boy, and when dressed in the Thomas livery, presented a highly-respectable appearance. She therefore determined to be magnanimous—to look over past events, and to show a Christian and forgiving spirit towards his delinquencies. She sent for Mrs. Ellis, with the intention of desiring her to use her maternal influence to induce him to apologize to aunt Rachel for his assault upon her corns, which apology Mrs. Thomas was willing to guarantee should be accepted; as for the indignities that

---

1 Kick (French).

2 Fellow servant.

3 I.e., imprisoned or confined against his will. See *OED* "durance" 5.

had been inflicted on herself, she thought it most politic to regard them in the light of accidents, and to say as little about that part of the affair as possible.

When Mrs. Ellis made her appearance on the day subsequent to the events just narrated, Mrs. Thomas enlarged to her upon the serious damage that aunt Rachel had received, and the urgent necessity that something should be done to mollify that important individual. When Charlie was brought into the presence of his mother and Mrs. Thomas, the latter informed him, that, wicked as had been his conduct towards herself, she was willing, for his mother's sake, to look over it; but that he must humble himself in dust and ashes before the reigning sovereign of the culinary kingdom, who, making the most of the injury inflicted on her toe, had declared herself unfit for service, and was at that moment ensconced in a large easy-chair, listening to the music of her favourite smoke-jack, whilst a temporary cook was getting up the dinner, under her immediate supervision and direction.

"Charlie, I'm quite ashamed of you," said his mother, after listening to Mrs. Thomas's lengthy statement. "What has come over you, child?"—Charlie stood biting his nails, and looking very sullen, but vouchsafed them no answer.—"Mrs. Thomas is so kind as to forgive you, and says she will look over the whole affair, if you will beg aunt Rachel's pardon. Come, now," continued Mrs. Ellis, coaxingly, "do, that's a good boy."

"Yes, do," added Mrs. Thomas, "and I will buy you a handsome new suit of livery."

This was too much for Charlie; the promise of another suit of the detested livery quite overcame him, and he burst into tears.

"Why, what ails the boy? He's the most incomprehensible child I ever saw! The idea of crying at the promise of a new suit of clothes!—any other child would have been delighted," concluded Mrs. Thomas.

"I don't want your old button-covered uniform," said Charlie, "and I won't wear it, neither! And as for aunt Rachel, I don't care how much she is hurt—I'm only sorry I didn't smash her other toe; and I'll see her skinned, and be skinned myself, before I'll ask her pardon!"

Both Mrs. Thomas and Charlie's mother stood aghast at this unexpected declaration; and the result of a long conference, held by the two, was that Charlie should be taken home, Mrs. Ellis being unable to withstand his tears and entreaties.

As he passed through the kitchen on his way out, he made a face at aunt Rachel, who, in return, threw at him one of the turnips she was peeling. It missed the object for which it was intended, and came plump into the eye of Robberts, giving to that respectable individual for some time thereafter the appearance of a prize-fighter in livery.

Charlie started for home in the highest spirits, which, however, became considerably lower on his discovering his mother's view of his late exploits was very different from his own. Mrs. Ellis's fondness and admiration of her son, although almost amounting to weakness, were yet insufficient to prevent her from feeling that his conduct, even after making due allowance for the provocation he had received, could not be wholly excused as mere boyish impetuosity and love of mischievous fun. She knew that his father would feel it his duty, not only to reprimand him, but to inflict some chastisement; and this thought was the more painful to her from the consciousness, that but for her own weak compliance with Mrs. Thomas's request, her boy would not have been placed in circumstances which his judgment and self-command had proved insufficient to carry him through. The day, therefore, passed less agreeably than Charlie had anticipated; for now that he was removed from the scene of his trials, he could not disguise from himself that his behaviour under them had been very different from what it ought to have been, and this had the salutary effect of bringing him into a somewhat humbler frame of mind. When his father returned in the evening, therefore, Charlie appeared so crest-fallen that even Caddy could scarcely help commiserating him, especially as his subdued state during the day had kept him from committing any of those offences against tidiness which so frequently exasperated her. Mr. Ellis, though very strict on what he thought points of duty, had much command of temper, and was an affectionate father. He listened, therefore, with attention to the details of Charlie's grievances, as well as of his misdemeanours, and some credit is due to him for the unshaken gravity he preserved throughout. Although he secretly acquitted his son of any really bad intention, he thought it incumbent on him to make Charlie feel in some degree the evil consequences of his unruly behaviour. After giving him a serious lecture, and pointing out the impropriety of taking such measures to deliver himself from the bondage in which his parents themselves had thought fit to place him, without even appealing to them, he insisted on his making the apologies due both to Mrs. Thomas and aunt Rachel (although he was fully aware that both had only got their deserts); and, further, intimated that he would not be reinstated in his parents' good graces until he had proved, by his good conduct and docility, that he was really sorry for his misbehaviour. It was a severe trial to Charlie to make these apologies; but he well knew that what his father had decided upon must be done—so he made a virtue of necessity, and, accompanied by his mother, on the following day performed his penance with as good a grace as he was able; and, in consideration of this submission, his father, when he came home in the evening, greeted him with all his usual kindness, and the recollection of this unlucky affair was at once banished from the family circle.

CHAPTER VIII.

Trouble in the Ellis Family.

SINCE the receipt of Mr. Garie's letter, Mrs. Ellis and Caddy had been busily engaged in putting the house in a state of preparation for their reception. Caddy, whilst superintending its decoration, felt herself in Elysium.[1] For the first time in her life she had the supreme satisfaction of having two unfortunate house-cleaners entirely at her disposal; consequently, she drove them about and worried them to an extent unparalleled in any of their former experience. She sought for and discovered on the windows (which they had fondly regarded as miracles of cleanliness) sundry streaks and smears, and detected infinite small spots of paint and white wash on the newly-scrubbed floors. She followed them upstairs and downstairs, and tormented them to that extent, that Charlie gave it as his private opinion that he should not be in the least surprised, on going up there, to find that the two old women had made away with Caddy, and hidden her remains in the coal-bin. Whilst she was thus engaged, to Charlie was assigned the duty of transporting to Winter-street her diurnal portion of food, without a hearty share of which she found it impossible to maintain herself in a state of efficiency; her labours in chasing the women about the house being of a rather exhausting nature.

When he made the visits in question, Charlie was generally reconnoitred by his sister from a window over the door, and was compelled to put his shoes through a system of purification, devised by her for his especial benefit. It consisted of three courses of scraper, and two of mat; this being considered by her as strictly necessary to bring his shoes to such a state of cleanliness as would entitle him to admission into the premises of which she was the temporary mistress.

Charlie, on two or three occasions finding a window open, made stealthy descents upon the premises without first having duly observed these quarantine regulations; whereupon he was attacked by Caddy, who, with the assistance of the minions under her command, so shook and pummelled him as to cause his precipitate retreat through the same opening by which he had entered, and that, too, in so short a space of time as to make the whole manœuvre appear to him in the light of a well-executed but

---

1 Heaven; a state of perfect happiness.

involuntary feat of ground and lofty tumbling.[1] One afternoon he started with his sister's dinner, consisting of a dish of which she was particularly fond, and its arrival was therefore looked for with unusual anxiety. Charlie, having gorged himself to an almost alarming extent, did not make the haste that the case evidently demanded; and as he several times stopped to act as umpire in disputed games of marbles (in the rules of which he was regarded as an authority), he necessarily consumed a great deal of time on the way.

Caddy's patience was severely tried by the long delay, and her temper, at no time the most amiable, gathered bitterness from the unprecedented length of her fast. Therefore, when he at length appeared, walking leisurely up Winter-street, swinging the kettle about in the most reckless manner, and setting it down on the pavement to play leap-frog over the fire-plugs, her wrath reached a point that boded no good to the young trifler.

Now, whilst Charlie had been giving his attention to the difficulties growing out of the games of marbles, he did not observe that one of the disputants was possessed of a tin kettle, in appearance very similar to his own, by the side of which, in the excitement of the moment, he deposited his own whilst giving a practical illustration of his view of the point under consideration. Having accomplished this to his entire satisfaction, he resumed what he supposed was his kettle, and went his way rejoicing.

Now, if Caddy Ellis had a fondness for one dish more than any other, it was for haricot,[2] with plenty of carrots; and knowing she was to have this for her dinner, she, to use her own pointed expression, "had laid herself out to have a good meal." She had even abstained from her customary lunch that she might have an appetite worthy of the occasion; and accordingly, long ere the dinner hour approached, she was hungry as a wolf. Notwithstanding this fact, when Charlie made his appearance at the door, she insisted on his going through all the accustomed forms with the mat and scraper before entering the house; an act of self-sacrifice on her part entirely uncalled for, as the day was remarkably fine, and Charlie's boots unusually clean.

He received two or three by no means gentle shoves and pokes as he entered, which he bore with unusual indifference, making

---

1   Americanism for acrobatic performance that takes place both on and off of a tightrope. See Richard Hopkins Thornton, *American Glossary*, 2 vols. (Philadelphia: Lippincott, 1912), 1:395.

2   Mutton stew.

not the slightest effort at retaliation, as was his usual practice. The fact is, Charlie was, as lions are supposed to be, quite disinclined for a fight after a hearty meal, so he followed Caddy upstairs to the second story. Here she had got up an extempore[1] dining-table, by placing a pasting board[2] across two chairs. Seating herself upon a stool, she jerked off the lid of the kettle, and, to her horror and dismay, found not the favourite haricot, but a piece of cheese-rind, a crust of dry bread, and a cold potato. Charlie, who was amusing himself by examining the flowers in the new carpet, did not observe the look of surprise and disgust that came over the countenance of his sister, as she took out, piece by piece, the remains of some schoolboy's repast.

"Look here," she at last burst forth, "do you call this *my* dinner?"

"Yes," said Charlie, in a deliberate tone, "and a very good one too, I should say; if you can't eat that dinner, you ought to starve; it's one of mother's best haricots."

"You don't call this cold potato and cheese-rind haricot, do you?" asked Caddy, angrily.

At this Charlie looked up, and saw before her the refuse scraps, which she had indignantly emptied upon the table. He could scarcely believe his eyes; he got up and looked in the kettle, but found no haricot. "Well," said he, with surprise, "if that don't beat me! I saw mother fill it with haricot myself; I'm clean beat about it."

"Tell me what you've done with it, then," almost screamed the angry girl.

"I really don't know what has become of it," he answered, with a bewildered air. "I saw—I saw—I—I—"

"You saw—you saw," replied the indignant Caddy, imitating his tone; and taking up the kettle, she began to examine it more closely. "Why, this isn't even our kettle; look at this lid. I'm sure it's not ours. You've been stopping somewhere to play, and exchanged it with some other boy, that's just what you've done."

---

1 Improvised.

2 The exact meaning is unclear. One possibility would be a pastry-board—a broad wooden surface used for rolling dough. Another would be a pasting-board, a considerably larger surface used by wallpaper hangers as a staging area to smooth lengths of paper and apply glue. Given that Caddy has been assigned to set up housekeeping for the Garies, either is plausible.

Just then it occurred to Charlie that at the place where he had adjusted the dispute about the marbles, he had observed in the hands of one of the boys a kettle similar to his own; and it flashed across his mind that he had then and there made the unfortunate exchange. He broke his suspicion to Caddy in the gentlest manner, at the same time edging his way to the door to escape the storm that he saw was brewing. The loss of her dinner—and of such a dinner—so enraged the hungry girl, as to cause her to seize a brush lying near and begin to belabour him without mercy. In his endeavour to escape from her his foot was caught in the carpet, and he was violently precipitated down the long flight of stairs. His screams brought the whole party to his assistance; even Kinch, who was sitting on the step outside, threw off his usual dread of Caddy, and rushed into the house. "Oh, take me up," piteously cried Charlie; "oh, take me up, I'm almost killed." In raising him, one of the old women took hold of his arm, which caused him to scream again. "Don't touch my arm, please don't touch my arm; I'm sure it's broke."

"No, no, it's not broke, only sprained, or a little twisted," said she; and, seizing it as she spoke, she gave it a pull and a wrench, for the purpose of making it all right again; at this Charlie's face turned deathly pale, and he fainted outright.

"Run for a doctor," cried the now thoroughly-alarmed Caddy; "run for the doctor! my brother's dead!" and bursting into tears, she exclaimed, "Oh, I've killed my brother, I've killed my brother!"

"Don't make so much fuss, child," soothingly replied one of the old women: "he's worth half a dozen dead folk yet. Lor' bless you, child, he's only fainted."

Water was procured and thrown in his face, and before Kinch returned with the doctor, he was quite restored to consciousness.

"Don't cry, my little man," said the physician, as he took out his knife and ripped up the sleeve of Charlie's coat. "Don't cry; let me examine your arm." Stripping up the shirt-sleeve, he felt it carefully over, and shaking his head (physicians always shake their heads) pronounced the arm broken, and that, too, in an extremely bad place. At this information Charlie began again to cry, and Caddy broke forth into such yells of despair as almost to drive them distracted.

The physician kindly procured a carriage, and saw Charlie comfortably placed therein; and held in the arms of Kinch, with the lamenting and disheartened Caddy on the opposite seat, he was slowly driven home. The house was quite thrown into confusion by their arrival under such circumstances; Mrs. Ellis, for a wonder, did not faint, but proceeded at once to do what was necessary. Mr. Ellis was sent for, and he immediately despatched Kinch for Dr. Burdett, their family physician, who came without a moment's delay. He examined Charlie's arm, and at first thought it would be necessary to amputate it.[1] At the mere mention of the word amputate, Caddy set up such a series of lamentable howls as to cause her immediate ejectment from the apartment. Dr. Burdett called in Dr. Diggs for a consultation, and between them it was decided that an attempt should be made to save the injured member. "Now, Charlie," said Dr. Burdett, "I'm afraid we must hurt you, my boy—but if you have any desire to keep this arm you must try to bear it."

"I'll bear anything to save my arm, doctor; I can't spare that," said he, manfully. "I'll want it by-and-by to help take care of mother and the girls."

"You're a brave little fellow," said Dr. Diggs, patting him on the head, "so then we'll go at it at once."

"Stop," cried Charlie, "let mother put her arm round my neck so, and Es, you hold the good hand. Now then, I'm all right—fire away!" and clenching his lips hard, he waited for the doctor to commence the operation of setting his arm. Charlie's mother tried to look as stoical as possible, but the corners of her mouth would twitch, and there was a nervous trembling of her under-lip; but she commanded herself, and only when Charlie gave a slight groan of pain, stooped and kissed his forehead; and when she raised her head again, there was a tear resting on the face of her son that was not his own. Esther was the picture of despair, and she wept bitterly for the misfortune which had befallen her pet brother; and when the operation was over, refused to answer poor Caddy's questions respecting Charlie's injuries, and scolded her with a warmth and volubility that was quite surprising to them all.

"You must not be too hard on Caddy," remarked Mr. Ellis. "She feels bad enough, I'll warrant you. It is a lesson that will not, I trust, be thrown away upon her; it will teach her to command her temper in future."

---

1 Before the development of antibiotics, it was not uncommon for a broken bone to lead to a fatal infection; compound fractures were particularly dangerous. Surgical amputation was in many cases the best option for saving the life of the patient.

Caddy was in truth quite crushed by the misfortune she had occasioned, and fell into such a state of depression and apathy as to be scarcely heard about the house; indeed, so subdued was she, that Kinch went in and out without wiping his feet, and tracked the mud all over the stair-carpet, and yet she uttered no word of remonstrance.

Poor little Charlie suffered much, and was in a high fever. The knocker was tied up, the windows darkened, and all walked about the house with sad and anxious countenances. Day after day the fever increased, until he grew delirious, and raved in the most distressing manner. The unfortunate haricot was still on his mind, and he was persecuted by men with strange-shaped heads and carrot eyes. Sometimes he imagined himself pursued by Caddy, and would cry in the most piteous manner to have her prevented from beating him. Then his mind strayed off to the marble-ground, where he would play imaginary games, and laugh over his success in such a wild and frightful manner as to draw tears from the eyes of all around him. He was greatly changed; the bright colour had fled from his cheek; his head had been shaved, and he was thin and wan, and at times they were obliged to watch him, and restrain him from tossing about, to the great peril of his broken arm.

At last his situation became so critical that Dr. Burdett began to entertain but slight hopes of his recovery; and one morning, in the presence of Caddy, hinted as much to Mr. Ellis.

"Oh, doctor, doctor," exclaimed the distracted girl, "don't say that! oh, try and save him! How could I live with the thought that I had killed my brother! oh, I can't live a day if he dies! Will God ever forgive me? Oh, what a wretch I have been! Oh, do think of something that will help him! He *mustn't* die, you *must* save him!" and crying passionately, she threw herself on the floor in an agony of grief. They did their best to pacify her, but all their efforts were in vain, until Mr. Ellis suggested, that since she could not control her feelings, she must be sent to stay with her aunt, as her lamentations and outcries agitated her suffering brother and made his condition worse. The idea of being excluded from the family circle at such a moment had more effect on Caddy than all previous remonstrances. She implored to have the sentence suspended for a time at least, that she might try to exert more self-command; and Mr. Ellis, who really pitied her, well knowing that her heart was not in fault, however reprehensible she was in point of temper, consented; and Caddy's behaviour from that moment proved the sincerity of her promises; and though she could not quite restrain occasional outbursts of senseless lamentation, still, when she felt such fits of despair coming on, she wisely retired to some remote corner of the house, and did not re-appear till she had regained her composure. The crisis was at length over, and Charlie was pronounced out of danger. No one was more elated by this announcement than our friend Kinch, who had, in fact, grown quite ashy in his complexion from confinement and grief; and was now thrown by this intelligence into the highest possible spirits. Charlie, although faint and weak, was able to recognize his friends, and derived great satisfaction from the various devices of Kinch to entertain him. That young gentleman quite distinguished himself by the variety and extent of his resources. He devised butting matches between himself and a large gourd, which he suspended from the ceiling, and almost blinded himself by his attempts to butt it sufficiently hard to cause it to rebound to the utmost length of the string, and might have made an idiot of himself for ever by his exertions, but for the timely interference of Mr. Ellis, who put a final stop to this diversion. Then he dressed himself in a short gown and nightcap, and made the pillow into a baby, and played the nurse with it to such perfection, that Charlie felt obliged to applaud by knocking with the knuckles of his best hand upon the head-board of his bedstead. On the whole, he was so overjoyed as to be led to commit all manner of eccentricities, and conducted himself generally in such a ridiculous manner, that Charlie laughed himself into a state of prostration, and Kinch was, in consequence, banished from the sick-room, to be re-admitted only on giving his promise to abstain from being as *funny as he could* any more. After the lapse of a short time Charlie was permitted to sit up, and held regular *levées*[1] of his schoolmates and little friends. He declared it was quite a luxury to have a broken arm, as it was a source of so much amusement. The old ladies brought him jellies and blanc-mange,[2] and he was petted and caressed to such an unparalleled extent, as to cause his delighted mother to aver that she lived in great fear of his being spoiled beyond remedy. At length he was permitted to come downstairs and sit by the window for a few hours each day. Whilst thus amusing himself one morning, a handsome carriage stopped before their house, and from it descended a fat and benevolent-

---

1 Morning receptions for visitors to distinguished persons, sometimes presided over from bed.
2 Milk-based pudding.

looking old lady, who knocked at the door and rattled the latch as if she had been in the daily habit of visiting there, and felt quite sure of a hearty welcome. She was let in by Esther, and, on sitting down, asked if Mrs. Ellis was at home. Whilst Esther was gone to summon her mother, the lady looked round the room, and espying Charlie, said, "Oh, there you are—I'm glad to see you; I hope you are improving."

"Yes, ma'am," politely replied Charlie, wondering all the time who their visitor could be.

"You don't seem to remember me—you ought to do so; children seldom forget any one who makes them a pleasant promise."

As she spoke, a glimmer of recollection shot across Charlie's mind, and he exclaimed, "You are the lady who came to visit the school."

"Yes; and I promised you a book for your aptness, and," continued she, taking from her reticule[1] a splendidly-bound copy of "Robinson Crusoe,"[2] "here it is."

Mrs. Ellis, as soon as she was informed that a stranger lady was below, left Caddy to superintend alone the whitewashing of Charlie's sick-room,[3] and having hastily donned another gown and a more tasty cap, descended to see who the visitor could be.

"You must excuse my not rising," said Mrs. Bird, for that was the lady's name; "it is rather a difficulty for me to get up and down often—so," continued she, with a smile, "you must excuse my seeming rudeness."

Mrs. Ellis answered, that any apology was entirely unnecessary, and begged she would keep her seat.

"I've come," said Mrs. Bird, "to pay your little man a visit. I was so much pleased with the manner in which he recited his exercises on the day of examination, that I promised him a book, and on going to the school to present it, I heard of his unfortunate accident. He looks very much changed—he has had a very severe time, I presume?"

"Yes, a very severe one. We had almost given him over, but it pleased God to restore him," replied Mrs. Ellis, in a thankful

---

1 Purse; handbag.

2 Enduringly popular novel by Daniel Defoe (1660–1731), first published in 1719.

3 Painting the walls with whitewash (a preparation of water, lime, and/or chalk) was long thought to help sanitize an indoor environment; it was a common step in preparing rooms for convalescence.

tone. "He is very weak yet," she continued, "and it will be a long time before he is entirely recovered."

"Who is your physician?" asked Mrs. Bird.

"Doctor Burdett," was the reply; "he has been our physician for years, and is a very kind friend of our family."

"And of mine, too," rejoined Mrs. Bird; "he visits my house every summer. What does he think of the arm?" she asked.

"He thinks in time it will be as strong as ever, and recommends sending Charlie into the country for the summer; but," said Mrs, Ellis, "we are quite at a loss where to send him."

"Oh! let me take him," said Mrs. Bird—"I should be delighted to have him. I've got a beautiful place—he can have a horse to ride, and there are wide fields to scamper over! Only let me have him, and I'll guarantee to restore him to health in a short time."

"You're very kind," replied Mrs. Ellis—"I'm afraid he would only be a burthen to you—be a great deal of trouble, and be able to do but little work."

"Work! Why, dear woman," replied Mrs. Bird, with some astonishment, "I don't want him to work—I've plenty of servants; I only want him to enjoy himself, and gather as much strength as possible. Come, make up your mind to let him go with me, and I'll send him home as stout as I am."

At the bare idea of Charlie's being brought to such a state of obesity, Kinch, who, during the interview, had been in the back part of the room, making all manner of faces, was obliged to leave the apartment, to prevent a serious explosion of laughter, and after their visitor had departed he was found rolling about the floor in a tempest of mirth.

After considerable conversation relative to the project, Mrs. Bird took her leave, promising to call soon again, and advising Mrs. Ellis to accept her offer. Mrs. Ellis consulted Dr. Burdett, who pronounced it a most fortunate circumstance, and said the boy could not be in better hands; and as Charlie appeared nothing loth,[1] it was decided he should go to Warmouth,[2] to the great grief of Kinch, who thought it a most unheard-of proceeding, and he regarded Mrs. Bird thenceforth as his personal enemy, and a wilful disturber of his peace.

---

1   I.e., Charlie has no objections.
2   As far as we can tell, Webb's Warmouth does not correspond to a particular place. From subsequent descriptions of Charlie's travels, it seems likely to serve as a generic representation of a small town in upstate New York or western New England.

CHAPTER IX.

Breaking up.

THE time for the departure of the Garies having been fixed, all in the house were soon engaged in the bustle of preparation. Boxes were packed with books, pictures, and linen; plate and china were wrapped and swaddled, to prevant breakage and bruises; carpets were taken up, and packed away; curtains taken down, and looking-glasses covered. Only a small part of the house was left in a furnished state for the use of the overseer, who was a young bachelor, and did not require much space.

In superintending all these arrangements Mrs. Garie displayed great activity; her former cheerfulness of manner had entirely returned, and Mr. Garie often listened with delight to the quick pattering of her feet, as she tripped lightly through the hall, and up and down the long stairs. The birds that sang about the windows were not more cheerful than herself, and when Mr. Garie heard her merry voice singing her lively songs, as in days gone by, he experienced a feeling of satisfaction at the pleasant result of his acquiescence in her wishes. He had consented to it as an act of justice due to her and the children; there was no pleasure to himself growing out of the intended change, beyond that of gratifying Emily, and securing freedom to her and the children. He knew enough of the North to feel convinced that he could not expect to live there openly with Emily, without being exposed to ill-natured comments, and closing upon himself the doors of many friends who had formerly received him with open arms. The virtuous dignity of the Northerner would be shocked, not so much at his having children by a woman of colour, but by his living with her in the midst of them, and acknowledging her as his wife. In the community where he now resided, such things were more common; the only point in which he differed from many other Southern gentlemen in this matter was in his constancy to Emily and the children, and the more than ordinary kindness and affection with which he treated them. Mr. Garie had for many years led a very retired life, receiving an occasional gentleman visitor; but this retirement had been entirely voluntary, therefore by no means disagreeable; but in the new home he had accepted, he felt that he might be shunned, and the reflection was anything but agreeable. Moreover, he was about to leave a place endeared to him by a thousand associations. Here he had passed the whole of his life, except about four years spent in travelling through Europe and America.

Mr. Garie was seated in a room where there were many things to recall days long since departed. The desk at which he was writing was once his father's, and he well remembered the methodical manner in which every drawer was carefully kept; over it hung a full-length portrait of his mother, and it seemed, as he gazed at it, that it was only yesterday that she had taken his little hand in her own, and walked with him down the long avenue of magnolias that were waving their flower-spangled branches in the morning breeze, and loading it with fragrance. Near him was the table on which her work-basket used to stand. He remembered how important he felt when permitted to hold the skeins of silk for her to wind, and how he would watch her stitch, stitch, hour after hour, at the screen that now stood beside the fire-place; the colours were faded, but the recollection of the pleasant smiles she would cast upon him from time to time, as she looked up from her work, was as fresh in his memory as if it were but yesterday. Mr. Garie was assorting and arranging the papers that the desk contained, when he heard the rattle of wheels along the avenue, and looking out of the window, he saw a carriage approaching.

The coachman was guiding his horses with one hand, and with the other he was endeavouring to keep a large, old-fashioned trunk from falling from the top. This was by no means an easy matter, as the horses appeared quite restive, and fully required his undivided attention. The rather unsteady motion of the carriage caused its inmate to put his head out of the window, and Mr. Garie recognized his uncle John, who lived in the north-western part of the State, on the borders of Alabama. He immediately left his desk, and hastened to the door to receive him.

"This is an unexpected visit, but none the less pleasant on that account," said Mr. Garie, his face lighting up with surprise and pleasure as uncle John alighted. "I had not the least expectation of being honoured by a visit from you. What has brought you into this part of the country? Business, of course? I can't conceive it possible that you should have ventured so far from home, at this early season, for the mere purpose of paying me a visit."

"You may take all the honour to yourself this time," smilingly replied uncle John, "for I have come over for your especial benefit; and if I accomplish the object of my journey, I shall consider the time anything but thrown away."

"Let me take your coat; and, Eph, see you to that trunk," said Mr. Garie. "You see everything is topsy-turvy with us, uncle John. We look like moving, don't we?"

"Like that or an annual house-cleaning," he replied, as he picked his way through rolls of carpet and matting, and between half-packed boxes; in doing which, he had several narrow escapes from the nails that protruded from them on all sides. "It's getting very warm; let me have something to drink," said he, wiping his face as he took his seat; "a julep—plenty of brandy and ice, and but little mint."

Eph, on receiving this order, departed in great haste in search of Mrs. Garie, as he knew that, whilst concocting one julep, she might be prevailed upon to mix another, and Eph had himself a warm liking for that peculiar Southern mixture, which liking he never lost any opportunity to gratify.

Emily hurried downstairs, on hearing of the arrival of uncle John, for he was regarded by her as a friend. She had always received from him marked kindness and respect, and upon the arrival of Mr. Garie's visitors, there was none she received with as much pleasure. Quickly mixing the drink, she carried it into the room where he and her husband were sitting. She was warmly greeted by the kind-hearted old man, who, in reply to her question if he had come to make them a farewell visit, said he hoped not: he trusted to make them many more in the same place.

"I'm afraid you won't have an opportunity," she replied. "In less than a week we expect to be on our way to New York.—I must go," continued she, "and have a room prepared for you, and hunt up the children. You'll scarcely know them, they have grown so much since you were here. I'll soon send them," and she hurried off to make uncle John's room comfortable.

"I was never more surprised in my life," said the old gentleman, depositing the glass upon the table, after draining it of its contents—"never more surprised than when I received your letter, in which you stated your intention of going to the North to live. A more ridiculous whim it is impossible to conceive—the idea is perfectly absurd! To leave a fine old place like this, where you have everything around you so nice and comfortable, to go north, and settle amongst a parcel of strange Yankees! My dear boy, you must give it up. I'm no longer your guardian—the law don't provide one for people of thirty years and upwards—so it is out of my power to say you shall not do it; but I am here to use all my powers of persuasion to induce you to relinquish the project."

"Uncle John, you don't seem to understand the matter. It is not a whim, by any means—it is a determination arising from a strict sense of duty; I feel that it is an act of justice to Emily and the children. I don't pretend to be better than most men; but my conscience will not permit me to be the owner of my own flesh and blood. I'm going north, because I wish to emancipate and educate my children—you know I can't do it here. At first I was as disinclined to favour the project as you are; but I am now convinced it is my duty, and, I must add, that my inclination runs in the same direction."

"Look here, Clarence, my boy," here interrupted uncle John; "you can't expect to live there as you do here; the prejudice against persons of colour is much stronger in some of the Northern cities than it is amongst us Southerners. You can't live with Emily there as you do here; you will be in everybody's mouth. You won't be able to sustain your old connections with your Northern friends—you'll find that they will cut you dead."

"I've looked at it well, uncle John. I've counted the cost, and have made up my mind to meet with many disagreeable things. If my old friends choose to turn their backs on me because my wife happens to belong to an oppressed race, that is not my fault. I don't feel that I have committed any sin by making the choice I have; and so their conduct or opinions won't influence my happiness much."

"Listen to me, Clary, for a moment," rejoined the old gentleman. "As long as you live here in Georgia you can sustain your present connection with impunity, and if you should ever want to break it off, you could do so by sending her and the children away; it would be no more than other men have done, and are doing every day. But go to the North, and it becomes a different thing. Your connection with Emily will inevitably become a matter of notoriety, and then you would find it difficult to shake her off there, as you could here, in case you wanted to marry another woman."

"Oh, uncle, uncle, how can you speak so indifferently about my doing such an ungenerous act; to characterize it in the very mildest terms? I feel that Emily is as much my wife in the eyes of God, as if a thousand clergymen had united us. It is not my fault that we are not legally married; it is the fault of the laws.[1] My father did not feel that my mother was any more his wife, than I do that Emily is mine."

---

1   See Appendix B1.

"Hush, hush; that is all nonsense, boy; and, besides, it is paying a very poor compliment to your mother to rank her with your mulatto mistress. I like Emily very much; she has been kind, affectionate, and faithful to you. Yet I really can't see the propriety of your making a shipwreck of your whole life on her account. Now," continued uncle John, with great earnestness, "I hoped for better things from you. You have talents and wealth; you belong to one of the oldest and best families in the State. When I am gone, you will be the last of our name; I had hoped that you would have done something to keep it from sinking into obscurity. There is no honour in the State to which you might not have aspired with a fair chance of success; but if you carry out your absurd determination, you will ruin yourself effectually."

"Well; I shall be ruined then, for I am determined to go. I feel it my duty to carry out my design," said Mr. Garie.

"Well, well, Clary," rejoined his uncle, "I've done my duty to my brother's son. I own, that although I cannot agree with you in your project, I can and do honour the unselfish motive that prompts it. You will always find me your friend under all circumstances, and now," concluded he, "it's off my mind."

The children were brought in and duly admired; a box of miniature carpenter's tools was produced; also, a wonderful man with a string through his waist—which string, when pulled, caused him to throw his arms and legs about in a most astonishing manner. The little folks were highly delighted with these presents, which uncle John had purchased at Augusta; they scampered off, and soon had every small specimen of sable humanity on the place at their heels, in ecstatic admiration of the wonderful articles of which they had so recently acquired possession.

As uncle John had absolutely refused all other refreshment than the julep before mentioned, dinner was ordered at a much earlier hour than usual. He ate very heartily, as was his custom; and, moreover, persisted in stuffing the children (as old gentlemen will do sometimes) until their mother was compelled to interfere to prevent their having a bilious attack[1] in consequence. Whilst the gentlemen were sitting over their dessert, Mr. Garie asked his uncle, if he had not a sister, with whom there was some mystery connected.

"No mystery," replied uncle John. "Your aunt made a very low marriage, and father cut her off from the family entirely. It happened when I was very young; she was the eldest of us all; there

---

1 I.e., a stomach-ache.

were four of us, as you know—your father, Bernard, I, and this sister of whom we are speaking. She has been dead for some years; she married a carpenter whom father employed on the place—a poor white man from New York. I have heard it said, that he was handsome, but drunken and vicious. They left one child—a boy; I believe he is alive in the North somewhere, or was, a few years since."

"And did she never make any overtures for a reconciliation?"

"She did, some years before father's death, but he was inexorable; he returned her letter, and died without seeing or forgiving her," replied uncle John.

"Poor thing; I suppose they were very poor?"

"I suppose they were. I have no sympathy for her. She deserved her fate, for marrying a greasy mechanic, in opposition to her father's commands, when she might have connected herself with any of the highest families in the State."

The gentlemen remained a long while that night, sipping their wine, smoking cigars, and discussing the probable result of the contemplated change. Uncle John seemed to have the worst forebodings as to the ultimate consequences, and gave it as his decided opinion, that they would all return to the old place in less than a year.

"You'll soon get tired of it," said he; "everything is so different there. Here you can get on well in your present relations; but mark me, you'll find nothing but disappointment and trouble where you are going."

The next morning he departed for his home; he kissed the children affectionately, and shook hands warmly with their mother. After getting into the carriage, he held out his hand again to his nephew, saying:— ·

"I am afraid you are going to be disappointed; but I hope you may not. Good bye, good bye—God bless you!" and his blue eyes looked very watery, as he was driven from the door.

That day, a letter arrived from Savannah, informing them that the ship in which they had engaged passage would be ready to sail in a few days; and they, therefore, determined that the first instalment of boxes and trunks should be sent to the city forthwith; and to Eph was assigned the melancholy duty of superintending their removal.

"Let me go with him, pa," begged little Clarence, who heard his father giving Eph his instructions.

"Oh, no," replied Mr. Garie; "the cart will be full of goods, there will be no room for you."

"But, pa, I can ride my pony; and, besides, you might let me go, for I shan't have many more chances to ride him—do let me go."

"Oh, yes, massa, let him go. Why dat ar chile can take care of his pony all by hissef. You should just seed dem two de oder day. You see de pony felt kinder big dat day, an' tuck a heap o' airs on hissef, an' tried to trow him—'twarn't no go—Massa Clary conquered him 'pletely. Mighty smart boy, dat," continued Eph, looking at little Clarence, admiringly, "mighty smart. I let him shoot off my pistol toder day, and he put de ball smack through de bull's eye—dat boy is gwine to be a perfect Ramrod."

"Oh, pa," laughingly interrupted little Clarence; "I've been telling him of what you read to me about Nimrod being a great hunter."[1]

"That's quite a mistake, Eph," said Mr. Garie, joining in the laugh.

"Well, I knowed it was suffin," said Eph, scratching his head; "suffin with a rod to it; I was all right on that pint—but you're gwine to let him go, ain't yer, massa?"

"I suppose, I must," replied Mr. Garie; "but mind now that no accident occurs to young Ramrod."

"I'll take care o' dat," said Eph, who hastened off to prepare the horses, followed by the delighted Clarence.

That evening, after his return from Savannah, Clarence kept his little sister's eyes expanded to an unprecedented extent by his narration of the wonderful occurrences attendant on his trip to town, and also of what he had seen in the vessel. He produced an immense orange, also a vast store of almonds and raisins, which had been given him by the good-natured steward. "But Em," said he, "we are going to sleep in such funny little places; even pa and mamma have got to sleep on little shelves stuck up against the wall; and they've got a thing that swings from the ceiling that they keep the tumblers and wine-glasses in—every glass has got a little hole for itself. Oh, it's so nice!"

"And have they got any nice shady trees on the ship?" asked the wondering little Em.

"Oh, no—what nonsense!" answered Clarence, swelling with the importance conferred by his superior knowledge. "Why, no, Em; who ever heard of such a thing as trees on a ship? they couldn't have trees on a ship if they wanted—there's no earth for them

---

1 "Nimrod ... was a mighty hunter" (Genesis 10:8–9). He was the grandson of Ham and the great-grandson of Noah.

to grow in. But I'll tell you what they've got—they've got masts a great deal higher than any tree, and I'm going to climb clear up to the top when we go to live on the ship."

"I wouldn't," said Em; "you might fall down like Ben did from the tree, and then you'd have to have your head sewed up as he had."

The probability that an occurrence of this nature might be the result of his attempt to climb the mast seemed to have considerable weight with Master Clarence, so he relieved his sister's mind at once by relinquishing the project.

The morning for departure at length arrived. Eph brought the carriage to the door at an early hour, and sat upon the box the picture of despair. He did not descend from his eminence to assist in any of the little arrangements for the journey, being very fearful that the seat he occupied might be resumed by its rightful owner, he having had a lengthy contest with the sable official who acted as coachman, and who had striven manfully, on this occasion, to take possession of his usual elevated station on the family equipage.[1] This, Eph would by no means permit, as he declared, "He was gwine to let nobody drive Massa dat day but hissef."

It was a mournful parting. The slaves crowded around the carriage kissing and embracing the children, and forcing upon them little tokens of remembrance. Blind Jacob, the patriarch of the place, came and passed his hands over the face of little Em for the last time, as he had done almost every week since her birth, that, to use his own language, "he might see how de piccaninny[2] growed." His bleared and sightless eyes were turned to heaven to ask a blessing on the little ones and their parents.

"Why, daddy Jake, you should not take it so hard," said Mr. Garie, with an attempt at cheerfulness. "You'll see us all again some day."

"No, no, massa, I'se feared I won't; I'se gettin' mighty old, massa, and I'se gwine home soon. I hopes I'll meet you all up yonder," said he, pointing heavenward. "I don't 'spect to see any of you here agin."

Many of the slaves were in tears, and all deeply lamented the departure of their master and his family, for Mr. Garie had always

---

1   Coach; carriage. See *OED* "equipage" 12.
2   Colloquial term used throughout the Atlantic world for black children. Here a word of affection, it was more often deployed in dehumanizing contexts.

been the kindest of owners, and Mrs. Garie was, if possible, more beloved than himself. She was first at every sick-bed, and had been comforter-general to all the afflicted and distressed in the place.

At last the carriage rolled away, and in a few hours they reached Savannah, and immediately went on board the vessel.

CHAPTER X.

Another Parting.

MRS. ELLIS had been for some time engaged in arranging and replenishing Charlie's wardrobe, preparatory to his journey to Warmouth with Mrs. Bird. An entire new suit of grey cloth had been ordered of the tailor, to whom Mrs. Ellis gave strict injunctions not to make them too small. Notwithstanding the unfavourable results of several experiments, Mrs. Ellis adhered with wonderful tenacity to the idea that a boy's clothes could never be made too large, and, therefore, when Charlie had a new suit, it always appeared as if it had been made for some portly gentleman, and sent home to Charlie by mistake.

This last suit formed no exception to the others, and Charlie surveyed with dismay its ample dimensions as it hung from the back of the chair. "Oh, gemini!" said he, "but that jacket is a rouser! I tell you what, mother, you'll have to get out a search-warrant to find me in that jacket; now, mind, I tell you!"

"Nonsense!" replied Mrs. Ellis, "it don't look a bit too large; put it on."

Charlie took up the coat, and in a twinkling had it on over his other. His hands were almost completely lost in the excessively long sleeves, which hung down so far that the tips of his fingers were barely visible. "Oh, mother!" he exclaimed, "just look at these sleeves—if such a thing were to happen that any one were to offer me a half dollar, they would change their mind before I could get my hand out to take it; and it will almost go twice round me, it is so large in the waist."

"Oh, you can turn the sleeves up; and as for the waist—you'll soon grow to it; it will be tight enough for you before long, I'll warrant," said Mrs. Ellis.

"But, mother," rejoined Charlie, "that is just what you said about the other blue suit, and it was entirely worn out before you had let down the tucks in the trowsers."

"Never mind the blue suit," persisted Mrs. Ellis, entirely unbiassed by this statement of facts. "You'll grow faster this time—you're going into the country, you must remember—boys always grow fast in the country; go into the other room and try on the trowsers."

Charlie retired into another room with the trowsers in question. Here he was joined by Kinch, who went into fits of laughter over Charlie's pea-jacket, as he offensively called the new coat.

"Why, Charlie," said he, "it fits you like a shirt on a bean-pole, or rather it's like a sentry's box—it don't touch you any where. But get into these pants," said he, almost choking with the laughter that Charlie's vexed look caused him to suppress—"get into the pants;" at the same time tying a string round Charlie's neck.

"What are you doing that for?" exclaimed Charlie, in an irritated tone; "I shouldn't have thought you would make fun of me!"

"Oh," said Kinch, assuming a solemn look, "don't they always tie a rope round a man's body when they are going to lower him into a pit? and how on earth do you ever expect we shall find you in the legs of them trowsers, unless something is fastened to you?" Here Charlie was obliged to join in the laugh that Kinch could no longer restrain.

"Stop that playing, boys," cried Mrs. Ellis, as their noisy mirth reached her in the adjoining room; "you forget I am waiting for you."

Charlie hastily drew on the trousers, and found that their dimensions fully justified the precaution Kinch was desirous of taking to secure him from sinking into oblivion.

"Oh, I can't wear these things," said Charlie, tears of vexation starting from his eyes. "Why, they are so large I can't even keep them up; and just look at the legs, will you—they'll have to be turned up a quarter of a yard at least."

"Here," said Kinch, seizing a large pillow, "I'll stuff this in. Oh, golly, how you look! if you ain't a sight to see!" and he shouted with laughter as he surveyed Charlie, to whom the pillow had imparted the appearance of a London alderman. "If you don't look like Squire Baker now, I'll give it up. You are as big as old Daddy Downhill. You are a regular Daniel Lambert!"[1]

The idea of looking like Squire Baker and Daddy Downhill, who were the "fat men" of their acquaintance, amused Charlie as much as it did his companion, and making the house ring with their mirth, they entered the room where Mr. Ellis and the girls had joined Mrs. Ellis.

"What on earth is the matter with the child?" exclaimed Mr. Ellis, as he gazed upon the grotesque figure Charlie presented. "What has the boy been doing to himself?" Hereupon Kinch

---

1 Englishman (1770–1809) renowned for prodigious heft—he weighed some 795 pounds at his death. His name remained a byword for obesity until well into the nineteenth century; see, for example, "A Great Idea" in Dickens's *Household Words* 5.126 (21 August 1852): 546–48.

explained how matters stood, to the infinite amusement of all parties.

"Oh, Ellen," said Mr. Ellis, "you must have them altered; they're a mile too big for him. I really believe they would fit me."

"They do look rather large," said Mrs. Ellis, reluctantly; "but it seems such a waste to take them in, as he grows so fast."

"He would not grow enough in two years to fill that suit," rejoined Mr. Ellis; "and he will have worn them out in less than six months;" and so, to the infinite satisfaction of Charlie, it was concluded that they should be sent back to the tailor's for the evidently necessary alterations.

The day for Charlie's departure at last arrived.

Kinch, who had been up since two o'clock in the morning, was found by Caddy at the early hour of five waiting upon the doorstep to accompany his friend to the wharf. Beside him lay a bag, in which there appeared to be some living object.

"What have you got in here?" asked Caddy, as she gave the bag a punch with the broom she was using.

"It's a present for Charlie," replied Kinch, opening the bag, and displaying, to the astonished gaze of Caddy, a very young pig.

"Why," said she, laughing, "you don't expect he can take that with him, do you?"

"Why not?" asked Kinch, taking up the bag and carrying it into the house. "It's just the thing to take into the country; Charlie can fatten him and sell him for a lot of money."

It was as much as Mrs. Ellis could do to convince Charlie and Kinch of the impracticability of their scheme of carrying off to Warmouth the pig in question. She suggested, as it was the exclusive property of Kinch, and he was so exceedingly anxious to make Charlie a parting gift, that she should purchase it, which she did, on the spot; and Kinch invested all the money in a large cross-bow, wherewith Charlie was to shoot game sufficient to supply both Kinch and his own parents. Had Charlie been on his way to the scaffold, he could not have been followed by a more solemn face than that presented by Kinch as he trudged on with him in the rear of the porter who carried the trunk.

"I wish you were not going," said he, as he put his arm affectionately over Charlie's shoulder, "I shall be so lonesome when you are gone; and what is more, I know I shall get licked every day in school, for who will help me with my sums?"

"Oh, any of the boys will, they all like you, Kinch; and if you only study a little harder, you can do them yourself," was Charlie's encouraging reply.

On arriving at the boat, they found Mrs. Bird waiting for them; so Charlie hastily kissed his mother and sisters, and made endless promises not to be mischievous, and, above all, to be as tidy as possible. Then tearing himself away from them, and turning to Kinch, he exclaimed, "I'll be back to see you all again soon, so don't cry, old fellow;" and at the same time thrusting his hand into his pocket, he drew out a number of marbles, which he gave him, his own lips quivering all the while. At last his attempts to suppress his tears and look like a man grew entirely futile, and he cried heartily as Mrs. Bird took his hand and drew him on board the steamer.

As it slowly moved from the pier and glided up the river,[1] Charlie stood looking with tearful eyes at his mother and sisters, who, with Kinch, waved their handkerchiefs as long as they could distinguish him, and then he saw them move away with the crowd.

Mrs. Bird, who had been conversing with a lady who accompanied her a short distance on her journey, came and took her little *protégé* by the hand, and led him to a seat near her in the after part of the boat, informing him, as she did so, that they would shortly exchange the steamer for the cars, and she thought he had better remain near her.

After some time they approached the little town where the passengers took the train for New York. Mrs. Bird, who had taken leave of her friend, held Charlie fast by the hand, and they entered the cars together. He looked a little pale and weak from the excitement of parting and the novelty of his situation. Mrs. Bird, observing his pallid look, placed him on a seat, and propped him up with shawls and cushions, making him as comfortable as possible.

The train had not long started, when the conductor came through to inspect the tickets, and quite started with surprise at seeing Charlie stretched at full length upon the velvet cushion. "What are you doing here?" exclaimed he, at the same time shaking him roughly, to arouse him from the slight slumber into which he had fallen. "Come, get up: you must go out of this."

"What do you mean by such conduct?" asked Mrs. Bird, very much surprised. "Don't wake him; I've got his ticket; the child is sick."

"I don't care whether he's sick or well—he can't ride in here. We don't allow niggers to ride in this car, no how you can fix it—

---

1 Probably the Delaware River.

so come, youngster," said he, gruffly, to the now aroused boy, "you must travel out of this."

"He shall do no such thing," replied Mrs. Bird, in a decided tone; "I've paid full price for his ticket, and he shall ride here; you have no legal right to eject him."

"I've got no time to jaw about rights, legal or illegal—all I care to know is, that I've my orders not to let niggers ride in these cars, and I expect to obey, so you see there is no use to make any fuss about it."

"Charlie," said Mrs. Bird, "sit here;" and she moved aside, so as to seat him between herself and the window. "Now," said she, "move him if you think best."

"I'll tell you what it is, old woman," doggedly remarked the conductor: "you can't play that game with me. I've made up my mind that no more niggers shall ride in this car, and I'll have him out of here, cost what it may."

The passengers now began to cluster around the contending parties, and to take sides in the controversy. In the end, the conductor stopped the train, and called in one or two of the Irish brake-men to assist him, if necessary, in enforcing his orders.

"You had better let the boy go into the negro car, madam," said one of the gentlemen, respectfully; "it is perfectly useless to contend with these ruffians. I saw a coloured man ejected from here last week, and severely injured; and, in the present state of public feeling, if anything happened to you or the child, you would be entirely without redress. The directors of this railroad control the State; and there is no such thing as justice to be obtained in any of the State courts in a matter in which they are concerned. If you will accept of my arm, I will accompany you to the other car—if you will not permit the child to go there alone, you had better go quietly with him."

"Oh, what is the use of so much talk about it? Why don't you hustle the old thing out," remarked a bystander, the respectability of whose appearance contrasted broadly with his manners; "she is some crack-brained Abolitionist. Making so much fuss about a little nigger! Let her go into the nigger car—she'll be more at home there."

Mrs. Bird, seeing the uselessness of contention, accepted the proffered escort of the gentleman before mentioned, and was followed out of the cars by the conductor and his blackguard assistants, all of them highly elated by the victory they had won over a defenceless old woman and a feeble little boy.

Mrs. Bird shrank back, as they opened the door of the car that had been set apart for coloured persons, and such objectionable whites as were not admitted to the first-class cars. "Oh, what a wretched place!" she exclaimed, as she surveyed the rough pine timbers and dirty floor; "I would not force a dog to ride in such a filthy place."

"Oh, don't stay here, ma'am; never mind me—I shall get on by myself well enough, I dare say," said Charlie; "it is too nasty a place for you to stay in."

"No, my child," she replied; "I'll remain with you. I could not think of permitting you to be alone in your present state of health. I declare," she continued, "it's enough to make any one an Abolitionist, or anything else of the kind, to see how inoffensive coloured people are treated!"

That evening they went on board the steamer that was to convey them to Warmouth, where they arrived very early the following morning.

Charlie was charmed with the appearance of the pretty little town, as they rode through it in Mrs. Bird's carriage, which awaited them at the landing. At the door of her residence they were met by two cherry-faced maids, who seemed highly delighted at the arrival of their mistress.

"Now, Charlie," said Mrs. Bird, as she sat down in her large arm-chair, and looked round her snug little parlour with an air of great satisfaction—"now we are at home, and you must try and make yourself as happy as possible. Betsey," said she, turning to one of the women, "here is a nice little fellow, whom I have brought with me to remain during the summer, of whom I want you to take the best care; for," continued she, looking at him compassionately, "the poor child has had the misfortune to break his arm recently, and he has not been strong since. The physician thought the country would be the best place for him, and so I've brought him here to stay with us. Tell Reuben to carry his trunk into the little maple chamber, and by-and-by, after I have rested, I will take a walk over the place with him."

"Here are two letters for you," said Betsey, taking them from the mantelpiece, and handing them to her mistress.

Mrs. Bird opened one, of which she read a part, and then laid it down, as being apparently of no importance. The other, however, seemed to have a great effect upon her, as she exclaimed, hurriedly, "Tell Reuben not to unharness the horses—I must go to Francisville immediately—dear Mrs. Hinton is very ill, and not expected to recover. You must take good care of Charlie until I return. If I do not come back to-night, you will know that she is worse, and that I am compelled to remain there;" and, on the carriage being brought to the door, she departed in haste to visit her sick friend.

CHAPTER XI.

The New Home.

WHEN Mrs. Garie embarked, she entertained the idea so prevalent among fresh-water sailors, that she was to be an exception to the rule of Father Neptune, in accordance with which all who intrude for the first time upon his domain are compelled to pay tribute to his greatness, and humbly bow in acknowledgment of his power.

Mrs. Garie had determined not to be sea-sick upon any account whatever, being fully persuaded she could brave the ocean with impunity, and was, accordingly, very brisk and blithe-looking, as she walked up and down upon the deck of the vessel. In the course of a few hours they sailed out of the harbour, and were soon in the open sea. She began to find out how mistaken she had been, as unmistakable symptoms convinced her of the vanity of all human calculations. "Why, you are not going to be ill, Em, after all your valiant declarations!" exclaimed Mr. Garie, supporting her unsteady steps, as they paced to and fro.

"Oh, no, no!" said she, in a firm tone; "I don't intend to give up to any such nonsense. I believe that people can keep up if they try. I do feel a little fatigued and nervous; it's caused, no doubt, by the long drive of this morning—although I think it singular that a drive should affect me in this manner." Thus speaking, she sat down by the bulwarks of the vessel, and a despairing look gradually crept over her face. At last she suddenly rose, to look at the water, as we may imagine. The effect of her scrutiny, however, was that she asked feebly to be assisted to her state-room, where she remained until their arrival in the harbour of New York.

The children suffered only for a short time, and as their father escaped entirely, he was able to watch that they got into no mischief. They were both great favourites with the captain and steward, and, between the two, were so stuffed and crammed with sweets as to place their health in considerable jeopardy.

It was a delightful morning when they sailed into the harbour of New York. The waters were dancing and rippling in the morning sun, and the gaily-painted ferry-boats were skimming swiftly across its surface in their trips to and from the city, which was just awaking to its daily life of bustling toil.

"What an immense city it is!" said Mrs. Garie—"how full of life and bustle! Why there are more ships at one pier here than there are in the whole port of Savannah!"

"Yes, dear," rejoined her husband; "and what is more, there always will be. Our folks in Georgia are not waked up yet; and when they do arouse themselves from their slumber, it will be too late. But we don't see half the shipping from here—this is only one side of the city—there is much more on the other. Look over there," continued he, pointing to Jersey city,—"that is where we take the cars for Philadelphia; and if we get up to dock in three or four hours, we shall be in time for the mid-day train."

In less time than they anticipated they were alongside the wharf; the trunks were brought up, and all things for present use were safely packed together and despatched, under the steward's care, to the office of the railroad.

Mr. and Mrs. Garie, after bidding good-bye to the captain, followed with the children, who were thrown into a great state of excitement by the noise and bustle of the crowded thoroughfare.

"How this whirl and confusion distracts me," said Mrs. Garie, looking out of the carriage-window. "I hope Philadelphia is not as noisy a place as this."

"Oh, no," replied Mr. Garie; "it is one of the most quiet and clean cities in the world, whilst this is the noisiest and dirtiest. I always hurry out of New York; it is to me such a disagreeable place, with its extortionate hackmen[1] and filthy streets."

On arriving at the little steamer in which they crossed the ferry,[2] they found it about to start, and therefore had to hurry on board with all possible speed.

Under the circumstances, the hackman felt that it would be flying in the face of Providence if he did not extort a large fare, and he therefore charged an extravagant price. Mr. Garie paid him, as he had no time to parley, and barely succeeded in slipping a *douceur*[3] into the steward's hand, when the boat pushed off from the pier.

In a few moments they had crossed the river, and were soon comfortably seated in the cars whirling over the track to Philadelphia.

As the conductor came through to examine the tickets, he paused for a moment before Mrs. Garie and the children. As he passed on, his assistant inquired, "Isn't that a nigger?"

"Yes, a half-white one," was the reply.

---

1   Drivers of hackney carriages; cabbies.
2   Here, not the boat but rather the place where the river is traversed.
3   A gratuity; a tip for services rendered.

"Why don't you order her out, then?—she has no business to ride in here," continued the first speaker.

"I guess we had better let her alone," suggested the conductor, "particularly as no one has complained; and there might be a row if she turned out to be the nurse to those children. The whole party are Southerners, that's clear; and these Southerners are mighty touchy about their niggers sometimes, and kick and cut like the devil about them. I guess we had better let her alone, unless some one complains about her being there."

As they drove through the streets of Philadelphia on the way to their new home, Mrs. Garie gave vent to many expressions of delight at the appearance of the city. "Oh, what a sweet place! everything is so bright and fresh-looking; why the pavement and doorsteps look as if they were cleaned twice a day. Just look at that house, how spotless it is; I hope ours resembles that. Ours is a new house, is it not?" she inquired.

"Not entirely; it has been occupied before, but only for a short time, I believe," was her husband's reply.

It had grown quite dark by the time they arrived at Winter-street, where Caddy had been anxiously holding watch and ward[1] in company with the servants who had been procured for them. A bright light was burning in the entry as the coachman stopped at the door.

"This is No. 27," said he, opening the door of the carriage, "shall I ring?"

"Yes, do," replied Mr. Garie; but whilst he was endeavouring to open the gate of the little garden in front, Caddy, who had heard the carriage stop, bounded out to welcome them. "This is Mr. Garie, I suppose," said she, as he alighted.

"Yes, I am; and you, I suppose, are the daughter of Mr. Ellis?"

"Yes, sir; I'm sorry mother is not here to welcome you; she was here until very late last night expecting your arrival, and was here again this morning," said Caddy, taking at the same time one of the little carpet bags, "Give me the little girl, I can take care of her too," she continued; and with little Em on one arm and the carpet bag on the other, she led the way into the house.

"We did not make up any fire," said she, "the weather is very warm to us. I don't know how it may feel to you, though."

"It is a little chilly," replied Mrs. Garie, as she sat down upon the sofa, and looked round the room with a smile of pleasure, and

---

1   Acting as a sentinel. See *OED* "watch" 7a.

added, "All this place wants, to make it the most bewitching of rooms, is a little fire."

Caddy hurried the new servants from place to place remorselessly, and set them to prepare the table and get the things ready for tea. She waylaid a party of labourers, who chanced to be coming that way, and hired them to carry all the luggage upstairs—had the desired fire made—mixed up some cornbread, and had tea on the table in a twinkling. They all ate very heartily, and Caddy was greatly praised for her activity.

"You are quite a housekeeper," said Mrs. Garie to Caddy. "Do you like it?"

"Oh, yes," she replied. "I see to the house at home almost entirely; mother and Esther are so much engaged in sewing, that they are glad enough to leave it in my hands, and I'd much rather do that than sew."

"I hope," said Mrs. Garie, "that your mother will permit you to remain with us until we get entirely settled."

"I know she will," confidently replied Caddy. "She will be up here in the morning. She will know you have arrived by my not having gone home this evening."

The children had now fallen asleep with their heads in close proximity to their plates, and Mrs. Garie declared that she felt very much fatigued and slightly indisposed, and thought the sooner she retired the better it would be for her. She accordingly went up to the room, which she had already seen and greatly admired, and was soon in the land of dreams.

As is always the case on such occasions, the children's nightdresses could not be found. Clarence was put to bed in one of his father's shirts, in which he was almost lost, and little Em was temporarily accommodated with a calico short gown of Caddy's, and, in default of a nightcap, had her head tied up in a Madras handkerchief, which gave her, when her back was turned, very much the air of an old Creole[1] who had been by some mysterious means deprived of her due growth.

The next morning Mrs. Garie was so much indisposed as to be unable to rise, and took her breakfast in bed. Her husband had

---

1 According to late eighteenth-century sumptuary laws in Louisiana and parts of the Caribbean, mixed-race women (Creoles) were required to wear their hair under headscarves called *tignons*. These were often fashioned from imported cloth, including light, colorful fabrics from the Indian city of Madras.

finished his meal, and was sitting in the parlour, when he observed a middle-aged coloured lady coming into the garden.

"Look, Caddy," cried he, "isn't this your mother?"

"Oh, yes, that is she," replied Caddy, and ran and opened the door, exclaiming, "Oh, mother, they're come;" and as she spoke, Mr. Garie came into the entry and shook hands heartily with her.

"I'm so much indebted to you," said he, "for arranging everything so nicely for us—there is not a thing we would wish to alter."

"I am very glad you are pleased; we did our best to make it comfortable," was her reply.

"And you succeeded beyond our expectation; but do come up," continued he, "Emily will be delighted to see you. She is quite unwell this morning; has not even got up yet;" and leading the way upstairs, he ushered Mrs. Ellis into the bedroom.

"Why, can this be you?" said she, surveying Emily with surprise and pleasure. "If I had met you anywhere, I should never have known you. How you have altered! You were not so tall as my Caddy when I saw you last; and here you are with two children—and pretty little things they are too!" said she, kissing little Em, who was seated on the bed with her brother, and sharing with him the remains of her mother's chocolate.

"And you look much younger that I expected to see you," replied Mrs. Garie. "Draw a chair up to the bed, and let us have a talk about old times. You must excuse my lying down; I don't intend to get up to-day; I feel quite indisposed."

Mrs. Ellis took off her bonnet, and prepared for a long chat; whilst Mr. Garie, looking at his watch, declared it was getting late, and started for down town, where he had to transact some business.

"You can scarcely think, Ellen, how much I feel indebted to you for all you have done for us; and we are so distressed to hear about Charlie's accident. You must have had a great deal of trouble."

"Oh, no, none to speak of—and had it been ever so much, I should have been just as pleased to have done it; I was so glad you were coming. What did put it in your heads to come here to live?" continued Mrs. Ellis.

"Oh, cousin George Winston praised the placed so highly, and you know how disagreeable Georgia is to live in. My mind was never at rest there respecting these," said she, pointing to the children; "so that I fairly teased Garie into it. Did you recognize George?"

"No, I didn't remember much about him. I should never have taken him for a coloured man; had I met him in the street, I should have supposed him to be a wealthy white Southerner. What a gentleman he is in his appearance and manners," said Mrs. Ellis.

"Yes, he is all that—my husband thinks there is no one like him. But we won't talk about him now; I want you to tell me all about yourself and family, and then tell you everything respecting my own fortunes." Hereupon ensued long narratives from both parties, which occupied the greater part of the morning.

Mr. Garie, on leaving the house, slowly wended his way to the residence of Mr. Walters. As he passed into the lower part of the city, his attention was arrested by the number of coloured children he saw skipping merrily along with their bags of books on their arms.

"This," said he to himself, "don't much resemble Georgia."[1]

After walking some distance he took out a card, and read, 257, Easton-street; and on inquiry found himself in the very street. He proceeded to inspect the numbers, and was quite perplexed by their confusion and irregularity.

A coloured boy happening to pass at the time, he asked him: "Which way do the numbers run, my little man?"

The boy looked up waggishly, and replied: "They don't run at all; they are permanently affixed to each door."

"But," said Mr. Garie, half-provoked, yet compelled to smile at the boy's pompous wit, "you know what I mean; I cannot find the number I wish; the street is not correctly numbered."

"The street is not numbered at all," rejoined the boy, "but the houses are," and he skipped lightly away.

Mr. Garie was finally set right about the numbers, and found himself at length before the door of Mr. Walters's house. "Quite a handsome residence," said he, as he surveyed the stately house, with its spotless marble steps and shining silver door-plate.

On ringing, his summons was quickly answered by a well-dressed servant, who informed him that Mr. Walters was at home, and ushered him into the parlour. The elegance of the room took Mr. Garie completely by surprise, as its furniture indicated not only great wealth, but cultivated taste and refined habits. The richly-papered walls were adorned by paintings from the hands of

---

1 [Webb's note:] It is a penal offence in Georgia to teach coloured children to read.

well-known foreign and native artists. Rich vases and well-executed bronzes were placed in the most favourable situations in the apartment; the elegantly-carved walnut table was covered with those charming little bijoux which the French only are capable of conceiving, and which are only at the command of such purchasers as are possessed of more money than they otherwise can conveniently spend.

Mr. Garie threw himself into a luxuriously-cushioned chair, and was soon so absorbed in contemplating the likeness of a negro officer which hung opposite, that he did not hear the soft tread of Mr. Walters as he entered the room. The latter, stepping slowly forward, caught the eye of Mr. Garie, who started up, astonished at the commanding figure before him.

"Mr. Garie, I presume?" said Mr. Walters.

"Yes," he replied, and added, as he extended his hand; "I have the pleasure of addressing Mr. Walters, I suppose?"

Mr. Walters bowed low as he accepted the proffered hand, and courteously requested his visitor to be seated.

As Mr. Garie resumed his seat, he could not repress a look of surprise, which Mr. Walters apparently perceived, for a smile slightly curled his lip as he also took a seat opposite his visitor.

Mr. Walters was above six feet in height, and exceedingly well-proportioned; of jet-black complexion, and smooth glossy skin. His head was covered with a quantity of woolly hair, which was combed back from a broad but not very high forehead. His eyes were small, black, and piercing, and set deep in his head. His aquiline nose, thin lips, and broad chin, were the very reverse of African in their shape, and gave his face a very singular appearance. In repose, his countenance was severe in its expression; but when engaged in agreeable conversation, the thin sarcastic-looking lips would part, displaying a set of dazzlingly white teeth, and the small black eyes would sparkle with animation. The neatness and care with which he was dressed added to the attractiveness of his appearance. His linen was the perfection of whiteness, and his snowy vest lost nothing by its contact therewith. A long black frock coat, black pants, and highly-polished boots, completed his attire.

"I hope," said he, "your house suits you; it is one of my own, and has never been rented except for a short time to a careful tenant, who was waiting for his own house to be finished. I think you will find it comfortable."

"Oh, perfectly so, I am quite sure. I must thank you for the prompt manner in which you have arranged everything for us. It seems more like coming to an old home than to a new residence," replied Mr. Garie.

"I am delighted to hear you say so," said Mr. Walters. "I shall be most happy to call and pay my respects to Mrs. Garie when agreeable to her. Depend upon it, we will do all in our power to make our quiet city pleasant to you both."

Mr. Garie thanked him, and after some further conversation, rose to depart.

As he was leaving the room, he stopped before the picture which had so engaged his attention, when Mr. Walters entered.

"So you, too, are attracted by that picture," said Mr. Walters, with a smile. "All white men look at it with interest. A black man in the uniform of a general officer is something so unusual that they cannot pass it with a glance."

"It is, indeed, rather a novelty," replied Mr. Garie, "particularly to a person from my part of the country. Who is it?"

"That is Toussaint l'Ouverture,"[1] replied Mr. Walters; "and I have every reason to believe it to be a correct likeness. It was presented to an American merchant by Toussaint himself—a present in return for some kindness shown him. This merchant's son, not having the regard for the picture that his father entertained for it, sold it to me. That," continued Mr. Walters, "looks like a man of intelligence. It is entirely different from any likeness I ever saw of him. The portraits generally represent him as a monkey-faced person, with a handkerchief about his head."

"This," said Mr. Garie, "gives me an idea of the man that accords with his actions."

Thus speaking, he continued looking at the picture for a short time, and then took his departure, after requesting Mr. Walters to call upon him at an early opportunity.

---

1   See Introduction, p. 15, note 1.

CHAPTER XII.

Mr. Garie's Neighbour.

WE must now introduce our readers into the back parlour of the house belonging to Mr. Garie's next-door neighbour, Mr. George Stevens.[1]

We find this gentleman standing at a window that overlooked his garden, enjoying a fragrant Havannah.[2] His appearance was not by any means prepossessing; he was rather above than below the middle height, with round shoulders, and long, thin arms, finished off by disagreeable-looking hands. His head was bald on the top, and the thin greyish-red hair, that grew more thickly about his ears, was coaxed up to that quarter, where an attempt had been made to effect such a union between the cords of the hair from each side as should cover the place in question.

The object, however, remained unaccomplished; as the hair was either very obstinate and would not be induced to lie as desired, or from extreme modesty objected to such an elevated position, and, in consequence, stopped half-way, as if undecided whether to lie flat or remain erect, producing the effect that would have been presented had he been decorated with a pair of horns. His baldness might have given an air of benevolence to his face, but for the shaggy eyebrows that over-shadowed his cunning-looking grey eyes. His cheekbones were high, and the cadaverous skin was so tightly drawn across them, as to give it a very parchment-like appearance. Around his thin compressed lips there was a continual nervous twitching, that added greatly to the sinister aspect of his face.

On the whole, he was a person from whom you would instinctively shrink; and had he been president or director of a bank in which you had money deposited, his general aspect would not have given you additional confidence in the stable character or just administration of its affairs.

Mr. George Stevens was a pettifogging attorney, who derived a tolerable income from a rather disreputable legal practice picked up among the courts that held their sessions in the various halls of the State-house. He was known in the profession as Slip-

---

1   The 1857 edition reads "Thomas Stevens," but this seems to have been an editor's or typesetter's error. It is the only appearance of Thomas in the text.
2   Cigar.

pery George, from the easy manner in which he glided out of scrapes that would have been fatal to the reputation of any other lawyer. Did a man break into a house, and escape without being actually caught on the spot with the goods in his possession, Stevens was always able to prove an *alibi* by a long array of witnesses. In fact, he was considered by the swell gentry of the city as their especial friend and protector, and by the members of the bar generally as anything but an ornament to the profession.

He had had rather a fatiguing day's labour, and on the evening of which we write, was indulging in his usual cigar, and amusing himself at the same time by observing the gambols of Clarence and little Em, who were enjoying a romp in their father's garden.

"Come here, Jule," said he, "and look at our new neighbour's children—rather pretty, ain't they?"

He was joined by a diminutive red-faced woman, with hair and eyes very much like his own, and a face that wore a peevish, pinched expression.

"Rather good-looking," she replied, after observing them for a few minutes, and then added, "Have you seen their parents?"

"No, not yet," was the reply. "I met Walters in the street this morning, who informed me they are from the South, and very rich; we must try and cultivate them—ask the children in to play with ours, and strike up an intimacy in that way, the rest will follow naturally, you know. By the way, Jule," continued he, "how I hate that nigger Walters, with his grand airs. I wanted some money of him the other day on rather ticklish securities for a client of mine, and the black wretch kept me standing in his hall for at least five minutes, and then refused me, with some not very complimentary remarks upon my assurance in offering him such securities. It made me so mad I could have choked him—it is bad enough to be treated with *hauteur* by a white man, but contempt from a nigger is almost unendurable."

"Why didn't you resent it in some way? I never would have submitted to anything of the kind from him," interrupted Mrs. Stevens.

"Oh, I don't dare to just now; I have to be as mild as milk with him. You forget about the mortgage; don't you know he has me in a tight place there, and I don't see how to get out of it either. If I am called Slippery George, I tell you what, Jule, there's not a better man of business in the whole of Philadelphia than that same Walters, nigger as he is; and no one offends him without paying dear for it in some way or other. I'll tell you something he did last week. He went up to Trenton on business, and at the hotel they refused to give him dinner because of his colour, and told him they did not permit niggers to eat at their tables. What does he do but buy the house over the landlord's head. The lease had just expired, and the landlord was anxious to negotiate another; he was also making some arrangements with his creditors, which could not be effected unless he was enabled to renew the lease of the premises he occupied. On learning that the house had been sold, he came down to the city to negotiate with the new owner, and to his astonishment found him to be the very man he had refused a meal to the week before. Blunt happened to be in Walters's office at the time the fellow called. Walters, he says, drew himself up to his full height, and looked like an ebony statue.

"'Sir,' said he, 'I came to your house and asked for a meal, for which I was able to pay; you not only refused it to me, but heaped upon me words such as fall only from the lips of blackguards. You refuse to have me in your house—I object to have you in mine: you will, therefore, quit the premises immediately.' The fellow sneaked out quite crestfallen, and his creditors have broken him up completely.

"I tell you what, Jule, if I was a black," continued he, "living in a country like this, I'd sacrifice conscience and everything else to the acquisition of wealth."

As he concluded, he turned from the window and sat down by a small table, upon which a lighted lamp had been placed, and where a few law papers were awaiting a perusal.

A little boy and girl were sitting opposite to him. The boy was playing with a small fly-trap, wherein he had already imprisoned a vast number of buzzing sufferers. In appearance he bore a close resemblance to his father; he had the same red hair and sallow complexion, but his grey eyes had a dull leaden hue.

"Do let them go, George, do!" said the little girl, in a pleading tone. "You'll kill them, shut up there."

"I don't care if I do," replied he, doggedly; "I can catch more—look here;" and as he spoke he permitted a few of the imprisoned insects to creep partly out, and then brought the lid down upon them with a force that completely demolished them.

The little girl shuddered at this wanton exhibition of cruelty, and offered him a paper of candy if he would liberate his prisoners, which he did rather reluctantly, but promising himself to replenish the box at the first opportunity.

"Ah!" said he, in a tone of exultation, "father took me with him to the jail to-day, and I saw all the people locked up. I mean to be a jailer some of these days. Wouldn't you like to keep a jail, Liz?" continued he, his leaden eyes receiving a slight accession of brightness at the idea.

"Oh, no!" replied she; "I would let all the people go, if I kept the jail."

A more complete contrast than this little girl presented to her parents and brother, cannot be imagined. She had very dark chestnut hair, and mild blue eyes, and a round, full face, which, in expression, was sweetness itself. She was about six years old, and her brother's junior by an equal number of years.

Her mother loved her, but thought her tame and spiritless in her disposition; and her father cherished as much affection for her as he was capable of feeling for any one but himself.

Mrs. Stevens, however, doted on their eldest hope, who was as disagreeable as a thoroughly spoiled and naturally evil-disposed boy could be.

As the evenings had now become quite warm, Mr. Garie frequently took a chair and enjoyed his evening cigar upon the doorstep of his house; and as Mr. Stevens thought his steps equally suited to this purpose, it was very natural he should resort there with the same object.

Mr. Stevens found no difficulty in frequently bringing about short neighbourly conversations with Mr. Garie. The little folk, taking their cue from their parents, soon became intimate, and ran in and out of each other's houses in the most familiar manner possible. Lizzy Stevens and little Em joined hearts immediately, and their intimacy had already been cemented by frequent consultations on the various ailments wherewith they supposed their dolls afflicted.

Clarence got on only tolerably with George Stevens; he entertained for him that deference that one boy always has for another who is his superior in any boyish pastime; but there was little affection lost between them—they cared very little for each other's society.

Mrs. Garie, since her arrival, had been much confined to her room, in consequence of her protracted indisposition. Mrs. Stevens had several times intimated to Mr. Garie her intention of paying his wife a visit; but never having received any very decided encouragement, she had not pressed the matter, though her curiosity was aroused, and she was desirous of seeing what kind of person Mrs. Garie could be.

Her son George in his visits had never been permitted farther than the front parlour; and all the information that could be drawn from little Lizzy, who was frequently in Mrs. Garie's bedroom, was that "she was a pretty lady, with great large eyes."

One evening, when Mr. Garie was occupying his accustomed seat, he was accosted from the other side by Mrs. Stevens, who, as usual, was very particular in her inquiries after the state of his wife's health; and on learning that she was so much improved as to be down-stairs, suggested that, perhaps, she would be willing to receive her.

"No doubt she will," rejoined Mr. Garie; and he immediately entered the house to announce the intended visit. The lamps were not lighted when Mrs. Stevens was introduced, and faces could not, therefore, be clearly distinguished.

"My dear," said Mr. Garie, "this is our neighbour, Mrs. Stevens."

"Will you excuse me for not rising?" said Mrs. Garie, extending her hand to her visitor. "I have been quite ill, or I should have been most happy to have received you before. My little folks are in your house a great deal—I hope you do not find them troublesome."

"Oh, by no means! I quite dote on your little Emily, she is such a sweet child—so very affectionate. It is a great comfort to have such a child near for my own to associate with—they have got quite intimate, as I hope we soon shall be."

Mrs. Garie thanked her for the kindness implied in the wish, and said she trusted they should be so.

"And how do you like your house?" asked Mrs. Stevens; "it is on the same plan as ours, and we find ours very convenient. They both formerly belonged to Walters; my husband purchased of him. Do you intend to buy?"

"It is very probable we shall, if we continue to like Philadelphia," answered Mr. Garie.

"I'm delighted to hear that," rejoined she—"very glad, indeed. It quite relieves my mind about one thing: ever since Mr. Stevens purchased our house we have been tormented with the suspicion that Walters would put a family of niggers in this; and if there is one thing in this world I detest more than another, it is coloured people, I think."

Mr. Garie here interrupted her by making some remark quite foreign to the subject, with the intention, no doubt, of drawing her off this topic. The attempt was, however, an utter failure, for she continued—"I think all those that are not slaves ought to be sent out of the country back to Africa, where they belong: they are, without exception, the most ignorant, idle, miserable set I ever saw."

"I think," said Mr. Garie, "I can show you at least one exception, and that too without much trouble. Sarah," he cried, "bring me a light."

"Oh," said Mrs. Stevens, "I suppose you refer to Walters—it is true he is an exception; but he is the only coloured person I ever saw that could make the least pretension to anything like refinement or respectability."

"Let me show you another," said Mr. Garie, as he took the lamp from the servant and placed it upon the table near his wife.

As the light fell on her face, their visitor saw that she belonged to the very class that she had been abusing in such unmeasured terms, and so petrified was she with confusion at the *faux pas* she had committed, that she was entirely unable to improvise the slightest apology.

Mrs. Garie, who had been reclining on the lounge, partially raised herself and gave Mrs. Stevens a withering look. "I presume, madam," said she, in a hurried and agitated tone, "that you are very ignorant of the people upon whom you have just been heaping such unmerited abuse, and therefore I shall not think so hardly of you as I should, did I deem your language dictated by pure hatred; but, be its origin what it may, it is quite evident that our further acquaintance could be productive of no pleasure to either of us—you will, therefore, permit me," continued she, rising with great dignity, "to wish you good evening;" and thus speaking, she left the room.

Mrs. Stevens was completely demolished by this unexpected *dénouement* of her long-meditated visit, and could only feebly remark to Mr. Garie that it was getting late, and she would go; and rising, she suffered herself to be politely bowed out of the house. In her intense anxiety to relate to her husband the scene which had just occurred, she could not take time to go round and through the gate, but leaped lightly over the low fence that divided the gardens, and rushed precipitately into the presence of her husband.

"Good heavens! George, what do you think?" she exclaimed; "I've had such a surprise!"

"I should think that you had, judging from appearances," replied he. "Why, your eyes are almost starting out of your head! What on earth has happened?" he asked, as he took the shade off the lamp to get a better view of his amiable partner.

"You would not guess in a year," she rejoined; "I never would have dreamed it—I never was so struck in my life!"

"Struck with what? Do talk sensibly, Jule, and say what all this is about," interrupted her husband, in an impatient manner. "Come, out with it—what has happened?"

"Why, would you have thought it," said she; "Mrs. Garie is a nigger woman—a real nigger—she would be known as such anywhere?"

It was now Mr. Stevens's turn to be surprised. "Why, Jule," he exclaimed, "you astonish me! Come, now, you're joking—you don't mean a real black nigger?"

"Oh, no, not jet black—but she's dark enough. She is as dark as that Sarah we employed as cook some time ago."

"You don't say so! Wonders will never cease—and he such a gentleman, too!" resumed her husband.

"Yes; and it's completely sickening," continued Mrs. Stevens, "to see them together; he calls her my dear, and is as tender and affectionate to her as if she was a Circassian[1]—and she nothing but a nigger—faugh! it's disgusting."

Little Clarence had been standing near, unnoticed by either of them during this conversation, and they were therefore greatly surprised when he exclaimed, with a burst of tears, "My mother is not a nigger any more than you are! How dare you call her such a bad name? I'll tell my father!"

Mr. Stevens gave a low whistle, and looking at his wife, pointed to the door. Mrs. Stevens laid her hand on the shoulder of Clarence, and led him to the door, saying, as she did so, "Don't come in here any more—I don't wish you to come into my house;" and then closing it, returned to her husband.

"You know, George," said she, "that I went in to pay her a short visit. I hadn't the remotest idea that she was a coloured woman, and I commenced giving my opinion respecting niggers very freely, when suddenly her husband called for a light, and I then saw to whom I had been talking. You may imagine my astonishment—I was completely dumb—and it would have done you good to have seen the air with which she left the room, after as good as telling me to leave the house."

"Well," said Mr. Stevens, "this is what may be safely termed an unexpected event. But, Jule," he continued, "you had better pack

---

1 Here, shorthand for both "white woman" and "Circassian beauty." Nineteenth-century racial science posited members of the Circassian tribes (from the Caucasus Mountains) as the purest examples of the white race, and literary convention held that Circassian women were surpassingly attractive.

these young folks off to bed, and then you can tell me the rest of it."

Clarence stood for some time on the steps of the house from which he had been so unkindly ejected, with his little heart swelling with indignation. He had often heard the term nigger used in its reproachful sense, but never before had it been applied to him or his, at least in his presence. It was the first blow the child received from the prejudice whose relentless hand was destined to crush him in after-years.

It was his custom, when any little grief pressed upon his childish heart, to go and pour out his troubles on the breast of his mother; but he instinctively shrunk from confiding this to her; for, child as he was, he knew it would make her very unhappy. He therefore gently stole into the house, crept quietly up to his room, lay down, and sobbed himself to sleep.

CHAPTER XIII.

Hopes consummated.

To Emily Winston we have always accorded the title of Mrs. Garie; whilst, in reality, she had no legal claim to it whatever. Previous to their emigration from Georgia, Mr. Garie had, on one or two occasions, attempted, but without success, to make her legally his wife.

He ascertained that, even if he could have found a clergyman willing to expose himself to persecution by marrying them, the ceremony itself would have no legal weight, as a marriage between a white and a mulatto was not recognized as valid by the laws of the state; and he had, therefore, been compelled to dismiss the matter from his mind, until an opportunity should offer for the accomplishment of their wishes.

Now, however, that they had removed to the north, where they would have no legal difficulties to encounter, he determined to put his former intention into execution. Although Emily had always maintained a studied silence on the subject, he knew that it was the darling wish of her heart to be legally united to him; so he unhesitatingly proceeded to arrange matters for the consummation of what he felt assured would promote the happiness of both. He therefore wrote to Dr. Blackly, a distinguished clergyman of the city, requesting him to perform the ceremony, and received from him an assurance that he would be present at the appointed time.

Matters having progressed thus far, he thought it time to inform Emily of what he had done. On the evening succeeding the receipt of an answer from the Rev. Dr. Blackly—after the children had been sent to bed—he called her to him, and, taking her hand, sat down beside her on the sofa.

"Emily," said he, as he drew her closer to him, "my dear, faithful Emily! I am about to do you an act of justice—one, too, that I feel will increase the happiness of us both. I am going to marry you, my darling! I am about to give you a lawful claim to what you have already won by your faithfulness and devotion. You know I tried, more than once, whilst in the south, to accomplish this, but, owing to the cruel and unjust laws existing there, I was unsuccessful. But now, love, no such difficulty exists; and here," continued he, "is an answer to the note I have written to Dr. Blackly, asking him to come next Wednesday night, and perform the ceremony.—You are willing, are you not, Emily?" he asked.

"Willing!" she exclaimed, in a voice tremulous with emotion— "willing! Oh, God! if you only knew how I have longed for it! It has been my earnest desire for years!" and, bursting into tears, she leaned, sobbing, on his shoulder.

After a few moments she raised her head, and, looking searchingly in his face, she asked: "But do you do this after full reflection on the consequences to ensue? Are you willing to sustain all the odium, to endure all the contumely, to which your acknowledged union with one of my unfortunate race will subject you? Clarence! it will be a severe trial—a greater one than any you have yet endured for me—and one for which I fear my love will prove but a poor recompense! I have thought more of these things lately; I am older now in years and experience. There was a time when I was vain enough to think that my affection was all that was necessary for your happiness; but men, I know, require more to fill their cup of content than the undivided affection of a woman, no matter how fervently beloved. You have talents, and, I have sometimes thought, ambition. Oh, Clarence! how it would grieve me, in after-years, to know that you regretted that for me you had sacrificed all those views and hopes that are cherished by the generality of your sex! Have you weighed it well?"

"Yes, Emily—well," replied Mr. Garie; "and you know the conclusion. My past should be a guarantee for the future. I had the world before me, and chose you—and with you I am contented to share my lot; and feel that I receive, in your affection, a full reward for any of the so-called sacrifices I may make. So, dry your tears, my dear," concluded he, "and let us hope for nothing but an increase of happiness as the result."

After a few moments of silence, he resumed: "It will be necessary, Emily, to have a couple of witnesses. Now, whom would you prefer? I would suggest Mrs. Ellis and her husband. They are old friends, and persons on whose prudence we can rely. It would not do to have the matter talked about, as it would expose us to disagreeable comments."

Mrs. Garie agreed perfectly with him as to the selection of Mr. and Mrs. Ellis; and immediately despatched a note to Mrs. Ellis, asking her to call at their house on the morrow.

When she came, Emily informed her, with some confusion of manner, of the intended marriage, and asked her attendance as witness, at the same time informing her of the high opinion her husband entertained of their prudence in any future discussion of the matter.

"I am really glad he is going to marry you, Emily," replied Mrs. Ellis, "and depend upon it we will do all in our power to aid it. Only yesterday, that inquisitive Mrs. Tiddy was at our house, and, in conversation respecting you, asked if I knew you to be married to Mr. Garie. I turned the conversation somehow, without giving her a direct answer. Mr. Garie, I must say, does act nobly towards you. He must love you, Emily, for not one white man in a thousand would make such a sacrifice for a coloured woman. You can't tell how we all like him—he is so amiable, so kind in his manner, and makes everyone so much at ease in his company. It's real good in him, I declare, and I shall begin to have some faith in white folks, after all.—Wednesday night," continued she; "very well—we shall be here, if the Lord spare us;" and, kissing Emily, she hurried off, to impart the joyful intelligence to her husband.

The anxiously looked for Wednesday evening at last arrived, and Emily arrayed herself in a plain white dress for the occasion. Her long black hair had been arranged in ringlets by Mrs. Ellis, who stood by, gazing admiringly at her.

"How sweet you look, Emily—you only want a wreath of orange blossoms to complete your appearance. Don't you feel a little nervous?" asked her friend.

"A little excited," she answered, and her hand shook as she put back one of the curls that had fallen across her face. Just then a loud ringing at the door announced the arrival of Dr. Blackly, who was shown into the front parlour.

Emily and Mrs. Ellis came down into the room where Mr. Garie was waiting for them, whilst Mr. Ellis brought in Dr. Blackly. The reverend gentleman gazed with some surprise at the party assembled. Mr. Garie was so thoroughly Saxon in appearance, that no one could doubt to what race he belonged, and it was equally evident that Emily, Mrs. Ellis, and her husband, were coloured persons.

Dr. Blackly looked from one to the other with evident embarrassment, and then said to Mr. Garie, in a low, hesitating tone:—

"I think there has been some mistake here—will you do me the favour to step into another room?"

Mr. Garie mechanically complied, and stood waiting to learn the cause of Dr. Blackly's strange conduct.

"You are a white man, I believe?" at last stammered forth the doctor.

"Yes, sir; I presume my appearance is a sufficient guarantee of that," answered Mr. Garie.

"Oh yes, I do not doubt it, and for that reason you must not be surprised if I decline to proceed with the ceremony."

"I do not see how my being a white man can act as a barrier to its performance," remarked Mr. Garie in reply.

"It would not, sir, if all the parties were of one complexion; but I do not believe in the propriety of amalgamation, and on no consideration could I be induced to assist in the union of a white man or woman with a person who has the slightest infusion of African blood in their veins. I believe the negro race," he continued, "to be marked out by the hand of God for servitude; and you must pardon me if I express my surprise that a gentleman of your evident intelligence should seek such a connection—you must be labouring under some horrible infatuation."

"Enough, sir," replied Mr. Garie, proudly; "I only regret that I did not know it was necessary to relate every circumstance of appearance, complexion, &c. I wished to obtain a marriage certificate, not a passport. I mistook you for a *Christian minister*, which mistake you will please to consider as my apology for having troubled you;" and thus speaking, he bowed Dr. Blackly out of the house. Mr. Garie stepped back to the door of the parlour and called out Mr. Ellis.

"We are placed in a very difficult dilemma," said he, as he was joined by the latter. "Would you believe it? that prejudiced old sinner has actually refused to marry us."

"It is no more than you might have expected of him—he's a thorough nigger-hater—keeps a pew behind the organ of his church for coloured people, and will not permit them to receive the sacrament until all the white members of his congregation are served. Why, I don't see what on earth induced you to send for him."

"I knew nothing of his sentiments respecting coloured people. I did not for a moment have an idea that he would hesitate to marry us. There is no law here that forbids it. What can we do?" said Mr. Garie, despairingly.

"I know a minister who will marry you with pleasure, if I can only catch him at home; he is so much engaged in visiting the sick and other pastoral duties."

"Do go—hunt him up, Ellis. It will be a great favour to me, if you can induce him to come. Poor Emily—what a disappointment this will be to her," said he, as he entered the room where she was sitting.

"What is the matter, dear?" she asked, as she observed Garie's anxious face. "I hope there is no new difficulty."

Mr. Garie briefly explained what had just occurred, and informed her, in addition, of Mr. Ellis having gone to see if he could get Father Banks, as the venerable old minister was called.

"It seems, dear," said she, despondingly, "as if Providence looked unfavourably on our design; for every time you have attempted it, we have been in some way thwarted;" and the tears chased one another down her face, which had grown pale in the excitement of the moment.

"Oh, don't grieve about it, dear; it is only a temporary disappointment. I can't think all the clergymen in the city are like Dr. Blackly. Some one amongst them will certainly oblige us. We won't despair; at least not until Ellis comes back."

They had not very long to wait; for soon after this conversation footsteps were heard in the garden, and Mr. Ellis entered, followed by the clergyman.

In a very short space of time they were united by Father Banks, who seemed much affected as he pronounced his blessing upon them.

"My children," he said, tremulously, "you are entering upon a path which, to the most favoured, is full of disappointment, care, and anxieties; but to you who have come together under such peculiar circumstances, in the face of so many difficulties, and in direct opposition to the prejudices of society, it will be fraught with more danger, and open to more annoyances, than if you were both of one race. But if men revile you, revile not again; bear it patiently for the sake of Him who has borne so much for you. God bless you, my children," said he, and after shaking hands with them all, he departed.

Mr. and Mrs. Ellis took their leave soon after, and then Mrs. Garie stole upstairs alone into the room where the children were sleeping. It seemed to her that night that they were more beautiful than ever, as they lay in their little beds quietly slumbering. She knelt beside them, and earnestly prayed their heavenly Father that the union which had just been consummated in the face of so many difficulties might prove a boon to them all.

"Where have you been, you runaway?" exclaimed her husband as she re-entered the parlour. "You stayed away so long, I began to have all sorts of frightful ideas—I thought of the 'mistletoe hung in the castle hall,'[1] and of old oak chests, and all kind of ter-

---

1 First line of Thomas Haynes Bayly's ballad "The Mistletoe Bough" (1833?), also published as "The Old Oak Chest." The ballad recounts the story of a young woman who hides in an obscure oaken trunk

rible things. I've been sitting here alone ever since the Ellises went: where have you been?"

"Oh, I've been upstairs looking at the children. Bless their young hearts! they looked so sweet and happy—and how they grow! Clarence is getting to be quite a little man; don't you think it time, dear, that he was sent to school? I have so much more to occupy my mind here than I had in Georgia, so many household duties to attend to, that I am unable to give that attention to his lessons which I feel is requisite. Besides, being so much at home, he has associated with that wretched boy of the Stevens's, and is growing rude and noisy; don't you think he had better be sent to school?"

"Oh yes, Emily, if you wish it," was Mr. Garie's reply. "I will search out a school to-morrow, or next day;" and taking out his watch, he continued, "it is near twelve o'clock—how the night has flown away—we must be off to bed. After the excitement of the evening, and your exertions of to-day, I fear that you will be indisposed to-morrow."

Clarence, although over nine years old, was so backward in learning, that they were obliged to send him to a small primary school which had recently been opened in the neighbourhood; and as it was one for children of both sexes, it was deemed advisable to send little Em with him.

"I do so dislike to have her go," said her mother, as her husband proposed that she should accompany Clarence; "she seems so small to be sent to school. I'm afraid she won't be happy."

"Oh! don't give yourself the least uneasiness about her not being happy there, for a more cheerful set of little folks I never beheld. You would be astonished to see how exceedingly young some of them are."

"What kind of a person is the teacher?" asked Mrs. Garie.

"Oh! she's a charming little creature; the very embodiment of cheerfulness and good humour. She has sparkling black eyes, a round rosy face, and can't be more than sixteen, if she is that old. Had I had such a teacher when a boy, I should have got on charmingly; but mine was a cross old widow, who wore spectacles and took an amazing quantity of snuff, and used to flog upon the slightest pretence. I went into her presence with fear and trem-

---

during a castle Christmas frolic, trips a "hidden spring," and becomes trapped. Her husband mounts a thorough search, but her "mouldering remains" are not found until many years later.

bling. I could never learn anything from her, and that must be my excuse for my present literary short-comings. But you need have no fear respecting Em getting on with Miss Jordan: I don't believe she could be unkind to any one, least of all to our little darling."

"Then you will take them down in the morning," suggested Mrs. Garie; "but on no account leave Emily unless she wishes to stay."

CHAPTER XIV.

Charlie at Warmouth.

AFTER the departure of Mrs. Bird to visit her sick friend, Betsey turned to Charlie and bid him follow her into the kitchen. "I suppose you haven't been to breakfast," said she, in a patronizing manner; "if you haven't, you are just in time, as we will be done ours in a little while, and then you can have yours."

Charlie silently followed her down into the kitchen, where a man-servant and the younger maid were already at breakfast; the latter arose, and was placing another plate upon the table, when Betsey frowned and nodded disapprovingly to her. "Let him wait," whispered she; "I'm not going to eat with niggers."

"Oh! he's such a nice little fellow," replied Eliza, in an under-tone; "let him eat with us."

Betsey here suggested to Charlie that he had better go up to the maple chamber, wash his face, and take his things out of his trunk, and that when his breakfast was ready she would call him.

"What on earth can induce you to want to eat with a nigger?" asked Betsey, as soon as Charlie was out of hearing. "I couldn't do it; my victuals would turn on my stomach. I never ate at the same table with a nigger in my life."

"Nor I neither," rejoined Eliza; "but I see no reason why I should not. The child appears to have good manners, he is neat and good-looking, and because God has curled his hair more than he has ours, and made his skin a little darker than yours or mine, that is no reason we should treat him as if he was not a human being,"

Alfred, the gardener, had set down his saucer and appeared very much astonished at this declaration of sentiment on the part of Eliza, and sneeringly remarked, "You're an Abolitionist, I suppose."

"No, I am not," replied she, reddening; "but I've been taught that God made all alike; one no better than the other. You know the Bible says God is no respecter of persons."

"Well, if it does," rejoined Alfred, with a stolid look, "it don't say that man isn't to be either, does it? When I see anything in my Bible that tells me I'm to eat and drink with niggers, I'll do it, and not before. I suppose you think that all the slaves ought to be free, and all the rest of the darned stuff these Abolitionists are preaching. Now if you want to eat with the nigger, you can;

nobody wants to hinder you. Perhaps he may marry you when he grows up—don't you think you had better set your cap at him?"[1]

Eliza made no reply to this low taunt, but ate her breakfast in silence.

"I don't see what Mrs. Bird brought him here for; she says he is sick,—had a broken arm or something; I can't imagine what use she intends to make of him," remarked Betsey.

"I don't think she intends him to be a servant here, at any rate," said Eliza; "or why should she have him put in the maple chamber, when there are empty rooms enough in the garret?"

"Well, I guess I know what she brought him for," interposed Alfred. "I asked her before she went away to get a little boy to help me do odd jobs, now that Reuben is about to leave; we shall want a boy to clean the boots, run on errands, drive up the cows, and do other little chores.[2] I'm glad he's a black boy; I can order him round more, you know, than if he was white, and he won't get his back up half as often either. You may depend upon it, that's what Mrs. Bird has brought him here for." The gardener, having convinced himself that his view of the matter was the correct one, went into the garden for his day's labour, and two or three things that he had intended doing he left unfinished, with the benevolent intention of setting Charlie at them the next morning.

Charlie, after bathing his face and arranging his hair, looked from the window at the wide expanse of country spread out before him, all bright and glowing in the warm summer sunlight. Broad well-cultivated fields stretched away from the foot of the garden to the river beyond, and the noise of the waterfall, which was but a short distance off, was distinctly heard, and the sparkling spray was clearly visible through the openings of the trees. "What a beautiful place,—what grand fields to run in; an orchard, too, full of blossoming fruit-trees! Well, this is nice," exclaimed Charlie, as his eye ran over the prospect; but in the midst of his rapture came rushing back upon him the remembrance of the cavalier treatment he had met with below-stairs, and he said with a sigh, as the tears sprang to his eyes, "But it is not home, after all." Just at this moment he heard his name called by Betsey, and he hastily descended into the kitchen. At one end of the partially-cleared table a clean plate and knife and fork had

---

1 I.e., take a romantic interest in him.
2 [Webb's note:] A Yankeeism, meaning little jobs about a farm.

been placed, and he was speedily helped to the remains of what the servants had been eating.

"You mustn't be long," said Betsey, "for to-day is ironing day, and we want the table as soon as possible."

The food was plentiful and good, but Charlie could not eat; his heart was full and heavy,—the child felt his degradation. "Even the servants refuse to eat with me because I am coloured," thought he. "Oh! I wish I was at home!"

"Why don't you eat?" asked Betsey.

"I don't think I want any breakfast; I'm not hungry," was the reply.

"I hope you are not sulky," she rejoined; "we don't like sulky boys here; why don't you eat?" she repeated.

The sharp, cold tones of her voice struck a chill into the child's heart, and his lip quivered as he stammered something farther about not being hungry; and he hurried away into the garden, where he calmed his feelings and allayed his home-sickness by a hearty burst of tears. After this was over, he wandered through the garden and fields until dinner; then, by reading his book and by another walk, he managed to get through the day.

The following morning, as he was coming down stairs, he was met by Alfred, who accosted him with, "Oh! you're up, are you; I was just going to call you." And looking at Charlie from head to foot, he inquired, "Is that your best suit?"

"No, it's my worst," replied Charlie. "I have two suits better than this;" and thinking that Mrs. Bird had arrived, he continued, "I'll put on my best if Mrs. Bird wants me."

"No, she ain't home," was the reply; "it's me that wants you; come down here; I've got a little job for you. Take this," said he, handing him a dirty tow apron, "and tie it around your neck; it will keep the blacking off your clothes, you know. Now," continued he, "I want you to clean these boots; these two pairs are Mr. Tyndall's—them you need not be particular with; but this pair is mine, and I want 'em polished up high,—now mind, I tell you. I'm going to wear a new pair of pants to meetin' to-morrow, and I expect to cut a dash, so you'll do 'em up slick, now won't you?"

"I'll do my best," said Charlie, who, although he did not dislike work, could not relish the idea of cleaning the servants' boots. "I'm afraid I shall find this a queer place," thought he. "I shall not like living here, I know—wait for my meals until the servants have finished, and clean their boots into the bargain. This is worse than being with Mrs. Thomas."

Charlie, however, went at it with a will, and was busily engaged in putting the finishing touches on Alfred's boots, when he heard his name called, and on looking up, saw Mrs. Bird upon the piazza above.

"Why, bless me! child, what are you about?—whose boots are those, and why are you cleaning them?"

"Oh!" he replied, his face brightening up at the sight of Mrs. Bird, "I'm so glad you've come; those are Mr. Tyndall's boots, and these," he continued, holding up the boots on which he was engaged, "are the gardener's."

"And who, pray, instructed you to clean them?"

"The gardener," replied Charlie.

"He did, did he?" said Mrs. Bird, indignantly. "Very well; now do you take off that apron and come to me immediately; before you do, however, tell Alfred I want him."

Charlie quickly divested himself of the tow apron, and after having informed the gardener that Mrs. Bird desired his presence in the parlour, he ran up there himself. Alfred came lumbering up stairs, after giving his boots an unusual scraping and cleansing preparatory to entering upon that part of the premises which to him was generally forbidden ground.

"By whose direction did you set the child at that dirty work?" asked Mrs. Bird, after he had entered the room.

"I hadn't anybody's direction to set him to work, but I thought you brought him here to do odd jobs. You know, ma'am, I ask-ed you some time ago to get a boy, and I thought this was the one."

"And if he had been, you would have taken a great liberty in assigning him any duties without first consulting me. But he is not a servant here, nor do I intend him to be such; and let me inform you, that instead of his cleaning *your* boots, it will be your duty henceforth to clean *his*. Now," continued she, "you know his position here, let me see that you remember yours. You can go."

This was said in so peremptory a manner, as to leave no room for discussion or rejoinder, and Alfred, with a chagrined look, went muttering down stairs.

"Things have come to a pretty pass," grumbled he. "I'm to wait on niggers, black their boots, and drive them out, too, I suppose. I'd leave at once if it wasn't such a good situation. Drat the old picture—what has come over her I wonder—she'll be asking old Aunt Charity, the black washerwoman, to dine with her next. She has either gone crazy or turned Abolitionist, I don't know which; something has happened to her, that's certain."

"Now, Charlie," said Mrs. Bird, as the door closed upon the crest-fallen gardener, "go to your room and dress yourself nicely. After I've eaten my breakfast, I am going to visit a friend, and I want you to accompany me; don't be long."

"Can't I eat mine first, Mrs. Bird?" he asked, in reply.

"I thought you had had yours, long ago," rejoined she.

"The others hadn't finished theirs when you called me, and I don't get mine until they have done," said Charlie.

"Until they have done; how happens that?" asked Mrs. Bird.

"I think they don't like to eat with me, because I'm coloured," was Charlie's hesitating reply.

"That is too much," exclaimed Mrs. Bird; "if it were not so very ridiculous, I should be angry. It remains for me, then," continued she, "to set them an example. I've not eaten my breakfast yet—come, sit down with me, and we'll have it together."

Charlie followed Mrs. Bird into the breakfast-room, and took the seat pointed out by her. Eliza, when she entered with the tea-urn, opened her eyes wide with astonishment at the singular spectacle she beheld. Her mistress sitting down to breakfast *vis-à-vis* to a little coloured boy! Depositing the urn upon the table, she hastened back to the kitchen to report upon the startling events that were occurring in the breakfast-room.

"Well, I never," said she; "that beats anything I ever did see; why, Mrs. Bird must have turned Abolitionist. Charlie is actually sitting at the same table with her, eating his breakfast as natural and unconcerned as if he was as white as snow! Wonders never will cease. You see I'm right though. I said that child wasn't brought here for a servant—we've done it for ourselves now—only think how mad she'll be when she finds he was made to wait for his meals until we have done. I'm glad I wasn't the one who refused to eat with him."

"I guess she has been giving Alfred a blowing up," said Betsy, "for setting him at boot cleaning; for he looked like a thunder-cloud when he came down stairs, and was muttering something about a consarned pet-nigger—he looked anything but pleased."

Whilst the lower powers were discussing what they were pleased to regard as an evidence of some mental derangement on the part of Mrs. Bird, that lady was questioning Charlie respecting his studies, and inquired if he would like to go to school in Warmouth.

"After a while, I think I should," he replied; "but for a week I'd like to be free to run about the fields and go fishing, and do lots of things. This is such a pretty place; and now that you have come I shall have nice times—I know I shall."

"You seem to have great confidence in my ability to make you happy. How do you know that I am as kind as you seem to suppose?" asked Mrs. Bird, with a smile.

"I know you are," answered Charlie, confidently; "you speak so pleasantly to me. And do you know, Mrs. Bird," continued he, "that I liked you from the first day, when you praised me so kindly when I recited my lessons before you. Did you ever have any little boys of your own?"

A change immediately came over the countenance of Mrs. Bird, as she replied: "Oh, yes, Charlie; a sweet, good boy about your own age:" and the tears stood in her eyes as she continued. "He accompanied his father to England years ago—the ship in which they sailed was never heard of—his name was Charlie too."

"I didn't know that, or I should not have asked," said Charlie, with some embarrassment of manner caused by the pain he saw he had inflicted. "I am very sorry," he continued.

Mrs. Bird motioned him to finish his breakfast, and left the table without drinking the tea she had poured out for herself.

There were but one or two families of coloured people living in the small town of Warmouth, and they of a very humble description; their faces were familiar to all the inhabitants, and their appearance was in accordance with their humble condition. Therefore, when Charlie made his *début*, in company with Mrs. Bird, his dress and manners differed so greatly from what they were accustomed to associate with persons of his complexion, that he created quite a sensation in the streets of the usually quiet and obscure little town.

He was attired with great neatness; and not having an opportunity of playing marbles in his new suit, it still maintained its spotless appearance. The fine grey broadcloth coat and pants fitted him to a nicety, the jaunty cap was set slightly on one side of his head giving him a somewhat saucy look, and the fresh colour now returning to his cheeks imparted to his face a much healthier appearance than it had worn for months.

He and his kind friend walked on together for some time, chatting about the various things that attracted their attention on the way, until they reached a cottage in the garden of which a gentleman was busily engaged in training a rosebush upon a new trellis.

So completely was he occupied with his pursuit that he did not observe the entrance of visitors, and quite started when he was gently tapped upon the shoulder by Mrs. Bird.

"How busy we are," said she, gaily, at the same time extending her hand—"so deeply engaged, that we can scarcely notice old friends that we have not seen for months."

"Indeed, this is a pleasant surprise," he remarked, when he saw by whom he had been interrupted. "When did you arrive?"

"Only this morning; and, as usual, I have already found something with which to bore you—you know, Mr. Whately, I always have something to trouble you about."

"Don't say trouble, my dear Mrs. Bird; if you will say 'give me something to occupy my time usefully and agreeably,' you will come much nearer the mark. But who is this you have with you?"

"Oh, a little *protégé* of mine, poor little fellow—he met with a sad accident recently—he broke his arm; and I have brought him down here to recruit. Charlie, walk around and look at the garden—I have a little matter of business to discuss with Mr. Whately, and when we shall have finished I will call you."

Mr. Whately led the way into his library, and placing a seat for Mrs. Bird, awaited her communication.

"You have great influence with the teacher of the academy, I believe," said she.

"A little," replied Mr. Whately, smiling.

"Not a little," rejoined Mrs. Bird, "but a great deal; and, my dear Mr. Whately, I want you to exercise it in my behalf. I wish to enter as a scholar that little boy I brought with me this morning."

"Impossible!" said Mr. Whately. "My good friend, the boy is coloured!"

"I am well aware of that," continued Mrs. Bird; "if he were not, there would not be the least trouble about his admission; nor am I sure there will be as it is, if you espouse his cause. One who has been such a benefactor to the academy as yourself, could, I suppose, accomplish anything."

"Yes; but that is stretching my influence unduly. I would be willing to oblige you in almost anything else, but I hesitate to attempt this. Why not send him to the public school?—they have a separate bench for black children; he can be taught there all that is necessary for *him* to know."

"He is far in advance of any of the scholars there. I attended the examination of the school to which he was attached," said Mrs. Bird, "and I was very much surprised at the acquirements of the pupils; this lad was distinguished above all the rest—he answered questions that would have puzzled older heads, with the greatest facility. I am exceedingly anxious to get him admitted to the academy, as I am confident he will do honour to the interest I take in him."

"And a very warm interest it must be, my dear Mrs. Bird, to induce you to attempt placing him in such an expensive and exclusive school. I am very much afraid you will have to give it up: many of the scholars' parents, I am sure, will object strenuously to the admission of a coloured boy as a scholar."

"Only tell me that you will propose him, and I will risk the refusal," replied Mrs. Bird—"it can be tried at all events; and if you will make the effort I shall be under deep obligations to you."

"Well, Mrs. Bird, let us grant him admitted—what benefit can accrue to the lad from an education beyond his station? He cannot enter into any of the learned professions: both whilst he is there, and after his education is finished, he will be like a fish out of water. You must pardon me if I say I think, in this case, your benevolence misdirected. The boy's parents are poor, I presume?"

"They certainly are not rich," rejoined Mrs. Bird; "and it is for that reason I wish to do all that I can for him. If I can keep him with me, and give him a good education, it may be greatly for his advantage; there may be a great change in public sentiment before he is a man—we cannot say what opening there may be for him in the future."

"Not unless it changes very much. I never knew prejudice more rampant than it is at this hour. To get the boy admitted as a right is totally out of the question: if he is received at all, it will be as a special favour, and a favour which—I am sure it will require all my influence to obtain. I will set about it immediately, and, rely upon it, I will do my best for your *protégé*."

Satisfied with the promise, which was as much as Mrs. Bird had dared to hope for, she called Charlie, then shook hands with Mr. Whately and departed.

CHAPTER XV.

Mrs. Stevens gains a Triumph.

THE Garies had now become thoroughly settled in Philadelphia, and, amongst the people of colour, had obtained a very extensive and agreeable acquaintance. At the South Mr. Garie had never borne the reputation of an active person. Having an ample fortune and a thoroughly Southern distaste for labour, he found it by no means inconvenient or unpleasant to have so much time at his disposal. His newspaper in the morning, a good book, a stroll upon the fashionable promenade, and a ride at dusk, enabled him to dispose of his time without being oppressed with *ennui*.

It was far happier for him that such was his disposition, as his domestic relations would have been the means of subjecting him to many unpleasant circumstances, from which his comparative retirement in a great measure screened him.

Once or twice since his settlement in the North his feelings had been ruffled, by the sneering remarks of some of his former friends upon the singularity of his domestic position; but his irritation had all fled before the smiles of content and happiness that beamed from the faces of his wife and children.

Mrs. Garie had nothing left to wish for; she was surrounded by every physical comfort and in the enjoyment of frequent intercourse with intelligent and refined people, and had been greatly attracted toward Esther Ellis with whom she had become very intimate.

One morning in November, these two were in the elegant little bed-room of Mrs. Garie, where a fire had been kindled, as the weather was growing very chilly and disagreeable.

"It begins to look quite like autumn," said Mrs. Garie, rising and looking out of the window. "The chrysanthemums are drooping and withered, and the dry leaves are whirling and skimming through the air. I wonder," she continued, "if the children were well wrapped up this morning?"

"Oh, yes; I met them at the corner, on their way to school, looking as warm and rosy as possible. What beautiful children they are! Little Em has completely won my heart; it really seems a pity for her to be put on the shelf, as she must be soon."

"How—what do you mean?" asked Mrs. Garie.

"Oh, this will explain," archly rejoined Esther, as she held up to view one of the tiny lace-trimmed frocks that she was making in anticipation of the event that has been previously hinted.

Mrs. Garie laughed, and turned to look out of the window again.

"Do you know, I found little Lizzy Stevens, your neighbour's daughter, shivering upon the steps in a neighbouring street, fairly blue with cold? She was waiting there for Clarence and Em. I endeavoured to persuade her to go on without them, but she would not. From what I could understand, she waits for them there every day."

"Her mother cannot be aware of it, then; for she has forbidden her children to associate with mine," rejoined Mrs. Garie. "I wonder she permits her little girl to go to the same school. I don't think she knows it, or it is very likely she would take her away."

"Has she ever spoken to you since the night of her visit?" asked Esther.

"Never! I have seen her a great many times since; she never speaks, nor do I. There she goes now. That," continued Mrs. Garie, with a smile, "is another illustration of the truthfulness of the old adage, 'Talk of'—well, I won't say who,—'and he is sure to appear.'"[1] And, thus speaking, she turned from the window, and was soon deeply occupied in the important work of preparing for the expected little stranger.

Mrs. Garie was mistaken in her supposition that Mrs. Stevens was unaware that Clarence and little Em attended the same school to which her own little girl had been sent; for the evening before the conversation we have just narrated she had been discussing the matter with her husband.

"Here," said she to him, "is Miss Jordan's bill for the last quarter. I shall never pay her another; I am going to remove Lizzy from that school."

"Remove her! what for? I thought I heard you say, Jule, that the child got on excellently well there,—that she improved very fast?"

"So she does, as far as learning is concerned; but she is sitting right next to one of those Garie children, and that is an arrangement I don't at all fancy. I don't relish the idea of my child attending the same school that niggers do; so I've come to the determination to take her away."

"I should do no such thing," coolly remarked Mr. Stevens. "I should compel the teacher to dismiss the Garies, or I should break up her school. Those children have no right to be there whatever. I don't care a straw how light their complexions are,

---

1 The full proverb is "Speak of the Devil and he shall appear," here euphemistically shortened.

they are niggers nevertheless, and ought to go to a nigger school; they are no better than any other coloured children. I'll tell you what you can do, Jule," continued he: "call on Mrs. Kinney, the Roths, and one or two others, and induce them to say that if Miss Jordan won't dismiss the Garies that they will withdraw their children; and you know if they do, it will break up the school entirely. If it was any other person's children but his, I would wink at it; but I want to give him a fall for his confounded haughtiness. Just try that plan, Jule, and you will be sure to succeed."

"I am not so certain about it, Stevens. Miss Jordan, I learn, is very fond of their little Em. I must say I cannot wonder at it. She is the most loveable little creature I ever saw. I will say that, if her mother is a nigger."

"Yes, Jule, all that may be; but I know the world well enough to judge that, when she becomes fully assured that it will conflict with her interests to keep them, she will give them up. She is too poor to be philanthropic, and, I believe, has sufficient good sense to know it."

"Well, I'll try your plan," said Mrs. Stevens; "I will put matters in train to-morrow morning."

Early the next morning, Mrs. Stevens might have been seen directing her steps to the house of Mrs. Kinney, with whom she was very intimate. She reached it just as that lady was departing to preside at a meeting of a female missionary society for evangelizing the Patagonians.[1]

"I suppose you have come to accompany me to the meeting," said she to Mrs. Stevens, as soon as they had exchanged the usual courtesies.

"Oh, dear, no; I wish I was," she replied. "I've got a troublesome little matter on my hands; and last night my husband suggested my coming to ask your advice respecting it. George has such a high opinion of your judgment, that he would insist on my troubling you."

Mrs. Kinney smiled, and looked gratified at this tribute to her importance.

"And moreover," continued Mrs. Stevens, "it's a matter in which your interest, as well as our own, is concerned."

---

1   The trope of the reformer more interested in the condition of people in distant lands—here, the highlands of Chile and Argentina—than in that of people closer to home was a common one in nineteenth-century novels. Cf. the "telescopic philanthropy" of Mrs. Jellyby in Dickens's *Bleak House* (1852–53).

Mrs. Kinney now began to look quite interested, and, untying the strings of her bonnet, exclaimed, "Dear me, what can it be?" "Knowing," said Mrs. Stevens, "that you entertain just the same sentiments that we do relative to associating with coloured people, I thought I would call and ask if you were aware that Miss Jordan receives coloured as well as white children in her school." "Why, no! My dear Mrs. Stevens, you astound me. I hadn't the remotest idea of such a thing. It is very strange my children never mentioned it."

"Oh, children are so taken up with their play, they forget such things," rejoined Mrs. Stevens. "Now," continued she, "husband said he was quite confident you would not permit your children to continue their attendance after this knowledge came to your ears. We both thought it would be a pity to break up the poor girl's school by withdrawing our children without first ascertaining if she would expel the little darkies. I knew, if I could persuade you to let me use your name as well as ours, and say that you will not permit your children to continue at her school unless she consents to our wishes, she, knowing the influence you possess, would, I am sure, accede to our demands immediately."

"Oh, you are perfectly at liberty to use my name, Mrs. Stevens, and say all that you think necessary to effect your object. But do excuse me for hurrying off," she continued, looking at her watch: "I was to have been at the meeting at ten o'clock, and it is now half-past. I hope you won't fail to call, and let me know how you succeed;" and, with her heart overflowing with tender care for the poor Patagonian, Mrs. Kinney hastily departed.

"That's settled," soliloquized Mrs. Stevens, with an air of intense satisfaction, as she descended the steps—"her four children would make a serious gap in the little school; and now, then," continued she, "for the Roths."

Mrs. Stevens found not the slightest difficulty in persuading Mrs. Roth to allow her name to be used, in connection with Mrs. Kinney's, in the threat to withdraw their children if the little Garies were not immediately expelled. Mrs. Roth swore by Mrs. Kinney, and the mere mention of that lady's name was sufficient to enlist her aid.

Thus armed, Mrs. Stevens lost no time in paying a visit to Miss Jordan's school. As she entered, the busy hum of childish voices was somewhat stilled; and Lizzy Stevens touched little Em, who sat next her, and whispered, "There is my mother."

Mrs. Stevens was welcomed very cordially by Miss Jordan, who offered her the seat of honour beside her.

"Your school seems quite flourishing," she remarked, after looking around the room, "and I really regret being obliged to make a gap in your interesting circle."

"I hope you don't intend to deprive me of your little girl," inquired Miss Jordan; "I should regret to part with her—not only because I am very fond of her, but in consideration of her own interest—she is coming on so rapidly."

"Oh, I haven't the slightest fault to find with her progress. *That*," said she, "is not the reason. I have another, of much more weight. Of course, every one is at liberty to do as they choose; and we have no right to dictate to you what description of scholars you should receive; but, if they are not such as we think proper companions for our children, you can't complain if we withdraw them."

"I really do not understand you, Mrs. Stevens," said the teacher, with an astonished look: "I have none here but the children of the most respectable persons—they are all as well behaved as school children generally are."

"I did not allude to behaviour; that, for all that I know to the contrary, is irreproachable; it is not character that is in question, but colour. I don't like my daughter to associate with coloured children."

"Coloured children!" repeated the now thoroughly bewildered teacher—"coloured children! My dear madam," continued she, smiling, "some one has been hoaxing you—I have no coloured pupils—I could not be induced to receive one on any account."

"I am very glad to hear you say so," rejoined Mrs. Stevens, "for that convinces me that my fears were groundless. I was under the impression you had imbibed some of those pestilent abolition sentiments coming into vogue. I see you are not aware of it, but you certainly have two coloured scholars; and there," said she, pointing to Clarence, "is one of them."

Clarence, who, with his head bent over his book, was sitting so near as to overhear a part of this conversation, now looked up, and found the cold, malignant, grey eyes of Mrs. Stevens fastened on him. He looked at her for a moment—then apparently resumed his studies.

The poor boy had, when she entered the room, an instinctive knowledge that her visit boded no good to them. He was beginning to learn the anomalous situation he was to fill in society. He had detested Mrs. Stevens ever since the night she had ejected him so rudely from her house, and since then had learned to some extent what was meant by the term *nigger woman*.

"You must certainly be misinformed," responded Miss Jordan. "I know their father—he has frequently been here. He is a Southerner, a thorough gentleman in his manners; and, if ever a man was white, I am sure he is."

"Have you seen their mother?" asked Mrs. Stevens, significantly.

"No, I never have," replied Miss Jordan; "she is in poor health; but she must unquestionably be a white woman—a glance at the children ought to convince you of that."

"It might, if I had not seen her, and did not know her to be a coloured woman. You see, my dear Miss Jordan," continued she, in her blandest tone, "I am their next-door neighbour and have seen their mother twenty times and more; she is a coloured woman beyond all doubt."

"I never could have dreamed of such a thing!" exclaimed Miss Jordan, as an anxious look overspread her face; then, after a pause, she continued: "I do not see what I am to do—it is really too unfortunate—I don't know how to act. It seems unjust and unchristian to eject two such children from my school, because their mother has the misfortune to have a few drops of African blood in her veins. I cannot make up my mind to do it. Why, you yourself must admit that they are as white as any children in the room."

"I am willing to acknowledge they are; but they have nigger blood in them, notwithstanding; and they are, therefore, as much niggers as the blackest, and have no more right to associate with white children than if they were black as ink. I have no more liking for white niggers than for black ones."

The teacher was perplexed, and, turning to Mrs. Stevens, said, imploringly: "This matter seems only known to you; let me appeal to your generosity—say nothing more about it. I will try to keep your daughter away from them, if you wish—but pray do not urge me to the performance of an act that I am conscious would be unjust."

Mrs. Stevens's face assumed a severe and disagreeable expression. "I hoped you would look at this matter in a reasonable light, and not compel those who would be your friends to appear in the light of enemies. If this matter was known to me alone, I should remove my daughter and say nothing more about it; but, unfortunately for you, I find that, by some means or other, both Mrs. Kinney and Mrs. Roth have become informed of the circumstance, and are determined to take their children away. I thought I would act a friend's part by you, and try to prevail on you to dismiss these two coloured children at once. I so far relied upon your right judgment as to assure them that you would not hesitate for a moment to comply with their wishes; and I candidly tell you, that it was only by my so doing that they were prevented from keeping their children at home to-day."

Miss Jordan looked aghast at this startling intelligence; if Mrs. Roth and Mrs. Kinney withdrew their patronage and influence, her little school (the sole support of her mother and herself) would be well-nigh broken up.

She buried her face in her hands, and sat in silence for a few seconds; then looking at Mrs. Stevens, with tearful eyes, exclaimed, "God forgive me if it must be so; nothing but the utter ruin that stares me in the face if I refuse induces me to accede to your request."

"I am sorry that you distress yourself so much about it. You know you are your own mistress, and can do as you choose," said Mrs. Stevens; "but if you will be advised by me, you will send them away at once."

"After school I will," hesitatingly replied Miss Jordan.

"I hate to appear so pressing," resumed Mrs. Stevens; "but I feel it my duty to suggest that you had better do it at once, and before the rest of the scholars. I did not wish to inform you to what extent this thing had gone; but it really has been talked of in many quarters, and it is generally supposed that you are cognisant of the fact that the Garies are coloured; therefore you see the necessity of doing something at once to vindicate yourself from the reproach of abolitionism."

At the pronunciation of this then terrible word in such connection with herself, Miss Jordan turned quite pale, and for a moment struggled to acquire sufficient control of her feelings to enable her to do as Mrs. Stevens suggested; at last, bursting into tears, she said, "Oh, I cannot—will not—do it. I'll dismiss them, but not in that unfeeling manner; that I cannot do."

The children were now entirely neglecting their lessons, and seemed much affected by Miss Jordan's tears, of which they could not understand the cause. She observing this, rang the bell, the usual signal for intermission.

Mrs. Stevens, satisfied with the triumph she had effected, took leave of Miss Jordan, after commending her for the sensible conclusion at which she had arrived, and promising to procure her two more pupils in the room of those she was about to dismiss.

Miss Jordan was a long time writing the note that she intended sending to Mr. Garie; and one of the elder girls returned to the school-room, wondering at the unusually long time that had been given for recreation.

"Tell Clarence and his sister to come here," said she to the girl who had just entered; and whilst they were on their way upstairs, she folded the note, and was directing it when Clarence entered.

"Clarence," said she, in a soft voice, "put on your hat; I have a note of some importance for you to take to your father—*your father* remember—don't give it to any one else." Taking out her watch, she continued, "It is now so late that you would scarcely get back before the time for dismissal, so you had better take little Emily home with you."

"I hope, ma'am, I haven't done anything wrong?" asked Clarence.

"Oh, no!" quickly replied she; "you're a dear, good boy, and have never given me a moment's pain since you came to the school." And she hurried out into the hall to avoid farther questioning.

She could not restrain the tears as she dressed little Em, whose eyes were large with astonishment at being sent home from school at so early an hour.

"Teacher, is school out?" asked she.

"No, dear, not quite; I wanted to send a note to your pa, and so I have let Clarry go home sooner than usual," replied Miss Jordan, kissing her repeatedly, whilst the tears were trickling down her cheek.

"Don't cry, teacher, I love you," said the little blue-eyed angel, whose lip began to quiver in sympathy; "don't cry, I'll come back again to-morrow."

This was too much for the poor teacher, who clasped the child in her arms, and gave way to a burst of uncontrollable sorrow. At last, conquering herself with an effort, she led the children down stairs, kissed them both again, and then opening the door she turned them forth into the street—turned away from her school these two little children, such as God received into his arms and blessed, because they were the children of a "*nigger woman.*"

CHAPTER XVI.

Mr. Stevens makes a Discovery.

"WELL, Jule, old Aunt Tabitha is gone at last, and I am not at all sorry for it, I assure you; she's been a complete tax upon me for the last eight years. I suppose you won't lament much, nor yet go into mourning for her," continued Mr. Stevens, looking at her jocularly.

"I'm not sorry, that I admit," rejoined Mrs. Stevens; "the poor old soul is better off, no doubt; but then there's no necessity to speak of the matter in such an off-hand manner."

"Now, Jule, I beg you won't attempt to put on the sanctified; that's too much from you, who have been wishing her dead almost every day for the last eight years. Why, don't you remember you wished her gone when she had a little money to leave; and when she lost that, you wished her off our hands because she had none. Don't pretend to be in the least depressed; that won't do with me."

"Well, never mind that," said Mrs. Stevens, a little confused; "what has become of her things—her clothing, and furniture?"

"I've ordered the furniture to be sold; and all there is of it will not realize sufficient to pay her funeral expenses. Brixton wrote me that she has left a bundle of letters directed to me, and I desired him to send them on."

"I wonder what they can be," said Mrs. Stevens.

"Some trash, I suppose; an early love correspondence, of but little value to any one but herself. I do not expect that they will prove of any consequence whatever."

"Don't you think one or the other of us should go to the funeral?" asked Mrs. Stevens.

"Nonsense. No! I have no money to expend in that way—it is as much as I can do to provide comfortably for the living, without spending money to follow the dead," replied he; "and besides, I have a case coming on in the Criminal Court next week that will absorb all my attention."

"What kind of a case is it?" she inquired.

"A murder case. Some Irishmen were engaged in a row, when one of the party received knock on his head that proved too much for him, and died in consequence. My client was one of the contending parties; and has been suspected, from some imprudent expressions of his, to have been the man who struck the fatal blow. His preliminary examination comes off to-morrow or next day, and I must be present as a matter of course."

At an early hour of the morning succeeding this conversation, Mr. Stevens might have been seen in his dingy office, seated at a rickety desk which was covered with various little bundles, carefully tied with red tape. The room was gloomy and cheerless, and had a mouldy disagreeable atmosphere. A fire burned in the coal stove, which, however, seemed only to warm, but did not dry the apartment; and the windows were covered with a thin coating of vapour.

Mr. Stevens was busily engaged in writing, when hearing footsteps behind him, he turned and saw Mr. Egan, a friend of his client, entering the room.

"Good morning, Mr. Egan," said he, extending his hand; "how is our friend McCloskey this morning?"

"Oh, it's far down in the mouth he is, be jabers[1]—the life a'most scared out of him!"

"Tell him to keep up a good heart and not to be frightened at trifles," laughingly remarked Mr. Stevens.

"Can't your honour come and see him?" asked Egan.

"I can't do that; but I'll give you a note to Constable Berry, and he will bring McCloskey in here as he takes him to court;" and Mr. Stevens immediately wrote the note, which Egan received and departed.

After the lapse of a few hours, McCloskey was brought by the accommodating constable to the office of Mr. Stevens.

"He'll be safe with you, I suppose, Stevens," said the constable, "but then there is no harm in seeing for one's self that all's secure;" and thus speaking, he raised the window and looked into the yard below. The height was too great for his prisoner to escape in that direction; then satisfying himself that the other door only opened into a closet, he retired, locking Mr. Stevens and his client in the room.

Mr. Stevens arose as soon as the door closed behind the constable, and stuffed a piece of damp sponge into the keyhole; he then returned and took a seat by his client.

"Now, McCloskey," said he, in a low tone, as he drew his chair closely in front of the prisoner, and fixed his keen grey eyes on him—"I've seen Whitticar. And I tell you what it is—you're in a very tight place. He's prepared to swear that he saw you with a

---

1 Irish dialect oath: "by Jesus."

slung shot[1] in your hand—that he saw you drop it after the man fell; he picked it up, and whilst the man was lying dead at his tavern, awaiting the coroner's inquest, he examined the wound, and saw in the skull two little dents or holes, which were undoubtedly made by the little prongs that are on the leaden ball of the weapon, as they correspond in depth and distance apart; and, moreover, the ball is attached to a twisted brace which proves to be the fellow to the one found upon a pair of your trousers. What can you say to all this?"

McCloskey here gave a smothered groan, and his usually red face grew deadly pale in contemplation of his danger.

"Now," said Mr. Stevens, after waiting long enough for his revelation to have its due effect upon him, "there is but one thing to be done. We must buy Whitticar off. Have you got any money? I don't mean fifty or a hundred dollars—that would be of no more use than as many pennies. We must have something of a lump— three or four hundred at the very least."

The prisoner drew his breath very hard at this, and remained silent.

"Come, speak out," continued Mr. Stevens, "circumstances won't admit of our delaying—this man's friends will raise Heaven and earth to secure your conviction; so you see, my good fellow, it's your money or your life. You can decide between the two— you know which is of the most importance to you."

"God save us, squire! how am I to raise that much money? I haven't more nor a hunther dollars in the world."

"You've got a house, and a good horse and dray," replied Mr. Stevens, who was well posted in the man's pecuniary resources. "If you expect me to get you out of this scrape, you must sell or mortgage your house, and dispose of your horse and dray. Somehow or other four hundred dollars must be raised, or you will be dangling at a rope's end in less than six months."

"I suppose it will have to go then," said McCloskey, reluctantly.

"Then give me authority," continued Mr. Stevens, "to arrange for the disposal of the property, and I will have your affairs all set straight in less than no time."

---

1 McCloskey's weapon is more like a sap or blackjack than a projectile sling-shot; it is swung, rather than fired. Such improvised weapons were common in nineteenth-century street violence: the "twisted brace" that attaches to the leaden weight is one of McCloskey's suspenders.

The constable here cut short any further colloquy by rapping impatiently on the door, then opening it, and exclaiming, "Come, now it is ten o'clock—time that you were in court;" and the two started out, followed by Mr. Stevens.

After having, by some of those mysterious plans with which lawyers are familiar, been enabled to put off the examination for a few days, Mr. Stevens returned to his office, and found lying upon his table the packet of letters he was expecting from New York.

Upon breaking the seal, and tearing off the outer covering, he discovered a number of letters, time-worn and yellow with age; they were tied tightly together with a piece of cord; cutting this, they fell scattered over the desk.

Taking one of them up, he examined it attentively, turning it from side to side to endeavour to decipher the half-effaced post-mark. "What a ninny I am, to waste time in looking at the cover of this, when the contents will, no doubt, explain the whole matter?" Thus soliloquising he opened the letter, and was soon deeply absorbed in its contents. He perused and re-perused it; then opened, one after another, the remainder that lay scattered before him. Their contents seemed to agitate him exceedingly; as he walked up and down the room with hasty strides, muttering angrily to himself, and occasionally returning to the desk to re-peruse the letters which had so strangely excited him.

Whilst thus engaged, the door was opened by no less a personage than Mr. Morton, who walked in and seated himself in a familiar manner.

"Oh, how are you, Morton. You entered with such a ghostly tread, that I scarcely heard you," said Mr. Stevens, with a start; "what has procured me the honour of a visit from you this morning?"

"I was strolling by, and thought I would just step in and inquire how that matter respecting the Tenth-street property has succeeded."

"Not at all—the old fellow is as obstinate as a mule; he won't sell except on his own terms, which are entirely out of all reason. I am afraid you will be compelled to abandon your building speculation in that quarter until his demise—he is old and feeble, and can't last many years; in the event of his death you may be able to effect some more favourable arrangement with his heirs."

"And perhaps have ten or fifteen years to wait—no, that won't do. I'd better sell out myself. What would *you* advise me to do, Stevens?"

Mr. Stevens was silent for a few moments; then having opened the door and looked into the entry, he closed it carefully, placed the piece of sponge in the key-hole, and returned to his seat at the desk, saying:—

"We've transacted enough business together to know one another pretty well. So I've no hesitation in confiding to you a little scheme I've conceived for getting into our hands a large proportion of property in one of the lower districts, at a very low figure; and 'tis probable, that the same plan, if it answers, will assist you materially in carrying out your designs. It will require the aid of two or three moneyed men like yourself; and, if successful, will without doubt be highly remunerative."

"*If* successful," rejoined Mr. Morton; "yes, there is the rub. How are you to guarantee success?"

"Hear my plan, and then you can decide. In the first place, you know as well as I that a very strong feeling exists in the community against the Abolitionists, and very properly too; this feeling requires to be guided into some proper current, and I think we can give it that necessary guidance, and at the same time render it subservient to our own purposes. You are probably aware that a large amount of property in the lower part of the city is owned by niggers; and if we can create a mob and direct it against them, they will be glad to leave that quarter, and remove further up into the city for security and protection. Once get the mob thoroughly aroused, and have the leaders under our control, and we may direct its energies against any parties we desire; and we can render the district so unsafe, that property will be greatly lessened in value—the houses will rent poorly and many proprietors will be happy to sell at very reduced prices. If you can furnish me the means to start with, I have men enough at my command to effect the rest. We will so control the elections in the district, through these men, as to place in office only such persons as will wink at the disturbances. When, through their agency, we have brought property down sufficiently low, we will purchase all that we can, re-establish order and quiet, and sell again at an immense advantage."

"Your scheme is a good one, I must confess, and I am ready to join you at any time. I will communicate with Carson, who, I think, will be interested, as he desired to invest with me in those Tenth-street improvements. I will call in to-morrow, and endeavour to persuade him to accompany me, and then we can discuss the matter more fully."

"Well, do; but one word before you go. You appear to know everybody—who is anybody—south of Mason and Dixon's line;

can you give me any information respecting a family by the name of Garie, who live or formerly did live in the vicinity of Savannah?"

"Oh, yes—I know them, root and branch; although there is but little of the latter left; they are one of the oldest families in Georgia—those of whom I have heard the most are of the last two generations. There now remains of the family but two persons—old John or Jack Garie as he is called, a bachelor—and who I have recently learned is at the point of death; and a crack-brained nephew of his, living in this city—said to be married to a nigger woman—actually married to her. Dr. Blackly informed me last week, that he sent for him to perform the ceremony, which he very properly refused to do. I have no doubt, however, that he has been successful in procuring the services of some one else. I am sorry to say, there are some clergymen in our city who would willingly assist in such a disgraceful proceeding. What ever could have induced a man with his prospects to throw himself away in that manner, I am at loss to determine—he has an independent fortune of about one hundred thousand dollars, besides expectations from his uncle, who is worth a considerable sum of money. I suppose these little darkies of his will inherit it," concluded Mr. Morton.

"Are there no other heirs?" asked Mr. Stevens, in a tone of deep interest.

"There may be. He had an aunt, who married an exceedingly low fellow from the North, who treated her shamefully. The mercenary scoundrel no doubt expected to have acquired a fortune with her, as it was generally understood that she was sole heiress of her mother's property—but it turned out to be an entire mistake. The circumstance made considerable stir at the time. I remember having heard my elders discuss it some years after its occurrence. But why do you take such an interest in it? You charged me with coming upon you like a ghost. I could return the compliment. Why, man, you look like a sheet. What ails you?"

"Me!—I—oh, nothing—nothing! I'm perfectly well—that is to say, I was up rather late last night, and am rather fatigued to-day—nothing more."

"You looked so strange, that I could not help being frightened—and you seemed so interested. You must have some personal motive for inquiring."

"No more than a lawyer often has in the business of his clients. I have been commissioned to obtain some information respecting these people—a mere matter of business, nothing more, believe me. Call in again soon, and endeavour to bring Carson; but pray be discreet—be very careful to whom you mention the matter."

"Never fear," said Mr. Morton, as he closed the door behind him, and sauntered lazily out of the house.

Mr. Morton speculated in stocks and town-lots in the same spirit that he had formerly betted at the race-course and cockpit[1] in his dear Palmetto State.[2] It was a pleasant sort of excitement to him, and without excitement of some kind, he would have found it impossible to exist. To have frequented gaming hells[3] and race-courses in the North would have greatly impaired his social position; and as he set a high value upon that, he was compelled to forego his favourite pursuits, and associate himself with a set of men who conducted a system of gambling operations upon 'Change,[4] of a less questionable but equally exciting character.

Mr. Stevens sat musing at his desk for some time after the departure of his visitor; then, taking up one of the letters that had so strongly excited him, he read and re-read it; then crushing it in his hand, arose, stamped his feet, and exclaimed, "I'll have it! if I—" here he stopped short and, looking round, caught a view of his face in the glass; he sank back into the chair behind him, horrified at the lividness of his countenance.

"Good God!" he soliloquized, "I look like a murderer already," and he covered his face with his hands, and turned away from the glass. "But I am wrong to be excited thus; men who accomplish great things approach them coolly, so must I. I must plot, watch, and wait;" and thus speaking, he put on his hat and left the office.

As Mr. Stevens approached his house, a handsome carriage drove up to the door of his neighbour, and Mr. Garie and his wife, who had been enjoying a drive along the bank of the river, alighted and entered their residence. The rustle of her rich silk dress grated harshly on his ear, and the soft perfume that wafted toward him as she glided by, was the very reverse of pleasant to him.

Mr. Garie bowed stiffly to him as they stood on the steps of their respective residences, which were only divided by the low iron fence; but, beyond the slight inclination of the head, took no further notice of him.

---

1 Cock-fighting ring.
2 South Carolina.
3 I.e., gaming hall. See *OED* "hell" 8.
4 I.e., in the context of a stock exchange.

"The cursed haughty brute," muttered Mr. Stevens, as he jerked the bell with violence; "how I hate him! I hated him before I knew—but now I—;" as he spoke, the door was opened by a little servant that Mrs. Stevens had recently obtained from a charity institution.

"You've kept me standing a pretty time," exclaimed he savagely, as he seized her ear and gave it a spiteful twist; "can't you manage to open the door quicker?"

"I was up in the garret, and didn't hear the bell," she replied, timidly.

"Then I'll improve your hearing," he continued malignantly, as he pulled her by the ear; "take that, now, and see if you'll keep me standing at the door an hour again."

Striding forward into the back parlour, he found his wife holding a small rattan[1] elevated over little Lizzy in a threatening attitude.

"Will you never mind me? I've told you again and again not to go, and still you persist in disobeying me. I'll cut you to pieces if you don't mind. Will you ever go again?" she almost screamed in the ears of the terrified child.

"Oh, no, mother, never; please don't whip me, I'll mind you;" and as she spoke, she shrank as far as possible into the corner of the room.

"What's all this—what's the matter, Jule? What on earth are you going to whip Liz for?"

"Because she deserves it," was the sharp reply; "she don't mind a word I say. I've forbid her again and again to go next door to visit those little niggers, and she will do it in spite of me. She slipped off this afternoon, and has been in their house over an hour; and it was only this morning I detected her kissing their Clarence through the fence."

"Faugh," said Mr. Stevens, with a look of disgust; "you kissed a nigger! I'm ashamed of you, you nasty little thing; your mother ought to have taken a scrubbing-brush and cleaned your mouth, never do such a thing again; come here to me."

As he spoke, he extended his hand and grasped the delicately-rounded arm of his little girl.

"What induces you to go amongst those people; hasn't your mother again and again forbidden you to do so. Why do you go,

---

1 A cane made from the wood of the rattan palm; it was commonly used to administer corporal punishment.

I say?" he continued, shaking her roughly by the arm, and frowning savagely. "Why don't you answer?—speak!"

The child, with the tears streaming down her lovely face, was only able to answer in her defence. "Oh, pa, I do love them so."

"You do, do you?" replied her exasperated father, stamping his foot, and pushing her from him; "go to bed, and if ever I hear of you going there again, you shall be well whipped." The tearful face lingered about the door in hope of a reprieve that did not come, and then disappeared for the night.

"The children must not be suffered to go in there, Jule; something I've learned to-day will—" here Mr. Stevens checked himself; and in answer to his wife's impatient "What have you learned?" replied, "Oh, nothing of consequence—nothing that will interest you," and sat with his slipper in his hand, engaged in deep thought.

Now for Mr. Stevens to commence a communication to his wife, and then break off in the middle of it, was as novel as disagreeable, as he was generally very communicative, and would detail to her in the evening, with pleasing minuteness, all the rogueries he had accomplished during the day; and his unwillingness to confide something that evidently occupied his mind caused his spouse to be greatly irritated.

Mr. Stevens drank his tea in silence, and during the evening continued absorbed in reflection; and, notwithstanding the various ill-natured remarks of his wife upon his strange conduct, retired without giving her the slightest clue to its cause.

CHAPTER XVII.

Plotting.

MR. STEVENS awoke at a very early hour the ensuing morning, and quite unceremoniously shook his wife to arouse her also. This he accomplished after considerable labour; for Mrs. Stevens was much more sleepy than usual, in consequence of her husband's restlessness the previous night.

"I declare," said she, rubbing her eyes, "I don't get any peace of my life. You lie awake, kicking about, half the night, muttering and whispering about no one knows what, and then want me to rise before day. What are you in such a hurry for this morning,— no more mysteries, I hope?"

"Oh, come, Jule, get up!" said her husband, impatiently. "I must be off to my business very early; I am overburthened with different things this morning."

Mrs. Stevens made a very hasty toilette, and descended to the kitchen, where the little charity-girl was bustling about with her eyes only half open. With her assistance, the breakfast was soon prepared, and Mr. Stevens called downstairs. He ate rapidly and silently, and at the conclusion of his meal, put on his hat, and wished his amiable spouse an abrupt good morning.

After leaving his house, he did not take the usual course to his office, but turned his steps toward the lower part of the city. Hastening onward, he soon left the improved parts of it in his rear, and entered upon a shabby district.

The morning was very chilly, and as it was yet quite early, but few people were stirring: they were labourers hurrying to their work, milkmen, and trundlers of breadcarts.

At length he stopped at the door of a tavern, over which was a large sign, bearing the name of Whitticar. On entering, he found two or three forlorn-looking wretches clustering round the stove, endeavouring to receive some warmth upon their half-clothed bodies,—their red and pimpled noses being the only parts about them that did not look cold. They stared wonderingly at Mr. Stevens as he entered; for a person so respectable as himself in appearance was but seldom seen in that house.

The boy who attended the bar inquired from behind the counter what he would take.

"Mr. Whitticar, if you please," blandly replied Mr. Stevens.

Hearing this, the boy bolted from the shop, and quite alarmed the family, by stating that there was a man in the shop, who said he wanted to *take* Mr. Whitticar, and he suspected that he was a policeman.

Whitticar, who was seldom entirely free from some scrape, went through another door to take a survey of the new comer, and on ascertaining who it was, entered the room.

"You've quite upset the family; we all took you for a constable," said he, approaching Mr. Stevens, who shook hands with him heartily, and then, laying his arm familiarly on his shoulder, rejoined,—

"I say, Whitticar, I want about five minutes' conversation with you. Haven't you some room where we can be quite private for a little while?"

"Yes; come this way," replied he. And, leading his visitor through the bar, they entered a small back room, the door of which they locked behind them.

"Now, Whitticar," said Mr. Stevens, "I want you to act the part of a friend by the fellow who got in that awkward scrape at this house. As you did not give the evidence you informed me you were possessed of, at the coroner's inquest, it is unnecessary for you to do so before the magistrate at examination. There is no use in hanging the fellow—it cannot result in any benefit to yourself; it will only attract disagreeable notice to your establishment, and possibly may occasion a loss of your licence. We will be willing to make it worth your while to absent yourself, for a short time at least, until the trial is over; it will put money in your purse, and save this poor devil's life besides. What do you say to receiving a hundred and fifty, and going off for a month or two?"

"Couldn't think of it, Mr. Stevens, no how. See how my business would suffer; everything would be at loose ends. I should be obliged to hire a man to take my place; and, in that case, I must calculate upon his stealing at least twenty-five per cent. of the receipts: and then there is his wages. No, no that won't do. Besides, I'm trying to obtain the nomination for the office of alderman—to secure it, I must be on the spot; nothing like looking out for oneself. I am afraid I can't accommodate you, squire, unless you can offer something better than one hundred and fifty."

"You've got no conscience," rejoined Mr. Stevens, "not a bit."

"Well, the less of that the better for me; it's a thing of very little use in the rum-selling business; it interferes with trade—so I can't afford to keep a conscience. If you really want me to go, make me a better offer; say two fifty, and I'll begin to think of it. The trial will be over in a month or six weeks, I suppose, and a spree of that length would be very pleasant."

"No, I won't do that, Whitticar,—that's flat; but I'll tell you what I will do. I'll make it two hundred, and what is more, I'll see to your nomination. I'm all right down here, you know; I own the boys in this district; and if you'll say you'll put some little matters through for me after you are elected, I'll call it a bargain."

"Then I'm your man," said Whitticar, extending his hand.

"Well, then," added Stevens, "come to my office this morning, and you shall have the money; after that I shall expect you to get out of town as quick as possible. Goodbye."

"So far all right," muttered Mr. Stevens, with an air of intense satisfaction, as he left the house; "he'll be of great use to me. When it becomes necessary to blind the public by a sham investigation, he will be the man to conduct it; when I want a man released from prison, or a little job of that kind done, he will do it—this act will put him in my power; and I am much mistaken if he won't prove of the utmost service in our riot scheme. Now, then, we will have an examination of McCloskey as soon as they like."

A few weeks subsequent to the events we have just written, we find Mr. Stevens seated in his dingy office in company with the McCloskey, who had recently been discharged from custody in default of sufficient evidence being found to warrant his committal for trial. He was sitting with his feet upon the stove, and was smoking a cigar in the most free-and-easy manner imaginable.

"So far, so good," said Mr. Stevens, as he laid down the letter he was perusing; "that simplifies the matter greatly; and whatever is to be done towards his removal, must be done quickly—now that the old man is dead there is but one to deal with."

During the interval that had elapsed between the interview of Mr. Stevens with Whitticar and the period to which we now refer, Mr. Stevens had been actively engaged in promoting his riot scheme; and already several disturbances had occurred, in which a number of inoffensive coloured people had been injured in their persons and property.

But this was only a faint indication of what was to follow; and as he had, through the agency of Mr. Morton and others, been able to prevent any but the most garbled statements of these affairs from getting abroad, there was but little danger of their operations being interfered with. Leading articles daily appeared in the public journals (particularly those that circulated amongst the lowest classes), in which the negroes were denounced, in the strongest terms. It was averred that their insolence, since the commencement of the abolition agitation, had become unbear-

able; and from many quarters was suggested the absolute necessity for inflicting some general chastisement, to convince them
that they were still negroes, and to teach them to remain in their
proper place in the body politic.

Many of these articles were written by Mr. Stevens, and their
insertion as editorials procured through the instrumentality of
Mr. Morton and his friends.

Mr. Stevens turned to his visitor, and inquired, "What was
done last night—much of anything?"

"A great deal, yer honour," replied McCloskey; "a nagur or
two half killed, and one house set on fire and nearly burned up."

"*Is that all?*" said Mr. Stevens, with a well-assumed look of disappointment. "Is that all? Why, you are a miserable set: you
should have beaten every darky out of the district by this time."

"They're not so aisily bate out—they fight like sevin divils. One
o' 'em, night before last, split Mikey Dolan's head clane open, and
it's a small chance of his life he's got to comfort himself wid."

"Chances of war—chances of war!" rejoined Mr. Stevens,—
"mere trifles when you get used to 'em: you mustn't let that stop
you—you have a great deal yet to do. What you have already
accomplished is a very small matter compared with what is
expected, and what I intend you to do: your work has only just
begun, man."

"Jist begun!" replied the astonished McCloskey; "haven't we
bin raising the very divil every night for the last week—running a
near chance of being kilt all the time—and all for nothing! It's
gettin' tiresome; one don't like to be fighting the nagurs all the
time for the mere fun of the thing—it don't pay, for divil a cent
have I got for all my trouble; and ye said ye would pay well, ye
remimber."

"So I shall," said Mr. Stevens, "when you do something worth
paying for—the quarter is not accomplished yet. I want the place
made so hot down there that the niggers can't stay. Go ahead,
don't give them any rest—I'll protect you from the consequences,
whatever they be: I've great things in store for you," continued
he, moving nearer and speaking in a confidential tone; "how
should you like to return to Ireland a moneyed man?"

"I should like it well enough, to be sure; but where's the
money to come from, squire?"

"Oh, there's money enough to be had if you have the courage
to earn it."

"I'm willin' enough to earn an honest penny, but I don't like
risking me neck for it, squire. It's clear ye'll not be after givin'

me a dale of money widout being sure of havin' the worth of it out o' me; and it's dirty work enough I've done, widout the doin' of any more: me conscience is a sore throuble to me about the other job. Be the powers I'm out o' that, and divil a like scrape will I get in agin wid my own consint."

"Your conscience has become troublesome very suddenly," rejoined Mr. Stevens, with a look of angry scorn; "it's strange it don't appear to have troubled you in the least during the last few weeks, whilst you have been knocking niggers on the head so freely."

"Well, I'm tired o' that work," interrupted McCloskey; "and what's more, I'll soon be lavin' of it off."

"We'll see about that," said Mr. Stevens. "You're a pretty fellow, now, ain't you—grateful, too—very! Here I've been successful in getting you out of a hanging scrape, and require a trifling service in return, and you retire. You'll find this trifling won't do with me," continued Mr. Stevens, with great sternness of manner. "You shall do as I wish: you are in my power! I need your services, and I will have them—make up your mind to that."

McCloskey was somewhat staggered at this bold declaration from Mr. Stevens; but he soon assumed his former assured manner, and replied, "I'd like to know how I'm in your power: as far as this riot business is concerned, you're as deep in the mud as I'm in the mire; as for the other, be St. Patrick, I'm clane out o' that!—they don't try a man twice for the same thing."

"Don't halloo so loud, my fine fellow," sneeringly rejoined Mr. Stevens, "you are not entirely out of the wood yet; you are by no means as safe as you imagine—you haven't been *tried* yet, you have only been examined before a magistrate! They lacked sufficient evidence to commit you for trial—that evidence I can produce at any time; so remember, if you please, you have not been tried yet: when you have been, and acquitted, be kind enough to let me know, will you?"

Mr. Stevens stood for a few moments silently regarding the change his language had brought over the now crest-fallen McCloskey;—he then continued—"Don't think you can escape me—I'll have a thousand eyes upon you; no one ever escapes me that I wish to retain. Do as I require, and I'll promote your interest in every possible way, and protect you; but waver, or hold back, and I'll hang you as unhesitatingly as if you were a dog."

This threat was given in a tone that left no doubt on the mind of the hearer but that Mr. Stevens would carry out his expressed intention; and the reflections thereby engendered by no means added to the comfort or sense of security that McCloskey had flattered himself he was in future to enjoy; he, therefore, began to discover the bad policy of offending one who might prove so formidable an enemy—of incensing one who had it in his power to retaliate by such terrible measures.

He therefore turned to Mr. Stevens, with a somewhat humbled manner, and said: "You needn't get so mad, squire—sure it's but natural that a man shouldn't want to get any deeper in the mire than he can help; and I've enough on my hands now to make them too red to look at wid comfort—sure it's not a shade deeper you'd have 'em?" he asked, looking inquiringly at Mr. Stevens, who was compelled to turn away his face for a moment to hide his agitation.

At last he mastered his countenance, and, in as cool a tone as he could assume, replied: "Oh, a little more on them will be scarcely a perceptible addition. You know the old adage, 'In for a penny, in for a pound.' You need have no fear," said he, lowering his voice almost to a whisper; "it can be done in a crowd—and at night—no one will notice it."

"I don't know about that, squire—in a crowd some one will be sure to notice it. It's too dangerous—I can't do it."

"Tut, tut, man; don't talk like a fool. I tell you there is no danger. You, in company with a mob of others, are to attack this man's house. When he makes his appearance, as he will be sure to do, shoot him down."

"Good God! squire," said McCloskey, his face growing pale at the prospect of what was required of him, "you talk of murder as if it was mere play!"

"And still, *I never murdered any one*," rejoined Mr. Stevens, significantly; "come, come—put your scruples in your pocket, and make up your mind to go through with it like a man. When the thing is done, you shall have five thousand dollars in hard cash, and you can go with it where you please. Now, what do you think of that?"

"Ah, squire, the money's a great timptation! but it's an awful job."

"No worse than you did for nothing," replied Mr. Stevens.

"But that was in a fair fight, and in hot blood; it isn't like planning to kill a man, squire."

"Do you call it a fair fight when you steal up behind a man, and break his skull with a slung shot?" asked Mr. Stevens.

McCloskey was unable to answer this, and sat moodily regarding his tempter.

"Come, make up your mind to it—you might as well," resumed Mr. Stevens, in a coaxing tone.

"Ye seem bent on not giving it up, and I suppose I'll have to do it," replied McCloskey, reluctantly; "but what has the man done to ye's, squire, that you're so down upon him?"

"Oh, he is one of those infernal Abolitionists, and one of the very worst kind; he lives with a nigger woman—and, what is more, he is married to her!"

"Married to a nigger!" exclaimed McCloskey—"it's a quare taste the animal has—but you're not afther killing him for that; there's something more behind: it's not for having a black wife instead of a white one you'd be afther murthering him—ye'll get no stuff like that down me."

"No, it is not for that alone, I acknowledge," rejoined Mr. Stevens, with considerable embarrassment. "He insulted me some time ago, and I want to be revenged upon him."

"It's a dear job to insult you, at that rate, squire; but where does he live?"

"In my neighbourhood—in fact, next door to me," replied Mr. Stevens with an averted face.

"Howly Mother! not away up there—sure it's crazy ye are. What, away up there in the city limits!—why, they would have the police and the sogers[1] at our heels in less than no time. Sure, you're out o' your sinses, to have me go up there with a mob. No, no—there's too much risk—I can't try that."

"I tell you there shall be no risk," impatiently replied Mr. Stevens. "It's not to be done to-night, nor to-morrow night; and, when I say do it, you *shall* do it, and as safely there as anywhere. Only come to the conclusion that a thing *must* be done, and it is half finished already. You have only to make up your mind that you will accomplish a design in spite of obstacles, and what you once thought to be insurmountable difficulties will prove mere straws in your path. But we are wasting time; I've determined you shall do it, and I hope you now know me well enough to be convinced that it is your best policy to be as obliging as possible. You had better go now, and be prepared to meet me to-night at Whitticar's."

After the door closed upon the retreating form of McCloskey, the careless expression that Mr. Stevens's countenance had worn during the conversation, gave place to one full of anxiety and apprehension, and he shuddered as he contemplated the fearful length to which he was proceeding.

---

1 I.e., soldiers.

"If I fail," said he—"pshaw! I'll *not* fail—I must not fail—for failure is worse than ruin; but cool—cool," he continued, sitting down to his desk—"those who work nervously do nothing right." He sat writing uninterruptedly until quite late in the afternoon, when the fading sunlight compelled him to relinquish his pen, and prepare for home.

Thrusting the papers into his pocket, he hurried toward the newspaper office from which were to emanate, as editorials, the carefully-concocted appeals to the passions of the rabble which he had been all the afternoon so busily engaged in preparing.

CHAPTER XVIII.

Mr. Stevens falls into bad Hands.

THE amiable partner of Mr. Stevens sat in high dudgeon, at being so long restrained from her favourite beverage by the unusually deferred absence of her husband. At length she was rejoiced by hearing his well-known step as he came through the garden, and the rattle of his latch-key as he opened the door was quite musical in her ears.

"I thought you was never coming," said she, querulously, as he entered the room; "I have been waiting tea until I am almost starved."

"You needn't have waited a moment, for you will be obliged to eat alone after all; I'm going out. Pour me out a cup of tea—I'll drink it whilst I'm dressing; and," continued Mr. Stevens, "I want you to get me that old brown over-coat and those striped trowsers I used to wear occasionally."

"Why, you told me," rejoined Mrs. Stevens, "that you did not require them again, and so I exchanged them for this pair of vases to-day."

"The devil you did!" said Mr. Stevens, angrily; "you let them lie about the house for nearly a year—and now, just as they were likely to be of some service to me, you've sold them. It's just like you—always doing something at the wrong time."

"How on earth, Stevens, was I to know you wanted them?"

"Well, there, Jule, they're gone; don't let's have any more talk about it. Get me another cup of tea; I must go out immediately."

After hastily swallowing the second cup, Mr. Stevens left his home, and walked to an omnibus-station, from whence he was quickly transported to a street in the lower part of the city, in which were a number of second-hand clothing stores. These places were supported principally by the country people who attended the market in the same street, and who fancied that the clothing they purchased at these shops must be cheap, because it was at second-hand.

Mr. Stevens stopped at the door of one of these establishments, and paused to take a slight survey of the premises before entering. The doorway was hung with coats of every fashion of the last twenty years, and all in various stages of decay. Some of them looked quite respectable, from much cleaning and patching; and others presented a reckless and forlorn aspect, as their worn and ragged sleeves swung about in the evening air. Old hats, some of which were, in all probability, worn at a period anterior to the Revolution, kept company with the well-blacked shoes that were ranged on shelves beside the doorway, where they served in the capacity of signs, and fairly indicated the style of goods to be purchased within.

Seeing that there were no buyers in the store, Mr. Stevens opened the door, and entered. The sounds of his footsteps drew from behind the counter no less a personage than our redoubtable friend Kinch, who, in the absence of his father, was presiding over the establishment.

"Well, Snowball," said Mr. Stevens, "do you keep this curiosity-shop?"

"My name is not Snowball, and this ain't a curiosity-shop," replied Kinch. "Do you want to buy anything?"

"I believe I do," answered Mr. Stevens. "Let me look at some coats—one that I can get on—I won't say fit me, I'm indifferent about that—let me see some of the worst you've got."

Kinch looked surprised at this request from a gentleman of Mr. Stevens's appearance, and handed out, quite mechanically, a coat that was but slightly worn.

"Oh, that won't do—I want something like this," said Mr. Stevens, taking down from a peg a very dilapidated coat, of drab colour, and peculiar cut. "What do you ask for this?"

"That's not fit for a gentleman like you, sir," said Kinch.

"I'm the best judge of that matter," rejoined Mr. Stevens. "What is the price of it?"

"Oh, that coat you can have for a dollar," replied Kinch.

"Then take it. Now hand out some trowsers."

The trowsers were brought; and from a large number Mr. Stevens selected a pair that suited him. Then adding an old hat to his list of purchases, he declared his fit-out complete.

"Can't you accommodate me with some place where I can put these on?" he asked of Kinch; "I'm going to have a little sport with some friends of mine, and I want to wear them."

Kinch led the way into a back room, where he assisted Mr. Stevens to array himself in his newly-purchased garments. By the change in his attire he seemed completely robbed of all appearance of respectability; the most disagreeable points of his *physique* seemed to be brought more prominently forward by the habiliments he had assumed, they being quite in harmony with his villainous countenance.

Kinch, who looked at him with wonder, was forced to remark, "Why, you don't look a bit like a gentleman now, sir."

Mr. Stevens stepped forward, and surveyed himself in the looking-glass. The transformation was complete—surprising even to himself. "I never knew before," said he, mentally, "how far a suit of clothes goes towards giving one the appearance of a gentleman."

He now emptied the pockets of the suit he had on;—in so doing, he dropped upon the floor, without observing it, one of the papers.

"Fold these up," said he, handing to Kinch the suit he had just taken off, "and to-morrow bring them to this address." As he spoke, he laid his card upon the counter, and, after paying for his new purchases, walked out of the shop, and bent his steps in the direction of Whitticar's tavern.

On arriving there, he found the bar-room crowded with half-drunken men, the majority of whom were Irishmen, armed with bludgeons of all sizes and shapes. His appearance amongst them excited but little attention, and he remained there some time before he was recognized by the master of the establishment.

"By the howly St. Patherick I didn't know you, squire; what have you been doing to yourself?"

"Hist!" cried Mr. Stevens, putting his fingers to his lips; "I thought it was best to see how matters were progressing, so I've run down for a little while. How are you getting on?"

"Fine, fine, squire," replied Whitticar; "the boys are ripe for anything. They talk of burning down a nigger church."

"Not to-night—they must not do such a thing to-night—we are not ready for that yet. I've made out a little list—some of the places on it they might have a dash at to-night, just to keep their hands in." As Mr. Stevens spoke, he fumbled in his pocket for the list in question, and was quite surprised to be unable to discover it.

"Can't you find it, squire?" asked Whitticar.

"I must have lost it on the way," replied Mr. Stevens. "I am sure I put it in this pocket," and he made another search. "No use—I'll have to give it up," said he, at length; "but where is McCloskey? I haven't seen him since I came in."

"He came here this afternoon, very far gone; he had been crooking his elbow pretty frequently, and was so very drunk that I advised him to go home and go to bed; so he took another dram and went away, and I haven't seen him since."

"That's bad, very bad—everything goes wrong this evening—I wanted him to-night particularly."

"Wouldn't the boys go out with you?" suggested Whitticar.

"No, no; that wouldn't do at all. I mustn't appear in these things. If I'm hauled up for participation, who is to be your lawyer—eh?"

"True for you," rejoined Whitticar; "and I'll just disperse the crowd as soon as I can, and there will be one peaceable night in the district at any rate."

Not liking to give directions to the mob personally, and his useful coadjutor McCloskey not being at hand, Mr. Stevens came to the conclusion he would return to his home, and on the next evening a descent should be made upon the places marked on the list.

Taking out his watch, he found it would be too late to return to the store where he had purchased his present adornments, so he determined to start for home.

The coat that temporarily adorned the person of Mr. Stevens was of peculiar cut and colour—it was, in fact, rather in the rowdy style, and had, in its pristine state, bedecked the person of a member of a notorious fire company.[1] These gentry had for a long time been the terror of the district in which they roamed, and had rendered themselves highly obnoxious to some of the rival factions on the borders of their own territory; they had the unpleasant habit of pitching into and maltreating, without the slightest provocation, any one whom their practised eyes discovered to be a rival; and by such outrages they had excited in the bosoms of their victims a desire for revenge that only awaited the occasion to manifest itself.

Mr. Stevens, in happy unconsciousness, that, owing to his habiliments, he represented one of the well-known and hated faction, walked on quite leisurely; but, unfortunately for him, his way home lay directly through the camp of their bitterest and most active enemies.

---

1 Before the advent of municipally funded firehouses, working-class volunteers organized themselves into neighborhood groups for the nominal purpose of fighting fires. In practice, such organizations tended to be as interested in promoting particular ethnic or economic agendas—sometimes with violent results—as they were in protecting against property damage or loss of life; they operated more as gangs than as providers of a civic service. Philadelphia's fire companies had an especially bad reputation among polite society: the actions of rival companies were blamed for a number of street riots, including the Pennsylvania Hall Riot of 1838.

Standing in front of a tavern-window, through which a bright light shone, were a group of young men, who bestowed upon Mr. Stevens more than passing attention.

"I'm blest," exclaimed one of them, "if there ain't a ranger! now that *is* a saucy piece of business, ain't it! That fellow has come up here to be able to go back and play brag-game."

"Let's wallop him, then," suggested another, "and teach him better than to come parading himself in our parts. I owe 'em something for the way they served me when I was down in their district."

"Well, come on," said the first speaker, "or he will get away whilst we are jawing about what we shall do."

Advancing to Mr. Stevens, he tapped that gentleman on the shoulder, and said, with mock civility, and in as bland a tone as he could assume, "It's really very obliging of you, mister, to come up here to be flogged—saves us the trouble of coming down to you. We would like to settle with you for that drubbing you gave one of our boys last week."

"You must be mistaken," replied Mr. Stevens: "I don't know anything of the affair to which you allude."

"You don't, eh! Well, take that, then, to freshen your memory," exclaimed one of the party, at the same time dealing him a heavy blow on the cheek, which made the lamp-lights around appear to dance about in the most fantastic style.

The first impulse of Mr. Stevens was to cry out for the watch-man; but a moment's reflection suggested the impolicy of that project, as he would inevitably be arrested with the rest; and to be brought before a magistrate in his present guise, would have entailed upon him very embarrassing explanations; he therefore thought it best to beg off—to throw himself, as it were, upon their sympathies.

"Stop, gentlemen—stop—for God's sake, stop," he cried, as soon as he could regain the breath that had been almost knocked out of him by the tremendous blow he had just received—"don't kill an innocent man; upon my honour I never saw you before, nor ever assaulted any of you in my life. My dear friends," he continued, in a dolorous tone, "please let me go—you are quite mistaken: I assure you I am not the man."

"No, we ain't mistaken, either: you're one of the rangers; I know you by your coat," replied one of the assaulters,

It now flashed upon Mr. Stevens that he had brought himself into these difficulties, by the assumption of the dress he then wore; he therefore quickly rejoined—"Oh, it is not *my* coat—I only put it on for a joke!"

"That's a likely tale," responded one of the party, who looked very incredulous; "I don't believe a word of it. That's some darned stuff you've trumped up, thinking to gammon[1] us—it won't go down; we'll just give you a walloping, if it's only to teach you to wear your own clothes,"—and suiting the action to the word, he commenced pommelling him unmercifully.

"Help! help!" screamed Mr. Stevens. "Don't kill me, gentlemen,—don't kill me!"

"Oh! we won't kill you—we'll only come as near it as we can, without quite finishing you," cried one of his relentless tormenters.

On hearing this, their victim made a frantic effort to break away, and not succeeding in it, he commenced yelling at the top of his voice. As is usual in such cases, the watchman was nowhere to be seen; and his cries only exasperated his persecutors the more.

"Hit him in the bread-crusher, and stop his noise," suggested one of the party farthest off from Mr. Stevens. This piece of advice was carried into immediate effect, and the unfortunate wearer of the obnoxious coat received a heavy blow in the mouth, which cut his lips and knocked out one of his front teeth.

His cries now became so loud as to render it necessary to gag him, which was done by one of the party in the most thorough and expeditious manner. They then dragged him into a wheelwright's shop near by, where they obtained some tar, with which they coated his face completely.

"Oh! don't he look like a nigger!" said one of the party, when they had finished embellishing their victim.

"Rub some on his hands, and then let him go," suggested another. "When he gets home I guess he'll surprise his mammy: I don't believe his own dog will know him!"

A shout of laughter followed this remark, in the midst of which they ungagged Mr. Stevens and turned him from the door.

"Now run for it—cut the quickest kind of time," exclaimed one of them, as he gave him a kick to add impetus to his forward movement.

This aid was, however, entirely unnecessary, for Mr. Stevens shot away from the premises like an arrow from a bow; and that, too, without any observation upon the direction in which he was going.

---

1 Trick; hoodwink.

As soon as he felt himself out of the reach of his tormentors, he sat down upon the steps of a mansion,[1] to consider what was best to be done. All the shops, and even the taverns, were closed—not a place was open where he could procure the least assistance; he had not even an acquaintance in the neighbourhood to whom he might apply.

He was, indeed, a pitiable object to look upon. The hat he had so recently purchased, bad as it was when it came into his possession, was now infinitely less presentable. In the severe trials it had undergone, in company with its unfortunate owner, it had lost its tip and half the brim. The countenance beneath it would, however, have absorbed the gazer's whole attention. His lips were swelled to a size that would have been regarded as large even on the face of a Congo negro, and one eye was puffed out to an alarming extent; whilst the coating of tar he had received rendered him such an object as the reader can but faintly picture to himself.

The door of the mansion was suddenly opened, and there issued forth a party of young men, evidently in an advanced state of intoxication. "Hallo! here's a darkey!" exclaimed one of them, as the light from the hall fell upon the upturned face of Mr. Stevens. "Ha, ha! Here's a darkey—now for some fun!"

Mr. Stevens was immediately surrounded by half a dozen well-dressed young men, who had evidently been enjoying an entertainment not conducted upon temperance principles. "Spirit of—hic—hic—night, whence co-co-comest thou?" stammered one; "sp-p-peak—art thou a creature of the mag-mag-na-tion-goblin-damned, or only a nigger?—speak!"[2]

Mr. Stevens, who at once recognized one or two of the parties as slight acquaintances, would not open his mouth, for fear that his voice might discover him, as to them, above all persons, he would have shrunk from making himself known, he therefore began to make signs as though he were dumb.

"Let him alone," said one of the more sober of the party; "he's a poor dumb fellow—let him go." His voice was disregarded, however, as the rest seemed bent on having some sport.

A half-hogshead, nearly filled with water, which stood upon the edge of the pavement, for the convenience of the builders who were at work next door, caught the attention of one of them.

---

1 Here, simply a freestanding house—not necessarily a grand one.

2 A pastiche of verbal figures cobbled together from *One Thousand and One Nights* (first English edition, 1706) and Shakespeare's *Hamlet* (1.4.40).

"Let's make him jump into this," he exclaimed, at the same time motioning to Mr. Stevens to that effect. By dint of great effort they made him understand what was required, and they then continued to make him jump in and out of the hogshead for several minutes; then, joining hands, they danced around him, whilst he stood knee-deep in the water, shivering, and making the most imploring motions to be set at liberty.

Whilst they were thus engaged, the door again opened, and the fashionable Mr. Morton (who had been one of the guests) descended the steps, and came to see what had been productive of so much mirth.

"What have you got here?" he asked, pressing forward, until he saw the battered form of Mr. Stevens; "oh, let the poor darkey go," he continued, compassionately, for he had just drunk enough to make him feel humane; "let the poor fellow go, it's a shame to treat him in this manner."

As he spoke, he endeavoured to take from the hands of one of the party a piece of chip, with which he was industriously engaged in streaking the face of Mr. Stevens with lime, "Let me alone, Morton—let me alone; I'm making a white man of him, I'm going to make him a glorious fellow-citizen, and have him run for Congress. Let me alone, I say."

Mr. Morton was able, however, after some persuasion, to induce the young men to depart; and as his home lay in a direction opposite to theirs, he said to Mr. Stevens, "Come on, old fellow, I'll protect you."

As soon as they were out of hearing of the others, Mr. Stevens exclaimed, "Don't you know me, Morton?"

Mr. Morton started back with surprise, and looked at his companion in a bewildered manner, then exclaimed, "No, I'll be hanged if I do. Who the devil are you?"

"I'm Stevens; you know me."

"Indeed I don't. Who's Stevens?"

"You don't know me! why, I'm George Stevens, the lawyer."

Mr. Morton thought that he now recognized the voice, and as they were passing under the lamp at the time, Mr. Stevens said to him, "Put your finger on my face, and you will soon see it is only tar." Mr. Morton did as he was desired, and found his finger smeared with the sticky article.

"What on earth have you been doing with yourself?" he asked, with great surprise; "what is all this masquerading for?"

Mr. Stevens hereupon related his visit at Whitticar's, and detailed the events that had subsequently occurred.

Mr. Morton gave vent to shouts of laughter as he listened to the recital of his friend. "By George!" he exclaimed, "I'll have to tell that; it is too good to keep."

"Oh, no, don't," said Mr. Stevens; "that won't do—you forget what I came out for?"

"True," rejoined Mr. Morton; "I suppose it will be best to keep mum about it. I'll go home with you, you might fall into the hands of the Philistines[1] again."

"Thank you—thank you," replied Mr. Stevens, who felt greatly relieved to have some company for his further protection; "and," continued he, "if I could only get some of this infernal stuff off my face, I should be so glad; let us try."

Accordingly they stopped at the nearest pump, and endeavoured to remove some of the obnoxious tar from his face; but, unfortunately, the only result obtained by their efforts was to rub it more thoroughly in, so they were compelled to give up in despair, and hasten onward.

Mr. Stevens rang so loudly at the door, as to quite startle his wife and the charity-girl, both of whom had fallen into a sound sleep, as they sat together awaiting his return. Mr. Morton, who, as we have said before, was not entirely sober, was singing a popular melody, and keeping time upon the door with the head of his cane. Now, in all her life, Mrs. Stevens had never heard her husband utter a note, and being greatly frightened at the unusual noise upon the door-step, held a hurried consultation with the charity-girl upon the best mode of proceeding.

"Call through the key-hole, ma'am," suggested she, which advice Mrs. Stevens immediately followed, and inquired, "Who's there?"

"Open the door, Jule, don't keep me out here with your darned nonsense; let me in quick."

"Yes, let him in," added Mr. Morton; "he's brought a gentleman from Africa with him."

Mrs. Stevens did not exactly catch the purport of the words uttered by Mr. Morton; and, therefore, when she opened the door, and her husband, with his well-blacked face, stalked into the entry, she could not repress a scream of fright at the hideous figure he presented.

"Hush, hush," he exclaimed, "don't arouse the neighbours—it's me; don't you know my voice."

---

1 Here used figuratively as "enemies" or "persecutors." See *OED* "Philistines" A1b.

Mrs. Stevens stared at him in a bewildered manner, and after bidding Mr. Morton "Good night," she closed and locked the door, and followed her husband into the back room.

In a short time he recapitulated the events of the night to his astonished and indignant spouse, who greatly commiserated his misfortunes. A bottle of sweet oil was brought into requisition, and she made a lengthened effort to remove the tar from her husband's face, in which she only partially succeeded; and it was almost day when he crawled off to bed, with the skin half scraped off from his swollen face.

CHAPTER XIX.

The Alarm.

IMMEDIATELY after the departure of Mr. Stevens, Master Kinch began to consider the propriety of closing the establishment for the night. Sliding down from the counter, where he had been seated, reflecting upon the strange conduct of his recent customer, he said, "I feels rather queer round about here," laying his hand upon his stomach; "and I'm inclined to think that some of them 'ere Jersey sausages and buckwheat cakes that the old man has been stuffing himself with, wouldn't go down slow. Rather shabby in him not to come back, and let me go home, and have a slap at the wittles. I expect nothing else, but that he has eat so much, that he's fell asleep at the supper-table, and won't wake up till bedtime. He's always serving me that same trick."

The old man thus alluded to was no other than Master Kinch's father, who had departed from the shop two or three hours previously, promising to return immediately after tea.

This promise appeared to have entirely faded from his recollection, as he was at that moment, as Kinch had supposed, fast asleep, and totally oblivious of the fact that such a person as his hungry descendant was in existence.

Having fully come to the conclusion to suspend operations for the evening, Kinch made two or three excursions into the street, returning each time laden with old hats, coats, and shoes. These he deposited on the counter without order or arrangement, muttering, as he did so, that the old man could sort 'em out in the morning to suit himself. The things being all brought from the street, he had only to close the shutters, which operation was soon effected, and our hungry friend on his way home.

The next morning Mr. De Younge (for the father of Kinch rejoiced in that aristocratic cognomen) was early at his receptacle for old clothes, and it being market-day, he anticipated doing a good business. The old man leisurely took down the shutters, assorted and hung out the old clothes, and was busily engaged in sweeping out the store, when his eye fell upon the paper dropped by Mr. Stevens the evening previous. "What's dis 'ere," said he, stooping to pick it up; "bill or suthin' like it, I s'pose. What a trial 'tis not to be able to read writin'; don't know whether 'tis worth keeping or not; best save it though till dat ar boy of mine comes, *he* can read it—he's a scholar. Ah, de children now-a-days has greater 'vantages than deir poor fathers had."

Whilst he was thus soliloquizing, his attention was arrested by the noise of footsteps in the other part of the shop, and looking up, he discerned the tall form of Mr. Walters.

"Why, bless me," said the old man, "dis is an early visit; where you come from, honey, dis time o' day?"

"Oh, I take a walk every morning, to breathe a little of the fresh air; it gives one an appetite for breakfast, you know. You'll let me take the liberty of sitting on your counter, won't you?" he continued; "I want to read a little article in a newspaper I have just purchased."

Assent being readily given, Mr. Walters was soon perusing the journal with great attention; at last he tossed it from him in an impatient manner, and exclaimed, "Of all lying rascals, I think the reporters for this paper are the greatest. Now, for instance, three or four nights since, a gang of villains assaulted one of my tenants—a coloured man—upon his own doorstep, and nearly killed him, and that, too, without the slightest provocation; they then set fire to the house, which was half consumed before it could be extinguished; and it is here stated that the coloured people were the aggressors, and whilst they were engaged in the *mêlée*, the house caught fire accidentally."

"Yes," rejoined Mr. De Younge; "things are gitting mighty critical even in dese 'ere parts; and I wouldn't live furder down town if you was to give me a house rent-free. Why, it's raly dangerous to go home nights down dere."

"And there is no knowing how long we may be any better off up here," continued Mr. Walters; "the authorities don't seem to take the least notice of them, and the rioters appear to be having it all their own way."

They continued conversing upon the topic for some time, Mr. De Younge being meanwhile engaged in sponging and cleaning some coats he had purchased the day before; in so doing, he was obliged to remove the paper he had picked up from the floor, and it occurred to him to ask Mr. Walters to read it; he therefore handed it to him, saying—

"Jist read dat, honey, won't you? I want to know if it's worth savin'. I've burnt up two or three receipts in my life, and had de bills to pay over; and I'se got rale careful, you know. 'Taint pleasant to pay money twice over for de same thing."

Mr. Walters took the paper extended to him, and, after glancing over it, remarked, "This handwriting is very familiar to me, *very*; but whose it is, I can't say; it appears to be a list of addresses, or something of that kind." And he read over various names of streets, and numbers of houses. "Why," he exclaimed, with a start of surprise, "here is my own house upon the list, 257, Easton-street; then here is 22, Christian-street; here also are numbers in Baker-street, Bedford-street, Sixth, Seventh, and Eighth Streets; in some of which houses I know coloured people live, for one or two of them are my own. This is a strange affair."

As he spoke, he turned over the paper, and read on the other side,—"Places to be attacked." "Why, this looks serious," he continued, with some excitement of manner. "'Places to be attacked,'—don't that seem to you as if it might be a list of places for these rioters to set upon? I really must look into this. Who could have left it here?"

"I raly don't know," replied the old man. "Kinch told me suthin' last night about some gemman comin' here and changing his clothes; p'raps 'twas him. I'd like to know who 'twas myself. Well, wait awhile, my boy will come in directly; maybe he can explain it."

He had scarcely finished speaking, when Master Kinch made his appearance, with his hat, as usual, placed upon nine hairs,[1] and his mouth smeared with the eggs and bacon with which he had been "staying and comforting" himself. He took off his hat on perceiving Mr. Walters, and, with great humility, "hoped that gentleman was well."

"Yes, very well, Kinch," replied Mr. Walters. "We were waiting for you. Can you tell where this came from?" he asked, handing him the mysterious paper.

"Never seen it before, that I know of," replied Kinch, after a short inspection.

"Well, who was here last night?" asked his father; "you said you sold suthin'?"

"So I did," replied Kinch; "sold a whole suit and the gentleman who put it on said he was going out for a lark. He was changing some papers from his pocket: perhaps he dropped it. I'm to take this suit back to him to-day. Here is his card."

"By heavens!" exclaimed Mr. Walters, after looking at the card, "I know the fellow,—George Stevens, 'Slippery George,'—every one knows him, and can speak no good of him either. Now I recognize the handwriting of the list; I begin to suspect something wrong by seeing his name in connection with this."

Hereupon Kinch was subjected to a severe cross-examination, which had the effect of deepening Mr. Walters's impression, that

---

1 I.e., perched jauntily (and precariously) atop his head.

some plot was being concocted that would result to the detriment of the coloured people; for he was confident that no good could be indicated by the mysterious conduct of Mr. Stevens.

After some deliberation, Kinch received instructions to take home the clothes as directed, and to have his eyes about him; and if he saw or heard anything, he was to report it.

In accordance with his instructions, Master Kinch made several journeys to Mr. Stevens's office, but did not succeed in finding that gentleman within; the last trip he made there fatigued him to such a degree, that he determined to wait his arrival, as he judged, from the lateness of the hour, that, if it was his intention to come at all that day, he would soon be there.

"I'll sit down here," said Kinch, who espied an old box in the back part of the entry, "and give myself a little time to blow."

He had not sat long before he heard footsteps on the stairs, and presently the sound of voices became quite audible.

"That's him," ejaculated Kinch, as Mr. Stevens was heard saying, in an angry tone,—"Yes; and a devil of a scrape I got into by your want of sobriety. Had you followed my directions, and met me at Whitticar's, instead of getting drunk as a beast, and being obliged to go home to bed, it wouldn't have happened."

"Well, squire," replied McCloskey, for he was the person addressed by Mr. Stevens, "a man can't be expected always to keep sober."

"He ought to when he has business before him," rejoined Mr. Stevens, sharply; "how the devil am I to trust you to do anything of importance, when I can't depend on your keeping sober a day at a time? Come up to this top landing," continued he, "and listen to me, if you think you are sober enough to comprehend what I say to you."

They now approached, and stood within a few feet of the place where Kinch was sitting, and Mr. Stevens said, with a great deal of emphasis, "Now, I want you to pay the strictest attention to what I say. I had a list of places made out for you last night, but, somehow or other, I lost it. But that is neither here nor there. This is what I want you to attend to particularly. Don't attempt anything to-night; you can't get a sufficient number of the boys together; but, when you do go, you are to take, first, Christian-street, between Eleventh and Twelfth,—there are several nigger families living in that block. Smash in their windows, break their furniture, and, if possible, set one of the houses on fire, and that will draw attention to that locality whilst you are operating elsewhere. By that time, the boys will be ripe for anything. Then you had better go to a house in Easton-street, corner of Shotwell: there is a rich nigger living there whose plunder is worth something. I owe him an old grudge, and I want you to pay it off for me."

"You keep me pretty busy paying your debts. What's the name of this rich nigger?"

"Walters," replied Mr. Stevens; "everybody knows him. Now about that other affair." Here he whispered so low, that Kinch could only learn they were planning an attack on the house of some one, but failed in discovering the name. McCloskey departed as soon as he had received full directions from Mr. Stevens, and his retreating steps might be still heard upon the stairs, when Mr. Stevens unlocked his office-door and entered.

After giving him sufficient time to get quietly seated, Kinch followed, and delivered the clothes left with him the evening previous. He was very much struck with Mr. Stevens's altered appearance, and, in fact, would not have recognized him, but for his voice.

"You don't seem to be well?" remarked Kinch, inquiringly.

"No, I'm not," he replied, gruffly; "I've caught cold." As Kinch was leaving the office, he called after him, "Did you find a paper in your shop this morning?"

"No, sir," replied Kinch, "*I didn't*;" but mentally he observed, "My daddy did though;" and, fearful of some other troublesome question, he took leave immediately.

Fatigued and out of breath, Kinch arrived at the house of Mr. Walters, where he considered it best to go and communicate what he had learned.

Mr. Walters was at dinner when he received from the maid a summons to the parlour to see a lad, who said his business was a matter "of life or death." He was obliged to smile at the air of importance with which Kinch commenced the relation of what he had overheard—but the smile gave place to a look of anxiety and indignation long ere he had finished, and at the conclusion of the communication he was highly excited and alarmed.

"The infernal scoundrel!" exclaimed Mr. Walters. "Are you sure it was my house?"

"Yes, sure," was Kinch's reply. "You are the only coloured person living in the square—and he said plain enough for anybody to understand, 'Easton-street, corner of Shotwell.' I heard every word but what they said towards the last in a whisper."

"You couldn't catch anything of it?" asked Mr. Walters.

"No, I missed that; they talked too low for me to hear."

After reflecting a few moments, Mr. Walters said: "Not a word of this is to be lisped anywhere except with my permission, and by my direction. Have you had your dinner?"

"No, sir," was the prompt reply.

"I want to despatch a note to Mr. Ellis, by you, if it won't trouble you too much. Can you oblige me?"

"Oh, yes, sir, by all means," replied Kinch, "I'll go there with pleasure."

"Then whilst I'm writing," continued Mr. Walters, "you can be eating your dinner, that will economize time, you know."

Kinch followed the servant who answered the bell into the dining-room which Mr. Walters had just left. On being supplied with a knife and fork, he helped himself bountifully to the roast duck, then pouring out a glass of wine, he drank with great enthusiasm, to "our honoured self," which proceeding caused infinite amusement to the two servants who were peeping at him through the dining-room door. "*Der*-licious," exclaimed Kinch, depositing his glass upon the table; "guess I'll try another;" and suiting the action to the word, he refilled his glass, and dispatched its contents in the wake of the other. Having laboured upon the duck until his appetite was somewhat appeased, he leant back in his chair and suffered his plate to be changed for another, which being done, he made an attack upon a peach pie, and nearly demolished it outright.

This last performance brought his meal to a conclusion, and with a look of weariness, he remarked, "I don't see how it is—but as soon as I have eat for a little while my appetite is sure to leave me—now I can't eat a bit more. But the worst thing is walking down to Mr. Ellis's. I don't feel a bit like it, but I suppose I must;" and reluctantly rising from the table, he returned to the parlour, where he found Mr. Walters folding the note he had promised to deliver.

As soon as he had despatched Kinch on his errand, Mr. Walters put on his hat and walked to the office of the mayor.

"Is his honour in?" he asked of one of the police, who was lounging in the anteroom.

"Yes, he is—what do *you* want with him?" asked the official, in a rude tone.

"That, sir, is none of your business," replied Mr. Walters; "if the mayor is in, hand him this card, and say I wish to see him."

Somewhat awed by Mr. Walters's dignified and decided manner, the man went quickly to deliver his message, and returned with an answer that his honour would be obliged to Mr. Walters if he would step into his office.

On following the officer, he was ushered into a small room—the private office of the chief magistrate of the city.

"Take a seat, sir," said the mayor, politely, "it is some time since we have met. I think I had the pleasure of transacting business with you quite frequently some years back if I am not mistaken."

"You are quite correct," replied Mr. Walters, "and being so favourably impressed by your courtesy on the occasions to which you refer, I have ventured to intrude upon you with a matter of great importance, not only to myself, but I think I may say to the public generally. Since this morning, circumstances have come under my notice that leave no doubt on my mind that a thoroughly-concerted plan is afoot for the distruction of the property of a large number of our coloured citizens—mine amongst the rest. You must be aware," he continued, "that many very serious disturbances have occurred lately in the lower part of the city."

"Yes, I've heard something respecting it," replied the mayor, "but I believe they were nothing more than trifling combats between the negroes and the whites in that vicinity."

"Oh, no, sir! I assure you," rejoined Mr. Walters, "they were and are anything but trifling. I regard them, however, as only faint indications of what we may expect if the thing is not promptly suppressed; there is an organized gang of villains, who are combined for the sole purpose of mobbing us coloured citizens; and, as we are inoffensive, we certainly deserve protection; and here," continued Mr. Walters, "is a copy of the list of places upon which it is rumoured an attack is to be made."

"I really don't see how I'm to prevent it, Mr. Walters; with the exception of your own residence, all that are here enumerated are out of my jurisdiction.[1] I can send two or three police for your protection if you think it necessary. But I really can't see my way clear to do anything further."

---

1 Given the novel's likely setting in the 1830s or 1840s, the Mayor's claim here is legally correct. The areas of Southwark and Moyamensing in the south and Kensington and the Northern Liberties District in the north (see map, Appendix C1)—where many black people in the Philadelphia municipal area lived—were not formally incorporated into the City itself until 1854. Still, it is worth noting the mayor's disingenuousness: Philadelphia officials frequently involved themselves in situations in the unincorporated districts, whether or not they had the legal authority to do so.

"Two or three police!" said Mr. Walters, with rising indignation at the apathy and indifference the mayor exhibited; "they would scarcely be of any more use than as many women. If that is the extent of the aid you can afford me, I must do what I can to protect myself."

"I trust your fears lead you to exaggerate the danger," said the mayor, as Mr. Walters arose to depart; "perhaps it is *only* rumour after all."

"I might have flattered myself with the same idea, did I not feel convinced by what has so recently occurred but a short distance from my own house; at any rate, if I am attacked, they will find I am not unprepared. Good day," and bowing courteously to the mayor, Mr. Walters departed.

CHAPTER XX.

The Attack.

MR. WALTERS lost no time in sending messengers to the various parties threatened by the mob, warning them either to leave their houses or to make every exertion for a vigorous defence. Few, however, adopted the latter extremity; the majority fled from their homes, leaving what effects they could not carry away at the mercy of the mob, and sought an asylum in the houses of such kindly-disposed whites as would give them shelter.

Although the authorities of the district had received the most positive information of the nefarious schemes of the rioters, they had not made the slightest efforts to protect the poor creatures threatened in their persons and property, but let the tide of lawlessness flow on unchecked.

Throughout the day parties of coloured people might have been seen hurrying to the upper part of the city: women with terror written on their faces, some with babes in their arms and children at their side, hastening to some temporary place of refuge, in company with men who were bending beneath the weight of household goods.

Mr. Walters had converted his house into a temporary fortress: the shutters of the upper windows had been loop-holed,[1] double bars had been placed across the doors and windows on the ground floor, carpets had been taken up, superfluous furniture removed, and an air of thorough preparation imparted. A few of Mr. Walters's male friends had volunteered their aid in defence of his house, and their services had been accepted.

Mr. Ellis, whose house was quite indefensible (it being situated in a neighbourhood swarming with the class of which the mob was composed), had decided on bringing his family to the house of Mr. Walters, and sharing with him the fortunes of the night, his wife and daughters having declared they would feel as safe there as elsewhere; and, accordingly, about five in the afternoon, Mrs. Ellis came up, accompanied by Kinch and the girls.

Caddy and Kinch, who brought up the rear, seemed very solicitous respecting the safety of a package that the latter bore in his arms.

---

1 I.e., slots have been cut into the shutters so that they may remain closed while the people hidden behind them may look out (or fire guns) into the street.

"What have you there?" asked Mr. Walters, with a smile; "it must be powder, or some other explosive matter, you take such wonderful pains for its preservation. Come, Caddy, tell us what it is; is it powder?"

"No, Mr. Walters, it isn't powder," she replied; "it's nothing that will blow the house up or burn it down."

"What is it, then? You tell us, Kinch."

"Just do, if you think best," said Caddy, giving him a threatening glance; whereupon, Master Kinch looked as much as to say, "If you were to put me on the rack you couldn't get a word out of me."

"I suppose I shall have to give you up," said Mr. Walters at last; "but don't stand here in the entry; come up into the drawing-room."

Mrs. Ellis and Esther followed him upstairs, and stood at the door of the drawing-room surveying the preparations for defence that the appearance of the room so abundantly indicated. Guns were stacked in the corner, a number of pistols lay upon the mantelpiece, and a pile of cartridges was heaped up beside a small keg of powder that stood upon the table opposite the fire-place.

"Dear me!" exclaimed Mrs. Ellis, "this looks dreadful; it almost frightens me out of my wits to see so many dangerous weapons scattered about."

"And how does it affect our quiet, Esther?" asked Mr. Walters.

"It makes me wish I were a man," she replied, with considerable vehemence of manner. All started at this language from one of her usually gentle demeanour.

"Why, Esther, how you talk, girl: what's come over you?"

"Talk!" replied she. "I say nothing that I do not feel. As we came through the streets to-day, and I saw so many inoffensive creatures, who, like ourselves, have never done these white wretches the least injury,—to see them and us driven from our homes by a mob of wretches, who can accuse us of nothing but being darker than themselves,—it takes all the woman out of my bosom, and makes me feel like a—" here Esther paused, and bit her lip to prevent the utterance of a fierce expression that hovered on the tip of her tongue.

She then continued: "One poor woman in particular I noticed: she had a babe in her arms, poor thing, and was weeping bitterly because she knew of no place to go to seek for shelter or protection. A couple of white men stood by jeering and taunting her. I felt as though I could have strangled them: had I been a man, I would have attacked them on the spot, if I had been sure they would have killed me the next moment."

"Hush! Esther, hush! my child; you must not talk so; it sounds unwomanly—unchristian. Why, I never heard you talk so before." Esther made no reply, but stood resting her forehead upon the mantelpiece. Her face was flushed with excitement, and her dark eyes glistened like polished jet.

Mr. Walters stood regarding her for a time with evident admiration, and then said, "You are a brave one, after my own heart." Esther hung down her head, confused by the ardent look he cast upon her, as he continued, "You have taken me by surprise; but it's always the way with you quiet people; events like these bring you out—seem to change your very natures, as it were. We must look out," said he, with a smile, turning to one of the young men, "or Miss Ellis will excel us all in courage. I shall expect great things from her if we are attacked to-night."

"Don't make a jest of me, Mr. Walters," said Esther, and as she spoke her eyes moistened and her lip quivered with vexation.

"No, no, my dear girl, don't misunderstand me," replied he, quickly; "nothing was farther from my thoughts. I truly meant all that I said. I believe you to be a brave girl."

"If you really think so," rejoined Esther, "prove it by showing me how to load these." As she spoke she took from the mantel one of the pistols that were lying there, and turned it over to examine it.

"Oh! put that down, Esther, put that down immediately," almost screamed Mrs. Ellis; "what with your speeches and your guns you'll quite set me crazy; do take it from her, Walters; it will certainly go off."

"There's not the least danger, Ellen," he replied; "there's nothing in it."

"Well, I'm afraid of guns, loaded or unloaded; they are dangerous, all of them, whether they have anything in them or not. Do you hear me, Esther; do put that down and come out of here."

"Oh, no, mother," said she, "do let me remain; there, I'll lay the pistols down and won't touch them again whilst you are in the room."

"You may safely leave her in my hands," interposed Mr. Walters. "If she wants to learn, let her; it won't injure her in the least, I'll take care of that." This assurance somewhat quieted Mrs. Ellis, who left the room and took up her quarters in another apartment.

"Now, Mr. Walters," said Esther, taking off her bonnet, "I'm quite in earnest about learning to load these pistols, and I wish you to instruct me. You may be hard pressed tonight, and unable to load for yourselves, and in such an emergency I could perhaps be of great use to you."

"But, my child," replied he, "to be of use in the manner you propose, you would be compelled to remain in quite an exposed situation."

"I am aware of that," calmly rejoined Esther.

"And still you are not afraid?" he asked, in surprise.

"Why should I be? I shall not be any more exposed than you or my father."

"That's enough—I'll teach you. Look here," said Mr. Walters, "observe how I load this." Esther gave her undivided attention to the work before her, and when he had finished, she took up another pistol and loaded it with a precision and celerity that would have reflected honour on a more practised hand.

"Well done!—capital!" exclaimed Mr. Walters, as she laid down the weapon. "You'll do, my girl; as I said before, you are one after my own heart. Now, whilst you are loading the rest, I will go downstairs, where I have some little matters to attend to." On the stair-way he was met by Kinch and Caddy, who were tugging up a large kettle of water. "Is it possible, Caddy," asked Mr. Walters, "that your propensity to dabble in soap and water has overcome you even at this critical time? You certainly can't be going to scrub?"

"No, I'm not going to scrub," she replied, "nor do anything like it. We've got our plans, haven't we, Kinch?"

"Let's hear what your plans are. I'd like to be enlightened a little, if convenient," said Mr. Walters.

"Well, it's *not* convenient, Mr. Walters, so you need not expect to hear a word about them. You'd only laugh if we were to tell you, so we're going to keep it to ourselves, ain't we, Kinch?"

The latter, thus appealed to, put on an air of profound mystery, and intimated that if they were permitted to pursue the even tenor of their way, great results might be expected; but if they were balked in their designs, he could not answer for the consequences.

"You and Esther have your plans," resumed Caddy, "and we have ours. We don't believe in powder and shot, and don't want anything to do with guns; for my part I'm afraid of them, so please let us go by—do, now, that's a good soul!"

"You seem to forget that I'm the commander of this fortress," said Mr. Walters, "and that I have a right to know everything that transpires within it; but I see you look obstinate, and as I haven't time to settle the matter now, you may pass on. I wonder what they can be about," he remarked, as they hurried on. "I must steal up by-and-by and see for myself."

One after another the various friends of Mr. Walters came in, each bringing some vague report of the designs of the mob. They all described the excitement as growing more intense; that the houses of various prominent Abolitionists had been threatened; that an attempt had been made to fire one of the coloured churches; and that, notwithstanding the rioters made little scruple in declaring their intentions, the authorities were not using the slightest effort to restrain them, or to protect the parties threatened. Day was fast waning, and the approaching night brought with it clouds and cold.

Whilst they had been engaged in their preparations for defence, none had time to reflect upon the danger of their situation; but now that all was prepared, and there was nothing to sustain the excitement of the last few hours, a chill crept over the circle who were gathered round the fire. There were no candles burning, and the uncertain glow from the grate gave a rather weird-like look to the group. The arms stacked in the corner of the room, and the occasional glitter of the pistol-barrels as the flames rose and fell, gave the whole a peculiarly strange effect.

"We look belligerent enough, I should think," remarked Mr. Walters, looking around him. "I wish we were well out of this: it's terrible to be driven to these extremities—but we are not the aggressors, thank God! and the results, be they what they may, are not of our seeking. I have a right to defend my own: I have asked protection of the law, and it is too weak, or too indifferent, to give it; so I have no alternative but to protect myself. But who is here? It has grown so dark in the room that I can scarcely distinguish any one. Where are all the ladies?"

"None are here except myself," answered Esther; "all the rest are below stairs."

"And where are you? I hear, but can't see you; give me your hand," said he, extending his own in the direction from which her voice proceeded. "How cold your hand is," he continued; "are you frightened?"

"Frightened!" she replied; "I never felt calmer in my life—put your finger on my pulse."

Mr. Walters did as he was desired, and exclaimed, "Steady as a clock. I trust nothing may occur before morning to cause it to beat more hurriedly."

"Let us put some wood on these coals," suggested Mr. Ellis; "it will make a slight blaze, and give us a chance to see each other." As he spoke he took up a few small fagots and cast them upon the fire.

The wood snapped and crackled, as the flames mounted the chimney and cast a cheerful glow upon the surrounding objects: suddenly a thoroughly ignited piece flew off from the rest and fell on the table in the midst of the cartridges. "Run for your lives!" shrieked one of the party. "The powder! the powder!" Simultaneously they nearly all rushed to the door.

Mr. Walters stood as one petrified. Esther alone, of the whole party, retained her presence of mind; springing forward, she grasped the blazing fragment and dashed it back again into the grate. All this passed in a few seconds, and in the end Esther was so overcome with excitement and terror, that she fainted outright. Hearing no report, those who had fled cautiously returned, and by their united efforts she was soon restored to consciousness.

"What a narrow escape!" said she, trembling, and covering her face with her hands; "it makes me shudder to think of it."

"We owe our lives to you, my brave girl," said Mr. Walters; "your presence of mind has quite put us all to the blush."

"Oh! move the powder some distance off, or the same thing may happen again. Please do move it, Mr. Walters; I shall have no peace whilst it is there."

Whilst they were thus engaged, a loud commotion was heard below stairs, and with one accord all started in the direction from whence the noise proceeded.

"Bring a light! bring a light!" cried Mrs. Ellis; "something dreadful has happened." A light was soon procured, and the cause of this second alarm fully ascertained.

Master Kinch, in his anxiety to give himself as warlike an appearance as possible, had added to his accoutrements an old sword that he had discovered in an out-of-the-way corner of the garret. Not being accustomed to weapons of this nature, he had been constantly getting it between his legs, and had already been precipitated by it down a flight of steps, to the imminent risk of his neck. Undaunted, however, by this mishap, he had clung to it with wonderful tenacity, until it had again caused a disaster the noise of which had brought all parties into the room where it had occurred.

The light being brought, Master Kinch crawled out from under a table with his head and back covered with batter, a pan of which had been overturned upon him, in consequence of his having been tripped up by his sword and falling violently against the table on which it stood.

"I said you had better take that skewer off," exclaimed Caddy "It's a wonder it hasn't broke your neck before now; but you are such a goose you would wear it," said she, surveying her aide-de-camp with derision, as he vainly endeavoured to scrape the batter from his face.

"Please give me some water," cried Kinch, looking from one to the other of the laughing group: "help a feller to get it off, can't you—it's all in my eyes, and the yeast is blinding me."

The only answer to this appeal was an additional shout of laughter, without the slightest effort for his relief. At last Caddy, taking compassion upon his forlorn condition, procured a basin of water, and assisted him to wash from his woolly pate what had been intended for the next day's meal.

"This is the farce after what was almost a tragedy," said Mr. Walters, as they ascended the stairs again; "I wonder what we shall have next!"

They all returned to their chairs by the drawing-room fire after this occurrence, and remained in comparative silence for some time, until loud cries of "Fire! fire!" startled them from their seats.

"The whole of the lower part of the city appears to be in a blaze," exclaimed one of the party who had hastened to the window; "look at the flames—they are ascending from several places. They are at their work; we may expect them here soon."

"Well, they'll find us prepared when they do come," rejoined Mr. Walters.

"What do you propose?" asked Mr. Ellis. "Are we to fire on them at once, or wait for their attack?"

"Wait for their attack, by all means," said he, in reply;—"if they throw stones, you'll find plenty in that room with which to return the compliment; if they resort to fire-arms, then we will do the same; I want to be strictly on the defensive—but at the same time we must defend ourselves fully and energetically."

In about an hour after this conversation a dull roar was heard in the distance, which grew louder and nearer every moment.

"Hist!" said Esther; "do you hear that noise? Listen! isn't that the mob coming?"

Mr. Walters opened the shutter, and then the sound became more distinct. On they came, nearer and nearer, until the noise of their voices became almost deafening.

There was something awful in the appearance of the motley crowd that, like a torrent, foamed and surged through the streets. Some were bearing large pine torches that filled the air with thick smoke and partially lighted up the surrounding gloom. Most of them were armed with clubs, and a few with guns and pistols.

As they approached the house, there seemed to be a sort of consultation between the ringleaders, for soon after every light was extinguished, and the deafening yells of "Kill the niggers!" "Down with the Abolitionists!" were almost entirely stilled.

"I wonder what that means," said Mr. Walters, who had closed the shutter, and was surveying, through an aperture that had been cut, the turbulent mass below. "Look out for something soon."

He had scarcely finished speaking, when a voice in the street cried, "One—two—three!" and immediately there followed a volley of missiles, crushing in the windows of the chamber above, and rattling upon the shutters of the room in which the party of defenders were gathered. A yell then went up from the mob, followed by another shower of stones.

"It is now our turn," said Mr. Walters, coolly. "Four of you place yourselves at the windows of the adjoining room; the rest remain here. When you see a bright light reflected on the crowd below, throw open the shutters, and hurl down stones as long as the light is shining. Now, take your places, and as soon as you are prepared stamp upon the floor."

Each of the men now armed themselves with two or more of the largest stones they could find, from the heap that had been provided for the occasion; and in a few seconds a loud stamping upon the floor informed Mr. Walters that all was ready. He now opened the aperture in the shutter, and placed therein a powerful reflecting light which brought the shouting crowd below clearly into view, and in an instant a shower of heavy stones came crashing down upon their upturned faces.

Yells of rage and agony ascended from the throng, who, not seeing any previous signs of life in the house, had no anticipation of so prompt and severe a response to their attack. For a time they swayed to and fro, bewildered by the intense light and crushing shower of stones that had so suddenly fallen upon them. Those in the rear, however, pressing forward, did not permit the most exposed to retire out of reach of missiles from the house; on perceiving which, Mr. Walters again turned the light upon them, and immediately another stony shower came rattling down, which caused a precipitate retreat.

"The house is full of niggers!—the house is full of niggers!" cried several voices—"Shoot them! kill them!" and immediately several shots were fired at the window by the mob below.

"Don't fire yet," said Mr. Walters to one of the young men who had his hand upon a gun. "Stop awhile. When we do fire, let it be to some purpose—let us make sure that some one is hit."

Whilst they were talking, two or three bullets pierced the shutters, and flattened themselves upon the ceiling above.

"Those are rifle bullets," remarked one of the young men— "do let us fire."

"It is too great a risk to approach the windows at present; keep quiet for a little while; and, when the light is shown again, fire. But, hark!" continued he, "they are trying to burst open the door. We can't reach them there without exposing ourselves, and if they should get into the entry it would be hard work to dislodge them."

"Let us give them a round; probably it will disperse those farthest off—and those at the door will follow," suggested one of the young men.

"We'll try it, at any rate," replied Walters. "Take your places, don't fire until I show the light—then pick your man, and let him have it. There is no use to fire, you know, unless you hit somebody. Are you ready?" he asked.

"Yes," was the prompt reply.

"Then here goes," said he, turning the light upon the crowd below—who, having some experience in what would follow, did their best to get out of reach; but they were too late—for the appearance of the light was followed by the instantaneous report of several guns which did fearful execution amidst the throng of ruffians. Two or three fell on the spot, and were carried off by their comrades with fearful execrations.

The firing now became frequent on both sides, and Esther's services came into constant requisition. It was in vain that her father endeavoured to persuade her to leave the room; notwithstanding the shutters had been thrown open to facilitate operations from within and the exposure thereby greatly increased, she resolutely refused to retire, and continued fearlessly to load the guns and hand them to the men.

"They've got axes at work upon the door, if they are not dislodged, they'll cut their way in" exclaimed one of the young men—"the stones are exhausted, and I don't know what we shall do."

Just then the splash of water was heard, followed by shrieks of agony.

"Oh, God! I'm scalded! I'm scalded!" cried one of the men upon the steps. "Take me away! take me away!"

In the midst of his cries another volume of scalding water came pouring down upon the group at the door, which was followed by a rush from the premises.

"What is that—who could have done that—where has that water come from?" asked Mr. Walters, as he saw the seething shower pass the window, and fall upon the heads below. "I must go and see."

He ran upstairs, and found Kinch and Caddy busy putting on more water, they having exhausted one kettle-full—into which they had put two or three pounds of cayenne pepper—on the heads of the crowd below.

"We gave 'em a settler, didn't we, Mr. Walters?" asked Caddy, as he entered the room. "It takes us; we fight with hot water. This," said she, holding up a dipper, "is my gun. I guess we made 'em squeal."

"You've done well, Caddy," replied he—"first-rate, my girl. I believe you've driven them off entirely," he continued, peeping out of the window. "They are going off, at any rate," said he, drawing in his head; "whether they will return or not is more than I can say. Keep plenty of hot water ready, but don't expose yourselves, children. Weren't you afraid to go to the window?" he asked.

"We didn't go near it. Look at this," replied Caddy, fitting a broom handle into the end of a very large tin dipper. "Kinch cut this to fit; so we have nothing to do but to stand back here, dip up the water, and let them have it; the length of the handle keeps us from being seen from the street. That was Kinch's plan."

"And a capital one it was too. Your head, Kinch, evidently has no batter within, if it has without; there is a great deal in that. Keep a bright look out," continued Mr. Walters; "I'm going downstairs. If they come again, let them have plenty of your warm pepper-sauce."

On returning to the drawing-room, Mr. Walters found Mr. Dennis, one of the company, preparing to go out. "I'm about to avail myself of the advantage afforded by my fair complexion, and play the spy," said he. "They can't discern at night what I am, and I may be able to learn some of their plans."

"A most excellent idea," said Mr. Walters; "but pray be careful. You may meet some one who will recognise you."

"Never fear," replied Mr. Dennis. "I'll keep a bright look out for that." And, drawing his cap far down over his eyes, to screen his face as much as possible, he sallied out into the street.

He had not been absent more than a quarter of an hour, when he returned limping into the house. "Have they attacked you—are you hurt?" asked the anxious group by which he was surrounded.

"I'm hurt, but not by them. I got on very well, and gleaned a great deal of information, when I heard a sudden exclamation, and, on looking round, I found myself recognized by a white man of my acquaintance. I ran immediately; and whether I was pursued or not, I'm unable to say. I had almost reached here, when my foot caught in a grating and gave my ankle such a wrench that I'm unable to stand." As he spoke, his face grew pale from the suffering the limb was occasioning. "I'm sorry, very sorry," he continued, limping to the sofa; "I was going out again immediately. They intend making an attack on Mr. Garie's house: I didn't hear his name mentioned, but I heard one of the men, who appeared to be a ringleader, say, 'We're going up to Winter-street, to give a coat of tar and feathers to a white man, who is married to a nigger woman.' They can allude to none but him. How annoying that this accident should have happened just now, of all times. They ought to be warned."

"Oh, poor Emily!" cried Esther, bursting into tears; "it will kill her, I know it will; she is so ill. Some one must go and warn them. Let me try; the mob, even if I met them, surely would not assault a woman."

"You mustn't think of such a thing, Esther," exclaimed Mr. Walters; "the idea isn't to be entertained for a moment. You don't know what ruthless wretches they are. Your colour discovered you would find your sex but a trifling protection. I'd go, but it would be certain death to me: my black face would quickly obtain for me a passport to another world if I were discovered in the street just now."

"I'll go," calmly spoke Mr. Ellis. "I can't rest here and think of what they are exposed to. By skulking through bye-streets and keeping under the shadows of houses I may escape observation—at any rate, I must run the risk." And he began to button up his coat. "Don't let your mother know I'm gone; stick by her, my girl," said he, kissing Esther; "trust in God,—He'll protect me."

Esther hung sobbing on her father's neck. "Oh, father, father," said she, "I couldn't bear to see you go for any one but Emily and the children."

"I know it, dear," he replied; "it's my duty. Garie would do the same for me, I know, even at greater risk. Good-bye! good-bye!" And, disengaging himself from the weeping girl, he started on his errand of mercy.

Walking swiftly forwards, he passed over more than two-thirds of the way without the slightest interruption, the streets through which he passed being almost entirely deserted. He had arrived within a couple of squares of the Garies, when suddenly, on turning a corner, he found himself in the midst of a gang of ruffians.

"Here's a nigger! here's a nigger!" shouted two or three of them, almost simultaneously, making at the same time a rush at Mr. Ellis, who turned and ran, followed by the whole gang. Fear lent him wings, and he fast outstripped his pursuers, and would have entirely escaped, had he not turned into a street which unfortunately was closed at the other end. This he did not discover until it was too late to retrace his steps, his pursuers having already entered the street.

Looking for some retreat, he perceived he was standing near an unfinished building. Tearing off the boards that were nailed across the window, he vaulted into the room, knocking off his hat, which fell upon the pavement behind him. Scarcely had he groped his way to the staircase of the dwelling when he heard the footsteps of his pursuers.

"He can't have got through," exclaimed one of them, "the street is closed up at the end; he must be up here somewhere."

Lighting one of their torches, they began to look around them, and soon discovered the hat lying beneath the window.

"He's in here, boys; we've tree'd the 'coon," laughingly exclaimed one of the ruffians. "Let's after him."

Tearing off the remainder of the boards, one or two entered, opened the door from the inside, and gave admission to the rest.

Mr. Ellis mounted to the second story, followed by his pursuers; on he went, until he reached the attic, from which a ladder led to the roof. Ascending this, he drew it up after him, and found himself on the roof of a house that was entirely isolated.

The whole extent of the danger flashed upon him at once. Here he was completely hemmed in, without the smallest chance for escape. He approached the edge and looked over, but could discover nothing near enough to reach by a leap.

"I must sell my life dearly," he said. "God be my helper now— He is all I have to rely upon." And as he spoke, the great drops of sweat fell from his forehead. Espying a sheet of lead upon the roof, he rolled it into a club of tolerable thickness, and waited the approach of his pursuers.

"He's gone on the roof," he heard one of them exclaim, "and pulled the ladder up after him." Just then, a head emerged from the trap-door, the owner of which, perceiving Mr. Ellis, set up a shout of triumph.

"We've got him! we've got him!—here he is!" which cries were answered by the exultant voices of his comrades below.

An attempt was now made by one of them to gain the roof; but he immediately received a blow from Mr. Ellis that knocked him senseless into the arms of his companions. Another attempted the same feat, and met a similar fate.

This caused a parley as to the best mode of proceeding, which resulted in the simultaneous appearance of three of the rioters at the opening. Nothing daunted, Mr. Ellis attacked them with such fierceness and energy that they were forced to descend, muttering the direst curses. In a few moments another head appeared, at which Mr. Ellis aimed a blow of great force; and the club descended upon a hat placed upon a stick. Not meeting the resistance expected, it flew from his hand, and he was thrown forward, nearly falling down the doorway.

With a shout of triumph, they seized his arm, and held him firmly, until one or two of them mounted the roof.

"Throw him over! throw him over!" exclaimed some of the fiercest of the crowd. One or two of the more merciful endeavoured to interfere against killing him outright; but the frenzy of the majority triumphed, and they determined to cast him into the street below.

Mr. Ellis clung to the chimney, shrieking,—"Save me! save me!—Help! help! Will no one save me!" His cries were unheeded by the ruffians, and the people at the surrounding windows were unable to afford him any assistance, even if they were disposed to do so.

Despite his cries and resistance, they forced him to the edge of the roof; he clinging to them the while, and shrieking in agonized terror. Forcing off his hold, they thrust him forward and got him partially over the edge, where he clung calling frantically for aid. One of the villains, to make him loose his hold, struck on his fingers with the handle of a hatchet found on the roof; not succeeding in breaking his hold by these means, with an oath he struck with the blade, severing two of the fingers from one hand and deeply mangling the other.

With a yell of agony, Mr. Ellis let go his hold, and fell upon a pile of rubbish below, whilst a cry of triumphant malignity went up from the crowd on the roof.

A gentleman and some of his friends kindly carried the insensible man into his house. "Poor fellow!" said he, "he is killed, I believe. What a gang of wretches. These things are dreadful; that such a thing can be permitted in a Christian city is perfectly appalling." The half-dressed family gathered around the mangled form of Mr. Ellis, and gave vent to loud expressions of sympathy. A doctor was quickly sent for, who stanched the blood that was flowing from his hands and head.

"I don't think he can live," said he, "the fall was too great. As far as I can judge, his legs and two of his ribs are broken. The best thing we can do, is to get him conveyed to the hospital; look in his pockets, perhaps we can find out who he is."

There was nothing found, however, that afforded the least clue to his name and residence; and he was, therefore, as soon as persons could be procured to assist, borne to the hospital, where his wounds were dressed, and the broken limbs set.

CHAPTER XXI.

More Horrors.

UNAWARE of the impending danger, Mr. Garie sat watching by the bedside of his wife. She had been quite ill; but on the evening of which we write, although nervous and wakeful, was much better. The bleak winds of the fast approaching winter dealt unkindly with her delicate frame, accustomed as she was to the soft breezes of her Southern home.

Mr. Garie had been sitting up looking at the fires in the lower part of the city. Not having been out all that day or the one previous, he knew nothing of the fearful state into which matters had fallen.

"Those lights are dying away, my dear," said he to his wife; "there must have been quite an extensive conflagration." Taking out his watch, he continued, "almost two o'clock; why, how late I've been sitting up. I really don't know whether it's worth while to go to bed or not, I should be obliged to get up again at five o'clock; I go to New York to-morrow, or rather to-day; there are some matters connected with Uncle John's will that require my personal attention. Dear old man, how suddenly he died."

"I wish, dear, you could put off your journey until I am better," said Mrs. Garie, faintly; "I do hate you to go just now."

"I would if I could, Emily; but it is impossible. I shall be back to-morrow, or the next day, at farthest. Whilst I'm there, I'll—"

"Hush!" interrupted Mrs. Garie, "stop a moment. Don't you hear a noise like the shouting of a great many people."

"Oh, it's only the firemen," replied he; "as I was about to observe—"

"Hush!" cried she again. "Listen now, that don't sound like the firemen in the least." Mr. Garie paused as the sound of a number of voices became more distinct.

Wrapping his dressing-gown more closely about him, he walked into the front room, which overlooked the street. Opening the window, he saw a number of men—some bearing torches— coming rapidly in the direction of his dwelling. "I wonder what all this is for; what can it mean," he exclaimed.

They had now approached sufficiently near for him to under-stand their cries. "Down with the Abolitionist—down with the Amalgamationist! give them tar and feathers!"

"It's a mob—and that word Amalgamationist—can it be pointed at me? It hardly seems possible; and yet I have a fear that there is something wrong."

"What is it, Garie? What is the matter?" asked his wife, who, with a shawl hastily thrown across her shoulders, was standing pale and trembling by the window.

"Go in, Emily, my dear, for Heaven's sake; you'll get your death of cold in this bleak night air—go in; as soon as I discover the occasion of the disturbance, I'll come and tell you. Pray go in." Mrs. Garie retired a few feet from the window, and stood listening to the shouts in the street.

The rioters, led on evidently by some one who knew what he was about, pressed forward to Mr. Garie's house; and soon the garden in front was filled with the shouting crowd.

"What do you all want—why are you on my premises, creating this disturbance?" cried Mr. Garie.

"Come down and you'll soon find out. You white-livered Abolitionist, come out, damn you! we are going to give you a coat of tar and feathers, and your black wench nine-and-thirty.[1] Yes, come down—come down!" shouted several, "or we will come up after you."

"I warn you," replied Mr. Garie, "against any attempt at violence upon my person, family, or property. I forbid you to advance another foot upon the premises. If any man of you enters my house, I'll shoot him down as quick as I would a mad dog."

"Shut up your gap; none of your cussed speeches," said a voice in the crowd; "if you don't come down and give yourself up, we'll come in and take you—that's the talk, ain't it, boys?" A general shout of approval answered this speech, and several stones were thrown at Mr. Garie, one of which struck him on the breast.

Seeing the utter futility of attempting to parley with the infuriated wretches below, he ran into the room, exclaiming, "Put on some clothes, Emily! shoes first—quick—quick, wife!—your life depends upon it. I'll bring down the children and wake the servants. We must escape from the house—we are attacked by a mob of demons. Hurry, Emily! do, for God sake!"

Mr. Garie aroused the sleeping children, and threw some clothes upon them, over which he wrapped shawls or blankets, or

---

1 I.e., 39 lashes. In the Jewish tradition, forty lashes were considered the maximum penalty for any offense (Deuteronomy 25.3). Because doling out too many lashes was held to be sinful, general practice meant that those doing so would stop at 39.

whatever came to hand. Rushing into the next room, he snatched a pair of loaded pistols from the drawer of his dressing-stand, and then hurried his terrified wife and children down the stairs.

"This way, dear—this way!" he cried, leading on toward the back door; "out that way through the gate with the children, and into some of the neighbour's houses. I'll stand here to keep the way."

"No, no, Garie," she replied, frantically; "I won't go without you."

"You must!" he cried, stamping his foot impatiently; "this is no time to parley—go, or we shall all be murdered. Listen, they've broken in the door. Quick—quick! go on;" and as he spoke, he pressed her and the children out of the door, and closed it behind them.

Mrs. Garie ran down the garden, followed by the children; to her horror, she found the gate locked, and the key nowhere to be found.

"What shall we do?" she cried. "Oh, we shall all be killed!" and her limbs trembled beneath her with cold and terror.

"Let us hide in here, mother," suggested Clarence, running toward the wood-house; "we'll be safe in there." Seeing that nothing better could be done, Mrs. Garie availed herself of the suggestion; and when she was fairly inside the place, fell fainting upon the ground.

As she escaped through the back door, the mob broke in at the front, and were confronting Mr. Garie, as he stood with his pistol pointed at them, prepared to fire.

"Come another step forward and I fire!" exclaimed he, resolutely; but those in the rear urged the advance of those in front, who approached cautiously nearer and nearer their victim. Fearful of opening the door behind him, lest he should show the way taken by his retreating wife, he stood uncertain how to act; a severe blow from a stone, however, made him lose all reflection, and he immediately fired. A loud shriek followed the report of his pistol, and a shower of stones was immediately hurled upon him.

He quickly fired again, and was endeavouring to open the door to effect his escape, when a pistol was discharged close to his head and he fell forward on the entry floor lifeless.

All this transpired in a few moments, and in the semi-darkness of the entry. Rushing forward over his lifeless form, the villains hastened upstairs in search of Mrs. Garie. They ran shouting through the house, stealing everything valuable that they could lay their hands upon, and wantonly destroying the furniture; they would have fired the house, but were prevented by McCloskey, who acted as leader of the gang.

For two long hours they ransacked the house, breaking all they could not carry off, drinking the wine in Mr. Garie's cellar, and shouting and screaming like so many fiends.

Mrs. Garie and the children lay crouching with terror in the wood-house, listening to the ruffians as they went through the yard cursing her and her husband and uttering the direst threats of what they would do should she fall into their hands. Once she almost fainted on hearing one of them propose opening the wood-house, to see if there was anything of value in it—but breathed again when they abandoned it as not worth their attention.

The children crouched down beside her—scarcely daring to whisper, lest they should attract the attention of their persecutors. Shivering with cold they drew closer around them the blanket with which they had been providentially provided.

"Brother, my feet are *so* cold," sobbed little Em. "I can't feel my toes. Oh, I'm so cold!"

"Put your feet closer to me, sissy," answered her brother, baring himself to enwrap her more thoroughly; "put my stockings on over yours;" and, as well as they were able in the dark, he drew his stockings on over her benumbed feet. "There, sis, that's better," he whispered, with an attempt at cheerfulness, "now you'll be warmer."

Just then Clarence heard a groan from his mother, so loud indeed that it would have been heard without but for the noise and excitement around the house—and feeling for her in the dark, he asked, "Mother, are you worse? are you sick?"

A groan was her only answer.

"Mother, mother," he whispered, "do speak, please do!" and he endeavoured to put his arm around her.

"Don't, dear—don't," said she, faintly, "just take care of your sister—you can't do me any good—don't speak, dear, the men will hear you."

Reluctantly the frightened child turned his attention again to his little sister; ever and anon suppressed groans from his mother would reach his ears—at last he heard a groan even fierce in its intensity; and then the sounds grew fainter and fainter until they entirely ceased. The night to the poor shivering creatures in their hiding place seemed interminably long, and the sound of voices in the house had not long ceased when the faint light of day pierced their cheerless shelter.

Hearing the voices of some neighbours in the yard, Clarence hastened out, and seizing one of the ladies by the dress, cried imploringly, "Do come to my mother, she's sick."

"Why, where did you come from, child?" said the lady, with a start of astonishment. "Where have you been?"

"In there," he answered, pointing to the wood-house. "Mother and sister are in there."

The lady, accompanied by one or two others, hastened to the wood-house.

"Where is she?" asked the foremost, for in the gloom of the place she could not perceive anything.

"Here," replied Clarence, "she's lying here." On opening a small window, they saw Mrs. Garie lying in a corner stretched upon the boards, her head supported by some blocks. "She's asleep," said Clarence. "Mother—mother," but there came no answer. "MOTHER," said he, still louder, but yet there was no response.

Stepping forward, one of the females opened the shawl, which was held firmly in the clenched hands of Mrs. Garie—and there in her lap partially covered by her scanty nightdress, was discovered a new-born babe, who with its mother had journeyed in the darkness, cold, and night, to the better land, that they might pour out their woes upon the bosom of their Creator.

The women gazed in mournful silence on the touching scene before them. Clarence was on his knees, regarding with fear and wonder the unnatural stillness of his mother—the child had never before looked on death, and could not recognize its presence. Laying his hand on her cold cheek, he cried, with faltering voice, "Mother, *can't* you speak?" but there was no answering light in the fixed stare of those glassy eyes, and the lips of the dead could not move. "Why don't she speak?" he asked.

"She can't, my dear; you must come away and leave her. She's better off, my darling—she's *dead*."

Then there was a cry of grief sprung up from the heart of that orphan boy, that rang in those women's ears for long years after; it was the first outbreak of a loving childish heart pierced with life's bitterest grief—a mother's loss.

The two children were kindly taken into the house of some benevolent neighbour, as the servants had all fled none knew whither. Little Em was in a profound stupor—the result of cold and terror, and it was found necessary to place her under the care of a physician.

After they had all gone, an inquest was held by the coroner, and a very unsatisfactory and untruthful verdict pronounced— one that did not at all coincide with the circumstances of the case, but such a one as might have been expected where there was a great desire to screen the affair from public scrutiny.

CHAPTER XXII.

An Anxious Day.

ESTHER ELLIS, devoured with anxiety respecting the safety of her father and the Garies, paced with impatient step up and down the drawing-room. Opening the window, she looked to see if she could discover any signs of day. "It's pitchy dark," she exclaimed, "and yet almost five o'clock. Father has run a fearful risk. I hope nothing has happened to him."

"I trust not. I think he's safe enough somewhere," said Mr. Walters. "He's no doubt been very cautious, and avoided meeting any one—don't worry yourself, my child, 'tis most likely he remained with them wherever they went; probably they are at the house of some of their neighbours."

"I can't help feeling dreadfully oppressed and anxious," continued she. "I wish he would come."

Whilst she was speaking, her mother entered the room. "Any news of your father?" she asked, in a tone of anxiety.

Esther endeavoured to conceal her own apprehensions, and rejoined, in as cheerful tone as she could assume—"Not yet, mother—it's too dark for us to expect him yet—he'll remain most likely until daylight."

"He shouldn't have gone had I been here—he's no business to expose himself in this way."

"But, mother," interrupted Esther, "only think of it—the safety of Emily and the children were depending on it—we mustn't be selfish."

"I know we oughtn't to be, my child," rejoined her mother, "but it's natural to the best of us—sometimes we can't help it."

Five—six—seven o'clock came and passed, and still there were no tidings of Mr. Ellis.

"I can bear this suspense no longer," exclaimed Esther. "If father don't come soon, I shall go and look for him. I've tried to flatter myself that he's safe; but I'm almost convinced now that something has happened to him, or he'd have come back long before this—he knows how anxious we would all be about him. I've tried to quiet mother and Caddy by suggesting various reasons for his delay, but, at the same time, I cannot but cherish the most dismal forebodings. I must go and look for him."

"No, no, Esther—stay where you are at present—leave that to me. I'll order a carriage and go up to Garie's immediately."

"Well, do, Mr. Walters, and hurry back: won't you?" she rejoined, as he left the apartment.

In a few moments he returned, prepared to start, and was speedily driven to Winter-street. He found a group of people gathered before the gate, gazing into the house. "The place has been attacked," said he, as he walked towards the front door—picking his way amidst fragments of furniture, straw, and broken glass. At the entrance of the house he was met by Mr. Balch, Mr. Garie's lawyer.

"This is a shocking affair, Walters," said he, extending his hand—he was an old friend of Mr. Walters.

"Very shocking, indeed," he replied, looking around. "But where is Garie? We sent to warn them of this. I hope they are all safe."

"Safe!" repeated Mr. Balch, with an air of astonishment. "Why, man, haven't you heard?"

"Heard what?" asked Mr. Walters, looking alarmed.

"That Mr. and Mrs. Garie are dead—both were killed last night."

The shock of this sudden and totally unexpected disclosure was such that Mr. Walters leaned against the doorway for support. "It can't be possible," he exclaimed at last, "not dead!"

"Yes, *dead*, I regret to say—he was shot through the head—and she died in the wood-house, of premature confinement, brought on by fright and exposure."[1]

"And the children?" gasped Walters.

"They are safe, with some neighbours—it's heart-breaking to hear them weeping for their mother." Here a tear glistened in the eye of Mr. Balch, and ran down his cheek. Brushing it off, he continued: "The coroner has just held an inquest, and they gave a most truthless verdict: nothing whatever is said of the cause of the murder, or of the murderers; they simply rendered a verdict—death caused by a wound from a pistol-shot, and hers—death from exposure. There seemed the greatest anxiety on the part of the coroner to get the matter over as quickly as possible, and few or no witnesses were examined. But I'm determined to sift the matter to the bottom; if the perpetrators of the murder can be discovered, I'll leave no means untried to find them."

"Do you know any one who sat on the inquest?" asked Walters.

---

1   I.e., Mrs. Garie has died from complications associated with the premature delivery of her child.

"Yes, one," was the reply, "Slippery George, the lawyer; you are acquainted with him—George Stevens. I find he resides next door."

"Do you know," here interrupted Mr. Walters, "that I've my suspicions that that villain is at the bottom of these disturbances, or at least has a large share in them. I have a paper in my possession, in his handwriting—it is in fact a list of the places destroyed by the mob last night—it fell into the hands of a friend of mine by accident—he gave it to me—it put me on my guard; and when the villains attacked my house last night they got rather a warmer reception than they bargained for."

"You astonish me! Is it possible your place was assaulted also?" asked Mr. Balch.

"Indeed, it was—and a hot battle we had of it for a short space of time. But how did you hear of this affair?"

"I was sent for by I can't tell whom. When I came and saw what had happened, I immediately set about searching for a will that I made for Mr. Garie a few weeks since; it was witnessed and signed at my office, and he brought it away with him. I can't discover it anywhere. I've ransacked every cranny. It must have been carried off by some one. You are named in it conjointly with myself as executor. All the property is left to her, poor thing, and his children. We must endeavour to find it somewhere—at any rate the children are secure; they are the only heirs—he had not, to my knowledge, a single white relative. But let us go in and see the bodies."

They walked together into the back room where the bodies were lying. Mrs. Garie was stretched upon the sofa, covered with a piano cloth; and her husband was laid upon a long table, with a silk window-curtain thrown across his face.

The two gazed in silence on the face of Mr. Garie—the brow was still knit, the eyes staring vacantly, and the marble whiteness of the face unbroken, save by a few gouts of blood near a small blue spot over the eye where the bullet had entered.

"He was the best-hearted creature in the world," said Walters, as he re-covered the face.

"Won't you look at her?" asked Mr. Balch.

"No, no—I can't," continued Walters; "I've seen horrors enough for one morning. I've another thing on my mind! A friend who assisted in the defence of my house started up here last night, to warn them of their danger, and when I left home he had not returned: it's evident he hasn't been here, and I greatly fear some misfortune has befallen him. Where are the children? Poor little orphans, I must see them before I go."

Accompanied by Mr. Balch, he called at the house where Clarence and Em had found temporary shelter. The children ran to him as soon as he entered the room. "Oh! Mr. Walters," sobbed Clarence, "my mother's dead—my mother's dead!"

"Hush, dears—hush!" he replied, endeavouring to restrain his own tears, as he took little Em in his arms. "Don't cry, my darling," said he, as she gave vent to a fresh outburst of tears.

"Oh, Mr. Walters!" said she, still sobbing, "*she was all the mother I had.*"

Mr. Balch here endeavoured to assist in pacifying the two little mourners.

"Why don't father come?" asked Clarence. "Have you seen him, Mr. Walters?"

Mr. Walters was quite taken aback by this inquiry, which clearly showed that the children were still unaware of the extent of their misfortunes. "I've seen him, my child," said he, evasively; "you'll see him before long." And fearful of further questioning, he left the house, promising soon to return.

Unable longer to endure her anxiety respecting her father, Esther determined not to await the return of Mr. Walters, which had already been greatly delayed, but to go herself in search of him. It had occurred to her that, instead of returning from the Garies direct to them, he had probably gone to his own home to see if it had been disturbed during the night.

Encouraged by this idea, without consulting any one, she hastily put on her cloak and bonnet, and took the direction of her home. Numbers of people were wending their way to the lower part of the city, to gratify their curiosity by gazing upon the havoc made by the rioters during the past night.

Esther found her home a heap of smoking ruins; some of the neighbours who recognized her gathered round, expressing their sympathy and regret. But she seemed comparatively careless respecting the loss of their property; and in answer to their kind expressions, could only ask, "Have you seen my father?—do you know where my father is?"

None, however, had seen him; and after gazing for a short time upon the ruins of what was once a happy home, she turned mournfully away, and walked back to Mr. Walters's.

"Has father come?" she inquired, as soon as the door was opened.

"Not yet!" was the discouraging reply: "and Mr. Walters, he hasn't come back, either, miss!"

Esther stood for some moments hesitating whether to go in, or to proceed in her search. The voice of her mother calling her from the stairway decided her, and she went in.

Mrs. Ellis and Caddy wept freely on learning from Esther the destruction of their home. This cause of grief, added to the anxiety produced by the prolonged absence of Mr. Ellis, rendered them truly miserable.

Whilst they were condoling with one another, Mr. Walters returned. He was unable to conceal his fears that something had happened to Mr. Ellis, and frankly told them so; he also gave a detailed account of what had befallen the Garies, to the great horror and grief of all.

As soon as arrangements could be made, Mr. Walters and Esther set out in search of her father. All day long they went from place to place, but gained no tidings of him; and weary and disheartened they returned at night, bringing with them the distressing intelligence of their utter failure to procure any information respecting him.

CHAPTER XXIII.

The Lost One Found.

ON the day succeeding the events described in our last chapter, Mr. Walters called upon Mr. Balch, for the purpose of making the necessary preparations for the interment of Mr. and Mrs. Garie.

"I think," said Mr. Balch, "we had better bury them in the Ash-grove cemetery; it's a lovely spot—all my people are buried there."

"The place is fine enough, I acknowledge," rejoined Mr. Walters; "but I much doubt if you can procure the necessary ground."

"Oh, yes, you can!" said Mr. Balch; "there are a number of lots still unappropriated."

"That may very likely be so; but are you sure we can get one if we apply?"

"Of course we can—what is to prevent?" asked Mr. Balch.

"You forget," replied Mr. Walters, "that Mrs. Garie was a coloured woman."

"If it wasn't such a solemn subject I really should be obliged to laugh at you, Walters," rejoined Mr. Balch, with a smile—"you talk ridiculously. What can her complexion have to do with her being buried there, I should like to know?"

"It has everything to do with it! Can it be possible you are not aware that they won't even permit a coloured person to walk through the ground, much less to be buried there!"

"You astonish me, Walters! Are you sure of it?"

"I give you my word of honour it is so! But why should you be astonished at such treatment of the dead, when you see how they conduct themselves towards the living? I have a friend," continued Mr. Walters, "who purchased a pew for himself and family in a white-church, and the deacons actually removed the floor from under it, to prevent his sitting there. They refuse us permission to kneel by the side of the white communicants at the Lord's Supper, and give us separate pews in obscure corners of their churches. All this you know—why, then, be surprised that they carry their prejudices into their graveyards?—the conduct is all of a piece."

"Well, Walters, I know the way things are conducted in our churches is exceedingly reprehensible; but I really did not know they stretched their prejudices to such an extent."

"I assure you they do, then," resumed Mr. Walters; "and in this very matter you'll find I'm correct. Ask Stormley, the undertaker, and hear what he'll tell you. Oh! a case in point.—About six months ago, one of our wealthiest citizens lost by death an old family servant, a coloured woman, a sort of half-housekeeper— half-friend. She resembled him so much, that it was generally believed she was his sister. Well, he tried to have her laid in their family vault, and it was refused; the directors thought it would be creating a bad precedent—they said, as they would not sell lots to coloured persons, they couldn't consistently permit them to be buried in those of the whites."

"Then Ash-grove must be abandoned; and in lieu of that what can you propose?" asked Mr. Balch.

"I should say we can't do better than lay them in the graveyard of the coloured Episcopal church."

"Let it be there, then. You will see to the arrangements, Walters. I shall have enough on my hands for the present, searching for that will: I have already offered a large reward for it—I trust it may turn up yet."

"Perhaps it may," rejoined Mr. Walters; "we must hope so, at least. I've brought the children to my house, where they are under the care of a young lady who was a great friend of their mother's; though it seems like putting too much upon the poor young creature, to throw them upon her for consolation, when she is almost distracted with her own griefs. I think I mentioned to you yesterday, that her father is missing; and, to add to their anxieties, their property has been all destroyed by the rioters. They have a home with me for the present, and may remain there as long as they please."

"Oh! I remember you told me something of them yesterday; and now I come to think of it, I saw in the Journal this morning, that a coloured man was lying at the hospital very much injured, whose name they could not ascertain. Can it be possible that he is the man you are in search of?"

"Let me see the article," asked Mr. Walters. Mr. Balch handed him the paper, and pointed out the paragraph in question.

"I'll go immediately to the hospital," said he, as he finished reading, "and see if it is my poor friend; I have great fears that it is. You'll excuse my leaving so abruptly—I must be off immediately."

On hastening to the hospital, Mr. Walters arrived just in time to be admitted to the wards; and on being shown the person whose name they had been unable to discover, he immediately recognized his friend.

"Ellis, my poor fellow," he exclaimed, springing forward.

"Stop, stop," cried the attendant, laying his hand upon Mr. Walters's shoulder; "he is hovering between life and death, the least agitation might be fatal to him. The doctor says, if he survives the night, he may probably get better; but he has small chance of life. I hardly think he will last twelve hours more, he's been dreadfully beaten; there are two or three gashes on his head, his leg is broken, and his hands have been so much cut, that the surgeon thinks they'll never be of any use to him, even if he recovers."

"What awful intelligence for his family!" said Mr. Walters; "they are already half distracted about him."

Mr. Ellis lay perfectly unconscious of what was passing around him, and his moans were deeply affecting to hear, unable to move but one limb—he was the picture of helplessness and misery.

"It's time to close; we don't permit visitors to remain after this hour," said the attendant; "come to-morrow, you can see your friend, and remain longer with him;" and bidding Mr. Walters good morning, he ushered him from the ward.

"How shall I ever find means to break this to the girls and their mother?" said he, as he left the gates of the hospital; "it will almost kill them; really I don't know what I shall say to them."

He walked homeward with hesitating steps, and on arriving at his house, he paused awhile before the door, mustering up courage to enter; at last he opened it with the air of a man who had a disagreeable duty to perform, and had made up his mind to go through with it. "Tell Miss Ellis to come to the drawing-room," said he to the servant; "merely say she's wanted—don't say I've returned."

He waited but a few moments before Esther made her appearance, looking sad and anxious. "Oh, it's you," she said, with some surprise. "You have news of father?"

"Yes, Esther, I have news; but I am sorry to say not of a pleasant character."

"Oh, Mr. Walters, nothing serious I hope has happened to him?" she asked, in an agitated tone.

"I'm sorry to say there has, Esther; he has met with an accident—a sad and severe one—he's been badly wounded." Esther turned deadly pale at this announcement, and leaned upon the table for support.

"I sent for you, Esther," continued Mr. Walters, "in preference to your mother, because I knew you to be courageous in danger, and I trusted you would be equally so in misfortune. Your father's case is a very critical one—very. It appears that after leaving here, he fell into the hands of the rioters, by whom he was shockingly beaten. He was taken to the hospital, where he now remains."

"Oh, let me go to him at once, do, Mr. Walters!"

"My dear child, it is impossible for you to see him to-day, it is long past the visiting hour; moreover, I don't think him in a state that would permit the least agitation. To-morrow you can go with me."

Esther did not weep, her heart was too full for tears. With a pale face, and trembling lips, she said to Mr. Walters, "God give us strength to bear up under these misfortunes; we are homeless—almost beggars—our friends have been murdered, and my father is now trembling on the brink of the grave; such troubles as these," said she, sinking into a chair, "are enough to crush any one."

"I know it, Esther; I know it, my child. I sympathize with you deeply. All that I have is at your disposal. You may command me in anything. Give yourself no uneasiness respecting the future of your mother and family, let the result to your father be what it may: always bear in mind that, next to God, I am your best friend. I speak thus frankly to you, Esther, because I would not have you cherish any hopes of your father's recovery; from his appearance, I should say there is but little, if any. I leave to you, my good girl, the task of breaking this sad news to your mother and sister; I would tell them, but I must confess, Esther, I'm not equal to it, the events of the last day or two have almost overpowered me."

Esther's lips quivered again, as she repeated the words, "Little hope; did the doctor say that?" she asked.

"I did not see the doctor," replied he; "perhaps there may be a favourable change during the night. I'd have you prepare for the worst, whilst you hope for the best. Go now and try to break it as gently as possible to your mother."

Esther left the room with heavy step, and walked to the chamber where her mother was sitting. Caddy also was there, rocking backwards and forwards in a chair, in an earnest endeavour to soothe to sleep little Em, who was sitting in her lap.

"Who was it, Esther?" asked her mother.

"Mr. Walters," she hesitatingly answered.

"Was it? Well, has he heard anything of your father?" she asked, anxiously.

Esther turned away her head, and remained silent.

"Why don't you answer?" asked her mother, with an alarmed look; "if you know anything of him, for God's sake tell me. Whatever it may be, it can't be worse than I expect; is he dead?" she asked.

"No—no, mother, he's not dead; but he's sick, very sick, mother. Mr. Walters found him in the hospital."

"In the hospital! how came he there? Don't deceive me, Esther, there's something behind all this; are you telling me the truth? is he still alive?"

"Mother, believe me, he is still alive, but how long he may remain so, God only knows." Mrs. Ellis, at this communication, leant her head upon the table, and wept uncontrollably. Caddy put down her little charge, and stood beside her mother, endeavouring to soothe her, whilst unable to restrain her own grief.

"Let us go to him, Esther," said her mother, rising; "I must see him—let us go at once."

"We can't, mother; Mr. Walters says it's impossible for us to see him to-day; they don't admit visitors after a certain hour in the morning."

"They *must* admit me: I'll tell them I'm his wife; when they know that, they *can't* refuse me." Quickly dressing themselves, Esther, Caddy, and their mother were about to start for the hospital, when Mr. Walters entered.

"Where are you all going?" he asked.

"To the hospital," answered Mrs. Ellis; "I must see my husband."

"I have just sent there, Ellen, to make arrangements to hear of him every hour. You will only have the grief of being refused admission if you go; they're exceedingly strict—no one is admitted to visit a patient after a certain hour; try and compose yourselves; sit down, I want to talk to you for a little while."

Mrs. Ellis mechanically obeyed; and on sitting down, little Em crept into her lap, and nestled in her arms.

"Ellen," said Mr. Walters, taking a seat by her; "it's useless to disguise the fact that Ellis is in a precarious situation—how long he may be sick it is impossible to say; as soon as it is practicable, should he get better, we will bring him here. You remember, Ellen, that years ago, when I was young and poor, Ellis often befriended me—now 'tis my turn. You must all make up your minds to remain with me—for ever, if you like—for the present, whether you like it or not. I'm going to be dreadfully obstinate, and have my own way completely about the matter. Here I've a large house, furnished from top to bottom with every comfort. Often I've wandered through it, and thought myself a selfish old fellow to be surrounded with so much luxury, and keep it entirely to myself. God has blessed me with abundance, and to what better use can it be appropriated than the relief of my friends? Now, Ellen, you shall superintend the whole of the establishment, Esther shall nurse her father, Caddy shall stir up the servants, and I'll look on and find my happiness in seeing you all happy. Now, what objection can you urge against that arrangement?" concluded he, triumphantly.

"Why, we shall put you to great inconvenience, and place ourselves under an obligation we can never repay," answered Mrs. Ellis.

"Don't despair of that—never mind the obligation; try and be as cheerful as you can; to-morrow we shall see Ellis, and perhaps find him better; let us at least hope for the best."

Esther looked with grateful admiration at Mr. Walters, as he left the room. "What a good heart he has, mother," said she, as he closed the door behind him; "just such a great tender heart as one should expect to find in so fine a form."

Mrs. Ellis and her daughters were the first who were found next day, at the office of the doorkeeper of the hospital waiting an opportunity to see their sick friends.

"You're early, ma'am," said a little bald-headed official, who sat at his desk fronting the door; "take a chair near the fire—it's dreadful cold this morning."

"Very cold," replied Esther, taking a seat beside her mother; "how long will it be before we can go in?"

"Oh, you've good an hour to wait—the doctor hasn't come yet," replied the door-keeper.

"How is my husband?" tremblingly inquired Mrs. Ellis.

"Who is your husband?—you don't know his number, do you? Never know names here—go by numbers."

"We don't know the number," rejoined Esther; "my father's name is Ellis; he was brought here two or three nights since—he was beaten by the mob."

"Oh, yes; I know now who you mean—number sixty—bad case that, shocking bad case—hands chopped—head smashed—leg broke; he'll have to cross over, I guess—make a die of it, I'm afraid."

Mrs. Ellis shuddered, and turned pale, as the man coolly discussed her husband's injuries, and their probable fatal termination. Caddy, observing her agitation, said, "Please, sir, don't talk of it; mother can't bear it."

The man looked at them compassionately for a few moments—then continued: "You mustn't think me hard-hearted—I see so much of these things, that I can't feel them as others do. This is a dreadful thing to you, no doubt, but it's an every-day song to me—people are always coming here mangled in all sorts of ways—so, you see, I've got used to it—in fact, I'd rather miss 'em now if they didn't come. I've sat in this seat every day for almost twenty years;" and he looked on the girls and their mother as he gave them this piece of information as if he thought they ought to regard him henceforth with great reverence.

Not finding them disposed to converse, the doorkeeper resumed the newspaper he was reading when they entered, and was soon deeply engrossed in a horrible steam-boat accident.

The sound of wheels in the courtyard attracting his attention, he looked up, and remarked: "Here's the doctor—as soon as he has walked the wards you'll be admitted."

Mrs. Ellis and her daughters turned round as the door opened, and, to their great joy, recognized Doctor Burdett.

"How d'ye do?" said he, extending his hand to Mrs. Ellis— "what's the matter? Crying!" he continued, looking at their tearful faces; "what has happened?"

"Oh, doctor," said Esther, "father's lying here, very much injured; and they think he'll die," said she, giving way to a fresh burst of grief.

"Very much injured—die—how is this?—I knew nothing of it—I haven't been here before this week."

Esther hereupon briefly related the misfortunes that had befallen her father.

"Dear me—dear me," repeated the kind old doctor. "There, my dear; don't fret—he'll get better, my child—I'll take him in hand at once. My dear Mrs. Ellis, weeping won't do the least good, and only make you sick yourself. Stop, do now—I'll go and see him immediately, and as soon as possible you shall be admitted."

They had not long to wait before a message came from Doctor Burdett, informing them that they could now be permitted to see the sufferer.

"You must control yourselves," said the doctor to the sobbing women, as he met them at the door; "you mustn't do anything to agitate him—his situation is extremely critical."

The girls and their mother followed him to the bedside of Mr. Ellis, who, ghastly pale, lay before them, apparently unconscious.

Mrs. Ellis gave but one look at her husband, and, with a faint cry, sank fainting upon the floor. The noise partially aroused him; he turned his head, and, after an apparent effort, recognized his daughters standing beside him: he made a feeble attempt to raise his mutilated hands, and murmured faintly, "You've come at last!" then closing his eyes, he dropped his arms, as if exhausted by the effort.

Esther knelt beside him, and pressed a kiss on his pale face. "Father!—father!" said she, softly. He opened his eyes again, and a smile of pleasure broke over his wan face, and lighted up his eyes, as he feebly said, "God bless you, darlings! I thought you'd never come. Where's mother and Caddy?"

"Here," answered Esther, "here, by me; your looks frightened her so, that she's fainted."

Doctor Burdett here interposed, and said: "You must all go now; he's too weak to bear more at present."

"Let me stay with him a little longer," pleaded Esther.

"No, my child, it's impossible," he continued; "besides, your mother will need your attention;" and, whilst he spoke, he led her into an adjoining room, where the others had preceded her.

CHAPTER XXIV.

Charlie distinguishes Himself.

CHARLIE had now been many weeks under the hospitable roof of Mrs. Bird, improving in health and appearance. Indeed, it would have been a wonder if he had not, as the kind mistress of the mansion seemed to do nought else, from day to day, but study plans for his comfort and pleasure. There was one sad drawback upon the contentment of the dear old lady, and that was her inability to procure Charlie's admission to the academy.

One morning Mr. Whately called upon her, and, throwing himself into a chair, exclaimed: "It's all to no purpose; their laws are as unalterable as those of the Medes and Persians[1]—arguments and entreaty are equally thrown away upon them; I've been closeted at least half a dozen times with each director; and as all I can say won't make your *protégé* a shade whiter, I'm afraid his admission to the academy must be given up."

"It's too bad," rejoined Mrs. Bird. "And who, may I ask, were the principal opposers?"

"They all opposed it, except Mr. Weeks and Mr. Bentham."

"Indeed!—why they are the very ones that I anticipated would go against it tooth and nail. And Mr. Glentworth—surely he was on our side?"

"He!—why, my dear madam, he was the most rabid of the lot. With his sanctified face and canting tongue!

"I'm almost ashamed to own it—but it's the truth, and I shouldn't hesitate to tell it—I found the most pious of the directors the least accessible; as to old Glentworth, he actually talked to me as if I was recommending the committal of some horrid sin. I'm afraid I shall be set down by him as a rabid Abolitionist, I got so warm on the subject. I've cherished as strong prejudices against coloured people as any one; but I tell you, seeing how contemptible it makes others appear, has gone a great way towards eradicating it in me. I found myself obliged to use the same arguments against it that are used by the Abolitionists, and in endeavouring to convince others of the absurdity of their prejudices, I convinced myself."

"I'd set my heart upon it," said Mrs. Bird, in a tone of regret; "but I suppose I'll have to give it up. Charlie didn't know I've

---

1   Daniel 6:8: "according to the law of the Medes and Persians, which altereth not."

made application for his admission, and has been asking me to let him go. A great many of the boys who attend there have become acquainted with him, and it was only yesterday that Mr. Glentworth's sons were teasing me to consent to his beginning there the next term. The boys," concluded she, "have better hearts than their parents."

"Oh, I begin to believe it's all sham, this prejudice; I'm getting quite disgusted with myself for having had it—or rather thinking I had it. As for saying it is innate, or that there is any natural antipathy to that class, it's all perfect folly; children are not born with it, or why shouldn't they shrink from a black nurse or playmate? It's all bosh," concluded he, indignantly, as he brought his cane down with a rap.

"Charlie's been quite a means of grace to you," laughingly rejoined Mrs. Bird, amused at his vehemence of manner. "Well, I'm going to send him to Sabbath-school next Sunday; and, if there is a rebellion against his admission there, I shall be quite in despair."

It is frequently the case, that we are urged by circumstances to the advocacy of a measure in which we take but little interest, and of the propriety of which we are often very sceptical; but so surely as it is just in itself, in our endeavours to convert others we convince ourselves; and, from lukewarm apologists, we become earnest advocates. This was just Mr. Whately's case: he had begun to canvass for the admission of Charlie with a doubtful sense of its propriety, and in attempting to overcome the groundless prejudices of others, he was convicted of his own.

Happily, in his ease, conviction was followed by conversion, and as he walked home from Mrs. Bird's, he made up his mind that, if they attempted to exclude Charlie from the Sabbath-school, he would give them a piece of his mind, and then resign his superintendency of it.

On arriving at home, he found waiting for him a young lady, who was formerly a member of his class in the Sabbath-school. "I've come," said she, "to consult you about forming an adult class in our school for coloured persons. We have a girl living with us, who would be very glad to attend, and she knows two or three others. I'll willingly take the class myself. I've consulted the pastor and several others, and no one seems to anticipate any objections from the scholars, if we keep them on a separate bench, and do not mix them up with the white children."

"I'm delighted to hear you propose it," answered Mr. Whately, quite overjoyed at the opening it presented, "the plan meets my warmest approval. I decidedly agree with you in the propriety of our making some effort for the elevation and instruction of this hitherto neglected class—any aid I can render—"

"You astonish me," interrupted Miss Cass, "though I must say very agreeably. You were the last person from whom I thought of obtaining any countenance. I did not come to you until armed with the consent of almost all the parties interested, because from you I anticipated considerable opposition," and in her delight, the young girl grasped Mr. Whately's hand, and shook it very heartily.

"Oh, my opinions relative to coloured people have lately undergone considerable modification; in fact," said he, with some little confusion, "quite a thorough revolution. I don't think we have quite done our duty by these people. Well, well, we must make the future atone for the past."

Miss Cass had entered upon her project with all the enthusiasm of youth, and being anxious that her class, "in point of numbers," should make a presentable appearance, had drafted into it no less a person than Aunt Comfort.

Aunt Comfort was a personage of great importance in the little village of Warmouth, and one whose services were called into requisition on almost every great domestic occasion.

At births she frequently officiated, and few young mothers thought themselves entirely safe if the black good-humoured face of Aunt Comfort was not to be seen at their bedside. She had a hand in the compounding of almost every bridecake,[1] and had been known to often leave houses of feasting, to prepare weary earth-worn travellers for their final place of rest. Every one knew, and all liked her, and no one was more welcome at the houses of the good people of Warmouth than Aunt Comfort.

But whilst rendering her all due praise for her domestic acquirements, justice compels us to remark that Aunt Comfort was not a literary character. She could get up a shirt to perfection, and made irreproachable chowder, but she was not a woman of letters. In fact, she had arrived at maturity at a time when negroes and books seldom came in familiar contact; and if the truth must be told, she cared very little about the latter. "But jist to 'blege Miss Cass," she consented to attend her class, averring as she did so, "that she didn't 'spect she was gwine to larn nothin' when she got thar."

Miss Cass, however, was of the contrary opinion, and anticipated that after a few Sabbaths, Aunt Comfort would prove to be

---

1 Wedding cake.

quite a literary phenomenon. The first time their class assembled the white children well-nigh dislocated their necks, in their endeavours to catch glimpses of the coloured scholars, who were seated on a backless bench, in an obscure corner of the room.

Prominent amongst them shone Aunt Comfort, who in honour of this extraordinary occasion, had retrimmed her cap, which was resplendent with bows of red ribbon as large as peonies. She had a Sunday-school primer in her hand, and was repeating the letters with the utmost regularity, as Miss Cass pronounced them. They got on charmingly until after crossing over the letter O, as a matter of course they came to P and Q.

"Look here," said Aunt Comfort, with a look of profound erudition, "here's anoder O. What's de use of having two of 'em"

"No, no, Aunt Comfort—that's Q—the letter Q."

"Umph," grunted the old woman, incredulously, "what's de use of saying dat's a Q, when you jest said not a minute ago 'twas O?"

"This is not the same," rejoined the teacher, "don't you see the little tail at the bottom of it?"

Aunt Comfort took off her silver spectacles, and gave the glasses of them a furious rub, then after essaying another look, exclaimed, "What, you don't mean dat 'ere little speck down at the bottom of it, does yer?"

"Yes, Aunt Comfort, that little speck, as you call it, makes all the difference—it makes O into Q."

"Oh, go 'way, child," said she, indignantly, "you isn't gwine to fool me dat ar way. I knows you of old, honey—you's up to dese 'ere things—you know you allus was mighty 'chevious, and I isn't gwine to b'lieve dat dat ar little speck makes all the difference— no such thing, case it don't—deys either both O's or both Q's. I'm clar o' dat—deys either one or tother."

Knowing by long experience the utter futility of attempting to convince Aunt Comfort that she was in the wrong, by anything short of a miracle, the teacher wisely skipped over the obnoxious letter, then all went smoothly on to the conclusion of the alphabet.

The lesson having terminated, Miss Cass looked up and discovered standing near her a coloured boy, who she correctly surmised was sent as an addition to her class. "Come here, and sit down," said she, pointing to a seat next Aunt Comfort. "What is your name?"

Charlie gave his name and residence, which were entered in due form on the teacher's book. "Now, Charles," she continued, "do you know your letters?"

"Yes, ma'am," was the answer.

"Can you spell?" she inquired. To this also Charlie gave an affirmative, highly amused at the same time at being asked such a question.

Miss Cass inquired no further into the extent of his acquirements, it never having entered her head that he could do more than spell. So handing him one of the primers, she pointed out a line on which to begin. The spirit of mischief entered our little friend, and he stumbled through b-l-a bla—b-l-i bli—b-l-o blo— b-l-u blu, with great gravity and slowness.

"You spell quite nicely, particularly for a little coloured boy," said Miss Cass, encouragingly, as he concluded the line; "take this next," she continued, pointing to another, "and when you have learned it, I will hear you again."

It was the custom of the superintendent to question the scholars upon a portion of Bible history, given out the Sabbath previous for study during the week. It chanced that upon the day of which we write, the subject for examination was one with which Charlie was quite familiar.

Accordingly, when the questions were put to the school, he answered boldly and quickly to many of them, and with an accuracy that astonished his fellow scholars.

"How did you learn the answers to those questions—you can't read?" said Miss Cass.

"Yes, but I can read," answered Charlie, with a merry twinkle in his eye.

"Why didn't you tell me so before?" she asked.

"Because you didn't ask me," he replied, suppressing a grin.

This was true enough, so Miss Cass, having nothing farther to say, sat and listened, whilst he answered the numerous and sometimes difficult questions addressed to the scholars.

Not so, Aunt Comfort. She could not restrain her admiration of this display of talent on the part of one of her despised race; she was continually breaking out with expressions of wonder and applause. "Jis' hear dat—massy on us—only jis' listen to de chile," said she, "talks jis' de same as if he was white. Why, boy, where you learn all dat?"

"Across the Red Sea," cried Charlie, in answer to a question from the desk of the superintendent.

"'Cross de Red Sea! Umph, chile, you been dere?" asked Aunt Comfort, with a face full of wonder.

"What did you say?" asked Charlie, whose attention had been arrested by the last question.

"Why I asked where you learned all dat 'bout de children of Israel."

"Oh, I learned that at Philadelphia," was his reply; "I learned it at school with the rest of the boys."

"You did!" exclaimed she, raising her hands with astonishment. "Is dere many more of 'em like you?"

Charlie did not hear this last question of Aunt Comfort's, therefore she was rather startled by his replying in a loud tone, "*Immense hosts.*"[1]

"Did I ever—jis' hear dat, dere's ''mense hostes' of 'em jest like him! only think of it. Is dey all dere yet, honey?"

"They were all drowned."

"Oh, Lordy, Lordy," rejoined she, aghast with horror; for Charlie's reply to a question regarding the fate of Pharaoh's army, had been by her interpreted as an answer to her question respecting his coloured schoolmates at Philadelphia.

"And how did you 'scape, honey," continued she, "from drowning 'long wid the rest of 'em?"

"Why I wasn't there, it was thousands of years ago."

"Look here. What do you mean?" she whispered; "didn't you say jest now dat you went to school wid 'em?"

This was too much for Charlie, who shook all over with suppressed laughter; nor was Miss Cass proof against the contagion—she was obliged to almost suffocate herself with her handkerchief to avoid a serious explosion.

"Aunt Comfort, you are mistaking him," said she, as soon as she could recover her composure; "he is answering the questions of the superintendent—not yours, and very well he has answered them, too," continued she. "I like to see little boys aspiring: I am glad to see you so intelligent—you must persevere, Charlie."

"Yes, you must, honey," chimed in Aunt Comfort, "very much like Miss Cass; I likes to see children—'specially children of colour—have *expiring* minds."

Charlie went quite off at this, and it was only by repeated hush—hushes, from Miss Cass, and a pinch in the back from Aunt Comfort, that he was restored to a proper sense of his position.

The questioning being now finished, Mr. Whately came to Charlie, praised him highly for his aptness, and made some inquiries respecting his knowledge of the catechism; also whether

---

1 The scripture lesson is on the escape of the Israelites from Egypt and the drowning of Pharaoh's Army in the Red Sea (Exodus 13–14), but the source of Charlie's quotation remains obscure.

he would be willing to join the class that was to be catechised in the church during the afternoon. To this, Charlie readily assented, and, at the close of the school, was placed at the foot of the class, preparatory to going into the Church.

The public catechizing of the scholars was always an event in the village; but now a novelty was given it, by the addition of a black lamb to the flock, and, as a matter of course, a much greater interest was manifested. Had a lion entered the doors of St. Stephen's church, he might have created greater consternation, but he could not have attracted more attention than did our little friend on passing beneath its sacred portals. The length of the aisle seemed interminable to him, and on his way to the altar he felt oppressed by the scrutiny of eyes through which he was compelled to pass. Mr. Dural, the pastor, looked kindly at him, as he stood in front of the chancel, and Charlie took heart from his cheering smile.

Now, to Aunt Comfort (who was the only coloured person who regularly attended the church) a seat had been assigned beside the organ; which elevated position had been given her that the congregation might indulge in their devotions without having their prejudices shocked by a too close contemplation of her ebony countenance.

But Aunt Comfort, on this occasion, determined to get near enough to hear all that passed, and, leaving her accustomed seat, she planted herself in one of the aisles of the gallery overlooking the altar, where she remained almost speechless with wonder and astonishment at the unprecedented sight of a woolly head at the foot of the altar.

Charlie got on very successfully until called upon to repeat the Lord's Prayer; and, strange to say, at this critical juncture, his memory forsook him, and he was unable to utter a word of it: for the life of him he could not think of anything but "Now I lay me down to sleep"—and confused and annoyed he stood unable to proceed. At this stage of affairs, Aunt Comfort's interest in Charlie's success had reached such a pitch that her customary awe of the place she was in entirely departed, and she exclaimed, "I'll give yer a start—'Our Farrer,'"—then overwhelmed by the consciousness that she had spoken out in meeting, she sank down behind a pew-door, completely extinguished. At this there was an audible titter, that was immediately suppressed; after which, Charlie recovered his memory, and, started by the opportune prompting of Aunt Comfort, he recited it correctly. A few questions more terminated the examination, and the children sat down in front of the altar until the conclusion of the service.

Mrs. Bird, highly delighted with the *début* of her *protégé*, bestowed no end of praises upon him, and even made the coachman walk home, that Charlie might have a seat in the carriage, as she alleged she was sure he must be much fatigued and overcome with the excitement of the day; then taking the reins into her own hands, she drove them safely home.

CHAPTER XXV.

The Heir.

WE must now return to Philadelphia, and pay a visit to the office of Mr. Balch. We shall find that gentleman in company with Mr. Walters: both look anxious, and are poring over a letter which is outspread before them.

"It was like a thunder-clap to me," said Mr. Balch: "the idea of there being another heir never entered my brain—I didn't even know he had a living relative."

"When did you get the letter?" asked Walters.

"Only this morning, and I sent for you immediately! Let us read it again—we'll make another attempt to decipher this incomprehensible name. Confound the fellow! why couldn't he write so that some one besides himself could read it! We must stumble through it," said he, as he again began the letter as follows:—

"Dear Sir,—Immediately on receipt of your favour, I called upon Mr. Thurston, to take the necessary steps for securing the property of your late client. To my great surprise, I found that another claimant had started up, and already taken the preliminary measures to entering upon possession. This gentleman, Mr.—

"Now, what would you call that name, Walters?—to me it looks like Stimmens, or Stunners, or something of the kind!"

"Never mind the name," exclaimed Walters—"skip that—let me hear the rest of the letter; we shall find out who he is soon enough, in all conscience."

"Well, then," resumed Mr. Balch—"This gentleman, Mr. ——, is a resident in your city; and he will, no doubt, take an early opportunity of calling on you, in reference to the matter. It is my opinion, that without a will in their favour, these children cannot oppose his claim successfully, if he can prove his consanguinity to Mr. Garie. His lawyer here showed me a copy of the letters and papers which are to be used as evidence, and, I must say, they *are* *entirely* without flaw. He proves himself, undoubtedly, to be the first cousin of Mr. Garie. You are, no doubt, aware that these children being the offspring of a slave-woman, cannot inherit, in this State (except under certain circumstances), the property of a white father.[1] I am, therefore, very much afraid that they are entirely at his mercy."

---

1 See Appendix B2.

"Well, then," said Walters, when Mr. Balch finished reading the letter, "it is clear there is an heir, and his claim *must* be well sustained, if such a man as Beckley, the first lawyer in the State, does not hesitate to endorse it; and as all the property (with the exception of a few thousands in my hands) lies in Georgia, I'm afraid the poor children will come off badly, unless this new heir proves to be a man of generosity—at all events, it seems we are completely at his mercy."

"We must hope for the best," rejoined Mr. Balch. "If he has any heart, he certainly will make some provision for them. The disappearance of that will is to me most unaccountable! I am confident it was at his house. It seemed so singular that none of his papers should be missing, except that—there were a great many others, deeds, mortgages, &c. scattered over the floor, but no will!"

The gentlemen were thus conversing, when they heard a tap at the door. "Come in!" cried Mr. Balch; and, in answer to the request, in walked Mr. George Stevens.

Mr. Walters and Mr. Balch bowed very stiffly, and the latter inquired what had procured him the honour of a visit.

"I have called upon you in reference to the property of the late Mr. Garie."

"Oh! you are acting in behalf of this new claimant, I suppose?" rejoined Mr. Balch.

"Sir!" said Mr. Stevens, looking as though he did not thoroughly understand him.

"I said," repeated Mr. Balch, "that I presumed you called in behalf of this new-found heir to Mr. Garie's property."

Mr. Stevens looked at him for a moment, then drawing himself up, exclaimed, "I AM THE HEIR!"

"You!—*you* the heir!" cried both the gentlemen, almost simultaneously.

"Yes, I am the heir!" coolly repeated Mr. Stevens, with an assured look. "I am the first cousin of Mr. Garie!"

"You his first cousin?—it is impossible!" said Walters.

"You'll discover it is not only possible, but true—I am, as I said, Mr. Garie's first cousin!"

"If you are that, you are more," said Walters, fiercely—"you're his murderer!" At this charge Mr. Stevens turned deathly pale. "Yes," continued Walters; "you either murdered him, or instigated others to do so! It was you who directed the rioters against both him and me—I have proof of what I say and can produce it. Now your motive is clear as day—you wanted his money, and destroyed him to obtain it! His blood is on your hands!" hissed Walters through his clenched teeth.

In the excitement consequent upon such a charge, Mr. Stevens, unnoticed by himself, had overturned a bottle of red ink, and its contents had slightly stained his hands. When Walters charged him with having Mr. Garie's blood upon them, he involuntarily looked down and saw his hands stained with red. An expression of intense horror flitted over his face when he observed it; but quickly regaining his composure, he replied, "It's only a little ink."

"Yes, I know *that* is ink," rejoined Walters, scornfully; "look at him, Balch," he continued, "he doesn't dare to look either of us in the face."

"It's false," exclaimed Stevens, with an effort to appear courageous; "it's as false as hell, and any man that charges me with it is a liar."

The words had scarcely passed his lips, when Walters sprang upon him with the ferocity of a tiger, and seizing him by the throat, shook and whirled him about as though he were a plaything.

"Stop, stop! Walters," cried Mr. Balch, endeavouring to loose his hold upon the throat of Mr. Stevens, who was already purple in the face; "let him go, this violence can benefit neither party. Loose your hold." At this remonstrance Walters dashed Stevens from him into the farthest corner of the room, exclaiming, "Now, go and prosecute me if you dare, and tell for what I chastised you; prosecute me for an assault, if you think you can risk the consequences."

Mr. Balch assisted him from the floor and placed him in a chair, where he sat holding his side, and panting for breath. When he was able to speak, he exclaimed, with a look of concentrated malignity, "Remember, we'll be even some day; I never received a blow and forgot it afterwards, bear that in mind."

"This will never do, gentlemen," said Mr. Balch, soothingly: "this conduct is unworthy of you. You are unreasonable both of you. When you have cooled down we will discuss the matter as we should."

"You'll discuss it alone then," said Stevens, rising, and walking to the door: "and when you have any further communication to make, you must come to me."

"Stop, stop, don't go," cried Mr. Balch, following him out at the door, which they closed behind them; "don't go away in a passion, Mr. Stevens. You and Walters are both too hasty. Come in here and sit down," said he, opening the door of a small adjoining room, "wait here one moment, I'll come back to you."

"This will never do, Walters," said he, as he re-entered his office; "the fellow has the upper hand of us, and we must humour him; we should suppress our own feelings for the children's sake. You are as well aware as I am of the necessity of some compromise—we are in his power for the present, and must act as circumstances compel us to."

"I can't discuss the matter with him," interrupted Walters, "he's an unmitigated scoundrel. I couldn't command my temper in his presence for five minutes. If you can arrange anything with him at all advantageous to the children, I shall be satisfied, it will be more than I expect; only bear in mind, that what I have in my hands belonging to Garie we must retain, he knows nothing of that."

"Very well," rejoined Mr. Balch, "depend upon it I'll do my best;" and closing the door, he went back to Mr. Stevens.

"Now, Mr. Stevens," said he, drawing up a chair, "we will talk over this matter dispassionately, and try and arrive at some amicable arrangement: be kind enough to inform me what your claims are."

"Mr. Balch, *you* are a gentleman," began Mr. Stevens, "and therefore I'm willing to discuss the matter thoroughly with you. You'll find me disposed to do a great deal for these children: but I wish it distinctly understood at the beginning, that whatever I may give them, I bestow as a favour. I concede nothing to them as a right, legally they have not the slightest claim upon me; of that you, who are an excellent lawyer, must be well aware."

"We won't discuss that point at present, Mr. Stevens. I believe you intimated you would be kind enough to say upon what evidence you purposed sustaining your claims?"

"Well, to come to the point, then," said Stevens; "the deceased Mr. Garie was, as I before said, my first cousin. His father and my mother were brother and sister. My mother married in opposition to her parents' desires; they cut her off from the family, and for years there was no communication between them. At my father's death, my mother made overtures for a reconciliation, which were contemptuously rejected, at length she died. I was brought up in ignorance of who my grandparents were; and only a few months since, on the death of my father's sister, did I make the discovery. Here," said he, extending the packet of letters which, the reader will remember once agitated him so strangely, "here are the letters that passed between my mother and her father."

Mr. Balch took up one and read:—

"Savannah, 18—

"Madam,—Permit me to return this letter (wherein you declare yourself the loving and repentant daughter of Bernard Garie) and at the same time inform you, that by your own acts you have deprived yourself of all claim to that relation. In opposition to my wishes, and in open defiance of my express commands, you chose to unite your fortune with one in every respect your inferior. If that union has not resulted as happily as you expected, you must sustain yourself by the reflection that you are the author of your own misfortunes and alone to blame for your present miserable condition.—Respectfully yours,

"Bernard Garie."

Mr. Balch read, one after another, letters of a similar purport—in fact, a long correspondence between Bernard Garie and the mother of Mr. Stevens. When he had finished, the latter remarked, "In addition to those, I can produce my mother's certificate of baptism, her marriage certificate, and every necessary proof of my being her son. If that does not suffice to make a strong case, I am at a loss to imagine what will."

Mr. Balch pondered a few moments, and then inquired, looking steadily at Mr. Stevens, "How long have you known of this relationship?"

"Oh, I've known it these three years."

"Three years! why, my dear sir, only a few moments ago you said a few months."

"Oh, did I?" said Mr. Stevens, very much confused; "I meant, or should have said, three years."

"Then, of course you were aware that Mr. Garie was your cousin when he took the house beside you?"

"Oh, yes—that is—yes—yes; I *was* aware of it."

"And did you make any overtures of a social character?" asked Mr. Balch.

"Well, yes—that is to say, my wife did."

"*Where were you the night of the murder?*"

Mr. Stevens turned pale at this question, and replied, hesitatingly, "Why, at home, of course."

"You were at home, and saw the house of your cousins assaulted, and made no effort to succour them or their children.

The next morning you are one of the coroner's inquest, and hurry through the proceedings, never once saying a word of your relationship to them, nor yet making any inquiry respecting the fate of the children. *It is very singular.*"

"I don't see what this cross-questioning is to amount to; it has nothing to do with my claim as heir."

"We are coming to that," rejoined Mr. Balch. "This, as I said, is very singular; and when I couple it with some other circumstances that have come to my knowledge, it is more than singular—*it is suspicious.* Here are a number of houses assaulted by a mob. Two or three days before the assault takes place, a list in your handwriting, and which is headed, '*Places to be attacked*,' is found, under circumstances that leave no doubt that it came directly from you. Well, the same mob that attacks these places—*marked out by you*—traverse a long distance to reach the house of your next-door neighbour. They break into it, and kill him; and you, who are aware at the time that he is your own cousin, do not attempt to interpose to prevent it, although it can be proved that you were all-powerful with the marauders. No! you allow him to be destroyed without an effort to save him, and immediately claim his property. Now, Mr. Stevens, people disposed to be suspicious—seeing how much you were to be the gainer by his removal, and knowing you had some connection with this mob—might not scruple to say that *you* instigated the attack by which he lost his life; and I put it to you—now don't you think that, if it was any one else, you would say that the thing looked suspicious?"

Mr. Stevens winced at this, but made no effort to reply.

Mr. Balch continued, "What I was going to remark is simply this. As we are in possession of these facts, and able to prove them by competent witnesses, we should not be willing to remain perfectly silent respecting it, unless you made what *we* regarded as a suitable provision for the children."

"I'm willing, as I said before, to do something; but don't flatter yourself I'll do any more than I originally intended from any fear of disclosures from you. I'm not to be frightened," said Mr. Stevens.

"I'm not at all disposed to attempt to frighten you: however, you know how far a mere statement of these facts would go towards rendering your position in society more agreeable.[1] A person who has been arrested on suspicion of murder is apt to be shunned and distrusted. It can't be helped; people are so very

---

1 Should probably read "disagreeable."

squeamish—they *will* draw back, you know, under such circumstances."

"I don't see how such a suspicion can attach itself to me," rejoined Stevens, sharply.

"Oh, well, we won't discuss that any further: let me hear what you will do for the children."

Mr. Balch saw, from the nervous and embarrassed manner of Mr. Stevens, that the indirect threat of exposing him had had considerable effect; and his downcast looks and agitation rather strengthened in his mind the suspicions that had been excited by the disclosures of Mr. Walters.

After a few moments' silence, Mr. Stevens said, "I'll settle three thousand dollars on each of the children. Now I think that is treating them liberally."

"Liberally!" exclaimed Balch, in a tone of contempt—"liberally! You acquire by the death of their father property worth one hundred and fifty thousand dollars, and you offer these children, who are the rightful heirs, three thousand dollars! That, sir, won't suffice."

"I think it should, then," rejoined Stevens. "By the laws of Georgia these children, instead of being his heirs, are my slaves. Their mother was a slave before them, and they were born slaves; and if they were in Savannah, I could sell them both to-morrow. On the whole, I think I've made you a very fair offer, and I'd advise you to think of it."

"No, Mr. Stevens; I shall accept no such paltry sum. If you wish a quick and peaceful possession of what you are pleased to regard as your rights, you must tender something more advantageous, or I shall feel compelled to bring this thing into court, even at the risk of loss; and there, you know, we should be obliged to make a clear statement of *everything* connected with this business. It might be advantageous to *us* to bring the thing fully before the court and public—but I'm exceedingly doubtful whether it would advance *your* interest."

Stevens winced at this, and asked, "What would you consider a fair offer?"

"I should consider *all* a just offer, half a fair one, and a quarter as little as you could have the conscience to expect us to take."

"I don't see any use in this chaffering, Mr. Balch," said Stevens; "you can't expect me to give you any such sums as you propose. Name a sum that you can reasonably expect to get."

"Well," said Mr. Balch, rising, "you must give us fifteen thousand dollars, and you should think yourself well off then. We could commence a suit, and put you to nearly that expense to defend it; to say nothing of the notoriety that the circumstance would occasion you. Both Walters and I are willing to spend both money and time in defence of these children's rights; I assure you they are not friendless."

"I'll give twelve thousand, and not a cent more, if I'm hung for it," said Mr. Stevens, almost involuntarily.

"Who spoke of hanging?" asked Mr. Balch.

"Oh!" rejoined Stevens, "that is only my emphatic way of speaking."

"Of course, you meant figuratively," said Mr. Balch, in a tone of irony; mentally adding, "as I hope you may be one day literally."

Mr. Stevens looked flushed and angry, but Mr. Balch continued, without appearing to notice him, and said: "I'll speak to Walters. Should he acquiesce in your proposal, I am willing to accept it; however, I cannot definitely decide without consulting him. To-morrow I will inform you of the result."

CHAPTER XXVI.

Home Again.

To Charlie the summer had been an exceedingly short one—time had flown so pleasantly away. Everything that could be done to make the place agreeable Mrs. Bird had effected. Amongst the number of her acquaintances who had conceived a regard for her young *protégé* was a promising artist to whom she had been a friend and patroness. Charlie paid him frequent visits, and would sit hour after hour in his studio, watching the progress of his work. Having nothing else at the time to amuse him, he one day asked the artist's permission to try his hand at a sketch. Being supplied with the necessary materials, he commenced a copy of a small drawing, and was working assiduously, when the artist came and looked over his shoulder.

"Did you ever draw before?" he asked, with a start of surprise.

"Never," replied Charlie, "except on my slate at school. I sometimes used to sketch the boys' faces."

"And you have never received any instructions?"

"Never—not even a hint," was the answer.

"And this is the first time you have attempted a sketch upon paper?"

"Yes; the very first."

"Then you are a little prodigy," said the artist, slapping him upon the shoulder. "I must take you in hand. You have nothing else to do; come here regularly every day, and I'll teach you. Will you come?"

"Certainly, if you wish it. But now, tell me, do you really think that drawing good?"

"Well, Charlie, if I had done it, it would be pronounced very bad for me; but, coming from your hands, it's something astonishing."

"Really, now—you're not joking me?"

"No, Charlie, I'm in earnest—I assure you I am; it is drawn with great spirit, and the boy that you have put in by the pump is exceedingly well done."

This praise served as a great incentive to our little friend, who, day after day thenceforth, was found at the studio busily engaged with his crayons, and making rapid progress in his new art.

He had been thus occupied some weeks, and one morning was hurrying to the breakfast-table, to get through his meal, that he might be early at the studio, when he found Mrs. Bird in her accustomed seat looking very sad.

"Why, what is the matter?" he asked, on observing the unusually grave face of his friend.

"Oh, Charlie, my dear! I've received very distressing intelligence from Philadelphia. Your father is quite ill."

"My father ill!" cried he, with a look of alarm.

"Yes, my dear! quite sick—so says my letter. Here are two for you."

Charlie hastily broke the seal of one, and read as follows:

"MY DEAR LITTLE BROTHER,—We are all in deep distress in consequence of the misfortunes brought upon us by the mob. Our home has been destroyed; and, worse than all, our poor father was caught, and so severely beaten by the rioters that for some days his life was entirely despaired of. Thank God! he is now improving, and we have every reasonable hope of his ultimate recovery. Mother, Caddy, and I, as you may well suppose, are almost prostrated by this accumulation of misfortunes, and but for the kindness of Mr. Walters, with whom we are living, I do not know what would have become of us. Dear Mr. and Mrs. Garie— [Here followed a passage that was so scored and crossed as to be illegible. After a short endeavour to decipher it, he continued:] We would like to see you very much, and mother grows every day more anxious for your return. I forgot to add, in connection with the mob, that Mr. Walters's house was also attacked, but unsuccessfully, the rioters having met a signal repulse. Mother and Caddy send a world of love to you. So does Kinch, who comes every day to see us, and is often extremely useful. Give our united kind regards to Mrs. Bird, and thank her in our behalf for her great kindness to you.—Ever yours,

"ESTHER.

"P.S.—Do try and manage to come home soon."

The tears trickled down Charlie's cheek as he perused the letter, which, when he had finished reading, he handed to Mrs. Bird, and then commenced the other. This proved to be from Kinch, who had spent all the spare time at his disposal since the occurrence of the mob in preparing it.

"To MR. CHARLES ELLIS, ESQ., at MRS. BIRD'S

"*Philadelphia.*

"DEER SIR AND HONNORED FRIEND.—I take This chance To Write To you To tell You that I am Well, And that we are all well Except Your father, who Is sick; and I hope you are Enjoying the same Blessin. We had An Awful fight, And I was There, and I was One of The Captings. I had a sord on; and the next Mornin we had a grate Brekfast. But nobody Eat anything but me, And I was obliged to eat, Or the Wittles would have spoiled. The Mob had Guns as Big as Cannun; And they Shot them Off, and the holes Are in The Shutter yet; And when You come Back, I will show them to You. Your Father is very bad; And I Have gone back to school, And I am Licked every day because I don't Know my Lesson. A great big boy, with white woolly hair and Pinkish Grey eyes, has got Your seat. I Put a Pin under him one Day, And he told On me; and We Are to Have a fight to-morrow. The boys Call Him 'Short and Dirty,' because he ain't tall, and never washes His Face. We Have got a new Teacher for the 5th Division. He's a Scorcher, And believes in Rat Tan.[1] I am to Wear My new Cloths Next Sunday. Excuse This long letter. Your Friend till death,

"KINCH SANDERS DE YOUNGE.

 "P.S. This is the best Skull and Cross-bones That I can make. Come home soon. Yours, &c.,

"K.S. DE YOUNGE, ESQ."

Charlie could not but smile through his tears, as he read this curious epistle, which was not more remarkable for its graceful composition than its wonderful chirography.[2] Some of the lines were written in blue ink, some in red, and others in that pale muddy black which is the peculiar colour of ink after passing through the various experiments of school-boys, who generally entertain the belief that all foreign substances, from molasses-candy to bread-crumbs, necessarily improve the colour and quality of that important liquid.

---

1 I.e., he believes in using corporal punishment; see above, p. 184, note 1.
2 Handwriting.

"Why every other word almost is commenced with a capital and I declare he's even made some in German text," cried Charlie, running his finger mirthfully along the lines, until he came to "Your father is very bad." Here the tears came welling up again—the shower had returned almost before the sun had departed; and, hiding his face in his hands, he leant sobbing on the table.

"Cheer up, Charlie!—cheer up, my little man! all may go well yet."

"Mrs. Bird," he sobbed, "you've been very kind to me; yet I want to go home. I must see mother and father. You see what Esther writes,—they want me to come home; do let me go."

"Of course you shall go, if you wish. Yet I should like you to remain with me, if you will."

"No, no, Mrs. Bird, I mustn't stay; it wouldn't be right for me to remain here, idle and enjoying myself, and they so poor and unhappy at home. I couldn't stay," said he, rising from the table,—"I must go."

"Well, my dear, you can't go now. Sit down and finish your breakfast, or you will have a head-ache."

"I'm not hungry—I can't eat," he replied; "my appetite has all gone." And stealing away from the room, he went up into his chamber, threw himself on the bed, and wept bitterly.

Mrs. Bird was greatly distressed at the idea of losing her little favourite. He had been so much with her that she had become strongly attached to him, and therefore looked forward to his departure with unfeigned regret. But Charlie could not be persuaded to stay; and reluctantly Mrs. Bird made arrangements for his journey home. Even the servants looked a little sorry when they heard of his intended departure; and Reuben the coachman actually presented him with a jack-knife as a token of his regard.

Mrs. Bird accompanied him to the steamer, and placed him under the special care of the captain; so that he was most comfortably provided for until his arrival in New York, where he took the cars direct for home.

Not having written to inform them on what day he might be expected, he anticipated giving them a joyful surprise, and, with this end in view, hastened in the direction of Mr. Walters's. As he passed along, his eye was attracted by a figure before him which he thought he recognized, and on closer inspection it proved to be his sister Caddy.

Full of boyish fun, he crept up behind her, and clasped his hands over her eyes, exclaiming, in an assumed voice, "Now, who am I?"

"Go away, you impudent, nasty thing!" cried Caddy, plunging violently. Charlie loosed his hold; she turned, and beheld her brother.

"Oh! Charlie, Charlie! is it you? Why, bless you, you naughty fellow, how you frightened me!" said she, throwing her arms round his neck, and kissing him again and again. "When did you come? Oh, how delighted mother and Ess will be!"

"I only arrived about half an hour ago. How are mother and father and Esther?"

"Mother and Ess are well, and father better. But I'm so glad to see you," she cried, with a fresh burst of tears and additional embraces.

"Why, Cad," said he, endeavouring to suppress some watery sensations of his own, "I'm afraid you're not a bit pleased at my return—you're actually crying about it."

"Oh, I'm so glad to see you that I can't help it," she replied, as she fell to crying and kissing him more furiously than before.

Charlie became much confused at these repeated demonstrations of joyful affection in the crowded street, and, gently disengaging her, remarked, "See, Caddy, everybody is looking at us; let us walk on."

"I had almost forgot I was sent on an errand—however, it's not of much consequence—I'll go home again with you;" and taking his hand, they trudged on together.

"How did you say father was?" he asked again.

"Oh, he's better bodily; that is, he has some appetite, sits up every day, and is gradually getting stronger; but he's all wrong here," said she, tapping her forehead. "Sometimes he don't know any of us—and it makes us all feel so bad." Here the tears came trickling down again, as she continued: "Oh, Charlie! what those white devils will have to answer for! When I think of how much injury they have done us, I *hate* them! I know it's wrong to hate anybody—but I can't help it; and I believe God hates them as much as I do!"

Charlie looked gloomy; and, as he made no rejoinder, she continued, "We didn't save a thing, not even a change of clothes; they broke and burnt up everything; and then the way they beat poor father was horrible—horrible! Just think—they chopped his fingers nearly all off, so that he has only the stumps left. Charlie,

Charlie!" she cried, wringing her hands, "it's heart-rending to see him—he can't even feed himself, and he'll never be able to work again!"

"Don't grieve, Cad," said Charlie, with an effort to suppress his own tears; "I'm almost a man now," continued he, drawing himself up—"don't be afraid, I'll take care of you all!"

Thus conversing, they reached Mr. Walters's. Caddy wanted Charlie to stop and look at the damage effected by the mob upon the outside of the house, but he was anxious to go in, and ran up the steps and gave the bell a very sharp pull. The servant who opened the door was about to make some exclamation of surprise, and was only restrained by a warning look from Charlie. Hurrying past them, Caddy led the way to the room where her mother and Esther were sitting. With a cry of joy Mrs. Ellis caught him in her arms, and, before he was aware of their presence, he found himself half smothered by her and Esther.

They had never been separated before his trip to Warmouth; and their reunion, under such circumstances, was particularly affecting. None of them could speak for a few moments, and Charlie clung round his mother's neck as though he would never loose his hold. "Mother, mother!" was all he could utter; yet in that word was comprised a world of joy and affection.

Esther soon came in for her share of caresses; then Charlie inquired, "Where's father?"

"In here," said Mrs. Ellis, leading the way to an adjoining room. "I don't think he will know you—perhaps he may." In one corner of the apartment, propped up in a large easy chair by a number of pillows, sat poor Mr. Ellis, gazing vacantly about the room and muttering to himself. His hair had grown quite white, and his form was emaciated in the extreme; there was a broad scar across his forehead, and his dull, lustreless eyes were deeply sunken in his head. He took no notice of them as they approached, but continued muttering and looking at his hands.

Charlie was almost petrified at the change wrought in his father. A few months before he had left him in the prime of healthful manhood; now he was bent and spectrelike, and old in appearance as if the frosts of eighty winters had suddenly fallen on him.

Mrs. Ellis laid her hand gently upon his shoulder, and said, "Husband, here's Charlie." He made no reply, but continued muttering and examining his mutilated hands. "It's Charlie," she repeated.

"Oh, ay! nice little boy!" he replied, vacantly; "whose son is he?"

Mrs. Ellis's voice quivered as she reiterated, "It's Charlie—our Charlie!—don't you know him?"

"Oh, yes! nice little boy—nice little boy. Oh!" he continued, in a suppressed and hurried tone, as a look of alarm crossed his face; "run home quick, little boy! and tell your mother they're coming, thousands of them; they've guns, and swords, and clubs. Hush! There they come—there they come!" And he buried his face in the shawl, and trembled in an agony of fright.

"Oh, mother, this is dreadful!" exclaimed Charlie. "Don't he know any of you?"

"Yes; sometimes his mind comes back—very seldom, though —only for a very little while. Come away: talking to him sometimes makes him worse." And slowly and sorrowfully the two left the apartment.

That evening, after Mr. Ellis had been safely bestowed in bed, the family gathered round the fire in the room of Mrs. Ellis, where Charlie entertained them with a description of Warmouth and of the manner in which he had passed the time whilst there. He was enthusiastic respecting Mrs. Bird and her kindness. "Mother, she is such a *dear* old lady: if I'd been as white as snow, and her own son, she couldn't have been kinder to me. She didn't want me to come away, and cried ever so much. Let me show you what she gave me!" Charlie thrust his hand into his pocket, and drew out a small wallet, from which he counted out four ten-dollar bills, two fives, and a two dollar and a half gold piece. "Ain't I rich!" said he, as, with the air of a millionaire, he tossed the money upon a table. "Now," he continued, "do you know what I'm about to do?" Not receiving any answer from his wondering sisters or mother, he added, "Why, just this!—here, mother, this is yours," said he, placing the four ten-dollar bills before her; "and here are five apiece for Esther and Cad; the balance is for your humble servant. Now, then," he concluded, "what do you think of that?"

Mrs. Ellis looked fondly at him, and, stroking his head, told him that he was a good son; and Esther and Caddy declared him to be the best brother in town.

"Now, girls," said he, with the air of a patriarch, "what do you intend to do with your money?"

"Mine will go towards buying me a dress, and Esther will save hers for a particular purpose," said Caddy. "I'll tell you something about her and Mr. Walters," continued she, with a mischievous look at her sister.

"Oh, Caddy—don't! Ain't you ashamed to plague me so?"

asked Esther, blushing to the roots of her hair. "Mother, pray stop her," cried she, pleadingly.

"Hush, Caddy!" interposed her mother, authoritatively; "you shall do no such thing."

"Well," resumed Caddy, "mother says I mustn't tell; but I can say this much—"

Esther here put her hand over her sister's mouth and effectually prevented any communication she was disposed to make.

"Never mind her, Ess!" cried Charlie; "you'll tell me all in good time, especially if it's anything worth knowing."

Esther made no reply, but, releasing her sister, hurried out of the room, and went upstairs to Charlie's chamber, where he found her on retiring for the night.

"I'm glad you're here; Ess," said he, "you'll indulge me. Here is the key—open my trunk and get me out a nightcap; I'm too tired, or too lazy, to get it for myself." Esther stooped down, opened the trunk, and commenced searching for the article of head-gear in question. "Come, Ess," said Charles, coaxingly, "tell me what this is about you and Mr. Walters."

She made no reply at first, but fumbled about in the bottom of the trunk, professedly in search of the nightcap, which she at that moment held in her hand. "Can't you tell me?" he again asked.

"Oh, there's nothing to tell, Charlie!" she answered,

"There must be something, Ess, or you wouldn't have blushed up so when Cad was about to speak of it. Do," said he, approaching her, and putting his arm round her neck—"do tell me all about it—I am sure there is some secret!"

"Oh, no, Charlie—there is no secret; it's only this——" Here she stopped, and, blushing, turned her head away.

"Ess, this is nonsense," said Charlie, impatiently: "if it's anything worth knowing, why can't you tell a fellow? Come," said he, kissing her, "tell me, now, like a dear old Ess as you are."

"Well, Charlie," said she, jerking the words out with an effort, "Mr.—Mr. Walters has asked me to marry him!"

"Phew—gemini! that is news!" exclaimed Charlie. "And are you going to accept him, Ess?"

"I don't know," she answered.

"Don't know!" repeated Charlie, in a tone of surprise. "Why, Ess, I'm astonished at you—such a capital fellow as he is! Half the girls of our acquaintance would give an eye for the chance."

"But he is so rich!" responded Esther.

"Well, now, that's a great objection, ain't it! I should say, all the better on that account," rejoined Charlie.

"The money is the great stumbling-block," continued she; "everybody would say I married him for that."

"Then *everybody* would lie, *as* everybody very often does! If I was you, Ess, and loved him, I shouldn't let his fortune stand in the way. I wish," continued he, pulling up his shirt-collar, "that some amiable young girl with a fortune of a hundred thousand dollars would make me an offer—I'd like to catch myself refusing her!"

The idea of a youth of his tender years marrying any one, seemed so ludicrous to Esther, that she burst into a hearty fit of laughter, to the great chagrin of our hero, who seemed decidedly of the opinion that his sister had not a proper appreciation of his years and inches.

"Don't laugh, Ess; but tell me—do you really intend to refuse him?"

"I can't decide yet, Charlie," answered she seriously; "if we were situated as we were before—were not such absolute paupers—I wouldn't hesitate to accept him; but to bring a family of comparative beggars upon him—I can't make up my mind to do that."

Charlie looked grave as Esther made this last objection; boy as he was, he felt its weight and justice. "Well, Ess," rejoined he, "I don't know what to say about it—of course, I can't advise. What does mother say?"

"She leaves it entirely to me," she answered. "She says I must act just as I feel is right."

"I certainly wouldn't have him at all, Ess, if I didn't love him; and if I did, I shouldn't let the money stand in the way—so, good night!"

Charlie slept very late the next morning, and was scarcely dressed when Esther knocked at his door, with the cheerful tidings that her father had a lucid interval and was waiting to see him.

Dressing himself hastily, he followed her into their father's room. When he entered, the feeble sufferer stretched out his mutilated arms towards him and clasped him round the neck, "They tell me," said he, "that you came yesterday, and that I didn't recognize you. I thought, when I awoke this morning, that I had a dim recollection of having seen some dear face; but my head aches so, that I often forget—yes, often forget. My boy," he continued, "you are all your mother and sisters have to depend upon now; I'm—I'm—" here his voice faltered, as he elevated his stumps of hands—"I'm helpless; but you must take care of them. I'm an old man now," said he, despondingly.

"I will, father; I'll try *so* hard" replied Charlie.

"It was cruel in them, wasn't it, son," he resumed. "See, they've made me helpless for ever!"

Charlie restrained the tears that were forcing themselves up, and rejoined, "Never fear, father! I'll do my best; I trust I shall soon be able to take care of you."

His father did not understand him—his mind was gone again, and he was staring vacantly about him. Charlie endeavoured to recall his attention, but failed, for he began muttering about the mob and his hands; they were compelled to quit the room, and leave him to himself, as he always became quiet sooner by being left alone.

CHAPTER XXVII.

Sudbury.

WE must now admit our readers to a consultation that is progressing between Mr. Balch and Mr. Walters, respecting the future of the two Garie children. They no doubt entered upon the conference with the warmest and most earnest desire of promoting the children's happiness; but, unfortunately, their decision failed to produce the wished-for result.

"I scarcely thought you would have succeeded so well with him," said Walters, "he is such an inveterate scoundrel; depend upon it nothing but the fear of the exposure resulting from a legal investigation would ever have induced that scamp to let twelve thousand dollars escape from his clutches. I am glad you have secured that much; when we add it to the eight thousand already in my possession it will place them in very comfortable circumstances, even if they never get any more."

"I think we have done very well," rejoined Mr. Balch; "we were as much in his power as he was in ours—not in the same way, however; a legal investigation, no matter how damaging it might have been to his reputation, would not have placed us in possession of the property, or invalidated his claim as heir. I think, on the whole, we may as well be satisfied, and trust in Providence for the future. So now, then, we will resume our discussion of that matter we had under consideration the other day. I cannot but think that my plan is best adapted to secure the boy's happiness."

"I'm sorry I cannot agree with you, Mr. Balch. I have tried to view your plan in the most favourable light, yet I cannot rid myself of a presentiment that it will result in the ultimate discovery of his peculiar position, and that most probably at some time when his happiness is dependent upon its concealment. An undetected forger, who is in constant fear of being apprehended, is happy in comparison with that coloured man who attempts, in this country, to hold a place in the society of whites by concealing his origin. He must live in constant fear of exposure; this dread will embitter every enjoyment, and make him the most miserable of men."

"You must admit," rejoined Mr. Balch, "that I have their welfare at heart. I have thought the matter over and over, and cannot, for the life of me, feel the weight of your objections. The children are peculiarly situated; everything seems to favour my views. Their mother (the only relative they had whose African origin was distinguishable) is dead and both of them are so exceedingly fair that it would never enter the brain of any one that they were connected with coloured people by ties of blood. Clarence is old enough to know the importance of concealing the fact, and Emily might be kept with us until her prudence also might be relied upon. You must acknowledge that as white persons they will be better off."

"I admit," answered Mr. Walters, "that in our land of liberty it is of incalculable advantage to be white; that is beyond dispute, and no one is more painfully aware of it than I. Often I have heard men of colour say they would not be white if they could— had no desire to change their complexions: I've written some down fools; others, liars. Why," continued he, with a sneering expression of countenance: "it is everything to be white; one feels that at every turn in our boasted free country, where all men are upon an equality. When I look around me, and see what I have made myself in spite of circumstances, and think what I might have been with the same heart and brain beneath a fairer skin, I am almost tempted to curse the destiny that made me what I am. Time after time, when scraping, toiling, saving, I have asked myself. To what purpose is it all?—perhaps that in the future white men may point at and call me, sneeringly, 'a nigger millionaire,' or condescend to borrow money of me. Ah! often, when some negro-hating white man has been forced to ask a loan at my hands, I've thought of Shylock and his pound of flesh, and ceased to wonder at him. There's no doubt, my dear sir, but what I fully appreciate the advantage of being white. Yet, with all I have endured, and yet endure from day to day, I esteem myself happy in comparison with that man, who, mingling in the society of whites, is at the same time aware that he has African blood in his veins, and is liable at any moment to be ignominiously hurled from his position by the discovery of his origin. He is never safe. I have known instances where parties have gone on for years and years undetected; but some untoward circumstance brings them out at last, and down they fall for ever."

"Walters, my dear fellow, you will persist in looking upon his being discovered as a thing of course: I see no reason for the anticipation of any such result. I don't see how he is to be detected—it may never occur. And do you feel justified in consigning them to a position which you know by painful experience to be one of the most disagreeable that can be endured. Ought we not to aid their escape from it if we can?"

Mr. Walters stood reflectively for some moments, and then exclaimed, "I'll make no farther objection; I would not have the boy say to me hereafter, 'But for your persisting in identifying me with a degraded people, I might have been better and happier than I am.' However, I cannot but feel that concealments of this kind are productive of more misery than comfort."

"We will agree to differ about that, Walters; and now, having your consent, I shall not hesitate to proceed in the matter, with full reliance that the future will amply justify my choice."

"Well, well! as I said before, I will offer no further objection. Now let me hear the details of your plan."

"I have written," answered Mr. Balch, "to Mr. Eustis, a friend of mine living at Sudbury,[1] where there is a large preparatory school for boys. At his house I purpose placing Clarence. Mr. Eustis is a most discreet man, and a person of liberal sentiments. I feel that I can confide everything to him without the least fear of his ever divulging a breath of it. He is a gentleman in the fullest sense of the term, and at his house the boy will have the advantage of good society, and will associate with the best people of the place."

"Has he a family?" asked Mr. Walters.

"He is a widower," answered Mr. Balch; "a maiden sister of his wife presides over his establishment; she will be kind to Clarence, I am confident; she has a motherly soft heart, and is remarkably fond of children. I have not the least doubt but that he will be very happy and comfortable there. I think it very fortunate, Walters," he continued, "that he has so few coloured acquaintances—no boyish intimacies to break up; and it will be as well to send him away before he has an opportunity of forming them. Besides, being here, where everything will be so constantly reviving the remembrance of his recent loss, he may grow melancholy and stupid. I have several times noticed his reserve, so unusual in a child. His dreadful loss and the horrors that attended it have made a deep impression—stupefied him, to a certain extent, I think. Well, well! we will get him off, and once away at school, and surrounded by lively boys, this dulness will soon wear off."

---

1   Possibly fictional; possibly Sudbury, Massachusetts, about 25 miles west of Boston. There does not seem to have been a corresponding Academy in Sudbury proper, but boarding schools like the one the narrative describes dotted the New England landscape.

The gentlemen having fully determined upon his being sent, it was proposed to bring him in immediately and talk to him relative to it. He was accordingly sent for, and came into the room, placing himself beside the chair of Mr. Walters.

Clarence had altered very much since the death of his parents. His face had grown thin and pale, and he was much taller than when he came to Philadelphia: a shade of melancholy had overspread his face; there was now in his eyes that expression of intense sadness that characterized his mother's. "You sent for me?" he remarked, inquiringly, to Mr. Walters.

"Yes, my boy," he rejoined, "we sent for you to have a little talk about school. Would you like to go to school again?"

"Oh, yes!" answered Clarence, his face lighting up with pleasure; "I should like it of all things; it would be much better than staying at home all day, doing nothing; the days are so long," concluded he, with a sigh.

"Ah! we will soon remedy that," rejoined Mr. Balch, "when you go to Sudbury."

"Sudbury!" repeated Clarence, with surprise; "where is that? I thought you meant to go to school here."

"Oh, no, my dear," said Mr. Balch, "I don't know of any good school here, such as you would like; we wish to send you to a place where you will enjoy yourself finely,—where you will have a number of boys for companions in your studies and pleasures."

"And is Em going with me?" he asked.

"Oh, no, that is not possible; it is a school for boys exclusively; you can't take your sister there," rejoined Mr. Walters.

"Then I don't want to go," said Clarence, decidedly; "I don't want to go where I can't take Em with me."

Mr. Balch exchanged glances with Mr. Walters, and looked quite perplexed at this new opposition to his scheme. Nothing daunted, however, by this difficulty, he, by dint of much talking and persuasion, brought Clarence to look upon the plan with favour, and to consent reluctantly to go without his sister.

But the most delicate part of the whole business was yet to come—they must impress upon the child the necessity of concealing the fact that he was of African origin. Neither seemed to know how to approach the subject. Clarence, however, involuntarily made an opening for them by inquiring if Emily was to go to Miss Jordan's school again.

"No, my dear," answered Mr. Balch, "Miss Jordan won't permit her to attend school there."

"Why?" asked Clarence.

"Because she is a coloured child," rejoined Mr. Balch. "Now, Clarence," he continued, "you are old enough, I presume, to know the difference that exists between the privileges and advantages enjoyed by the whites, and those that are at the command of the coloured people. White boys can go to better schools, and they can enter college and become professional men, lawyers, doctors, &c., or they may be merchants—in fact, they can be anything they please. Coloured people can enjoy none of these advantages; they are shut out from them entirely. Now which of the two would you rather be—coloured or white?"

"I should much rather be white, of course," answered Clarence; "but I am coloured, and can't help myself," said he, innocently.

"But, my child, we are going to send you where it is not known that you are coloured; and you must *never, never* tell it, because if it became known, you would be expelled from the school, as you were from Miss Jordan's."

"I didn't know we were expelled," rejoined Clarence. "I know she sent us home, but I could not understand what it was for. I'm afraid they will send me from the other school. Won't they know I am coloured?"

"No, my child, I don't think they will discover it unless you should be foolish enough to tell it yourself, in which case both Mr. Walters and myself would be very much grieved."

"But suppose some one should ask me," suggested Clarence.

"No one will ever ask you such a question," said Mr. Balch, impatiently; "all you have to do is to be silent yourself on the subject. Should any of your schoolmates ever make inquiries respecting your parents, all you have to answer is, they were from Georgia, and you are an orphan."

Clarence's eyes began to moisten as Mr. Balch spoke of his parents, and after a few moments he asked, with some hesitation, "Am I never to speak of mother? I love to talk of mother."

"Yes, my dear, of course you can talk of your mother," answered Mr. Balch, with great embarrassment; "only, you know, my child, you need not enter into particulars as regards her appearance; that is, you—ah!—need not say she was a coloured woman. You *must not* say that; you understand?"

"Yes, sir," answered Clarence.

"Very well, then; bear that in mind. You must know, Clarence," continued he, "that this concealment is necessary for your welfare, or we would not require it; and you must let me impress it upon you, that it is requisite that you attend strictly to our directions."

Mr. Walters remained silent during most of this conversation. He felt a repugnance to force upon the child a concealment the beneficial results of which were the reverse of obvious, so he merely gave Clarence some useful advice respecting his general conduct, and then permitted him to leave the room.

The morning fixed upon for their departure for Sudbury turned out to be cold and cheerless; and Clarence felt very gloomy as he sat beside his sister at their early breakfast, of which he was not able to eat a morsel. "Do eat something Clary," said she, coaxingly; "only look what nice buckwheat cakes these are; cook got up ever so early on purpose to bake them for you."

"No, sis," he replied, "I can't eat. I feel so miserable, everything chokes me."

"Well, eat a biscuit, then," she continued, as she buttered it and laid it on his plate; "do eat it, now."

More to please her than from a desire to eat, he forced down a few mouthfuls of it, and drank a little tea; then, laying his arm round her neck, he said, "Em, you must try hard to learn to write soon, so that I may hear from you at least once a week."

"Oh! I shall soon know how, I'm in g's and h's now. Aunt Esther—she says I may call her Aunt Esther—teaches me every day. Ain't I getting on nicely?"

"Oh, yes, you learn very fast," said Esther, encouragingly, as she completed the pile of sandwiches she was preparing for the young traveller; then, turning to look at the timepiece on the mantel, she exclaimed, "Quarter to seven—how time flies! Mr. Balch will soon be here. You must be all ready, Clarence, so as not to keep him waiting a moment."

Clarence arose from his scarcely tasted meal, began slowly to put on his overcoat, and make himself ready for the journey. Em tied on the warm woollen neck-comforter, kissing him on each cheek as she did so, and whilst they were thus engaged, Mr. Balch drove up to the door.

Charlie, who had come down to see him off, tried (with his mouth full of buckwheat cake) to say something consolatory, and gave it as his experience, "that a fellow soon got over that sort of thing; that separations must occur sometimes," &c.—and, on the whole, endeavoured to talk in a very manly and philosophical strain; but his precepts and practice proved to be at utter variance, for when the moment of separation really came and he saw the tearful embrace of Em and her brother, he caught the infection of grief, and cried as heartily as the best of them. There was but little time, however, to spare for leave-takings, and the young traveller and his guardian were soon whirling over the road towards New York.

By a singular chance, Clarence found himself in the same car in which he had formerly rode when they were on their way to Philadelphia: he recognized it by some peculiar paintings on the panel of the door, and the ornamental border of the ceiling. This brought back a tide of memories, and he began contrasting that journey with the present. Opposite was the seat on which his parents had sat, in the bloom of health, and elate with joyous anticipations; he remembered—oh! so well—his father's pleasant smile, his mother's soft and gentle voice. Both now were gone. Death had made rigid that smiling face—her soft voice was hushed for ever—and the cold snow was resting on their bosoms in the little churchyard miles away. Truly the contrast between now and then was extremely saddening, and the child bowed his head upon the seat, and sobbed in bitter grief.

"What is the matter?" asked Mr. Balch; "not crying again, I hope. I thought you were going to be a man, and that we were not to have any more tears. Come!" continued he, patting him encouragingly on the back, "cheer up! You are going to a delightful place, where you will find a number of agreeable playmates, and have a deal of fun, and enjoy yourself amazingly."

"But it won't be *home*," replied Clarence.

"True," replied Mr. Balch, a little touched, "it won't seem so at first; but you'll soon like it, I'll guarantee that."

Clarence was not permitted to indulge his grief to any great extent, for Mr. Balch soon succeeded in interesting him in the various objects that they passed on the way.

On the evening of the next day they arrived at their destination, and Clarence alighted from the cars, cold, fatigued, and spiritless. There had been a heavy fall of snow a few days previous, and the town of Sudbury, which was built upon the hill-side, shone white and sparkling in the clear winter moonlight.

It was the first time that Clarence had ever seen the ground covered with snow, and he could not restrain his admiration at the novel spectacle it presented to him. "Oh, look!—oh, do look! Mr. Balch," he exclaimed, "how beautifully white it looks; it seems as if the town was built of salt."

It was indeed a pretty sight. Near them stood a clump of fantastic-shaped trees, their gnarled limbs covered with snow, and brilliant with the countless icicles that glistened like precious stones in the bright light that was reflected upon them from the windows of the station. A little farther on, between them and the town, flowed a small stream, the waters of which were dimpling and sparkling in the moonlight. Beside its banks arose stately cotton-mills, and from their many windows hundreds of lights were shining. Behind them, tier above tier, were the houses of the town; and crowning the hill was the academy, with its great dome gleaming on its top like a silver cap upon a mountain of snow. The merry sleigh-bells and the crisp tramp of the horses upon the frozen ground were all calculated to make a striking impression on one beholding such a scene for the first time.

Clarence followed Mr. Balch into the sleigh, delighted and bewildered with the surrounding objects. The driver whipped up his horses, they clattered over the bridge, dashed swiftly through the town, and in a very short period arrived at the dwelling of Mr. Eustis.

The horses had scarcely stopped, when the door flew open, and a stream of light from the hall shone down the pathway to the gate. Mr. Eustis came out on the step to welcome them. After greeting Mr. Balch warmly, he took Clarence by the hand, and led him into the room where his sister was sitting.

"Here is our little friend," said he to her, as she arose and approached them; "try and get him warm, Ada—his hands are like ice."

Miss Ada Bell welcomed Clarence in the most affectionate manner, assisted him to remove his coat, unfastened his woollen neck-tie, and smoothed down his glossy black hair; then, warming a napkin, she wrapped it round his benumbed hands, and held them in her own until the circulation was restored and they were supple and comfortable again.

Miss Ada Bell appeared to be about thirty-five. She had good regular features, hazel eyes, and long chestnut curls: a mouth with the sweetest expression, and a voice so winning and affectionate in its tone that it went straight to the hearts of all that listened to its music.

"Had you a pleasant journey?" she asked.

"It was rather cold," answered Clarence, "and I am not accustomed to frosty weather."

"And did you leave all your friends well?" she continued, as she chafed his hands.

"Quite well, I thank you," he replied.

"I hear you have a little sister; were you not sorry to leave her behind?"

This question called up the tearful face of little Em and her last embrace. He could not answer; he only raised his mournful dark eyes to the face of Miss Ada, and as he looked at her they grew moist, and a tear sparkled on his long lashes. Miss Ada felt that she had touched a tender chord, so she stooped down and kissed his forehead, remarking, "You have a good face, Clarence, and no doubt an equally good heart; we shall get on charmingly together, I know." Those kind words won the orphan's heart, and from that day forth Clarence loved her. Tea was soon brought upon the table, and they all earnestly engaged in the discussion of the various refreshments that Miss Ada's well-stocked larder afforded. Everything was so fresh and nicely flavoured that both the travellers ate very heartily; then, being much fatigued with their two days' journey, they seized an early opportunity to retire.

★★★

Here we leave Clarence for many years; the boy will have become a man ere we re-introduce him, and, till then, we bid him adieu.

CHAPTER XXVIII.

Charlie seeks Employment.

CHARLIE had been at home some weeks, comparatively idle; at least he so considered himself, as the little he did in the way of collecting rents and looking up small accounts for Mr. Walters he regarded as next to nothing, it not occupying half his time. A part of each day he spent in attendance on his father, who seemed better satisfied with his ministrations than with those of his wife and daughters. This proved to be very fortunate for all parties, as it enabled the girls to concentrate their attention on their sewing—of which they had a vast deal on hand.

One day, when Esther and Charlie were walking out together, the latter remarked: "Ess, I wish I could find some regular and profitable employment, or was apprenticed to some good trade that would enable me to assist mother a little; I'd even go to service if I could do no better—anything but being idle whilst you are all so hard at work. It makes me feel very uncomfortable."

"I would be very glad if you could procure some suitable employment. I don't wish you to go to service again, that is out of the question. Of whom have you made inquiry respecting a situation?"

"Oh, of lots of people; they can tell me of any number of families who are in want of a footman, but no one appears to know of a person who is willing to receive a black boy as an apprentice to a respectable calling. It's too provoking; I really think, Ess, that the majority of white folks imagine that we are only fit for servants, and incapable of being rendered useful in any other capacity. If that terrible misfortune had not befallen father, I should have learned his trade."

"Ah" sighed Esther, "but for that we should all have been happier. But, Charlie," she added, "how do you know that you cannot obtain any other employment than that of a servant? Have you ever applied personally to any one?"

"No, Esther, I haven't; but you know as well as I that white masters won't receive coloured apprentices."

"I think a great deal of that is taken for granted," rejoined Esther, "try some one yourself."

"I only wish I knew of any one to try," responded Charlie, "I'd hazard the experiment at any rate."

"Look over the newspaper in the morning," advised Esther; "there are always a great many wants advertised—amongst them you may perhaps find something suitable."

"Well, I will Ess—now then we won't talk about that any more—pray tell me, if I'm not too inquisitive, what do you purpose buying with your money—a wedding-dress, eh?" he asked, with a merry twinkle in his eye.

Esther blushed and sighed, as she answered: "No, Charlie, that is all over for the present. I told him yesterday I could not think of marrying now, whilst we are all so unsettled. It grieved me to do it, Charlie, but I felt that it was my duty. Cad and I are going to add our savings to mother's; that, combined with what we shall receive for father's tools, good-will, &c., will be sufficient to furnish another house; and as soon as we can succeed in that, we will leave Mr. Walters, as it is embarrassing to remain under present circumstances."

"And what is to become of little Em?—she surely won't remain alone with him?"

"Mr. Walters has proposed that when we procure a house she shall come and board with us. He wants us to take one of his houses, and offers some fabulous sum for the child's board, which it would be unreasonable in us to take. Dear, good man, he is always complaining that we are too proud, and won't let him assist us when he might. If we find a suitable house I shall be delighted to have her. I love the child for her mother's sake and her own."

"I wonder if they will ever send her away, as they did Clarence?" asked Charlie.

"I do not know," she rejoined. "Mr. Balch told me that he should not insist upon it if the child was unwilling."

The next day Charlie purchased all the morning papers he could obtain, and sat down to look over the list of wants. There were hungry people in want of professed cooks; divers demands for chamber-maids, black or white; special inquiries for waiters and footmen, in which the same disregard of colour was observable; advertisements for partners in all sorts of businesses, and for journeymen in every department of mechanical operations; then there were milliners wanted, sempstresses,[1] and even theatrical assistants, but nowhere in the long columns could he discover: "Wanted, a boy." Charlie searched them over and over, but the stubborn fact stared him in the face—there evidently were no boys wanted; and he at length concluded that he either belonged to a very useless class, or that there was an unaccountable prejudice existing in the city against the rising generation.

---

1 Seamstresses.

Charlie folded up the papers with a despairing sigh, and walked to the post-office to mail a letter to Mrs. Bird that he had written the previous evening. Having noticed a number of young men examining some written notices that were posted up, he joined the group, and finding it was a list of wants he eagerly read them over.

To his great delight he found there was one individual at least, who thought boys could be rendered useful to society, and who had written as follows: "Wanted, a youth of about thirteen years of age who writes a good hand, and is willing to make himself useful in an office.—Address, Box No. 77, Post-office."

"I'm their man!" said Charlie to himself, as he finished perusing it—"I'm just the person. I'll go home and write to them immediately;" and accordingly he hastened back to the house, sat down, and wrote a reply to the advertisement. He then privately showed it to Esther, who praised the writing and composition, and pronounced the whole very neatly done.

Charlie then walked down to the post-office to deposit his precious reply; and after dropping it into the brass mouth of the mail-box, he gazed in after it, and saw it glide slowly down into the abyss below.

How many more had stopped that day to add their contributions to the mass which Charlie's letter now joined? Merchants on the brink of ruin had deposited missives whose answer would make or break them; others had dropped upon the swelling heap tidings that would make poor men rich—rich men richer; maidens came with delicately written notes, perfumed and gilt-edged, eloquent with love—and cast them amidst invoices and bills of lading. Letters of condolence and notes of congratulation jostled each other as they slid down the brass throat; widowed mothers' tender epistles to wandering sons; the letters of fond wives to absent husbands; erring daughters' last appeals to outraged parents; offers of marriage; invitations to funerals; hope and despair; joy and sorrow; misfortune and success—had glided in one almost unbroken stream down that ever-distended and insatiable brass throat.

Charlie gave one more look at the opening, then sauntered homeward, building by the way houses of fabulous dimensions, with the income he anticipated from the situation if he succeeded in procuring it. Throughout the next day he was in a state of feverish anxiety and expectation, and Mrs. Ellis two or three times inquired the meaning of the mysterious whisperings and glances that were exchanged between him and Esther. The day wore away, and yet no answer—the next came and passed, still no communication; and Charlie had given up in despair, when he was agreeably surprised by the following:—

"Messrs. Twining, Western, and Twining will be much obliged to Charles Ellis, if he will call at their office, 567, Water-street, to-morrow morning at eleven o'clock, as they would like to communicate further with him respecting a situation in their establishment."

Charlie flew up stairs to Esther's room, and rushing in precipitately, exclaimed, "Oh! Ess—I've got it, I've got it—see here," he shouted, waving the note over his head; "Hurrah! Hurrah! Just read it, Ess, only just read it!"

"How can I, Charlie?" said she, with a smile, "if you hold it in your hand and dance about in that frantic style—give it me. There now—keep quiet a moment, and let me read it." After perusing it attentively, Esther added, "Don't be too sanguine, Charlie. You see by the tenor of the note that the situation is not promised you; they only wish to see you respecting it. You may not secure it, after all—some obstacle may arise of which we are not at present aware."

"Go on, old raven—croak away!" said Charlie, giving her at the same time a facetious poke.

"There's many a slip between the cup and the lip,"[1] she added.

"Oh, Ess!" he rejoined, "don't throw cold water on a fellow in that style—don't harbour so many doubts. Do you think they would take the trouble to write if they did not intend to give me the situation? Go away, old raven," concluded he, kissing her, "and don't let us have any more croaking."

Charlie was bounding from the room, when he was stopped by his sister, who begged him not to say anything to their mother respecting it, but wait until they knew the issue of the interview; and, if he secured the situation, it would be a very agreeable surprise to her.

We will now visit, in company with the reader, the spacious offices of Messrs. Twining, Western, and Twining, where we shall find Mr. Western about consigning to the waste-paper basket a large pile of letters. This gentleman was very fashionably dressed, of dark complexion, with the languid air and drawling intonation of a Southerner.

At an adjoining desk sat an elderly sharp-faced gentleman, who was looking over his spectacles at the movements of his

---

1 Proverbial; see Whiting 399.

partner. "What a mass of letters you are about to destroy," he remarked.

Mr. Western took from his mouth the cigar he was smoking, and after puffing from between his lips a thin wreath of smoke, replied: "Some of the most atwocious scwawls that man ever attempted to pewuse,—weplies to the advertisement. Out of the whole lot there wasn't more than a dozen amongst them that were weally pwesentable. Here is one wemawkably well witten: I have desiwed the witer to call this morning at eleven. I hope he will make as favouwable an impwession as his witing has done. It is now almost eleven—I pwesume he will be here soon."

Scarcely had Mr. Western finished speaking, ere the door opened, and Esther entered, followed by Charlie. Both the gentlemen rose, and Mr. Twining offered her a chair.

Esther accepted the proffered seat, threw up her veil, and said, in a slightly embarrassed tone, "My brother here, took the liberty of replying to an advertisement of yours, and you were kind enough to request him to call at eleven to-day."

"We sent a note to *your* brother?" said Mr. Twining, in a tone of surprise.

"Yes, sir, and here it is," said she, extending it to him.

Mr. Twining glanced over it, and remarked, "This is your writing, Western;" then taking Charlie's letter from the desk of Mr. Western, he asked, in a doubting tone, "Is this your own writing and composition?"

"My own writing and composing," answered Charlie.

"And it is vewy cweditable to you, indeed," said Mr. Western.

Both the gentlemen looked at the note again, then at Charlie, then at Esther, and lastly at each other; but neither seemed able to say anything, and evident embarrassment existed on both sides.

"And so you thought you would twy for the situation," at last remarked Mr. Western to Charlie.

"Yes, sir," he answered. "I was and am very anxious to obtain some employment."

"Have you a father?" asked Mr. Twining.

"Yes, sir; but he was badly injured by the mob last summer, and will never be able to work again."

"That's a pity," said Western, sympathisingly; "and what have you been doing?"

"Nothing very recently. I broke my arm last spring, and was obliged to go into the country for my health. I have not long returned."

"Do your pawents keep house?"

"Not at present. We are staying with a friend. Our house was burned down by the rioters."

This conversation recalled so vividly their past trials, that Esther's eyes grew watery, and she dropped her veil to conceal a tear that was trembling on the lid.

"How vewy unfortunate!" said Mr. Western, sympathisingly; "vewy twying, indeed!" then burying his chin in his hand, he sat silently regarding them for a moment or two.

"Have you come to any decision about taking him?" Esther at last ventured to ask of Mr. Twining.

"Taking him!—oh, dear me, I had almost forgot. Charles, let me see you write something—here, take this seat."

Charlie sat down as directed, and dashed off a few lines, which he handed to Mr. Twining, who looked at it over and over; then rising, he beckoned to his partner to follow him into an adjoining room.

"Well, what do you say?" asked Western, after they had closed the door behind them. "Don't you think we had better engage him?"

"Engage *him!*" exclaimed Twining—"why, you surprise me, Western—the thing's absurd; engage a coloured boy as under clerk! I never heard of such a thing."

"I have often," drawled Western; "there are the gweatest number of them in New Orleans."

"Ah, but New Orleans is a different place; such a thing never occurred in Philadelphia."

"Well, let us cweate a pwecedent, then. The boy wites wemark-ably well, and will, no doubt, suit us exactly. It will be a chawity to take him. We need not care what others say—evewybody knows who we are and what we are!"

"No, Western; I know the North better than you do; it would-n't answer at all here. We cannot take the boy—it is impossible; it would create a rumpus amongst the clerks, who would all feel dreadfully insulted by our placing a nigger child on an equality with them. I assure you the thing is out of the question."

"Well, I must say you Northern people are perfectly incomp-wehensible. You pay taxes to have niggers educated, and made fit for such places—and then won't let them fill them when they are pwepared to do so. I shall leave you, then, to tell them we can't take him. I'm doosed sowwy[1] for it—I like his looks."

---

1 Deuced (euphemism for "damned") sorry.

Whilst Mr. Western and his partner were discussing in one room, Charlie and Esther were awaiting with some anxiety their decision in the other.

"I think they are going to take me," said Charlie; "you saw how struck they appeared to be with the writing."

"They admired it, I know, my dear; but don't be too sanguine."

"I feel *sure* they are going to take me," repeated he with a hopeful countenance.

Esther made no reply, and they remained in silence until Mr. Twining returned to the room.

After two or three preparatory ahems, he said to Esther; "I should like to take your brother very much; but you see, in consequence of there being so much excitement just now, relative to Abolitionism and kindred subjects, that my partner and myself—that is, I and Mr. Western—think—or rather feel—that just now it would be rather awkward for us to receive him. We should like to take him; but his *colour*, miss—his complexion is a *fatal* objection. It grieves me to be obliged to tell you this; but I think, under the circumstances it would be most prudent for us to decline to receive him. We are *very* sorry—but our clerks are all young men, and have a great deal of prejudice, and I am sure he would be neither comfortable nor happy with them. If I can serve you in any other way—"

"There is nothing that you can do that I am aware of," said Esther, rising; "I thank you, and am sorry that we have occupied so much of your time."

"Oh, don't mention it," said Mr. Twining, evidently happy to get rid of them; and, opening the door, he bowed them out of the office.

The two departed sadly, and they walked on for some distance in silence. At last Esther pressed his hand, and, in a choking voice, exclaimed, "Charlie, my dear boy, I'd give my life if it would change your complexion—if it would make you white! Poor fellow! your battle of life will be a hard one to fight!"

"I know it, Ess; but I shouldn't care to be white if I knew I would not have a dear old Ess like you for a sister," he answered, pressing her hand affectionately. "I don't intend to be conquered," he continued; "I'll fight it out to the last—this won't discourage me. I'll keep on trying," said he, determinedly—"if one won't, perhaps another will."

For two or three days Charlie could hear of nothing that would be at all suitable for him. At last, one morning he saw an advertisement for a youth to learn the engraver's business—one who had some knowledge of drawing preferred; to apply at Thomas Blatchford's, bank-note engraver. "Thomas Blatchford," repeated Mr. Walters, as Charlie read it over—"why that is *the* Mr. Blatchford, the Abolitionist. I think you have some chance there most decidedly—I would advise you to take those sketches of yours and apply at once."

Charlie ran upstairs, and selecting the best-executed of his drawings, put them in a neat portfolio, and, without saying anything to Esther or his mother, hastened away to Mr. Blatchford's. He was shown into a room where a gentleman was sitting at a table examining some engraved plates.

"Is this Mr. Blatchford's?" asked Charlie.

"That is my name, my little man—do you want to see me?" he kindly inquired.

"Yes, sir. You advertised for a boy to learn the engraving business, I believe."

"Well; and what then?"

"I have come to apply for the situation."

"*You—you* apply?" said he, in a tone of surprise.

"Yes, sir," faltered Charlie; "Mr. Walters recommended me to do so."

"Ah, you know Mr. Walters, then," he rejoined.

"Yes, sir; he is a great friend of my father's—we are living with him at present."

"What have you in your portfolio, there?" enquired Mr. Blatchford. Charlie spread before him the sketches he had made during the summer, and also some ornamental designs suitable for the title-pages of books. "Why, these are excellently well done," exclaimed he, after examining them attentively; "who taught you?"

Charlie hereupon briefly related his acquaintance with the artist, and his efforts to obtain employment, and their results, besides many other circumstances connected with himself and family. Mr. Blatchford became deeply interested, and, at the end of a long conversation, delighted Charlie by informing him that if he and his mother could agree as to terms he should be glad to receive him as an apprentice.

Charlie could scarcely believe the evidence of his own ears, and leaving his portfolio on the table was hastening away.

"Stop! stop!" cried Mr. Blatchford, with a smile; "you have not heard all I wish to say. I would be much obliged to your mother if she would call at my house this evening, and then we can settle the matter definitely."

Charlie seemed to tread on air as he walked home. Flying up to Esther—his usual confidant—he related to her the whole affair, and gave at great length his conversation with Mr. Blatchford.

"That looks something like," said she; "I am delighted with the prospect that is opening to you. Let us go and tell mother,"—and, accordingly, off they both started, to carry the agreeable intelligence to Mrs. Ellis.

That evening Charlie, his mother, and Mr. Walters went to the house of Mr. Blatchford. They were most kindly received, and all the arrangements made for Charlie's apprenticeship. He was to remain one month on trial; and if, at the end of that period, all parties were satisfied, he was to be formally indentured.

Charlie looked forward impatiently to the following Monday, on which day he was to commence his apprenticeship. In the intervening time he held daily conferences with Kinch, as he felt their intimacy would receive a slight check after he entered upon his new pursuit.

"Look here, old fellow," said Charlie; "it won't do for you to be lounging on the door-steps of the office, nor be whistling for me under the windows. Mr. Blatchford spoke particularly against my having playmates around in work hours; evenings I shall always be at home, and then you can come and see me as often as you like."

Since his visit to Warmouth, Charlie had been much more particular respecting his personal appearance, dressed neater, and was much more careful of his clothes. He had also given up marbles, and tried to persuade Kinch to do the same.

"I'd cut marbles, Kinch," said he to him one evening, when they were walking together, "if I were you; it makes one such a fright—covers one with chalk-marks and dirt from head to foot. And another thing, Kinch; you have an abundance of good clothes—do wear them, and try and look more like a gentleman."

"Dear me!" said Kinch, rolling up the white of his eyes—"just listen how we are going on! Hadn't I better get an eye-glass and pair of light kid gloves?"

"Oh, Kinch!" said Charlie, gravely, "I'm not joking—I mean what I say. You don't know how far rough looks and an untidy person go against one. I do wish you would try and keep yourself decent."

"Well, there then—I will," answered Kinch. "But, Charlie, I'm afraid, with your travelling and one thing or other, you will forget your old playmate by-and-by, and get above him."

Charlie's eyes moistened; and, with a boy's impulsiveness, he threw his arm over Kinch's shoulder, and exclaimed with emphasis, "Never, old fellow, never—not as long as my name is Charlie Ellis. You mustn't be hurt at what I said, Kinch—I think more of these things than I used to—I see the importance of them. I find that any one who wants to get on must be particular in little things as well as great, and I must try and be a man now—for you know things don't glide on as smoothly with us as they used. I often think of our fun in the old house—ah, perhaps we'll have good times in another of our own yet!"—and with this Charlie and his friend separated for the night.

CHAPTER XXIX.

Clouds and Sunshine.

THE important Monday at length arrived, and Charlie hastened to the office of Mr. Blatchford, which he reached before the hour for commencing labour. He found some dozen or more journeymen assembled in the work-room; and noticed that upon his entrance there was an interchange of significant glances, and once or twice he overheard the whisper of "nigger."

Mr. Blatchford was engaged in discussing some business matter with a gentleman, and did not observe the agitation that Charlie's entrance had occasioned. The conversation having terminated, the gentleman took up the morning paper, and Mr. Blatchford, noticing Charlie, said, "Ah! you have come, and in good time, too. Wheeler," he continued, turning to one of the workmen, "I want you to take this boy under your especial charge: give him a seat at your window, and overlook his work."

At this there was a general uprising of the workmen, who commenced throwing off their caps and aprons. "What is all this for?" asked Mr. Blatchford in astonishment—"why this commotion?"

"We won't work with niggers!" cried one; "No nigger apprentices!" cried another; and "No niggers—no niggers!" was echoed from all parts of the room.

"Silence!" cried Mr. Blatchford, stamping violently—"silence, every one of you!" As soon as partial order was restored, he turned to Wheeler, and demanded, "What is the occasion of all this tumult—what does it mean?"

"Why, sir, it means just this: the men and boys discovered that you intended to take a nigger apprentice, and have made up their minds if you do they will quit in a body."

"It cannot be possible," exclaimed the employer, "that any man or boy in my establishment has room in his heart for such narrow contemptible prejudices. Can it be that you have entered into a conspiracy to deprive an inoffensive child of an opportunity of earning his bread in a respectable manner? Come, let me persuade you—the boy is well-behaved and educated!"

"Damn his behaviour and education!" responded a burly fellow; "let him be a barber or shoe-black—that is all niggers are good for. If he comes, we go—that's so, ain't it, boys?"

There was a general response of approval to this appeal; and Mr. Blatchford, seeing the utter uselessness of further parleying, left the room, followed by Charlie and the gentleman with whom he had been conversing.

Mr. Blatchford was placed in a most disagreeable position by this revolt on the part of his workmen; he had just received large orders from some new banks which were commencing operations, and a general disruption of his establishment at that moment would have ruined him. To accede to his workmen's demands he must do violence to his own conscience; but he dared not sacrifice his business and bring ruin on himself and family, even though he was right.

"What would you do, Burrell?" he asked of the gentleman who had followed them out.

"There is no question as to what you must do. You mustn't ruin yourself for the sake of your principles. You will have to abandon the lad; the other alternative is not to be thought of for a moment."

"Well, Charles, you see how it is," said Mr. Blatchford, reluctantly. Charlie had been standing intently regarding the conversation that concerned him so deeply. His face was pale and his lips quivering with agitation.

"I'd like to keep you, my boy, but you see how I'm situated, I must either give up you or my business; the latter I cannot afford to do." With a great effort Charlie repressed his tears, and bidding them good morning in a choking voice, hastened from the room.

"It's an infernal shame!" said Mr. Blatchford, indignantly; "and I shall think meanly of myself for ever for submitting to it; but I can't help myself, and must make the best of it."

Charlie walked downstairs with lingering steps, and took the direction of home. "All because I'm coloured," said he, bitterly, to himself—"all because I'm coloured! What *will* mother and Esther say? How it will distress them—they've so built upon it! I wish," said he, sadly, "that I was dead!" No longer able to repress the tears that were welling up, he walked towards the window of a print-store, where he pretended to be deeply interested in some pictures whilst he stealthily wiped his eyes. Every time he turned to leave the window, there came a fresh flood of tears; and at last he was obliged to give way entirely, and sobbed as if his heart would break.

He was thus standing when he felt a hand laid familiarly on his shoulder, and, on turning round, he beheld the gentleman he had left in Mr. Blatchford's office. "Come, my little man," said he, "don't take it so much to heart. Cheer up—you may find some other person willing to employ you. Come, walk on with me—

where do you live?" Charlie dried his eyes and gave him his address as they walked on up the street together.

Mr. Burrell talked encouragingly, and quite succeeded in soothing him ere they separated. "I shall keep a look out for you," said he, kindly; "and if I hear of anything likely to suit you, I shall let you know."

Charlie thanked him and sauntered slowly home. When he arrived, and they saw his agitated looks, and his eyes swollen from the effect of recent tears, there was a general inquiry of "What has happened? Why are you home so early; are you sick?"

Charlie hereupon related all that had transpired at the office—his great disappointment and the occasion of it—to the intense indignation and grief of his mother and sisters.

"I wish there were no white folks," said Caddy, wrathfully; "they are all, I believe, a complete set of villains and everything else that is bad."

"Don't be so sweeping in your remarks, pray don't, Caddy," interposed Esther; "you have just heard what Charlie said of Mr. Blatchford—his heart is kindly disposed, at any rate; you see he is trammelled by others."

"Oh! well, I don't like any of them—I hate them all!" she continued bitterly, driving her needle at the same time into the cloth she was sewing, as if it was a white person she had in her lap and she was sticking pins in him. "Don't cry, Charlie," she added; "the old white wretches, they shouldn't get a tear out of me for fifty trades!" But Charlie could not be comforted; he buried his head in his mother's lap, and wept over his disappointment until he made himself sick.

That day, after Mr. Burrell had finished his dinner, he remarked to his wife, "I saw something this morning, my dear, that made a deep impression on me. I haven't been able to get it out of my head for any length of time since; it touched me deeply, I assure you."

"Why, what could it have been? Pray tell me what it was."

Thereupon, he gave his wife a graphic account of the events that had transpired at Blatchford's in the morning; and in conclusion, said, "Now, you know, my dear, that no one would call *me* an *Abolitionist*; and I suppose I have some little prejudice, as well as others, against coloured people; but I had no idea that sensible men would have carried it to that extent, to set themselves up, as they did, in opposition to a little boy anxious to earn his bread by learning a useful trade."

Mrs. Burrell was a young woman of about twenty-two, with a round good-natured face and plump comfortable-looking figure; she had a heart overflowing with kindness, and was naturally much affected by what he related. "I declare it's perfectly outrageous," exclaimed she, indignantly; "and I wonder at Blatchford for submitting to it. I wouldn't allow myself to be dictated to in that manner—and he such an Abolitionist too! Had I been him, I should have stuck to my principles at any risk. Poor little fellow! I so wonder at Blatchford; I really don't think he has acted manly."

"Not so fast, my little woman, if you please—that is the way with almost all of you, you let your hearts run away with your heads. You are unjust to Blatchford; he could not help himself, he was completely in their power. It is almost impossible at present to procure workmen in our business, and he is under contract to finish a large amount of work within a specified time; and if he should fail to fulfil his agreement it would subject him to immense loss—in fact, it would entirely ruin him. You are aware, my dear, that I am thoroughly acquainted with the state of his affairs; he is greatly in debt from unfortunate speculations, and a false step just now would overset him completely; he could not have done otherwise than he has, and do justice to himself and his family. I felt that he could not; and in fact advised him to act as he did."

"Now, George Burrell, you didn't," said she, reproachfully.

"Yes I did, my dear, because I thought of his family; I really believe though, had I encouraged him, he would have made the sacrifice."

"And what became of the boy?"

"Oh, poor lad, he seemed very much cut down by it—I was quite touched by his grief. When I came out, I found him standing by a shop window crying bitterly. I tried to pacify him, and told him I would endeavour to obtain a situation for him somewhere—and I shall."

"Has he parents?" asked Mrs. Burrell.

"Yes; and, by the way, don't you remember whilst the mob was raging last summer, we read an account of a man running to the roof of a house to escape from the rioters? You remember they chopped his hands off and threw him over?"

"Oh, yes, dear, I recollect; don't—don't mention it," said she, with a shudder of horror. "I remember it perfectly."

"Well, this little fellow is his son," continued Mr. Burrell.

"Indeed! and what has become of his father—did he die?"

"No, he partially recovered, but is helpless, and almost an idiot. I never saw a child, apparently so anxious to get work; he talked more like a man with a family dependent upon him for support, than a youth. I tell you what, I became quite interested in him; he was very communicative, and told me all their circumstances; their house was destroyed by the mob, and they are at present residing with a friend."

Just then the cry of a child was heard in the adjoining room, and Mrs. Burrell rushed precipitately away, and soon returned with a fat, healthy-looking boy in her arms, which, after kissing, she placed in her husband's lap. He was their first-born and only child, and, as a matter of course, a great pet, and regarded by them as a most wonderful boy; in consequence, papa sat quite still, and permitted him to pull the studs out of his shirt, untie his cravat, rumple his hair, and take all those little liberties to which babies are notoriously addicted.

Mrs. Burrell sat down on a stool at her husband's feet, and gazed at him and the child in silence for some time.

"What's the matter, Jane; what has made you so grave?"

"I was trying to imagine, Burrell, how I should feel if you, I, and baby were coloured; I was trying to place myself in such a situation. Now we know that our boy, if he is honest and upright—is blest with great talent or genius—may aspire to any station in society that he wishes to obtain. How different it would be if he were coloured!—there would be nothing bright in the prospective for him. We could hardly promise him a living at any respectable calling. I think, George, we treat coloured people with great injustice, don't you?"

Mr. Burrell hemmed and ha'd at this direct query, and answered, "Well, we don't act exactly right toward them, I must confess."

Mrs. Burrell rose, and took the vacant knee of her husband, and toying with the baby, said, "Now, George Burrell, I want to ask a favour of you. Why can't *you* take this boy?"

"I take him! why, my dear, I don't want an apprentice."

"Yes, but you must *make* a want. You said he was a bright boy, and sketched well. Why, I should think that he's just what you ought to have. There is no one at your office that would oppose it. Cummings and Dalton were with your father before you, they would never object to anything reasonable that you proposed. Come, dear! do now make the trial—won't you?"

Mr. Burrell was a tender-hearted, yielding sort of an individual; and what was more, his wife was fully aware of it; and like a young witch as she was, she put on her sweetest looks, and begged so imploringly, that he was almost conquered. But when she took up the baby, and made him put his chubby arms round his father's neck, and say "pese pop-pop," he was completely vanquished, and surrendered at discretion.

"I'll see what can be done," said he, at last.

"And will you do it afterwards?" she asked, archly.

"Yes, I will, dear, I assure you," he rejoined.

"Then I know it will be done," said she, confidently; "and none of us will be the worse off for it, I am sure."

After leaving home, Mr. Burrell went immediately to the office of Mr. Blatchford; and after having procured Charlie's portfolio, he started in the direction of his own establishment. He did not by any means carry on so extensive a business as Mr. Blatchford, and employed only two elderly men as journeymen. After he had sat down to work, one of them remarked, "Tucker has been here, and wants some rough cuts executed for a new book. I told him I did not think you would engage to do them; that you had given up that description of work."

"I think we lose a great deal, Cummings, by being obliged to give up those jobs," rejoined Mr. Burrell.

"Why don't you take an apprentice then," he suggested; "it's just the kind of work for them to learn upon."

"Well I've been thinking of that," replied he, rising and producing the drawings from Charlie's portfolio. "Look here," said he, "what do you think of these as the work of a lad of twelve or fourteen, who has never had more than half a dozen lessons?"

"I should say they were remarkably well done," responded Cummings. "Shouldn't you say so, Dalton?" The party addressed took the sketches, and examined them thoroughly, and gave an approving opinion of their merits.

"Well," said Mr. Burrell, "the boy that executed those is in want of a situation, and I should like to take him: but I thought I would consult you both about it first. I met with him under very singular circumstances, and I'll tell you all about it." And forthwith he repeated to them the occurrences of the morning, dwelling upon the most affecting parts, and concluding by putting the question to them direct, as to whether they had any objections to his taking him.

"Why no, none in the world," readily answered Cummings. "Laws me! colour is nothing after all; and black fingers can handle a graver as well as white ones, I expect."

"I thought it best to ask you, to avoid any after difficulty. You have both been in the establishment so long, that I felt that you ought to be consulted."

"You needn't have taken that trouble," said Dalton. "You might have known that anything done by your father's son, would be satisfactory to us. I never had anything to do with coloured people, and haven't anything against them; and as long as you are contented I am."

"Well, we all have our little prejudices against various things; and as I did not know how you both would feel, I thought I wouldn't take any decided steps without consulting you; but now I shall consider it settled, and will let the lad know that I will take him."

In the evening, he hastened home at an earlier hour than usual, and delighted his wife by saying—"I have succeeded to a charm, my dear—there wasn't the very slightest objection. I'm going to take the boy, if he wishes to come."

"Oh, I'm delighted," cried she, clapping her hands. "Cry hurrah for papa!" said she to the baby; "cry hurrah for papa!"

The scion of the house of Burrell gave vent to some scarcely intelligible sounds, that resembled "Hoo-rogler pop-pop!" which his mother averred was astonishingly plain, and deserving of a kiss; and, snatching him up, she gave him two or three hearty ones, and then planted him in his father's lap again.

"My dear," said her husband, "I thought, as you proposed my taking this youth, you might like to have the pleasure of acquainting him with his good fortune. After tea, if you are disposed, we will go down there; the walk will do you good."

"Oh, George Burrell," said she, her face radiant with pleasure, "you are certainly trying to outdo yourself. I have been languishing all day for a walk! What a charming husband you are! I really ought to do something for you. Ah, I know what—I'll indulge you; you may smoke all the way there and back. I'll even go so far as to light the cigars for you myself."

"That *is* a boon," rejoined her husband with a smile; "really 'virtue rewarded,'[1] I declare."

Tea over, the baby kissed and put to bed, Mrs. Burrell tied on the most bewitching of bonnets, and donning her new fur-trimmed cloak, declared herself ready for the walk; and off they started. Mr. Burrell puffed away luxuriously as they walked along, stopping now and then at her command, to look into such

---

1 Proverbial phrase describing poetic justice, as in Samuel Richardson's novel *Pamela; or Virtue Rewarded* (1740).

shop-windows as contained articles adapted to the use of infants, from india-rubber rings and ivory rattles, to baby coats and shoes.

At length they arrived at the door of Mr. Walters, and on looking up at the house, he exclaimed, "This is 257, but it can't be the place; surely coloured people don't live in as fine an establishment as this." Then, running up the steps, he examined the plate upon the door. "The name corresponds with the address given me," said he; "I'll ring. Is there a lad living here by the name of Charles Ellis?" he asked of the servant who opened the door.

"Yes, sir," was the reply. "Will you walk in?"

When they were ushered into the drawing-room, Mr. Burrell said,—"Be kind enough to say that a gentleman wishes to see him."

The girl departed, closing the door behind her, leaving them staring about the room. "How elegantly it is furnished!" said she. "I hadn't an idea that there were any coloured people living in such style."

"Some of them are very rich," remarked her husband.

"But you said this boy was poor."

"So he is. I understand they are staying with the owner of this house."

Whilst they were thus conversing the door opened, and Esther entered. "I am sorry," said she, "that my brother has retired. He has a very severe head-ache, and was unable to remain up longer. His mother is out: I am his sister, and shall be most happy to receive any communication for him."

"I regret to hear of his indisposition," replied Mr. Burrell; "I hope it is not consequent upon his disappointment this morning?"

"I fear it is. Poor fellow! he took it very much to heart. It was a disappointment to us all. We were congratulating ourselves on having secured him an eligible situation."

"I assure you the disappointment is not all on one side; he is a very promising boy, and the loss of his prospective services annoying. Nothing but stern necessity caused the result."

"Oh, we entirely acquit you, Mr. Blatchford, of all blame in the matter. We are confident that what happened was not occasioned by any indisposition on your part to fulfil your agreement."

"My dear," interrupted Mrs. Burrell, "she thinks you are Mr. Blatchford."

"And are you not?" asked Esther, with some surprise.

"Oh, no; I'm an intimate friend of his, and was present this morning when the affair happened."

"Oh, indeed," responded Esther.

"Yes; and he came home and related it all to me,—the whole affair," interrupted Mrs. Burrell. "I was dreadfully provoked; I assure you, I sympathized with him very much. I became deeply interested in the whole affair; I was looking at my little boy,—for I have a little boy," said she, with matronly dignity,—"and I thought, suppose it was *my* little boy being treated so, how should I like it? So bringing the matter home to myself in that way made me feel all the more strongly about it; and I just told George Burrell he must take him, as he is an engraver; and I and the baby gave him no rest until he consented to do so. He will take him on the same terms offered by Mr. Blatchford; and then we came down to tell you; and—and," said she, quite out of breath, "that is all about it."

Esther took the little woman's plump hand in both her own, and, for a moment, seemed incapable of even thanking her. At last she said, in a husky voice, "You can't think what a relief this is to us. My brother has taken his disappointment so much to heart—I can't tell you how much I thank you. God will reward you for your sympathy and kindness. You must excuse me," she continued, as her voice faltered; "we have latterly been so unaccustomed to receive such sympathy and kindness from persons of your complexion, that this has quite overcome me."

"Oh, now, don't! I'm sure it's no more than our duty, and I'm as much pleased as you can possibly be—it has given me heartfelt gratification, I assure you."

Esther repeated her thanks, and followed them to the door, where she shook hands with Mrs. Burrell, who gave her a pressing invitation to come and see her baby.

"How easy it is, George Burrell," said the happy little woman, "to make the hearts of others as light as our own—mine feels like a feather," she added, as she skipped along, clinging to his arm. "What a nice, lady-like girl his sister is—is her brother as handsome as she?"

"Not quite, he answered; "still, he is very good-looking. I'll bring him home with me to-morrow at dinner, and then you can see him."

Chatting merrily, they soon arrived at home. Mrs. Burrell ran straightway upstairs to look at that "blessed baby;" she found him sleeping soundly, and looking as comfortable and happy as it is possible for a sleeping baby to look—so she bestowed upon him a perfect avalanche of kisses, and retired to her own peaceful pillow.

And now, having thus satisfactorily arranged for our young friend Charlie, we will leave him for a few years engaged in his new pursuits.

CHAPTER XXX.

Many Years After.

OLD Father Time is a stealthy worker. In youth we are scarcely able to appreciate his efforts, and oftentimes think him an exceedingly slow and limping old fellow. When we ripen into maturity, and are fighting our own way through the battle of life, we deem him swift enough of foot, and sometimes rather hurried; but when old age comes on, and death and the grave are foretold by trembling limbs and snowy locks, we wonder that our course has been so swiftly run, and chide old Time for a somewhat hasty and precipitate individual.

The reader must imagine that many years have passed away since the events narrated in the preceding chapters transpired, and permit us to re-introduce the characters formerly presented, without any attempt to describe how that long period has been occupied.

First of all, let us resume our acquaintance with Mr. Stevens. To effect this, we must pay that gentleman a visit at his luxurious mansion in Fifth Avenue, the most fashionable street of New York—the place where the upper ten thousand of that vast, bustling city most do congregate. As he is an old acquaintance (we won't say friend), we will disregard ceremony, and walk boldly into the library where that gentleman is sitting.

He is changed—yes, sadly changed. Time has been hard at work with him, and, dissatisfied with what his unaided agency could produce, has called in conscience to his aid, and their united efforts have left their marks upon him. He looks old—aye, very old. The bald spot on his head has extended its limits until there is only a fringe of thin white hair above the ears. There are deep wrinkles upon his forehead; and the eyes, half obscured by the bushy grey eyebrows, are bloodshot and sunken; the jaws hollow and spectral, and his lower lip drooping and flaccid. He lifts his hand to pour out another glass of liquor from the decanter at his side, when his daughter lays her hand upon it, and looks appealingly in his face.

She has grown to be a tall, elegant woman, slightly thin, and with a careworn and fatigued expression of countenance. There is, however, the same sweetness in her clear blue eyes, and as she moves her head, her fair flaxen curls float about her face as dreamily and deliciously as ever they did of yore. She is still in black, wearing mourning for her mother, who not many months before had been laid in a quiet nook on the estate at Savannah.

"Pray, papa, don't drink any more," said she, persuasively—"it makes you nervous, and will bring on one of those frightful attacks again."

"Let me alone," he remonstrated harshly—"let me alone, and take your hand off the glass; the doctor has forbidden laudanum, so I will have brandy instead—take off your hand and let me drink, I say."

Lizzie still kept her hand upon the decanter, and continued gently: "No, no, dear pa—you promised me you would only drink two glasses, and you have already taken three—it is exceedingly injurious. The doctor insisted upon it that you should decrease the quantity, and you are adding to it instead."

"Devil take the doctor!" exclaimed he roughly, endeavouring to disengage her hold—"give me the liquor, I say."

His daughter did not appear the least alarmed at this violence of manner, nor suffer her grasp upon the neck of the decanter to be relaxed; but all the while spoke soothing words to the angry old man, and endeavoured to persuade him to relinquish his intention of drinking any more.

"You don't respect your old father," he cried, in a whining tone—"you take advantage of my helplessness, all of you—you ill-treat me and deny me the very comforts of life! I'll tell—I'll tell the doctor," he continued, as his voice subsided into an almost inaudible tone, and he sank back into the chair in a state of semi-stupor.

Removing the liquor from his reach, his daughter rang the bell, and then walked towards the door of the room.

"Who procured that liquor for my father?" she asked of the servant who entered.

"I did, miss," answered the man, hesitatingly.

"Let this be the last time you do such a thing," she rejoined, eyeing him sternly, "unless you wish to be discharged. I thought you all fully understood that on no consideration was my father to have liquor, unless by the physician's or my order—it aggravates his disease and neutralizes all the doctor's efforts—and, unless you wish to be immediately discharged, never repeat the same offence. Now, procure some assistance—it is time my father was prepared for bed."

The man bowed and left the apartment; but soon returned, saying there was a person in the hall who had forced his way into the house, and who positively refused to stir until he saw Mr. Stevens.

"He has been here two or three times," added the man, "and he is very rough and impudent."

"This is most singular conduct," exclaimed Miss Stevens. "Did he give his name?"

"Yes, miss; he calls himself McCloskey."

At the utterance of this well-known name, Mr. Stevens raised his head, and stared at the speaker with a look of stupid fright, and inquired, "Who here—what name is that?—speak louder—what name?"

"McCloskey," answered the man, in a louder tone.

"What! he—*he!*" cried Mr. Stevens, with a terrified look. "Where—where is he?" he continued, endeavouring to rise—"where is he?"

"Stop, pa," interposed his daughter, alarmed at his appearance and manner. "Do stop—let me go."

"No—no!" said the old man wildly, seizing her by the dress to detain her—"*you* must not go—that would never do! He might tell her," he muttered to himself—"No, no—I'll go!"—and thus speaking, he made another ineffectual attempt to reach the door.

"Dear father! do let me go!" she repeated, imploringly. "You are incapable of seeing any one—let me inquire what he wants!" she added, endeavouring to loose his hold upon her dress.

"No—you shall not!" he replied, clutching her dress still tighter, and endeavouring to draw her towards him.

"Oh, father!" she asked distractedly, "what can this mean? Here," said she, addressing the servant, who stood gazing in silent wonder on this singular scene, "help my father into his chair again, and then tell this strange man to wait awhile."

The exhausted man, having been placed in his chair, motioned to his daughter to close the door behind the servant, who had just retired.

"He wants money," said he, in a whisper—"he wants money! He'll make beggars of us all—and yet I'll have to give him some. Quick! give me my cheque-book—let me give him something before he has a chance to talk to any one—quick! quick!"

The distracted girl wrung her hands with grief at what she imagined was a return of her father's malady, and exclaimed, "Oh! if George only would remain at home—it is too much for me to have the care of father whilst he is in such a state." Then pretending to be in search of the cheque-book, she turned over the pamphlets and papers upon his desk, that she might gain time, and think how it was best to proceed.

Whilst she was thus hesitating, the door of the room was suddenly opened, and a shabbily dressed man, bearing a strong odour of rum about him, forced his way into the apartment, saying, "I will see him. D——n it, I don't care a haporth[1] how sick he is—let me go, or by the powers I'll murther some of yes." The old man's face was almost blanched with terror when he heard the voice and saw the abrupt entry of the intruder. He sprang from the chair with a great effort, and then, unable to sustain himself, sunk fainting on the floor.

"Oh, you have killed my father—you have killed my father! Who are you, and what do you want, that you dare thrust yourself upon him in this manner?" said she, stooping to assist in raising him; "cannot you see he is entirely unfit for any business?"

Mr. Stevens was replaced in his chair, and water thrown in his face to facilitate his recovery.

Meanwhile, McCloskey had poured himself out a glass of brandy and water, which he stood sipping as coolly as if everything in the apartment was in a state of the most perfect composure. The singular terror of her father, and the boldness and assurance of the intruder, were to Miss Stevens something inexplicable—she stood looking from one to the other, as though seeking an explanation, and on observing symptoms of a return to consciousness on the part of her parent, she turned to McCloskey, and said, appealingly: "You see how your presence has agitated my father. Pray let me conjure you—go. Be your errand what it may, I promise you it shall have the earliest attention. Or," said she, "tell me what it is; perhaps I can see to it—I attend a great deal to father's business. Pray tell me!"

"No, no!" exclaimed the old man, who had caught the last few words of his daughter. "No, no—not a syllable! Here, I'm well— I'm well enough. I'll attend to you. There, there—that will do," he continued, addressing the servant; "leave the room. And you," he added, turning to his daughter, "do you go too. I am much better now, and can talk to him. Go! go!" he cried, impatiently, as he saw evidences of a disposition to linger, on her part; "if I want you I'll ring. Go!—this person won't stay long."

"Not if I get what I came for, miss," said McCloskey, insolently; "otherwise, there is no knowing how long I may stay." With a look of apprehension, Lizzie quitted the room, and the murderer and his accomplice were alone together.

---

1 Common contraction for "half-pennyworth."

Mr. Stevens reached across the table, drew the liquor towards him, and recklessly pouring out a large quantity, drained the glass to the bottom—this seemed to nerve him up and give him courage, for he turned to McCloskey and said, with a much bolder air than he had yet shown in addressing him, "So, you're back again, villain! are you? I thought and hoped you were dead;" and he leaned back in his chair and closed his eyes as if to shut out some horrid spectre.

"I've been divilish near it, squire, but Providence has preserved me, ye see—jist to be a comfort to ye in yer old age. I've been shipwrecked, blown up in steamboats, and I've had favers and choleray and the divil alone knows what—but I've been marcifully presarved to ye, and hope ye'll see a good dale of me this many years to come."

Mr. Stevens glared at him fiercely for a few seconds, and then rejoined, "You promised me solemnly, five years ago, that you would never trouble me again, and I gave you money enough to have kept you in comfort—ay, luxury—for the remainder of your life. Where is it all now?"

"That's more than I can tell you, squire. I only know how it comes. I don't trouble myself how it goes—that's your look out. If ye are anxious on that score you'd better hire a bookkeeper for me—he shall send yer honour a quarterly account, and then it won't come on ye so sudden when it's all out another time."

"Insolent!" muttered Mr. Stevens.

McCloskey gave Mr. Stevens an impudent look, but beyond that took no farther notice of his remark, but proceeded with the utmost coolness to pour out another glass of brandy—after which he drew his chair closer to the grate, and placed his dirty feet upon the mantelpiece in close proximity to an alabaster clock.

"You make yourself very much at home," said Stevens, indignantly.

"Why shouldn't I?" answered his tormentor, in a tone of the most perfect good humour. "Why shouldn't I—in the house of an ould acquaintance and particular friend—just the place to feel at home, eh, Stevens?" then, folding his arms and tilting back his chair, he asked, coolly: "You haven't a cigar, have ye?"

"No," replied Stevens, surlily; "and if I had, you should not have it. Your insolence is unbearable; you appear," continued he, with some show of dignity, "to have forgotten who I am, and who you are."

"Ye're mistaken there, squire. Divil a bit have I. I'm McCloskey, and you are Slippery George—an animal that's known over the 'varsal world as a Philadelphia lawyer[1]—a man that's chated his hundreds, and if he lives long enough, he'll chate as many more, savin' his friend Mr. McCloskey, and him he'll not be afther chating, because he won't be able to get a chance, although he'd like to if he could—divil a doubt of that."

"It's false—I never tried to cheat you," rejoined Stevens, courageously, for the liquor was beginning to have a very inspir-iting effect. "It's a lie—I paid you all I agreed upon, and more besides; but you are like a leech—never satisfied. You have had from me altogether nearly twenty thousand dollars, and you'll not get much more—now, mind I tell you."

"The divil I won't," rejoined he, angrily; "that is yet to be seen. How would you like to make yer appearance at court some fine morning, on the charge of murther, eh?" Mr. Stevens gave a per-ceptible shudder, and looked round, whereupon McCloskey said, with a malevolent grin, "Ye see I don't stick at words, squire; I call things by their names."

"So I perceive," answered Stevens. "You were not so bold once."

"Ha, ha!" laughed McCloskey. "I know *that* as well as you—then *I* was under the thumb—that was before we were sailing in the one boat; now ye see, squire, the boot is on the other leg."

Mr. Stevens remained quiet for a few moments, whilst his ragged visitor continued to leisurely sip his brandy and contem-plate the soles of his boots as they were reflected in the mirror above—they were a sorry pair of boots, and looked as if there would soon be a general outbreak of his toes—so thin and dilap-idated did the soles appear.

"Look at thim boots, and me suit ginerally, and see if your conscience won't accuse ye of ingratitude to the man who made yer fortune—or rather lets ye keep it, now ye have it. Isn't it a shame now for me, the best friend you've got in the world, to be tramping the streets widdout a penny in his pocket, and ye livin' in clover, with gold pieces as plenty as blackberries. It don't look right, squire, and mustn't go on any longer."

"What do you want—whatever will satisfy you?" asked Stevens. "If I give you ever so much now, what guarantee have I that you'll not return in a month or so, and want as much more?"

"I'll pledge ye me honour," said McCloskey, grandly.

---

1   Both literal (Stevens has practiced law in Philadelphia) and proverbial. In the early United States, a "Philadelphia lawyer" was shorthand for an attorney of particular cunning; see Whiting 334.

"Your honour!" rejoined Stevens, "that is no security."

"Security or no security," said McCloskey, impatiently, "you'll have to give me the money—it's not a bit of use now this disputin, bekase ye see I'm bound to have it, and ye are wise enough to know ye'd better give it to me. What if ye have give me thousands upon thousands," continued he, his former good-humoured expression entirely vanishing; "it's nothing more than you ought to do for keeping yer secrets for ye—and as long as ye have money, ye may expect to share it with me: so make me out a good heavy cheque, and say no more about it."

"What do you call a heavy cheque?" asked Stevens, in a despairing tone.

"Five or six thousand," coolly answered his visitor.

"Five or six thousand!" echoed Mr. Stevens, "it is impossible."

"It had better not be," said McCloskey, looking angry; "it had better not be—I'm determined not to be leading a beggar's life, and you to be a rolling in wealth."

"I can't give it, and won't give it—if it must come to that," answered Stevens, desperately. "It is you that have the fortune— I am only your banker at this rate. I can't give it to you—I haven't got that much money."

"You must find it then, and pretty quick at that," said McCloskey. "I'm not to be fooled with—I came here for money, and I must and will have it."

"I am willing to do what is reasonable," rejoined Mr. Stevens, in a more subdued tone. "You talk of thousands as most men do of hundreds. I really haven't got it."

"Oh, bother such stuff as that," interrupted McCloskey, incredulously. "I don't believe a word of it—I've asked them that know, and every one says you've made a mint of money by speculation—that since ye sold out in the South and came here to live, there's no end to the money ye've made; so you see it don't do to be making a poor mouth to me. I've come here for a check for five thousand dollars, and shan't go away without it," concluded he, in a loud and threatening tone.

During this conversation, Lizzie Stevens had been standing at the door, momentarily expecting a recall to the apartment. She heard the low rumble of their voices, but could not distinguish words. At length, hearing McCloskey's raised to a higher key, she could no longer restrain her impatience, and gently opening the door, looked into the room. Both their faces were turned in the opposite direction, so that neither noticed the gentle intrusion of

Lizzie, who, fearing to leave her father longer alone, ventured into the apartment.

"You need not stand looking at me in that threatening manner. You may do as you please—go tell what you like; but remember, when I fall, so do you; I have not forgotten that affair in Philadelphia from which I saved you—don't place me in a situation that will compel me to recur to it to your disadvantage."

"Ah, don't trouble yerself about that, squire; I don't—that is entirely off my mind; for now Whitticar is dead, where is yer witnesses?"

"Whitticar dead!" repeated Stevens.

"Yes; and what's more, he's buried—so he's safe enough, squire; and I shouldn't be at all surprised if you'd be glad to have me gone too."

"I would to God you had been, before I put myself in your power."

"'Twas your own hastiness. When it came to the pinch, I wasn't equal to the job, so ye couldn't wait for another time, but out with yer pistol, and does it yerself." The wretched man shuddered and covered his face, as McCloskey coolly recounted his murder of Mr. Garie, every word of which was too true to be denied.

"And haven't I suffered," said he, shaking his bald head mournfully; "haven't I suffered—look at my grey hairs and half-palsied frame, decrepit before I'm old—sinking into the tomb with a weight of guilt and sin upon me that will crush me down to the lowest depth of hell. Think you," he continued, "that because I am surrounded with all that money can buy, that I am happy, or ever shall be, with this secret gnawing at my heart; every piece of gold I count out, I see his hands outstretched over it, and hear him whisper 'Mine!' He gives me no peace night or day; he is always by me; I have no rest. And you must come, adding to my torture, and striving to tear from me that for which I bartered conscience, peace, soul, everything that would make life desirable. If there is mercy in you, leave me with what I give you, and come back no more. Life has so little to offer, that rather than bear this continued torment and apprehension I daily suffer, I will cut my throat, and then *your* game is over."

Lizzie Stevens stood rooted to the spot whilst her father made the confession that was wrung from him by the agony of the moment.

"Well, well!" said McCloskey, somewhat startled and alarmed

at Stevens's threat of self-destruction—"well, I'll come down a thousand—make it four."

"That I'll do," answered the old man, tremblingly; and reaching over, he drew towards him the cheque-book. After writing the order for the sum, he was placing it in the hand of McCloskey, when, hearing a faint moan, he looked towards the door, and saw his daughter fall fainting to the ground.

CHAPTER XXXI.

The Thorn rankles.

WE left the quiet town of Sudbury snow-clad and sparkling in all the glory of a frosty moonlight night; we now return to it, and discover it decked out in its bravest summer garniture. A short distance above the hill upon which it is built, the water of the river that glides along its base may be seen springing over the low dam that obstructs its passage, sparkling, glistening, dancing in the sunlight, as it falls splashing on the stones below; and then, as though subdued by the fall and crash, it comes murmuring on, stopping now and then to whirl and eddy round some rock or protruding stump, and at last glides gently under the arch of the bridge, seemingly to pause beneath its shadow and ponder upon its recent tumble from the heights above. Seated here and there upon the bridge are groups of boys, rod in hand, endeavouring, with the most delicious-looking and persuasive of baits, to inveigle finny innocents from the cool depths below.

The windows of the mills are all thrown open, and now and then the voices of some operatives, singing at their work, steal forth in company with the whir and hum of the spindles, and mingle with the splash of the waterfall; and the united voices of nature, industry, and man, harmonize their swelling tones, or go floating upward on the soft July air. The houses upon the hill-side seem to be endeavouring to extricate themselves from bowers of full-leafed trees; and with their white fronts, relieved by the light green blinds, look cool and inviting in the distance. High above them all, as though looking down in pride upon the rest, stands the Academy, ennobled in the course of years by the addition of extensive wings and a row of stately pillars.

On the whole, the town looked charmingly peaceful and attractive, and appeared just the quiet nook that a weary worker in cities would select as a place of retirement after a busy round of toils or pleasure.

There were little knots of idlers gathered about the railroad station, as there always is in quiet towns—not that they expect any one; but that the arrival and departure of the train is one of the events of the day, and those who have nothing else particular to accomplish feel constrained to be on hand to witness it. Every now and then one of them would look down the line and wonder why the cars were not in sight.

Amongst those seemingly the most impatient was Miss Ada Bell, who looked but little older than when she won the heart of the orphan Clarence, years before, by that kind kiss upon his childish brow. It was hers still—she bound it to her by long years of affectionate care, almost equalling in its sacrificing tenderness that which a mother would have bestowed upon her only child. Clarence, her adopted son, had written to her, that he was wretched, heart-sore, and ill, and longed to come to her, his almost mother, for sympathy, advice, and comfort: so she, with yearning heart, was there to meet him.

At last the faint scream of the steam-whistle was heard, and soon the lumbering locomotive came puffing and snorting on its iron path, dashing on as though it could never stop, and making the surrounding hills echo with the unearthly scream of its startling whistle, and arousing to desperation every dog in the quiet little town. At last it stopped, and stood giving short and impatient snorts and hisses, whilst the passengers were alighting.

Clarence stepped languidly out, and was soon in the embrace of Miss Ada.

"My dear boy, how thin and pale you look!" she exclaimed; "come, get into the carriage; never mind your baggage, George will look after that; your hands are hot—very hot, you must be feverish."

"Yes, Aunt Ada," for so she had insisted on his calling her, "I am ill—sick in heart, mind, and everything. Cut up the horses,"[1] said he, with slight impatience of manner; "let us get home quickly. When I get in the old parlour, and let you bathe my head as you used to, I am sure I shall feel better. I am almost exhausted from fatigue and heat."

"Very well then, dear, don't talk now," she replied, not in the least noticing his impatience of manner; "when you are rested, and have had your tea, will be time enough."

They were soon in the old house, and Clarence looked round with a smile of pleasure on the room where he had spent so many happy hours. Good Aunt Ada would not let him talk, but compelled him to remain quiet until he had rested himself, and eaten his evening meal.

He had altered considerably in the lapse of years, there was but little left to remind one of the slight, melancholy-looking boy, that once stood a heavy-hearted little stranger in the same room, in days gone by. His face was without a particle of red to relieve

---

1 I.e., whip them especially hard.

its uniform paleness; his eyes, large, dark, and languishing, were half hidden by unusually long lashes; his forehead broad, and surmounted with clustering raven hair; a glossy moustache covered his lip, and softened down its fulness; on the whole, he was strikingly handsome, and none would pass him without a second look.

Tea over, Miss Ada insisted that he should lie down upon the sofa again, whilst she sat by and bathed his head. "Have you seen your sister lately?" she asked.

"No, Aunt Ada," he answered, hesitatingly, whilst a look of annoyance darkened his face for a moment; "I have not been to visit her since last fall—almost a year."

"Oh! Clarence, how can you remain so long away?" said she, reproachfully.

"Well, I can't go there with any comfort or pleasure," he answered, apologetically; "I can't go there; each year as I visit the place, their ways seem more strange and irksome to me. Whilst enjoying her company, I must of course come in familiar contact with those by whom she is surrounded. Sustaining the position that I do—passing as I am for a white man—I am obliged to be very circumspect, and have often been compelled to give her pain by avoiding many of her dearest friends when I have encountered them in public places, because of their complexion. I feel mean and cowardly whilst I'm doing it; but it is necessary—I can't be white and coloured at the same time; the two don't mingle, and I must consequently be one or the other. My education, habits, and ideas, all unfit me for associating with the latter; and I live in constant dread that something may occur to bring me out with the former. I don't avoid coloured people, because I esteem them my inferiors in refinement, education, or intelligence; but because they are subjected to degradations that I shall be compelled to share by too freely associating with them.

"It is a pity," continued he, with a sigh, "that I was not suffered to grow up with them, then I should have learnt to bear their burthens, and in the course of time might have walked over my path of life, bearing the load almost unconsciously. Now it would crush me, I know. It was a great mistake to place me in my present false position," concluded he, bitterly; "it has cursed me. Only a day ago I had a letter from Em, reproaching me for my coldness; yet, God help me! What am I to do!"

Miss Ada looked at him sorrowfully, and continued smoothing down his hair, and inundating his temples with Cologne; at last she ventured to inquire, "How do matters progress with you and Miss Bates? Clary, you have lost your heart there!"

"Too true," he replied, hurriedly; "and what is more—little Birdie (I call her little Birdie) has lost hers too. Aunt Ada, we are engaged!"

"With her parents' consent?" she asked.

"Yes, with her parents' consent; we are to be married in the coming winter."

"Then they know *all*, of course—they know you are coloured?" observed she.

"They know all!" cried he, starting up. "*Who* said they did—*who* told them?—tell me that, I say! Who has *dared* to tell them I am a coloured man?"

"Hush, Clarence, hush!" replied she, attempting to soothe him. "I do not know that any one has informed them; I only inferred so from your saying you were engaged. I thought *you* had informed them yourself. Don't you remember you wrote that you should?—and I took it for granted that you had."

"Oh! yes, yes; so I did! I fully intended to, but found myself too great a coward. *I dare not*—I cannot risk losing her. I am fearful that if she knew it she would throw me off for ever."

"Perhaps not, Clarence—if she loves you as she should; and even if she did, would it not be better that she should know it now, than have it discovered afterwards, and you both be rendered miserable for life."

"No, no, Aunt Ada—I cannot tell her! It must remain a secret until after our marriage; then, if they find it out, it will be to their interest to smooth the matter over, and keep quiet about it."

"Clary, Clary—that is *not* honourable!"

"I know it—but how can I help it? Once or twice I thought of telling her, but my heart always failed me at the critical moment. It would kill me to lose her. Oh! I love her, Aunt Ada," said he, passionately—"love her with all the energy and strength of my father's race, and all the doating tenderness of my mother's. I could have told her long ago, before my love had grown to its present towering strength, but craft set a seal upon my lips, and bid me be silent until her heart was fully mine, and then nothing could part us; yet now even, when sure of her affections, the dread that her love would not stand the test, compels me to shrink more than ever from the disclosure."

"But, Clarence, you are not acting generously; I know your conscience does not approve your actions."

"Don't I know that?" he answered, almost fiercely; "yet I dare not tell—I must shut this secret in my bosom, where it gnaws, gnaws, gnaws, until it has almost eaten my heart away. Oh, I've thought of that, time and again; it has kept me awake night after night, it haunts me at all hours; it is breaking down my health and strength—wearing my very life out of me; no escaped galley slave ever felt more than I do, or lived in more constant fear of detection: and yet I must nourish this tormenting secret, and keep it growing in my breast until it has crowded out every honourable and manly feeling; and then, perhaps, after all my sufferings and sacrifice of candour and truth, out it will come at last, when I least expect or think of it."

Aunt Ada could not help weeping, and exclaimed, commiseratingly, "My poor, poor boy!" as he strode up and down the room.

"The whole family, except her, seem to have the deepest contempt for coloured people; they are constantly making them a subject of bitter jests; they appear to have no more feeling or regard for them than if they were brutes—and I," continued he, "I, miserable, contemptible, false-hearted knave, as I am, I—I— yes, I join them in their heartless jests, and wonder all the while my mother does not rise from her grave and *curse* me as I speak!"

"Oh! Clarence, Clarence, my dear child!" cried the terrified Aunt Ada, "you talk deliriously; you have brooded over this until it has almost made you crazy. Come here—sit down." And seizing him by the arm, she drew him on the sofa beside her, and began to bathe his hot head with the Cologne again.

"Let me walk, Aunt Ada," said he after a few moments,—"let me walk, I feel better whilst I am moving; I can't bear to be quiet." And forthwith he commenced striding up and down the room again with nervous and hurried steps. After a few moments he burst out again—

"It seems as if fresh annoyances and complications beset me every day. Em writes me that she is engaged. I was in hopes, that, after I had married, I could persuade her to come and live with me, and so gradually break off her connection with coloured people; but that hope is extinguished now: she is engaged to a coloured man."

Aunt Ada could see no remedy for this new difficulty, and could only say, "Indeed!"

"I thought something of the kind would occur when I was last at home, and spoke to her on the subject, but she evaded giving me any definite answer; I think she was afraid to tell me—she has written, asking my consent."

"And will you give it?" asked Aunt Ada.

"It will matter but little if I don't; Em has a will of her own, and I have no means of coercing her; besides, I have no reasonable objection to urge: it would be folly in me to oppose it, simply because he is a coloured man—for, what am I myself? The only difference is, that his identity with coloured people is no secret, and he is not ashamed of it; whilst I conceal my origin, and live in constant dread that some one may find it out." When Clarence had finished, he continued to walk up and down the room, looking very careworn and gloomy.

Miss Bell remained on the sofa, thoughtfully regarding him. At last, she rose up and took his hand in hers, as she used to when he was a boy, and walking beside him, said, "The more I reflect upon it, the more necessary I regard it that you should tell this girl and her parents your real position before you marry her. Throw away concealment, make a clean breast of it! you may not be rejected when they find her heart is so deeply interested. If you marry her with this secret hanging over you, it will embitter your life, make you reserved, suspicious, and consequently ill-tempered, and destroy all your domestic happiness. Let me persuade you, tell them ere it be too late. Suppose it reached them through some other source, what would they then think of you?"

"Who else would tell them? Who else knows it? You, you," said he suspiciously—"*you* would not betray me! I thought you loved me, Aunt Ada."

"Clarence, my dear boy," she rejoined, apparently hurt by his hasty and accusing tone, "you *will* mistake me—I have no such intention. If they are never to learn it except through *me*, your secret is perfectly safe. Yet I must tell you that I feel and think that the true way to promote her happiness and your own, is for you to disclose to them your real position, and throw yourself upon their generosity for the result."

Clarence pondered for a long time over Miss Bell's advice, which she again and again repeated, placing it each time before him in a stronger light, until, at last, she extracted from him a promise that he would do it. "I know you are right, Aunt Ada," said he; "I am convinced of that—it is a question of courage with me. I know it would be more honourable for me to tell her now. I'll try to do it—I will make an effort, and summon up the courage necessary—God be my helper!"

"That's a dear boy!" she exclaimed, kissing him affectionately; "I know you will feel happier when it is all over; and even if she should break her engagement, you will be infinitely better off than if it was fulfilled and your secret subsequently discovered. Come, now," she concluded, "I am going to exert my old authority, and send you to bed; to-morrow, perhaps, you may see this in a more hopeful light."

Two days after this, Clarence was again in New York, amid the heat and dust of that crowded, bustling city. Soon after his arrival, he dressed himself, and started for the mansion of Mr. Bates, trembling as he went, for the result of the communication he was about to make.

Once on the way he paused, for the thought had occurred to him that he would write to them; then reproaching himself for his weakness and timidity, he started on again with renewed determination.

"I'll see her myself," he soliloquized. "I'll tell little Birdie all, and know my fate from her own lips. If I must give her up, I'll know the worst from her."

When Clarence was admitted, he would not permit himself to be announced, but walked tiptoe upstairs and gently opening the drawing-room door, entered the room.

Standing by the piano, turning over the leaves of some music, and merrily humming an air, was a young girl of extremely *petite* and delicate form. Her complexion was strikingly fair; and the rich curls of dark auburn that fell in clusters on her shoulders, made it still more dazzling by the contrast presented. Her eyes were grey, inclining to black; her features small, and not over-remarkable for their symmetry, yet by no means disproportionate. There was the sweetest of dimples on her small round chin, and her throat white and clear as the finest marble. The expression of her face was extremely childlike; she seemed more like a schoolgirl than a young woman of eighteen on the eve of marriage. There was something deliciously airy and fairylike in her motions, and as she slightly moved her feet in time to the music she was humming, her thin blue dress floated about her, and undulated in harmony with her graceful motions.

After gazing at her for a few moments, Clarence called gently, "Little Birdie." She gave a timid joyous little cry of surprise and pleasure, and fluttered into his arms.

"Oh, Clary, love, how you startled me! I did not dream there was any one in the room. It was so naughty in you," said she, childishly, as he pushed back the curls from her face and kissed her. "When did you arrive?"

"Only an hour ago," he answered.

"And you came here at once? Ah, that was so lover-like and kind," she rejoined, smiling.

"You look like a sylph to-night, Anne," said he, as she danced about him. "Ah," he continued, after regarding her for a few seconds with a look of intense admiration, "you want to rivet my chains the tighter,—you look most bewitching. Why are you so much dressed to-night?—jewels, sash, and satin slippers," he continued; "are you going out?"

"No, Clary," she answered. "I was to have gone to the theatre; but just at the last moment I decided not to. A singular desire to stay at home came over me suddenly. I had an instinctive feeling that I should lose some greater enjoyment if I went; so I remained at home; and here, love, are you. But what is the matter? you look sad and weary."

"I am a little fatigued," said he, seating himself and holding her hand in his: "a little weary; but that will soon wear off; and as for the sadness," concluded he, with a forced smile, "that *must* depart now that I am with you, Little Birdie."

"I feel relieved that you have returned safe and well," said she, looking up into his face from her seat beside him; "for, Clary, love, I had such a frightful dream, such a singular dream about you. I have endeavoured to shake it out of my foolish little head; but it won't go, Clary,—I can't get rid of it. It occurred after you left us at Saratoga.[1] Oh, it was nothing though," said she, laughing and shaking her curls,—"nothing; and now you are safely returned, I shall not think of it again. Tell me what you have seen since you went away; and how is that dear Aunt Ada of yours you talk so much about?"

"Oh, she is quite well," answered he; "but tell, Anne, tell me about that dream. What was it, Birdie?—come tell me."

"I don't care to," she answered, with a slight shudder,—"I don't want to, love."

"Yes, yes,—do, sweet," importuned he; "I want to hear it."

"Then if I must," said she, "I will. I dreamed that you and I were walking on a road together, and 'twas such a beautiful road,

---

1 Saratoga Springs, New York (often shortened to Saratoga), became a fashionable spa and resort town in the nineteenth century. Its mineral baths were thought to have restorative powers and were particularly popular among middle- and upper-class tourists.

with flowers and fruit, and lovely cottages on either side. I thought you held my hand; I felt it just as plain as I clasp yours now. Presently a rough ugly man overtook us, and bid you let me go; and that you refused, and held me all the tighter. Then he gave you a diabolical look, and touched you on the face, and you broke out in loathsome black spots, and screamed in such agony and frightened me so, that I awoke all in a shiver of terror, and did not get over it all the next day."

Clarence clutched her hand tighter as she finished, so tight indeed, that she gave a little scream of pain and looked frightened at him. "What is the matter?" she inquired; "your hand is like ice, and you are paler than ever. You haven't let that trifling dream affect you so? It is nothing."

"I am superstitious in regard to dreams," said Clarence, wiping the perspiration from his forehead. "Go," he asked, faintly, "play me an air, love,—something quick and lively to dispel this. I wish you had not told me."

"But you begged me to," said she, pouting, as she took her seat at the instrument.

"How ominous," muttered he,—"became covered with black spots; that is a foreshadowing. How can I tell her," he thought. "It seems like wilfully destroying my own happiness." And he sat struggling with himself to obtain the necessary courage to fulfil the purpose of his visit, and became so deeply engrossed with his own reflections as to scarcely even hear the sound of the instrument.

"It is too bad," she cried, as she ceased playing: "here I have performed some of your favourite airs, and that too without eliciting a word of commendation. You are inexpressibly dull to-night; nothing seems to enliven you. What is the matter?"

"Oh," rejoined he, abstractedly, "am I? I was not aware of it."

"Yes, you are," said Little Birdie, pettishly; "nothing seems to engage your attention." And, skipping off to the table, she took up the newspaper, and exclaimed,—"Let me read you something very curious."

"No, no, Anne dear," interrupted he; "sit here by me. I want to say something serious to you—something of moment to us both."

"Then it's something very grave and dull, I know," she remarked; "for that is the way people always begin. Now I don't want to hear anything serious to-night; I want to be merry. You *look* serious enough; and if you begin to *talk* seriously you'll be perfectly unbearable. So you must hear what I am going to read to you first." And the little tyrant put her finger on his lip, and looked so bewitching, that he could not refuse her. And the important secret hung on his lips, but was not spoken.

"Listen," said she, spreading out the paper before her and running her tiny finger down the column. "Ah, I have it," she exclaimed at last, and began:—

"'We learn from unimpeachable authority that the Hon. —— ——, who represents a district of our city in the State legislature, was yesterday united to the Quateroon[1] daughter of the late Gustave Almont. She is said to be possessed of a large fortune, inherited from her father; and they purpose going to France to reside,—a sensible determination; as, after such a *mésalliance*, the honourable gentleman can no longer expect to retain his former social position in our midst.—*New Orleans Watchman.*'"

"Isn't it singular," she remarked, "that a man in his position should make such a choice?"

"He loved her, no doubt," suggested Clarence; "and she was almost white."

"How could he love her?" asked she, wonderingly. "Love a coloured woman! I cannot conceive it possible," said she, with a look of disgust; "there is something strange and unnatural about it."

"No, no," he rejoined, hurriedly, "it was love, Anne,—pure love; it is not impossible. I—I—" "am coloured," he would have said; but he paused and looked full in her lovely face. He could not tell her,—the words slunk back into his coward heart unspoken.

She stared at him in wonder and perplexity, and exclaimed,— "Dear Clarence, how strangely you act! I am afraid you are not well. Your brow is hot," said she, laying her hand on his forehead; "you have been travelling too much for your strength."

"It is not that," he replied. "I feel a sense of suffocation, as if all the blood was rushing to my throat. Let me get the air." And he rose and walked to the window. Anne hastened and brought him a glass of water, of which he drank a little, and then declared himself better.

After this, he stood for a long time with her clasped in his arms; then giving her one or two passionate kisses, he strained her closer to him and abruptly left the house, leaving Little Birdie startled and alarmed by his strange behaviour.

---

1   Also spelled "quadroon," a mixed-race person with a single black grandparent.

CHAPTER XXXII.

Dear Old Ess again.

LET US visit once more the room from which Mr. Walters and his friends made so brave a defence. There is but little in its present appearance to remind one of that eventful night,—no reminiscences of that desperate attack, save the bullet-hole in the ceiling, which Mr. Walters declares shall remain unfilled as an evidence of the marked attention he has received at the hands of his fellow-citizens.

There are several noticeable additions to the furniture of the apartment; amongst them an elegantly-carved work-stand, upon which some unfinished articles of children's apparel are lying; a capacious rocking-chair, and grand piano.

Then opposite to the portrait of Toussaint is suspended another picture, which no doubt holds a higher position in the regard of the owner of the mansion than the African warrior aforesaid. It is a likeness of the lady who is sitting at the window,—Mrs. Esther Walters, *née* Ellis. The brown baby in the picture is the little girl at her side,—the elder sister of the other brown baby who is doing its best to pull from its mother's lap the doll's dress upon which she is sewing. Yes, that is "dear old Ess," as Charlie calls her yet, though why he will persist in applying the adjective we are at a loss to determine.

Esther looks anything but old—a trifle matronly, we admit— but old we emphatically say she is not; her hair is parted plainly, and the tiniest of all tiny caps sits at the back of her head, looking as if it felt it had no business on such raven black hair, and ought to be ignominiously dragged off without one word of apology. The face and form are much more round and full, and the old placid expression has been undisturbed in the lapse of years.

The complexion of the two children was a sort of compromise between the complexions of their parents—chubby-faced, chestnut-coloured, curly-headed, rollicking little pests, who would never be quiet, and whose little black buttons of eyes were always peering into something, and whose little plugs of fingers would, in spite of every precaution to prevent, be diving into mother's work-box, and various other highly inconvenient and inappropriate places.

"There!" said Esther, putting the last stitch into a doll she had been manufacturing; "now, take sister, and go away and play." But little sister, it appeared, did not wish to be taken, and she made the best of her way off, holding on by the chairs, and tottering over the great gulfs between them, until she succeeded in reaching the music-stand, where she paused for a while before beginning to destroy the music. Just at this critical juncture a young lady entered the room, and held up her hands in horror, and baby hastened off as fast as her toddling limbs could carry her, and buried her face in her mother's lap in great consternation.

Emily Garie made two or three slight feints of an endeavour to catch her, and then sat down by the little one's mother, and gave a deep sigh.

"Have you answered your brother's letter?" asked Esther.

"Yes, I have," she replied; "here it is,"—and she laid the letter in Esther's lap. Baby made a desperate effort to obtain it, but suffered a signal defeat, and her mother opened it, and read—

"DEAR BROTHER,—I read your chilling letter with deep sorrow. I cannot say that it surprised me; it is what I have anticipated during the many months that I have been silent on the subject of my marriage. Yet, when I read it, I could not but feel a pang to which heretofore I have been a stranger. Clarence, you know I love you, and should not make the sacrifice you demand a test of my regard. True, I cannot say (and most heartily I regret it) that there exists between us the same extravagant fondness we cherished as children—but that is no fault of mine. Did you not return to me, each year, colder and colder—more distant and unbrotherly—until you drove back to their source the gushing streams of a sister's love that flowed so strongly towards you? You ask me to resign Charles Ellis and come to you. What can you offer me in exchange for his true, manly affection?—to what purpose drive from my heart a love that has been my only solace, only consolation, for your waning regard! We have grown up together—he has been warm and kind, when you were cold and indifferent—and now that he claims the reward of long years of tender regard, and my own heart is conscious that he deserves it, you would step between us, and forbid me yield the recompense that it will be my pride and delight to bestow. It grieves me to write it; yet I must, Clary—for between brother and sister there is no need of concealments; and particularly at such a time should everything be open, clear, explicit. Do not think I wish to reproach you. What you are, Clarence, your false position and unfortunate education have made you. I write it with pain—your demand seems extremely selfish. I fear it is not of *me* but of *yourself* you are thinking, when you ask me to sever, at once and for ever, my connection with a people who, you say, can only degrade me. Yet how much happier am I, sharing their degradation, than you appear to be! Is it regard for me that induces the desire that I should share the life of constant dread that I cannot but feel you endure—or do you fear that my present connections will interfere with your own plans for the future?

"Even did I grant it was my happiness alone you had in view, my objections would be equally strong. I could not forego the claims of early friendship, and estrange myself from those who have endeared themselves to me by long years of care—nor pass coldly and unrecognizingly by play-mates and acquaintances, because their complexions were a few shades darker than my own. This I could never do—to me it seems ungrateful: yet I would not reproach you because you can—for the circumstances by which you have been sur-rounded have conspired to produce that result—and I presume you regard such conduct as necessary to sustain you in your present position. From the tenor of your letter I should judge that you entertained some fear that I might compromise you with your future bride, and intimate that *my* choice may deprive you of *yours*. Surely that need not be. *She* need not even know of my existence. Do not entertain a fear that I, or my future husband, will ever interfere with your happiness by thrusting ourselves upon you, or endanger your social position by proclaiming our relationship. Our paths lie so widely apart that they need never cross. You walk on the side of the oppressor—I, thank God, am with the oppressed.

"I am happy—more happy, I am sure, than you could make me, even by surrounding me with the glittering lights that shine upon your path, and which, alas! may one day go sud-denly out, and leave you wearily groping in the darkness. I trust, dear brother, my words may not prove a prophecy; yet, should they be, trust me, Clarence, you may come back again, and a sister's heart will receive you none the less warmly that you selfishly desired her to sacrifice the happi-ness of a lifetime to you. I shall marry Charles Ellis. I ask you to come and see us united—I shall not reproach you if you do not; yet I shall feel strange without a single relative to kiss or bless me in that most eventful hour of a woman's life. God bless you, Clary! I trust your union may be as happy as I anticipate my own will be—and, if it is not, it will not be because it has lacked the earnest prayers of your neglected but still loving sister."

"Esther, I thought I was too cold in that—tell me, do you think so?"

"No, dear, not at all; I think it a most affectionate reply to a cold, selfish letter."

"Oh, I'm glad to hear you say that. I can trust better to your tenderness of others' feelings than to my own heart. I felt strongly, Esther, and was fearful that it might be too harsh or reproachful. I was anxious lest my feelings should be too strikingly displayed; yet it was better to be explicit—don't you think so?"

"Undoubtedly," answered Esther; and handing back the letter, she took up baby, and seated herself in the rocking-chair.

Now baby had a prejudice against caps, inveterate and unconquerable; and grandmamma, nurse, and Esther were compelled to bear the brunt of her antipathies. We have before said that Esther's cap *looked* as though it felt itself in an inappropriate position—that it had got on the head of the wrong individual—and baby, no doubt in deference to the cap's feelings, tore it off, and threw it in the half-open piano, from whence it was extricated with great detriment to the delicate lace.

Emily took a seat near the window, and drawing her worktable towards her, raised the lid. This presenting another opening for baby, she slid down from her mother's lap, and hastened towards her. She just arrived in time to see it safely closed, and toddled back to her mother, as happy as if she had succeeded in running riot over its contents, and scattering them all over the floor.

Emily kept looking down the street, as though in anxious expectation of somebody; and whilst she stood there, there was an opportunity of observing how little she had changed in the length of years. She is little Em magnified, with a trifle less of the child in her face. Her hair has a slight kink, is a little more wavy than is customary in persons of entire white blood; but in no other way is her extraction perceptible. Only the initiated, searching for evidences of African blood, would at all notice this slight peculiarity.

Her expectation was no doubt about to be gratified, for a smile broke over her face, as she left the window and skipped downstairs; when she re-entered, she was accompanied by her intended husband.

There was great commotion amongst the little folk in consequence of this new arrival. Baby kicked, and screamed out "Unker Char," and went almost frantic because her dress became entangled in the buckle of her mamma's belt, and her sister received a kiss before she could be extricated.

Charlie is greatly altered—he is tall, remarkably athletic, with a large, handsomely-shaped head, covered with close-cut, woolly hair; high forehead, heavy eyebrows, large nose, and a mouth of ordinary size, filled with beautifully white teeth, which he displays at almost every word he speaks; chin broad, and the whole expression of his face thoughtful and commanding, yet replete with good humour. No one would call him handsome, yet there was something decidedly attractive in his general appearance. No one would recognize him as the Charlie of old, whose escapades had so destroyed the comfort and harmony of Mrs. Thomas's establishment; and only once, when he held up the baby, and threatened to let her tear the paper ornaments from the chandelier, was there a twinkle of the Charlie of old looking out of his eyes.

"How are mother and father to-day?" asked Esther.

"Oh, both well. I left them only a few minutes ago at the dinner table. I had to hurry off to go to the office."

"So I perceive," observed Esther, archly, "and of course, coming here, which is four squares out of your way, will get you there much sooner."

Emily blushed, and said, smilingly, Esther was "a very impertinent person;" and in this opinion Charlie fully concurred. They then walked to the window, where they stood, saying, no doubt, to each other those little tender things which are so profoundly interesting to lovers, and so exceedingly stupid to every one else. Baby, in high glee, was seated on Charlie's shoulder, where she could clutch both hands in his hair and pull until the tears almost started from his eyes.

"Emily and you have been talking a long while, and I presume you have fully decided on what day you are both to be rescued from your misery, and when I am to have the exquisite satisfaction of having my house completely turned upside down for your mutual benefit," said Esther. "I trust it will be as soon as possible, as we cannot rationally expect that either of you will be bearable until it is all over, and you find yourselves ordinary mortals again. Come now, out with it. When is it to be?"

"I say next week," cried Charlie.

"Next week, indeed," hastily rejoined Emily. "I could not think of such a thing—so abrupt."

"So abrupt," repeated Charlie, with a laugh. "Why, haven't I been courting you ever since I wore roundabouts,[1] and hasn't everybody been expecting us to be married every week within the last two years. Fie, Em, it's anything but abrupt."

Emily blushed still deeper, and looked out of the window, down the street and up the street, but did not find anything in the prospect at either side that at all assisted her to come to a decision, so she only became more confused and stared the harder; at last she ventured to suggest that day two months.

"This day two months—outrageous!" said Charlie. "Come here, dear old Ess, and help me to convince this deluded girl of the preposterous manner in which she is conducting herself."

"I must join her side if you *will* bring me into the discussion. I think she is right, Charlie—there is so much to be done: the house to procure and furnish, and numberless other things that you hasty and absurd men know nothing about."

By dint of strong persuasion from Charlie, Emily finally consented to abate two weeks of the time, and they decided that a family council should be held that evening at Mrs. Ellis's, when the whole arrangements should be definitely settled.

A note was accordingly despatched by Esther to her mother—that she, accompanied by Emily and the children, would come to them early in the afternoon, and that the gentlemen would join them in the evening at tea-time. Caddy was, of course, completely upset by the intelligence; for, notwithstanding that she and the maid-of-all-work lived in an almost perpetual state of house-cleaning, nothing appeared to her to be in order, and worse than all, there was nothing to eat.

"Nothing to eat!" exclaimed Mrs. Ellis. "Why, my dear child, there are all manner of preserves, plenty of fresh peaches to cut and sugar down, and a large pound-cake in the house, and any quantity of bread can be purchased at the baker's."

"Bread—plain bread!" rejoined Caddy, indignantly, quite astonished at her mother's modest idea of a tea—and a company-tea at that. "Do you think, mother, I'd set Mr. Walters down to plain bread, when we always have hot rolls and short-cake at their house? It is not to be thought of for a moment: they must have some kind of hot cake, be the consequences what they may."

Caddy bustled herself about, and hurried up the maid-of-all-

---

1 Short, close-fitting jackets buttoned to the neck; worn chiefly by young boys.

work in an astonishing manner, and before the company arrived had everything prepared, and looked as trim and neat herself as if she had never touched a rolling-pin, and did not know what an oven was used for.

Behold them all assembled. Mrs. Ellis at the head of the table with a grandchild on each side of her, and her cap-strings pinned upon the side next to baby. Esther sits opposite her husband, who is grown a little grey, but otherwise is not in the least altered; next to her is her father, almost buried in a large easy-chair, where he sits shaking his head from time to time, and smiling vacantly at the children; then come Emily and Charlie at the foot, and at his other hand Caddy and Kinch—Kinch the invincible—Kinch the dirty—Kinch the mischievous, now metamorphosed into a full-blown dandy, with faultless linen, elegant vest, and fashionably-cut coat. Oh, Kinch, what a change—from the most shabby and careless of all boys to a consummate exquisite, with heavy gold watch and eye-glass, and who has been known to dress regularly twice a day!

There was a mighty pouring out of tea at Mrs. Ellis's end of the table, and baby of course had to be served first with some milk and bread. Between her and the cat intimate relations seemed to exist, for by their united efforts the first cup was soon disposed of, and baby was clamouring for the second before the elder portions of the family had been once served round with tea.

Charlie and Emily ate little and whispered a great deal; but Kinch, the voracity of whose appetite had not at all diminished in the length of years, made up for their abstinence by devouring the delicious round short-cakes with astonishing rapidity. He did not pretend to make more than two bites to a cake, and they slipped away down his throat as if it was a railroad tunnel and they were a train of cars behind time.

Caddy felt constrained to get up every few moments to look after something, and to assure herself by personal inspection that the reserved supplies in the kitchen were not likely to be exhausted. Esther occupied herself in attending upon her helpless father, and fed him as tenderly and carefully as if he was one of her babies.

"I left you ladies in council. What was decided?" said Charlie, "don't be at all bashful as regards speaking before Kinch, for he is in the secret and has been these two months. Kinch is to be groomsman, and has had three tailors at work on his suit for a fortnight past. He told me this morning that if you did not hurry matters up, his wedding coat would be a week out of fashion before he should get a chance to wear it."

"How delightful—Kinch to be groomsman," said Esther; "that is very kind in you, Kinch, to assist us to get Charlie off our hands."

"And who is to be bridesmaid?" asked Walters.

"Oh, Caddy of course—I couldn't have any one but Caddy," blushingly answered Emily.

"That is capital," cried Charlie, giving Kinch a facetious poke, "just the thing, isn't it, Kinch—it will get her accustomed to these matters. You remember what you told me this morning, eh, old boy?" he concluded, archly.

Kinch tried to blush, but being very dark-complexioned his efforts in that direction were not at all apparent, so he evidenced his confusion by cramming a whole short-cake into his mouth, and almost caused a stoppage in the tunnel; Caddy became excessively red in the face, and was sure they wanted more cakes.

But Mr. Walters was equally confident they did not, and put his back against the door and stood there, whilst Mrs. Ellis gravely informed them that she soon expected to be her own housekeeper, for that she had detected Caddy and Kinch in a fur-niture establishment, pricing a chest of drawers and a wash-stand; and that Kinch had unblushingly told her they had for some time been engaged to be married, but somehow or other had forgotten to mention it to her.

This caused a general shout of laughter around the table, in which baby tumultuously joined, and rattled her spoon against the tea-urn until she almost deafened them.

This noise frightened Mr. Ellis, who cried, "There they come! there they come!" and cowered down in his great chair, and looked so exceedingly terrified, that the noise was hushed instantly, and tears sprang into the eyes of dear old Ess, who rose and stood by him, and laid his withered face upon her soft warm bosom, smoothed down the thin grey hair, and held him close to her throbbing tender heart, until the wild light vanished from his bleared and sunken eyes, and the vacant childish smile came back on his thin, wan face again, when she said, "Pray don't laugh so very loud, it alarms father; he is composed now, pray don't startle him so again."

This sobered them down a little, and they quietly recom-menced discussing the matrimonial arrangements; but they were all in such capital spirits that an occasional hearty and good-humoured laugh could not be suppressed.

Mr. Walters acted in his usual handsome manner, and facetiously collaring Charlie, took him into a corner and informed him that he had an empty house that he wished him to occupy, and that if he ever whispered the word rent, or offered him any money before he was worth twenty thousand dollars, he should believe that he wanted to pick a quarrel with him, and should refer him to a friend, and then pistols and coffee[1] would be the inevitable result.

Then it came out that Caddy and Kinch had been courting for some time, if not with Mrs. Ellis's verbal consent, with at least no objection from that good lady; for Master Kinch, besides being an exceedingly good-natured fellow, was very snug in his boots,[2] and had a good many thousand dollars at his disposal, bequeathed him by his father.

The fates had conspired to make that old gentleman rich. He owned a number of lots on the outskirts of the city, on which he had been paying taxes a number of years, and he awoke one fine morning to find them worth a large sum of money. The city council having determined to cut a street just beside them, and the property all around being in the hands of wealthy and fashionable people, his own proved to be exceedingly valuable.

It was a sad day for the old man, as Kinch and his mother insisted that he should give up business, which he did most reluctantly, and Kinch had to be incessantly on the watch thereafter, to prevent him from hiring cellars, and sequestering their old clothes to set up in business again. They were both gone now, and Kinch was his own master, with a well-secured income of a thousand dollars a year, with a prospect of a large increase.

They talked matters over fully, and settled all their arrangements before the time for parting, and then, finding the baby had scrambled into Mrs. Ellis's lap and gone fast asleep, and that it was long after ten o'clock, each departed, taking their several ways for home.

---

1 American idiomatic shorthand for a sunrise duel.
2 Financially comfortable.

CHAPTER XXXIII.

The Fatal Discovery.

THERE is great bustle and confusion in the house of Mr. Bates. Mantua-makers[1] and milliners are coming in at unearthly hours, and consultations of deep importance are being duly held with maiden aunts and the young ladies who are to officiate as bridesmaids at the approaching ceremony. There are daily excursions to drapers' establishments, and jewellers, and, in fact, so much to be done and thought of, that little Birdie is in constant confusion, and her dear little curly head is almost turned topsy-turvy. Twenty times in each day is she called upstairs to where the sempstresses are at work, to have something tried on or fitted. Poor little Birdie! she declares she never can stand it: she did not dream that to be married she would have been subjected to such a world of trouble, or she would never have consented,—*never!*

And then Clarence, too, comes in every morning, and remains half the day, teasing her to play, to talk, or sing. Inconsiderate Clarence! when she has so much on her mind; and when at last he goes, and she begins to felicitate herself that she is rid of him, back he comes again in the evening, and repeats the same annoyance. O, naughty, tiresome, Clarence! how can you plague little Birdie so? Perhaps you think she doesn't dislike it; you may be right, very likely she doesn't.

She sometimes wonders why he grows paler and thinner each day, and his nervous and sometimes distracted manner teases her dreadfully; but she supposes all lovers act thus, and expects they cannot help it—and then little Birdie takes a sly peep in the glass, and does not so much wonder after all.

Yet if she sometimes deems his manner startling and odd, what would she say if she knew that, night after night, when he left her side, he wandered for long hours through the cold and dreary streets, and then went to his hotel, where he paced his room until almost day?

Ah, little Birdie, a smile will visit his pale face when you chirp tenderly to him, and a faint tinge comes upon his cheek when you lay your soft tiny hand upon it; yet all the while there is that desperate secret lying next his heart, and, like a vampire, sucking away, drop by drop, happiness and peace.

---

1   Dressmakers; a mantua was a kind of loose gown.

Not so with little Birdie; she is happy—oh, *so* happy: she rises with a song upon her lips, and is chirping in the sunshine she herself creates, the live-long day. Flowers of innocence bloom and flourish in her peaceful lithesome heart. Poor, poor, little Birdie! those flowers are destined to wither soon, and the sunlight fade from thy happy face for ever.

One morning, Clarence, little Birdie, and her intended brides-maid, Miss Ellstowe, were chatting together, when a card was handed to the latter, who, on looking at it, exclaimed, "Oh, dear me! an old beau of mine; show him up," and scampering off to the mirror, she gave a hasty glance, to see that every curl was in its effective position.

"Who is it?" asked little Birdie, all alive with curiosity; "do say who it is."

"Hush!" whispered Miss Ellstowe, "here he comes, my dear; he is very rich—a great catch; are my curls all right?"

Scarcely had she asked the question, and before an answer could be returned, the servant announced Mr. George Stevens, and the gentleman walked into the room.

Start not, reader, it is not the old man we left bent over the prostrate form of his unconscious daughter, but George Stevens, junior, the son and heir of the old man aforesaid. The heart of Clarence almost ceased to beat at the sound of that well-known name, and had not both the ladies been so engrossed in observing the new-comer, they must have noticed the deep flush that suffused his face, and the deathly pallor that succeeded it.

Mr. Stevens was presented to Miss Bates, and Miss Ellstowe turned to present him to Clarence. "Mr. Garie—Mr. Stevens," said she. Clarence bowed.

"Pardon me, I did not catch the name," said the former, politely.

"Mr. Clarence Garie," she repeated, more distinctly.

George Stevens bowed, and then sitting down opposite Clarence, eyed him for a few moments intently. "I think we have met before," said he at last, in a cold, contemptuous tone, not unmingled with surprise, "have we not?"

Clarence endeavoured to answer, but could not; he was, for a moment, incapable of speech; a slight gurgling noise was heard in his throat, as he bowed affirmatively.

"We were neighbours at one time, I think," added George Stevens.

"We were," faintly ejaculated Clarence.

"It is a great surprise to me to meet *you* here," pursued George Stevens.

"The surprise is mutual, I assure you, sir," rejoined Clarence, coldly, and with slightly agitated manner.

Hereupon ensued an embarrassing pause in the conversation, during which the ladies could not avoid observing the livid hue of Clarence's face. There was a perfect tumult raging in his breast; he knew that now his long-treasured secret would be brought out; this was to be the end of his struggle to preserve it—to be exposed at last, when on the brink of consummating his happiness. As he sat there, looking at George Stevens, he became a murderer in his heart; and if an invisible dagger could have been placed in his hands, he would have driven it to the hilt in his breast, and stilled for ever the tongue that was destined to betray him.

But it was too late; one glance at the contemptuous, malignant face of the son of his father's murderer, told him his fate was sealed—that it was now too late to avert exposure. He grew faint, dizzy, ill,—and rising, declared hurriedly he must go, staggered towards the door, and fell upon the carpet, with a slight stream of blood spirting from his mouth.[1]

Little Birdie screamed, and ran to raise him; George Stevens and Miss Ellstowe gave their assistance, and by their united efforts he was placed upon the sofa. Little Birdie wiped the bloody foam from his mouth with her tiny lace handkerchief, bathed his head, and held cold water to his lips; but consciousness was long returning, and they thought he was dying.

Poor torn heart! pity it was thy beatings were not stilled then for ever. It was not thy fate; long, long months of grief and despair were yet to come before the end approached and day again broke upon thee.

Just at this crisis Mr. Bates came in, and was greatly shocked and alarmed by Clarence's deathly appearance. As he returned to consciousness he looked wildly about him, and clasping little Birdie's hand in his, gazed at her with a tender imploring countenance: yet it was a despairing look—such a one as a shipwrecked seaman gives when, in sight of land, he slowly relaxes his hold upon the sustaining spar that he has no longer the strength to clutch, and sinks for ever beneath the waters.

---

1 The description of Clary's symptoms is consistent with other nineteenth-century representations of the physiological consequences of terrible grief or shock.

A physician was brought in, who declared he had ruptured a minor blood-vessel, and would not let him utter a whisper, and, assisted by Mr. Bates, placed him in his carriage, and the three were driven as swiftly as possible to the hotel where Clarence was staying. Little Birdie retired to her room in great affliction, followed by Miss Ellstowe, and George Stevens was left in the room alone.

"What can the fellow have been doing here?" he soliloquized; "on intimate terms too, apparently; it is very singular; I will wait Miss Ellstowe's return, and ask an explanation."

When Miss Ellstowe re-entered the room, he immediately inquired, "What was that Mr. Garie doing here? He seems on an exceedingly intimate footing, and your friend apparently takes a wonderful interest in him."

"Of course she does; that is her *fiancé*."

"*Impossible!*" rejoined he, with an air of astonishment.

"Impossible!—why so? I assure you he is. They are to be married in a few weeks. I am here to officiate as bridesmaid."

"Phew!" whistled George Stevens; and then, after pausing a moment, he asked, "Do you know anything about this Mr. Garie—anything, I mean, respecting his family?"

"Why, no—that is, nothing very definite, more than that he is an orphan, and a gentleman of education and independent means."

"Humph!" ejaculated George Stevens, significantly.

"Humph!" repeated Miss Ellstowe, "what do you mean? Do you know anything beyond that? One might suppose you did, from your significant looks and gestures."

"Yes, I *do* know something about this Mr. Garie," he replied, after a short silence. "But tell me what kind of people are these you are visiting—Abolitionists, or anything of that sort?"

"How absurd, Mr. Stevens, to ask such a question; of course they are not," said she, indignantly; "do you suppose I should be here if they were? But why do you ask—is this Mr. Garie one?"

"No, my friend," answered her visitor; "*I wish that was all.*"

"That was all!—how strangely you talk—you alarm me," continued she, with considerable agitation. "If you know anything that will injure the happiness of my friend—anything respecting Mr. Garie that she or her father should know—make no secret of it, but disclose it to me at once. Anne is my dearest friend, and I, of course, must be interested in anything that concerns her happiness. Tell me, what is it you know?"

"It is nothing, I assure you, that it will give me any pleasure to tell," answered he.

"Do speak out, Mr. Stevens. Is there any stain on his character, or that of his family? Did he ever do anything dishonourable?"

"*I wish that was all*," coolly repeated George Stevens. "I am afraid he is a villain, and has been imposing himself upon this family for what he is not."

"Good Heavens! Mr. Stevens, how is he a villain or impostor?"

"You all suppose him to be a white man, do you not?" he asked.

"Of course we do," she promptly answered.

"Then you are all grievously mistaken, for he is not. Did you not notice how he changed colour, how agitated he became, when I was presented? It was because he knew that his exposure was at hand. I know him well—in fact, he is the illegitimate son of a deceased relative of mine, by a mulatto slave."

"It cannot be possible," exclaimed Miss Ellstowe, with a wild stare of astonishment. "Are you sure of it?"

"Sure of it! of course I am. I should indeed be a rash man to make such a terrible charge unless perfectly able to substantiate it. I have played with him frequently when a child, and my father made a very liberal provision for this young man and his sister, after the death of their father, who lost his life through imprudently living with this woman in Philadelphia, and consequently getting himself mixed up with these detestable Abolitionists."

"Can this be true?" asked Miss Ellstowe, incredulously.

"I assure you it is. We had quite lost sight of them for a few years back, and I little supposed we should meet under such circumstances. I fear I shall be the cause of great discomfort, but I am sure in the end I shall be thanked. I could not, with any sense of honour or propriety, permit such a thing as this marriage to be consummated, without at least warning your friends of the real position of this fellow. I trust, Miss Ellstowe, you will inform them of what I have told you."

"How can I? Oh, Mr. Stevens!" said she, in a tone of deep distress, "this will be a terrible blow—it will almost kill Anne. No, no; the task must not devolve on me—I cannot tell them. Poor little thing! it will break her heart, I am afraid."

"Oh, but you must, Miss Ellstowe; it would seem very impertinent in me—a stranger—to meddle in such a matter; and, besides, they may be aware of it, and not thank me for my interference."

"No, I assure you they are not; I am confident they have not the most distant idea of such a thing—they would undoubtedly regard it as an act of kindness on your part. I shall insist upon your remaining until the return of Mr. Bates, when I shall beg you to repeat to him what you have already revealed to me."

"As you insist upon it, I suppose I must," repeated he, after some reflection; "but I must say I do not like the office of informer," concluded he, with assumed reluctance.

"I am sorry to impose it upon you; yet, rest assured, they will thank you. Excuse me for a few moments—I will go and see how Anne is."

Miss Ellstowe returned, after a short interval, with the information that little Birdie was much more composed, and would, no doubt, soon recover from her fright.

"To receive a worse blow," observed George Stevens. "I pity the poor little thing—only to think of the disgrace of being engaged to a nigger. It is fortunate for them that they will make the discovery ere it be too late. Heavens! only think what the consequences might have been had she married this fellow, and his peculiar position became known to them afterwards! She would have been completely 'done for.'"[1]

Thus conversing respecting Clarence, they awaited the return of Mr. Bates. After the lapse of a couple of hours he entered the drawing-room. Mr. Stevens was presented to him by Miss Ellstowe, as a particular friend of herself and family.

"I believe you were here when I came in before; I regret I was obliged to leave so abruptly," courteously spoke Mr. Bates, whilst bowing to his new acquaintance; "the sudden and alarming illness of my young friend will, I trust, be a sufficient apology."

"How is he now?" asked Miss Ellstowe.

"Better—much better," answered he, cheerfully; "but very wild and distracted in his manner—alarmingly so, in fact. He clung to my hand, and wrung it when we parted, and bid me good bye again and again, as if it was for the last time. Poor fellow! he is frightened at that hemorrhage, and is afraid it will be fatal; but there is not any danger, he only requires to be kept quiet—he will soon come round again, no doubt. I shall have to ask you to excuse me again," said he, in conclusion; "I must go and see my daughter."

Mr. Bates was rising to depart, when George Stevens gave Miss Ellstowe a significant look, who said, in a hesitating tone, "Mr. Bates, one moment before you go. My friend, Mr. Stevens,

---

1 Doomed.

has a communication to make to you respecting Mr. Garie, which will, I fear, cause you, as it already has me, deep distress."

"Indeed!" rejoined Mr. Bates, in a tone of surprise; "What is it? Nothing that reflects upon his character, I hope."

"I do not know how my information will influence your conduct towards him, for I do not know what your sentiments may be respecting such persons. I know society in general do not receive them, and my surprise was very great to find him here."

"I do not understand you; what do you mean?" demanded Mr. Bates, in a tone of perplexity; "has he ever committed any crime?"

"He is a coloured man," answered George Stevens, briefly. Mr. Bates became almost purple, and gasped for breath; then, after staring at his informant for a few seconds incredulously, repeated the words "Coloured man!" in a dreamy manner, as if in doubt whether he had really heard them.

"Yes, coloured man," said George Stevens, confidently; "it grieves me to be the medium of such disagreeable intelligence; and I assure you I only undertook the office upon the representation of Miss Ellstowe, that you were not aware of the fact, and would regard my communication as an act of kindness."

"It—it *can't* be," exclaimed Mr. Bates, with the air of a man determined not to be convinced of a disagreeable truth; "it cannot be possible."

Hereupon George Stevens related to him what he had recently told Miss Ellstowe respecting the parentage and position of Clarence. During the narration, the old man became almost frantic with rage and sorrow, bursting forth once or twice with the most violent exclamations; and when George Stevens concluded, he rose and said, in a husky voice—

"I'll kill him, the infernal hypocrite! Oh! the impostor to come to my house in this nefarious manner, and steal the affections of my daughter—the devilish villain! a bastard! a contemptible black-hearted nigger. Oh, my child—my child! it will break your heart when you know what deep disgrace has come upon you. I'll go to him," added he, his face flushed, and his white hair almost erect with rage; "I'll murder him—there's not a man in the city will blame me for it;" and he grasped his cane as though he would go at once, and inflict summary vengeance upon the offender.

"Stop, sir, don't be rash," exclaimed George Stevens; "I would not screen this fellow from the effects of your just and very natural indignation—he is abundantly worthy of the severest punishment you can bestow; but if you go in your present excited state, you might be tempted to do something which would make this whole affair public, and injure, thereby, your daughter's future. You'll pardon me, I trust, and not think me presuming upon my short acquaintance in making the suggestion."

Mr. Bates looked about him bewilderedly for a short time, and then replied, "No, no, you need not apologize, you are right—I thank you; I myself should have known better. But my poor child! what will become of her?" and in an agony of sorrow he resumed his seat, and buried his face in his hands.

George Stevens prepared to take his departure, but Mr. Bates pressed him to remain. "In a little while," said he, "I shall be more composed, and then I wish you to go with me to this worthless scoundrel. I must see him at once, and warn him what the consequences will be should he dare approach my child again. Don't fear me," he added, as he saw George Stevens hesitated to remain; "that whirlwind of passion is over now. I promise you I shall do nothing unworthy of myself or my child."

It was not long before they departed together for the hotel at which Clarence was staying. When they entered his room, they found him in his bed, with the miniature of little Birdie in his hands. When he observed the dark scowl on the face of Mr. Bates, and saw by whom he was accompanied, he knew his secret was discovered; he saw it written on their faces. He trembled like a leaf, and his heart seemed like a lump of ice in his bosom. Mr. Bates was about to speak, when Clarence held up his hand in the attitude of one endeavouring to ward off a blow, and whispered hoarsely—

"Don't tell me—not yet—a little longer! I see you know all. I see my sentence written on your face! Let me dream a little longer ere you speak the words that must for ever part me and little Birdie. I know you have come to separate us—but don't tell me yet; for when you do," said he, in an agonized tone, "it will kill me!"

"I wish to God it would!" rejoined Mr. Bates. "I wish you had died long ago; then you would have never come beneath my roof to destroy its peace for ever. You have acted basely, palming yourself upon us—counterfeit as you were! and taking in exchange her true love and my honest, honourable regard."

Clarence attempted to speak, but Mr. Bates glared at him, and continued—"There are laws to punish thieves and counterfeits— but such as you may go unchastised, except by the abhorrence of all honourable men. Had you been unaware of your origin, and had the revelation of this gentleman been as new to you as to me, you would have deserved sympathy; but you have been acting a lie, claiming a position in society to which you knew you had no right, and deserve execration and contempt. Did I treat you as my feelings dictated, you would understand what is meant by the weight of a father's anger; but I do not wish the world to know that my daughter has been wasting her affections upon a worthless nigger; that is all that protects you! Now, hear me," he added, fiercely,—"if ever you presume to darken my door again, or attempt to approach my daughter, I will shoot you, as sure as you sit there before me!"

"And serve you perfectly right!" observed George Stevens.

"Silence, sir!" rejoined Clarence, sternly. "How dare you interfere? He may say what he likes—reproach me as he pleases—*he* is *her* father—I have no other reply; but if you dare again to utter a word, I'll——" and Clarence paused and looked about him as if in search of something with which to enforce silence.

Feeble-looking as he was, there was an air of determination about him which commanded acquiescence, and George Stevens did not venture upon another observation during the interview.

"I want my daughter's letters—every line she ever wrote to you; get them at once—I want them now," said Mr. Bates, imperatively.

"I cannot give them to you immediately, they are not accessible at present. Does she want them?" he asked, feebly—"has she desired to have them back?"

"Never mind that!" said the old man, sternly; "no evasions. Give me the letters!"

"To-morrow I will send them," said Clarence. "I will read them all over once again," thought he.

"I cannot believe you," said Mr. Bates.

"I promise you upon my honour I will send them to-morrow!"

"*A nigger's honour!*" rejoined Mr. Bates, with a contemptuous sneer.

"Yes, sir—a nigger's honour!" repeated Clarence, the colour mounting to his pale cheeks. "A few drops of negro blood in a man's veins do not entirely deprive him of noble sentiments. 'Tis true my past concealment does not argue in my favour.—I concealed that which was no fault of my own, but what the injustice of society has made a crime."

"I am not here for discussion; and I suppose I must trust to your *honour*," interrupted Mr. Bates, with a sneer. "But remember, if the letters are not forthcoming to-morrow I shall be here again, and then," concluded he in a threatening tone, "my visit will not be as harmless as this has been!"

After they had gone, Clarence rose and walked feebly to his desk,[1] which, with great effort and risk, he removed to the bed-side; then taking from it little Birdie's letters, he began their perusal.

Ay! read them again—and yet again; pore over their con-tents—dwell on those passages replete with tenderness, until every word is stamped upon thy breaking heart—linger by them as the weary traveller amid Sahara's sand pauses by some sparkling fountain in a shady oasis, tasting of its pure waters ere he launches forth again upon the arid waste beyond. This is the last green spot upon thy way to death; beyond whose grim portals, let us believe, thou and thy "little Birdie" may meet again.

---

1 Here, a box that holds writing materials.

CHAPTER XXXIV.

"Murder will out."[1]

THE city clocks had just tolled out the hour of twelve, the last omnibus had rumbled by, and the silence without was broken only at rare intervals when some belated citizen passed by with hurried footsteps towards his home. All was still in the house of Mr. Stevens—so quiet, that the ticking of the large clock in the hall could be distinctly heard at the top of the stairway, breaking the solemn stillness of the night with its monotonous "click, click—click, click!"

In a richly furnished chamber overlooking the street a dim light was burning; so dimly, in fact, that the emaciated form of Mr. Stevens was scarcely discernible amidst the pillows and covering of the bed on which he was lying. Above him a brass head of curious workmanship held in its clenched teeth the canopy that overshadowed the bed; and as the light occasionally flickered and brightened, the curiously carved face seemed to light up with a sort of sardonic grin; and the grating of the curtain-rings, as the sick man tossed from side to side in his bed, would have suggested the idea that the odd supporter of the canopy was gnashing his brazen teeth at him.

On the wall, immediately opposite the light, hung a portrait of Mrs. Stevens; not the sharp, hard face we once introduced to the reader, but a smoother, softer countenance—yet a worn and melancholy one in its expression. It looked as if the waves of grief had beaten upon it for a long succession of years, until they had tempered down its harsher peculiarities, giving a subdued appearance to the whole countenance.

"There is twelve o'clock—give me my drops again, Lizzie," he remarked, faintly. At the sound of his voice Lizzie emerged from behind the curtains, and essayed to pour into a glass the proper quantity of medicine. She was twice obliged to pour back into the phial what she had just emptied forth, as the trembling of her hands caused her each time to drop too much; at last, having succeeded in getting the exact number of drops, she handed him the glass, the contents of which he eagerly drank.

"There!" said he, "thank you; now, perhaps, I may sleep. I have not slept for two nights—such has been my anxiety about that

---

1 Proverbial; see for instance William Henry Porter, *Common and Scriptural Proverbs Explained* (Boston: James Munroe, 1845), 131.

man; nor you either, my child—I have kept you awake also. You can sleep, though, without drops. To-morrow, when you are prepared to start, wake me, if I am asleep, and let me speak to you before you go. Remember, Lizzie, frighten him if you can! Tell him, I am ill myself—that I can't survive this continued worriment and annoyance. Tell him, moreover, I am not made of gold, and will not be always giving. I don't believe he is sick—dying—do you?" he asked, looking into her face, as though he did not anticipate an affirmative answer.

"No, father, I don't think he is really ill; I imagine it is another subterfuge to extract money. Don't distress yourself unnecessarily; perhaps I may have some influence with him—I had before, you know!"

"Yes, yes, dear, you managed him very well that time—very well," said he, stroking down her hair affectionately. "I—I—my child, I could never have told you of that dreadful secret; but when I found that you knew it all, my heart experienced a sensible relief. It was a selfish pleasure, I know; yet it eased me to share my secret; the burden is not half so heavy now."

"Father, would not your mind be easier still, if you could be persuaded to make restitution to his children? This wealth is valueless to us both. You can never ask forgiveness for the sin whilst you cling thus tenaciously to its fruits."

"Tut, tut—no more of that!" said he, impatiently; "I cannot do it without betraying myself. If I gave it back to them, what would become of you and George, and how am I to stop the clamours of that cormorant?[1] No, no! it is useless to talk of it—I cannot do it!"

"There would be still enough left for George, after restoring them their own, and you might give this man my share of what is left. I would rather work day and night," said she, determinedly, "than ever touch a penny of the money thus accumulated."

"I've thought all that over, long ago, but I dare not do it—it might cause inquiries to be made that might result to my disadvantage. No, I cannot do that; sit down, and let us be quiet now."

Mr. Stevens lay back upon his pillow, and for a moment seemed to doze; then starting up again suddenly, he asked, "Have you told George about it? Have you ever confided anything to him?"

"No, papa," answered she soothingly, "not a breath; I've been secret as the grave."

---

1 A proverbially greedy seabird; here used as a figure for an avaricious person. See *OED* "cormorant" 2a.

"That's right!" rejoined he—"that is right! I love George, but not as I do you. He only comes to me when he wants money. He is not like you, darling—you take care of and nurse your poor old father. Has he come in yet?"

"Not yet; he never gets home until almost morning, and is then often fearfully intoxicated."

The old man shook his head, and muttered, "The sins of the fathers shall[1]—what is that? Did you hear that noise?—hush!"

Lizzie stood quietly by him for a short while, and then walked on tiptoe to the door—"It is George," said she, after peering into the gloom of their entry; "he has admitted himself with his night-key."

The shuffling sound of footsteps was now quite audible upon the stairway, and soon the bloated face of Mr. Stevens's hopeful son was seen at the chamber door. In society and places where this young gentleman desired to maintain a respectable character he could be as well behaved, as choice in his language, and as courteous as anybody; but at home, where he was well known, and where he did not care to place himself under any restraint, he was a very different individual.

"Let me in, Liz," said he, in a thick voice; "I want the old man to fork over some money—I'm cleaned out."

"No, no—go to bed, George," she answered, coaxingly, "and talk to him about it in the morning."

"I'm coming in *now*," said he, determinedly; "and besides, I want to tell you something about that nigger Garie."

"Tell us in the morning," persisted Lizzie.

"No—I'm going to tell you now," rejoined he, forcing his way into the room—"it's too good to keep till morning. Pick up that wick, let a fellow see if you are all alive!"

Lizzie raised the wick of the lamp in accordance with his desire, and then sat down with an expression of annoyance and vexation on her countenance.

George threw himself into an easy chair, and began, "I saw that white nigger Garie to-night, he was in company with a gentleman, at that—the assurance of that fellow is perfectly incomprehensible. He was drinking at the bar of the hotel; and as it is no secret why he and Miss Bates parted, I enlightened the company on the subject of his antecedents. He threatened to

---

1 Paraphrase of Old Testament warning that the sins of the fathers will be visited on their children (see Exodus 20:5, Numbers 14:18, Deuteronomy 5:9).

challenge me! Ho! ho!—fight with a nigger—that is too good a joke!" And laughing heartily, the young ruffian leant back in his chair. "I want some money to-morrow, dad," continued he. "I say, old gentleman, wasn't it a lucky go that darkey's father was put out of the way so nicely, eh?—We've been living in clover ever since—haven't we?"

"How dare you address me in that disrespectful manner? Go out of the room, sir!" exclaimed Mr. Stevens, with a disturbed countenance.

"Come, George, go to bed," urged his sister wearily. "Let father sleep—it is after twelve o'clock. I am going to wake the nurse, and then retire myself."

George rose stupidly from his chair, and followed his sister from the room. On the stairway he grasped her arm rudely, and said, "I don't understand how it is that you and the old man are so cursed thick all of a sudden. You are thick as two thieves, always whispering and talking together. Act fair, Liz—don't persuade him to leave you all the money. If you do, we'll quarrel—that's flat. Don't try and cozen him out of my share as well as your own—you hear!"

"Oh, George!" rejoined she reproachfully—"I never had such an idea."

"Then what are you so much together for? Why is there so much whispering and writing, and going off on journeys all alone? What does it all mean, eh?"

"It means nothing at all, George. You are not yourself to-night," said she evasively; "you had better go to bed."

"It is *you* that are not yourself," he retorted. "What makes you look so pale and worried—and why do you and the old man start if the door cracks, as if the devil was after you? What is the meaning of that?" asked he with a drunken leer. "You had better look out," concluded he; "I'm watching you both, and will find out all your secrets by-and-by."

"Learn all our secrets! Ah, my brother!" thought she, as he disappeared into his room, "you need not desire to have their fearful weight upon you, or you will soon grow as anxious, thin, and pale as I am."

The next day at noon Lizzie started on her journey, after a short conference with her father.

Night had settled upon her native city, when she was driven through its straight and seemingly interminable thoroughfares. The long straight rows of lamps, the snowy steps, the scrupulously clean streets, the signs over the stores, were like the faces of old acquaintances, and at any other time would have caused agreeable recollections; but the object of her visit pre-occupied her mind, to the exclusion of any other and more pleasant associations.

She ordered the coachman to take her to an obscure hotel, and, after having engaged a room, she left her baggage and started in search of the residence of McCloskey.

She drew her veil down over her face very closely, and walked quickly through the familiar streets, until she arrived at the place indicated in his letter. It was a small, mean tenement, in a by-street, in which there were but one or two other houses. The shutters were closed from the upper story to the lowest, and the whole place wore an uninhabited appearance. After knocking several times, she was about to give up in despair, when she discovered through the glass above the door the faint glimmer of a light, and shortly after a female voice demanded from the inside, "Who is there?"

"Does Mr. McCloskey live here?" asked Lizzie.

Hearing a voice not more formidable than her own, the person within partially opened the door; and, whilst shading with one hand the candle she held in the other, gazed out upon the speaker.

"Does Mr. McCloskey live here?" repeated Lizzie.

"Yes, he does," answered the woman, in a weak voice; "but he's got the typers."

"Has the what?" inquired Lizzie, who did not exactly understand her.

"Got the typers—got the fever, you know."

"The typhus fever!" said Lizzie, with a start; "then he is really sick."

"Really sick!" repeated the woman—"*really* sick! I should think he was! Why, he's been a raving and swearing awful for days; he stormed and screamed so loud that the neighbours complained. Law! they had to even shave his head."[1]

"Is he any better?" asked Lizzie, with a sinking heart. "Can I see him?"

"P'raps you can, if you go to the hospital to-morrow; but whether you'll find him living or dead is more than I can say. I

1　Because the heat that accumulated around the head was thought to be particularly dangerous and uncomfortable for patients with typhoid fever, shaving was a common treatment protocol. See John Armstrong, *Practical Illustrations of Typhus Fever* ... (London: Printed for Baldwin, Cradock, and Joy, 1819), 554.

couldn't keep him here—I wasn't able to stand him. I've had the fever myself—he took it from me. You must come in," continued the woman, "if you want to talk—I'm afraid of catching cold, and can't stand at the door. Maybe you're afraid of the fever," she further observed, as she saw Lizzie hesitate on the door-step.

"Oh, no, I'm not afraid of that," answered Lizzie quickly—"I am not in the least afraid."

"Come in, then," reiterated the woman, "and I'll tell you all about it."

The woman looked harmless enough, and Lizzie hesitated no longer, but followed her through the entry into a decently furnished room. Setting the candlestick upon the mantelpiece, she offered her visitor a chair, and then continued—

"He came home this last time in an awful state. Before he left some one sent him a load of money, and he did nothing but drink and gamble whilst it lasted. I used to tell him that he ought to take care of his money, and he'd snap his fingers and laugh. He used to say that he owned the goose that laid the golden eggs, and could have money whenever he wanted it. Well, as I was a saying, he went; and when he came back he had an awful attack of *delirium tremens*, and then he took the typers. Oh, laws mercy!" continued she, holding up her bony hands, "how that critter raved! He talked about killing people."

"He did!" interrupted Lizzie, with a gesture of alarm, and laying her hand upon her heart, which beat fearfully—"did he mention any name?"

The woman did not stop to answer this question, but proceeded as if she had not been interrupted. "He was always going on about two orphans and a will, and he used to curse and swear awfully about being obliged to keep something hid. It was dreadful to listen to—it would almost make your hair stand on end to hear him."

"And he never mentioned names?" said Lizzie inquiringly.

"No, that was so strange; he never mentioned no names— *never*. He used to rave a great deal about two orphans and a will, and he would ransack the bed, and pull up the sheets, and look under the pillows, as if he thought it was there. Oh, he acted very strange, but never mentioned no names. I used to think he had something in his trunk, he was so very special about it. He was better the day they took him off; and the trunk went with him— he would have it; but since then he's had a dreadful relapse, and there's no knowin' whether he is alive or dead."

"I must go to the hospital," said Lizzie, rising from her seat, and greatly relieved to learn that nothing of importance had fallen from McCloskey during his delirium. "I shall go there as quickly as I can," she observed, walking to the door.

"You'll not see him to-night if you do," rejoined the woman. "Are you a relation?"

"Oh, no," answered Lizzie; "my father is an acquaintance of his. I learned that he was ill, and came to inquire after him."

Had the woman not been very indifferent or unobservant, she would have noticed the striking difference between the manner and appearance of Lizzie Stevens and the class who generally came to see McCloskey. She did not, however, appear to observe it, nor did she manifest any curiosity greater than that evidenced by her inquiring if he was a relative.

Lizzie walked with a lonely feeling through the quiet streets until she arrived at the porter's lodge of the hospital. She pulled the bell with trembling hands, and the door was opened by the little bald-headed man whose loquacity was once (the reader will remember) so painful to Mrs. Ellis. There was no perceptible change in his appearance, and he manifestly took as warm an interest in frightful accidents as ever. "What is it—what is it?" he asked eagerly, as Lizzie's pale face became visible in the bright light that shone from the inner office. "Do you want a stretcher?"

The rapidity with which he asked these questions, and his eager manner, quite startled her, and she was for a moment unable to tell her errand.

"Speak up, girl—speak up! Do you want a stretcher—is it burnt or run over. Can't you speak, eh?"

It now flashed upon Lizzie that the venerable janitor was labouring under the impression that she had come to make application for the admission of a patient, and she quickly answered—

"Oh, no; it is nothing of the kind, I am glad to say."

"Glad to say," muttered the old man, the eager, expectant look disappearing from his face, giving place to one of disappointment—"glad to say; why there hasn't been an accident to-day, and here you've gone and rung the bell, and brought me here to the door for nothing. What do you want then?"

"I wish to inquire after a person who is here."

"What's his number?" gruffly inquired he.

"That I cannot tell," answered she; "his name is McCloskey."

"I don't know anything about him. Couldn't tell who he is unless I go all over the books to-night. We don't know people by their names here; come in the morning—ten o'clock, and don't never ring that bell again," concluded he, sharply, "unless you want a stretcher: ringing the bell, and no accident!" and grumbling at being disturbed for nothing, he abruptly closed the door in Lizzie's face.

Anxious and discomfited, she wandered back to her hotel; and after drinking a weak cup of tea, locked her room-door, and retired to bed. There she lay, tossing from side to side—she could not sleep—her anxiety respecting her father's safety; her fears, lest in the delirium of fever McCloskey should discover their secret, kept her awake far into the night, and the city clocks struck two ere she fell asleep.

When she awoke in the morning the sun was shining brightly into her room; for a few moments she could not realize where she was; but the events of the past night soon came freshly to her; looking at her watch, she remembered that she was to go to the hospital at ten, and it was already half-past nine; her wakefulness the previous night having caused her to sleep much later than her usual hour.

Dressing herself in haste, she hurried down to breakfast; and after having eaten a slight meal, ordered a carriage, and drove to the hospital.

The janitor was in his accustomed seat, and nodded smilingly to her as she entered. He beckoned her to him, and whispered, "I inquired about him. McCloskey, fever-ward, No. 21, died this morning at two o'clock and forty minutes."

"Dead!" echoed Lizzie, with a start of horror.

"Yes, dead," repeated he, with a complacent look; "any relation of yours—want an order for the body?"

Lizzie was so astounded by this intelligence, that she could not reply; and the old man continued mysteriously. "Came to before he died—wish he hadn't—put me to a deal of trouble—sent for a magistrate—then for a minister—had something on his mind— couldn't die without telling it, you know; then there was oaths, depositions—so much trouble. Are you his relation—want an order for the body?"

"Oaths! magistrate!—a confession no doubt," thought Lizzie; her limbs trembled; she was so overcome with terror that she could scarcely stand; clinging to the railing of the desk by which she was standing for support, she asked, hesitatingly, "He had something to confess then?"

The janitor looked at her for a few moments attentively, and seemed to notice for the first time her ladylike appearance and manners; a sort of reserve crept over him at the conclusion of his scrutiny, for he made no answer to her question, but simply asked, with more formality than before, "Are you a relation—do you want an order for the body?"

Ere Lizzie could answer his question, a man, plainly dressed, with keen grey eyes that seemed to look restlessly about in every corner of the room, came and stood beside the janitor. He looked at Lizzie from the bow on the top of her bonnet to the shoes on her feet; it was not a stare, it was more a hasty glance—and yet she could not help feeling that he knew every item of her dress, and could have described her exactly.

"Are you a relative of this person," he asked, in a clear sharp voice, whilst his keen eyes seemed to be piercing her through in search of the truth.

"No, sir," she answered, faintly.

"A friend then, I presume," continued he, respectfully.

"An acquaintance," returned she. The man paused for a few moments, then taking out his watch, looked at the time, and hastened from the office.

This man possessed Lizzie with a singular feeling of dread— why she could not determine; yet, after he was gone, she imagined those cold grey eyes were resting on her, and bidding the old janitor, who had grown reserved so suddenly, good morning, she sprang into her carriage as fast as her trembling limbs could carry her, and ordered the coachman to drive back to the hotel.

"Father must fly!" soliloquized she; "the alarm will, no doubt, lend him energy. I've heard of people who have not been able to leave their rooms for months becoming suddenly strong under the influence of terror. We must be off to some place of concealment until we can learn whether he is compromised by that wretched man's confession."

Lizzie quickly paid her bill, packed her trunk, and started for the station in hopes of catching the mid-day train for New York.

The driver did not spare his horses, but at her request drove them at their utmost speed—but in vain. She arrived there only time enough to see the train move away; and there, standing on the platform,[1] looking at her with a sort of triumphant satisfaction, was the man with the keen grey eyes. "Stop! stop!" cried she.

"Too late, miss," said a bystander, sympathizingly; "just too late—no other train for three hours."

---

1 Here, presumably, a small, flat area projecting from the tail of the caboose; see *OED* "platform" 2b.

"Three hours!" said Lizzie, despairingly; "three hours! Yet I must be patient—there is no remedy," and she endeavoured to banish her fears and occupy herself in reading the advertisements that were posted up about the station. It was of no avail, that keen-looking man with his piercing grey eyes haunted her; and she could not avoid associating him in her thoughts with her father and McCloskey. What was he doing on the train, and why did he regard her with that look of triumphant satisfaction.

Those were to her the three longest hours of her life. Wearily and impatiently she paced up and down the long saloon, watching the hands of the clock as they appeared to almost creep over the dial-plate. Twenty times during those three hours did she compare the clock with her watch, and found they moved on unvaryingly together.

At last the hour for the departure of the train arrived; and seated in the car, she was soon flying at express speed on the way towards her home. "How much sooner does the other train arrive than we?" she asked of the conductor.

"Two hours and a half, miss," replied he, courteously; "we gain a half-hour upon them."

"A half-hour—that is something gained," thought she; "I may reach my father before that man. Can he be what I suspect?"

On they went—thirty—forty—fifty miles an hour, yet she thought it slow. Dashing by villages, through meadows, over bridges,—rattling, screaming, puffing, on their way to the city of New York. In due time they arrived at the ferry, and after crossing the river were in the city itself. Lizzie took the first carriage that came to hand, and was soon going briskly through the streets towards her father's house. The nearer she approached it, the greater grew her fears; a horrible presentiment that something awful had occurred, grew stronger and stronger as she drew nearer home. She tried to brave it off—resist it—crush it—but it came back upon her each time with redoubled force.

On she went, nearer and nearer every moment, until at last she was in the avenue itself. She gazed eagerly from the carriage, and thought she observed one or two persons run across the street opposite her father's house. It could not be!—she looked again—yes, there was a group beneath his window. "Faster! faster!" she cried frantically; "faster if you can." The door was at last reached; she sprang from the carriage and pressed through the little knot of people who were gathered on the pavement. Alas! her presentiments were correct. There, lying on the pavement, was the mangled form of her father, who had desperately sprung from the balcony above, to escape arrest from the man with the keen grey eyes, who, with the warrant in his hand, stood contemplating the lifeless body.

"Father! father!" cried Lizzie, in an anguished voice; "father, speak once!" Too late! too late! the spirit had passed away—the murderer had rushed before a higher tribunal—a mightier Judge—into the presence of One who tempers justice with mercy.

CHAPTER XXXV.

The Wedding.

THE night that Lizzie Stevens arrived in Philadelphia was the one decided upon for the marriage of Emily Garie and Charles Ellis; and whilst she was wandering so lonely through the streets of one part of the city, a scene of mirth and gaiety was transpiring in another, some of the actors in which would be made more happy by events that would be productive of great sorrow to her.

Throughout that day bustle and confusion had reigned supreme in the house of Mr. Walters. Caddy, who had been there since the break of day, had taken the domestic reins entirely from the hands of the mistress of the mansion, and usurped command herself. Quiet Esther was well satisfied to yield her full control of the domestic arrangements for the festivities, and Caddy was nothing loath to assume them.

She entered upon the discharge of her self-imposed duties with such ardour as to leave no doubt upon the minds of the parties most interested but that they would be thoroughly performed, and with an alacrity too that positively appalled quiet Esther's easy-going servants.

Great doubts had been expressed as to whether Caddy could successfully sustain the combined characters of *chef de cuisine* and bridesmaid, and a failure had been prophesied. She therefore felt it incumbent upon her to prove these prognostications unfounded, and demonstrate the practicability of the undertaking. On the whole, she went to work with energy, and seemed determined to establish the fact that her abilities were greatly underrated, and that a woman could accomplish more than one thing at a time when she set about it.

The feelings of all such persons about the establishment of Mr. Walters as were "constitutionally tired" received that day divers serious shocks at the hands of Miss Caddy—who seemed endowed with a singular faculty which enabled her to discover just what people did *not* want to do, and of setting them at it immediately.

For instance, Jane, the fat girl, hated going upstairs excessively. Caddy employed her in bringing down glass and china from a third-story pantry; and, moreover, only permitted her to bring a small quantity at a time, which rendered a number of trips strictly necessary, to the great aggravation and serious discomfort of the fat girl in question.

On the other hand, Julia, the slim chambermaid, who would have been delighted with such employment, and who would have undoubtedly refreshed herself on each excursion upstairs with a lengthened gaze from the window, was condemned to the polishing of silver and dusting of plates and glass in an obscure back pantry, which contained but one window, and that commanding a prospect of a dead wall.

Miss Caddy felt in duty bound to inspect each cake, look over the wine, and (to the great discomfiture of the waiter) decant it herself, not liking to expose him to any unnecessary temptation. She felt, too, all the more inclined to assume the office of butler from the fact that, at a previous party of her sister's, she had detected this same gentleman with a bottle of the best sherry at his mouth, whilst he held his head thrown back in a most surprising manner, with a view, no doubt, of contemplating the ceiling more effectually from that position.

Before night such was the increasing demand for help in the kitchen that Caddy even kidnapped the nurse, and locked the brown baby and her sister in the bath-room, where there was no window in their reach, nor any other means at hand from which the slightest injury could result to them. Here they were supplied with a tub half filled with water, and spent the time most delightfully in making boats of their shoes, and lading them with small pieces of soap, which they bit off from the cake for the occasion; then, coasting along to the small towns on the borders of the tub, they disposed of their cargoes to imaginary customers to immense advantage.

Walters had declared the house uninhabitable, and had gone out for the day. Esther and Emily busied themselves in arranging the flowers in the drawing-room and hall, and hanging amidst the plants on the balcony little stained glass lamps; all of which Caddy thought very well in its way, but which she was quite confident would be noticed much less by the guests than the supper—in which supposition she was undoubtedly correct.

Kinch also lounged in two or three times during the day, to seek consolation at the hands of Esther and Emily. He was in deep distress of mind—in great perturbation. His tailor had promised to send home a vest the evening previous and had not fulfilled his agreement. After his first visit Kinch entered the house in the most stealthy manner, for fear of being encountered by Caddy; who, having met him in the hall during the morning, posted him off for twenty pounds of sugar, a ball of twine, and a stone jar, despite his declaration of pre-engagements, haste, and limited knowledge of the articles in question.

Whilst Lizzie Stevens was tremblingly ringing the bell at the lodge of the hospital, busy hands were also pulling at that of Mr. Walters's dwelling. Carriage after carriage rolled up, and deposited their loads of gay company, who skipped nimbly over the carpet that was laid down from the door to the curbstone. Through the wide hall and up the stairway, flowers of various kinds mingled their fragrance and loaded the air with their rich perfume; and expressions of delight burst from the lips of the guests as they passed up the brilliantly-lighted stairway and thronged the spacious drawing-rooms.

There were but few whites amongst them, and they particular friends. There was Mrs. Bird, who had travelled from Warmouth to be present at the ceremony; Mr. Balch, the friend and legal adviser of the bride's father; Father Banks, who was to tie the happy knot; and there, too, was Mrs. Burrell, and that baby, now grown to a promising lad, and who would come to the wedding because Charlie had sent him a regular invitation written like that sent his parents.

Mr. and Mrs. Ellis were of course there,—the latter arrayed in a rich new silk made up expressly for the occasion—and the former almost hidden in his large easy chair. The poor old gentleman scarcely seemed able to comprehend the affair, and apparently laboured under the impression that it was another mob, and looked a little terrified at times when the laughter or conversation grew louder than usual.

The hour for the ceremony was fast approaching, and Esther left the assembled guests and went up into Emily Garie's room to assist the young ladies in preparing the bride. They all besought her to be calm, not to agitate herself upon any consideration; and then bustled about her, and flurried themselves in the most ridiculous manner, with a view, no doubt, of tranquillizing her feelings more effectually.

"Little Em," soon to be Mrs. Ellis, was busily engaged in dressing; the toilet-table was covered with lighted candles, and all the gas-burners in the room were in full blaze, bringing everything out in bold relief.

"We are having quite an illumination; the glare almost blinds me," said Emily. "Put out some of the candles."

"No, no, my dear," rejoined one of the young ladies engaged in dressing her; "we cannot sacrifice a candle. We don't need them to discern your charms, Em; only to enable us to discover how to deck them to the best advantage. How sweet you look!"

Emily gazed into the mirror; and from the blush that suffused her face and the look of complacency that followed, it was quite evident that she shared her friend's opinion.

She did, indeed, look charming. There was a deeper colour than usual on her cheeks, and her eyes were illumined with a soft, tender light. Her wavy brown hair was parted smoothly on the front, and gathered into a cluster of curls at the back. Around her neck glistened a string of pearls, a present from Mr. Winston, who had just returned from South America. The pure white silk fitted to a nicety, and the tiny satin slippers seemed as if they were made upon her feet, and never intended to come off again. Her costume was complete, with the exception of the veil and wreath, and Esther opened the box that she supposed contained them, for the purpose of arranging them on the bride.

"Where have you put the veil, my dear?" she asked, after raising the lid of the box, and discovering that they were not there.

"In the box, are they not?" answered one of the young ladies.

"No, they are not there," continued Esther, as she turned over the various articles with which the tables were strewed. All in vain; the veil and wreath could be nowhere discovered.

"Are you sure it came home?" asked one.

"Of course," replied another; "I had it in my hand an hour ago."

Then a thorough search was commenced, all the drawers ransacked, and everything turned over again and again; and just when they were about to abandon the search in despair, one of the party returned from the adjoining room, dragging along the brown baby, who had the veil wrapped about her chubby shoulders as a scarf, and the wreath ornamenting her round curly head. Even good-natured Esther was a little ruffled at this daring act of baby's, and hastily divested that young lady of her borrowed adornments, amidst the laughter of the group.

Poor baby was quite astonished at the precipitate manner in which she was deprived of her finery, and was for a few moments quite overpowered by her loss; but, perceiving a drawer open in the toilet-table, she dried her eyes, and turned her attention in that direction, and in tossing its contents upon the floor amply solaced herself for the deprivation she had just undergone.

"Caddy is a famous chief bridesmaid—hasn't been here to give the least assistance," observed Esther; "she is not even dressed herself. I will ring, and ask where she can be—in the kitchen or supper-room I've no doubt. Where is Miss Ellis?" she asked of the servant who came to answer her summons.

"Downstairs, mem—the boy that brought the ice-cream

kicked over a candy ornament, and Miss Ellis was very busy a shaking of him when I came up."

"Do beg her to stop," rejoined Esther, with a laugh, "and tell her I say she can shake him in the morning—we are waiting for her to dress now; and also tell Mr. DeYounge to come here to the door—I want him."

Kinch soon made his appearance, in accordance with Esther's request, and fairly dazzled her with his costume. His blue coat was brazen with buttons, and his white cravat tied with choking exactness; spotless vest, black pants, and such patent leathers as you could have seen your face in with ease.

"How fine you look, Kinch," said Esther admiringly.

"Yes," he answered; "the new vest came home—how do you like it?"

"Oh, admirable! But, Kinch, can't you go down, and implore Caddy to come up and dress—time is slipping away very fast?"

"Oh, I daren't," answered Kinch, with a look of alarm—"I don't dare to go down now that I'm dressed. She'll want me to carry something up to the supper-room if I do—a pile of dishes, or something of the kind. I'd like to oblige you, Mrs. Walters, but it's worth my new suit to do it."

Under these circumstances, Kinch was excused; and a deputation, headed by Mr. Walters, was sent into the lower regions to wait upon Caddy, who prevailed upon her to come up and dress, which she did, being all the while very red in the face, and highly indignant at being sent for so often.

"Good gracious!" she exclaimed, "what a pucker you are all in!"

"Why, Caddy, it's time to be," replied Esther—"it wants eight minutes of the hour."

"And that is just three minutes more than I should want for dressing if I was going to be married myself," rejoined she; and hastening away, she returned in an incredibly short time, all prepared for the ceremony.

Charlie was very handsomely got up for the occasion. Emily, Esther, Caddy—in fact, all of them—agreed that he never looked better in his life. "That is owing to me—all my doings," said Kinch exultingly. "He wanted to order his suit of old Forbes, who hasn't looked at a fashion-plate[1] for the last ten years, and I

---

1 Engraved illustration of popular dress. Many nineteenth-century American periodicals that were aimed at mass audiences (such as *Godey's Lady's Book* and, later, *Harper's Bazaar*) devoted considerable resources to promoting the currency, exclusivity, and fineness of their particular plates.

wouldn't let him. I took him to my man, and see what he has made of him—turned him out looking like a bridegroom, instead of an old man of fifty! It's all owing to me," said the delighted Kinch, who skipped about the entry until he upset a vase of flowers that stood on a bracket behind him; whereupon Caddy ran and brought a towel, and made him take off his white gloves and wipe up the water, in spite of his protestations that the shape of his pantaloons would not bear the strain of stooping.

At last the hour arrived, and the bridal party descended to the drawing-room in appropriate order, and stood up before Father Banks. The ceremony was soon over, and Emily was clasped in Mrs. Ellis's arms, who called her "daughter," and kissed her cheek with such warm affection that she no longer felt herself an orphan, and paid back with tears and embraces the endearments that were lavished upon her by her new relatives.

Father Banks took an early opportunity to give them each some good advice, and managed to draw them apart for that purpose. He told them how imperfect and faulty were all mankind—that married life was not all *couleur de rose*[1]—that the trials and cares incident to matrimony fully equalled its pleasures; and besought them to bear with each other patiently, to be charitable to each other's faults—and a reasonable share of earthly happiness must be the result.

Then came the supper. Oh! such a supper!—such quantities of nice things as money and skill alone can bring together. There were turkeys innocent of a bone, into which you might plunge your knife to the very hilt without coming in contact with a splinter—turkeys from which cunning cooks had extracted every bone leaving the meat alone behind, with the skin not perceptibly broken. How brown and tempting they looked, their capacious bosoms giving rich promise of high-seasoned dressing within, and looking larger by comparison with the tiny reed-birds beside them, which lay cosily on the golden toast, looking as much as to say, "If you want something to remember for ever, come and give me a bite!"

Then there were dishes of stewed terrapin, into which the initiated dipped at once, and to which they for some time gave their undivided attention, oblivious, apparently, of the fact that there was a dish of chicken-salad close beside them.

Then there were oysters in every variety—silver dishes containing them stewed, their fragrant macey odour wafting itself

---

1   Rose-colored (Fr.); winsome and delightful.

upward, and causing watery sensations about the mouth. Waiters were constantly rushing into the room, bringing dishes of them fried so richly brown, so smoking hot, that no man with a heart in his bosom could possibly refuse them. Then there were glass dishes of them pickled, with little black spots of allspice floating on the pearly liquid that contained them. And lastly, oysters broiled, whose delicious flavour exceeds my powers of description—these, with ham and tongue, were the solid comforts. There were other things, however, to which one could turn when the appetite grew more dainty; there were jellies, blancmange, chocolate cream, biscuit glacé, peach ice, vanilla ice, orange-water ice, brandy peaches, preserved strawberries and pines;[1] not to say a word of towers of candy, bonbons, kisses,[2] champagne, Rhine wine, sparkling Catawba,[3] liquors, and a man in the corner making sherry cobblers of wondrous flavour, under the especial supervision of Kinch; on the whole, it was an American supper, got up regardless of expense—and whoever has been to such an entertainment knows very well what an American supper is.

What a merry happy party it was—how they all seemed to enjoy themselves—and how they all laughed, when the bride essayed to cut the cake, and could not get the knife through the icing—and how the young girls put pieces away privately, that they might place them under their pillows to dream upon![4] What a happy time they had!

Father Banks enjoyed himself amazingly; he eat quantities of stewed terrapin, and declared it the best he ever tasted. He talked gravely to the old people—cheerfully and amusingly to the young; and was, in fact, having a most delightful time—when a servant whispered to him that there was a person in the entry who wished to see him immediately.

"Oh dear!" he exclaimed to Mr. Balch, "I was just congratulating myself that I should have one uninterrupted evening, and you see the result—called off at this late hour."

Father Banks followed the servant from the room, and inquired of the messenger what was wanted.

---

1 Possibly pine strawberries (see *OED* "pine" 3c) or pieces of pineapple.
2 A small, sweet candy.
3 American sparkling wine made from Catawba grapes; it was exceedingly popular in the nineteenth century.
4 Euro-American folk tradition holds that a woman who places wedding cake under her pillow will dream of her true love.

"You must come to the hospital immediately, sir; the man with the typhus-fever—you saw him yesterday—he's dying; he says he must see you—that he has something important to confess. I'm to go for a magistrate as well."

"Ah!" said Father Banks, "you need go no further, Alderman Balch is here—he is quite competent to receive his depositions."

"I'm heartily glad of it," replied the man, "it will save me another hunt. I had a hard time finding you. I've been to your house and two or three other places, and was at last sent here. I'll go back and report that you are coming and will bring a magistrate with you."

"Very good," rejoined Father Banks, "do so. I will be there immediately." Hastening back to the supper room, he discovered Mr. Balch in the act of helping himself to a brandy peach, and apprised him of the demand for his services. "Now, Banks," said he, good-humouredly, "that is outrageous. Why did you not let him go for some one else? It is too bad to drag me away just when the fun is about to commence." There was no alternative, however, and Mr. Balch prepared to follow the minister to the bedside of McCloskey.

When they arrived at the hospital, they found him fast sinking—the livid colour of his face, the sunken glassy eyes, the white lips, and the blue tint that surrounded the eyes and mouth told at once the fearful story. Death had come. He was in full possession of his faculties, and told them all. How Stevens had saved him from the gallows—and how he agreed to murder Mr. Garie—of his failure when the time of action arrived, and how, in consequence, Stevens had committed the deed, and how he had paid him time after time to keep his secret.

"In my trunk there," said he, in a dying whisper,—"in my trunk is the will. I found it that night amongst his papers. I kept it to get money out of his children with when old Stevens was gone. Here," continued he, handing his key from beneath the pillow, "open my trunk and get it."

Mr. Balch eagerly unlocked the trunk, and there, sure enough, lay the long-sought-for and important document.

"I knew it would be found at last. I always told Walters so; and now," said he, exultingly, "see my predictions are verified."

McCloskey seemed anxious to atone for the past by making an ample confession. He told them all he knew of Mr. Stevens's present circumstances—how his property was situated, and every detail necessary for their guidance. Then his confession was sworn to and witnessed; and the dying man addressed himself to the affairs of the next world, and endeavoured to banish entirely from his mind all thoughts of this.

After a life passed in the exercise of every Christian virtue—after a lengthened journey over its narrow stony pathway, whereon temptations have been met and triumphed over—where we have struggled with difficulties, and borne afflictions without murmur or complaint, cheering on the weary we have found sinking by the wayside, comforting and assisting the fallen, endeavouring humbly and faithfully to do our duty to God and humanity—even after a life thus passed, when we at last lie down to die the most faithful and best may well shrink and tremble when they approach the gloomy portals of death. At such an hour memory, more active than every other faculty, drags all the good and evil from the past and sets them in distinct array before us. Then we discover how greatly the latter exceeds the former in our lives, and how little of our Father's work we have accomplished after all our toils and struggles. 'Tis then the most devoted servant of our common Master feels compelled to cry, "Mercy! O my Father!—for justice I dare not ask."

If thus the Christian passes away—what terror must fill the breast of one whose whole life has been a constant warfare upon the laws of God and man? How approaches he the bar of that awful Judge, whose commands he has set at nought, and whose power he has so often contemned? With a fainting heart, and tongue powerless to crave the mercy his crimes cannot deserve!

McCloskey struggled long with death—died fearfully hard. The phantoms of his victims seemed to haunt him in his dying hour, interposing between him and God; and with distorted face, clenched hands, and gnashing teeth, he passed away to his long account.

From the bedside of the corpse Mr. Balch went—late as it was—to the office of the chief of police. There he learned, to his great satisfaction, that the governor was in town; and at an early hour the next morning he procured a requisition for the arrest of Mr. Stevens, which he put into the hands of the man with the keen grey eyes for the purpose of securing the criminal; and with the result of his efforts the reader is already acquainted.

CHAPTER XXXVI.

And the Last.

WITH such celerity did Mr. Balch work in behalf of his wards, that he soon had everything in train for the recovery of the property.

At first George Stevens was inclined to oppose the execution of the will, but he was finally prevailed upon by his advisers to make no difficulty respecting it, and quietly resign what he must inevitably sooner or later relinquish. Lizzie Stevens, on the contrary, seemed rather glad that an opportunity was afforded to do justice to her old playmates, and won the good opinion of all parties by her gentleness and evident anxiety to atone for the wrong done them by her father. Even after the demands of the executors of Mr. Garie were fully satisfied, such had been the thrift of her father that there still remained a comfortable support for her and her brother.

To poor Clarence this accession of fortune brought no new pleasure; he already had sufficient for his modest wants; and now that his greatest hope in life had been blighted, this addition of wealth became to him rather a burden than a pleasure.

He was now completely excluded from the society in which he had so long been accustomed to move; the secret of his birth had become widely known, and he was avoided by his former friends and sneered at as a "nigger." His large fortune kept some two or three whites about him, but he knew they were leeches seeking to bleed his purse, and he wisely avoided their society.

He was very wretched and lonely: he felt ashamed to seek the society of coloured men now that the whites despised and rejected him, so he lived apart from both classes of society, and grew moody and misanthropic.

Mr. Balch endeavoured to persuade him to go abroad—to visit Europe: he would not. He did not confess it, but the truth was, he could not tear himself away from the city where little Birdie dwelt, where he now and then could catch a glimpse of her to solace him in his loneliness. He was growing paler and more fragile-looking each day, and the doctor at last frankly told him that, if he desired to live, he must seek some warmer climate for the winter.

Reluctantly Clarence obeyed; in the fall he left New York, and during the cold months wandered through the West India islands. For a while his health improved, but when the novelty produced by change of scene began to decline he grew worse again, and brooded more deeply than ever over his bitter disappointment, and consequently derived but little benefit from the change; the spirit was too much broken for the body to mend—his heart was too sore to beat healthily or happily.

He wrote often now to Emily and her husband, and seemed desirous to atone for his past neglect. Emily had written to him first; she had learned of his disappointment, and gave him a sister's sympathy in his loneliness and sorrow.

The chilly month of March had scarcely passed away when they received a letter from him informing them of his intention to return. He wrote, "I am no better, and my physician says that a longer residence here will not benefit me in the least—that I came *too late*. I cough, cough, cough, incessantly, and each day become more feeble. I am coming home, Emmy; coming home, I fear, to die. I am but a ghost of my former self. I write you this that you may not be alarmed when you see me. It is too late now to repine, but, oh! Em, if my lot had only been cast with yours—had we never been separated—I might have been to-day as happy as you are."

It was a clear bright morning when Charlie stepped into a boat to be conveyed to the ship in which Clarence had returned to New York: she had arrived the evening previous, and had not yet come up to the dock. The air came up the bay fresh and invigorating from the sea beyond, and the water sparkled as it dripped from the oars, which, with monotonous regularity, broke the almost unruffled surface of the bay. Some of the ship's sails were shaken out to dry in the morning sun, and the cordage hung loosely and carelessly from the masts and yards. A few sailors lounged idly about the deck, and leaned over the side to watch the boat as it approached. With their aid it was soon secured alongside, and Charlie clambered up the ladder, and stood upon the deck of the vessel. On inquiring for Clarence, he was shown into the cabin, where he found him extended on a sofa.

He raised himself as he saw Charlie approach, and, extending his hand, exclaimed,—"How kind! I did not expect you until we reached the shore."

For a moment, Charlie could not speak. The shock caused by Clarence's altered appearance was too great,—the change was terrible. When he had last seen him, he was vigorous-looking, erect, and healthful; now he was bent and emaciated to a frightful extent. The veins on his temples were clearly discernible; the muscles of his throat seemed like great cords; his cheeks were hollow, his sunken eyes were glassy bright and surrounded with a dark rim, and his breathing was short and evidently painful. Charlie held his thin fleshless hand in his own, and gazed in his face with an anguished expression.

"I look badly,—don't I Charlie?" said he, with assumed indifference; "worse than you expected, eh?"

Charlie hesitated a little, and then answered,—"Rather bad; but it is owing to your sea-sickness, I suppose; that has probably reduced you considerably; then this close cabin must be most unfavourable to your health. Ah, wait until we get you home, we shall soon have you better."

"Home!" repeated Clarence,—"home! How delightful that word sounds! I feel it is going *home* to go to you and Em." And he leant back and repeated the word "home," and paused afterward, as one touches some favourite note upon an instrument, and then silently listens to its vibrations. "How is Em?" he asked at length.

"Oh, well—very well," replied Charlie. "She has been busy as a bee ever since she received your last letter; such a charming room as she has prepared for you!"

"Ah, Charlie," rejoined Clarence, mournfully, "I shall not live long to enjoy it, I fear."

"Nonsense!" interrupted Charlie, hopefully; "don't be so desponding, Clary: here is spring again,—everything is thriving and bursting into new life. You, too, will catch the spirit of the season, and grow in health and strength again. Why, my dear fellow," continued he, cheerfully, "you can't help getting better when we once get hold of you. Mother's gruels, Doctor Burdett's prescriptions, and Em's nursing, would lift a man out of his coffin. Come, now, don't let us hear anything more about dying."

Clarence pressed his hand and looked at him affectionately, as though he appreciated his efforts to cheer him and felt thankful for them; but he only shook his head and smiled mournfully.

"Let me help your man to get you up. When once you get ashore you'll feel better, I've no doubt. We are not going to an hotel, but to the house of a friend who has kindly offered to make you comfortable until you are able to travel."

With the assistance of Charlie and the servant, Clarence was gradually prepared to go ashore. He was exceedingly weak, could scarcely totter across the deck; and it was with some difficulty that they at last succeeded in placing him safely in the boat. After they landed, a carriage was soon procured, and in a short time thereafter Clarence was comfortably established in the house of Charlie's friend.

Their hostess, a dear old motherly creature, declared that she knew exactly what Clarence needed; and concocted such delicious broths, made such strengthening gruels, that Clarence could not avoid eating, and in a day or two he declared himself better than be had been for a month, and felt quite equal to the journey to Philadelphia.

The last night of their stay in New York was unusually warm; and Clarence informed Charlie he wished to go out for a walk. "I wish to go a long distance,—don't think me foolish when I tell you where. I want to look at the house where little Birdie lives. It may be for the last time. I have a presentiment that I shall see her if I go,—I am sure I shall," added he, positively, as though he felt a conviction that his desire would be accomplished.

"I would not, Clary," remonstrated Charlie. "Your health won't permit the exertion; it is a long distance, too, you say; and, moreover, don't you think, my dear fellow, that it is far more prudent to endeavour, if possible, to banish her from your mind entirely. Don't permit yourself to think about her, if you can help it. You know she is unattainable by you, and you should make an effort to conquer your attachment."

"It is too late—too late now, Charlie," he replied, mournfully. "I shall continue to love her as I do now until I draw my last breath. I know it is hopeless—I know she can never be more to me than she already is; but I cannot help loving her. Let us go; I may see her once again. Ah, Charlie, you cannot even dream what inexpressible pleasure the merest glimpse of her affords me! Come, let us go."

Charlie would not permit him to attempt to walk; and they procured a carriage, in which they rode to within a short distance of the house. The mansion of Mr. Bates appeared quite gloomy as they approached it. The blinds were down, and no lights visible in any part of the house.

"I am afraid they are out of town," remarked Charlie, when Clarence pointed out the house; "everything looks so dull about it. Let us cross over to the other pavement."[1] And they walked over to the other side of the street, and gazed upward at the house.

"Let us sit down here," suggested Clarence,—"here, on this broad stone; it is quite dark now, and no one will observe us."

"No, no!" remonstrated Charlie; "the stone is too damp and cold."

---

1 Sidewalk (chiefly British).

"Is it?" said Clarence vacantly. And taking out his handkerchief, he spread it out, and, in spite of Charlie's dissuasions, sat down upon it.

"Charlie," said he, after gazing at the house a long time in silence, "I have often come here and remained half the night looking at her windows. People have passed by and stared at me as though they thought me crazy; I was half crazy then, I think. One night, I remember, I came and sat here for hours; far in the night I saw her come to the window, throw up the casement, and look out. That was in the summer, before I went away, you know. There she stood in the moonlight, gazing upward at the sky, so pale, so calm and holy-looking, in her pure white dress, that I should not have thought it strange if the heavens had opened, and angels descended and borne her away with them on their wings." And Clarence closed his eyes as he concluded, to call back upon the mirror of his mind the image of little Birdie as she appeared that night.

They waited a long while, during which there was no evidence exhibited that there was any one in the house. At last, just as they were about to move away, they descried the glimmer of a light in the room which Clarence declared to be her room. His frame trembled with expectation, and he walked to and fro opposite the house with an apparent strength that surprised his companion. At length the light disappeared again, and with it Clarence's hopes.

"Now then we *must* go," said Charlie, "it is useless for you to expose yourself in this manner. I insist upon your coming home."

Reluctantly Clarence permitted himself to be led across the street again. As they were leaving the pavement, he turned to look back again, and, uttering a cry of surprise and joy, he startled Charlie by clutching his arm.

"Look! look!" he cried, "there she is—my little Birdie." Charlie looked up at the window almost immediately above them, and observed a slight pale girl, who was gazing up the street in an opposite direction.

"Little Birdie—little Birdie," whispered Clarence, tenderly. She did not look toward them, but after standing there a few seconds, moved from between the curtains and disappeared.

"Thank God for that!" exclaimed Clarence, passionately, "I knew—I knew I should see her. *I knew it*," repeated he, exultingly; and then, overcome with joy, he bowed his head upon Charlie's shoulder and wept like a child. "Don't think me foolish, Charlie," apologized he, "I cannot help it. I will go home now. Oh, brother, I feel so much happier." And with a step less faint and trembling, he walked back to the carriage.

The following evening he was at home, but so enfeebled with the exertions of the last two days, as to be obliged to take to his bed immediately after his arrival. His sister greeted him affectionately, threw her arms about his neck and kissed him tenderly; years of coldness and estrangement were forgotten in that moment, and they were once more to each other as they were before they parted.

Emily tried to appear as though she did not notice the great change in his appearance, and talked cheerfully and encouragingly in his presence; but she wept bitterly, when alone, over the final separation which she foresaw was not far distant.

The next day Doctor Burdett called, and his grave manner and apparent disinclination to encourage any hope, confirmed the hopeless impression they already entertained.

Aunt Ada came from Sudbury at Emily's request; she knew her presence would give pleasure to Clarence, she accordingly wrote her to come, and she and Emily nursed by turns the failing sufferer.

Esther and her husband, Mrs. Ellis and Caddy, and even Kinch, were unremitting in their attentions, and did all in their power to amuse and comfort him.

Day by day he faded perceptibly, grew more and more feeble, until at last Doctor Burdett began to number days instead of weeks as his term of life. Clarence anticipated death with calmness—did not repine or murmur. Father Banks was often with him cheering him with hopes of a happier future beyond the grave.

One day he sent for his sister and desired her to write a letter for him. "Em," said he, "I am failing fast; these fiery spots on my cheek, this scorching in my palms, these hard-drawn, difficult breaths, warn me that the time is very near. Don't weep, Em!" continued he, kissing her—"there, don't weep—I shall be better off—happier—I am sure! Don't weep now—I want you to write to little Birdie for me. I have tried, but my hand trembles so that I cannot write legibly—I gave it up. Sit down beside me here, and write; here is the pen." Emily dried her eyes, and mechanically sat down to write as he desired. Motioning to him that she was ready, he dictated—

"MY DEAR LITTLE BIRDIE,—I once resolved never to write to you again, and partially promised your father that I would not; then I did not dream that I should be so soon compelled to break my resolution. Little Birdie, I am dying! My physician informs me that I have but a few more days to live. I have been trying to break away from earth's affairs and fix my thoughts on other and better things. I have given up all but you, and feel that I cannot relinquish you until I see you once again. Do not refuse me, little Birdie! Show this to your father—he must consent to a request made by one on the brink of the grave."

"There, that will do; let me read it over," said he, extending his hand for the note. "Yes, I will sign it now—then do you add our address. Send it now, Emily—send it in time for to-night's mail."

"Clary, do you think she will come?" inquired his sister.

"Yes," replied he, confidently; "I am sure she will if the note reaches her." Emily said no more, but sealed and directed the note, which she immediately despatched to the post-office; and on the following day it reached little Birdie.

From the time when the secret of Clarence's birth had been discovered, until the day she had received his note, she never mentioned his name. At the demand of her father she produced his letters, miniature, and even the little presents he had given her from time to time, and laid them down before him without a murmur; after this, even when he cursed and denounced him, she only left the room, never uttering a word in his defence. She moved about like one who had received a stunning blow—she was dull, cold, apathetic. She would smile vacantly when her father smoothed her hair or kissed her cheek; but she never laughed, or sang and played, as in days gone by; she would recline for hours on the sofa in her room gazing vacantly in the air, and taking apparently no interest in anything about her. She bent her head when she walked, complained of coldness about her temples, and kept her hand constantly upon her heart.

Doctors were at last consulted; they pronounced her physically well, and thought that time would restore her wonted animation; but month after month she grew more dull and silent, until her father feared she would become idiotic, and grew hopeless and unhappy about her. For a week before the receipt of the note from Clarence, she had been particularly apathetic and indifferent, but it seemed to rouse her into life again. She started up after reading it, and rushed wildly through the hall into her father's library.

"See here!" exclaimed she, grasping his arm—"see there—I knew it! I've felt day after day that it was coming to that! You separated us, and now he is dying—dying!" cried she. "Read it—read it!"

Her father took the note, and after perusing it laid it on the table, and said coldly, "Well?"

"Well!" repeated she, with agitation—"Oh, father, it is not well! Father!" said she, hurriedly, "you bid me give him up—told me he was unworthy—pointed out to me fully and clearly why we could not marry: I was convinced we could not, for I knew you would never let it be. Yet I have never ceased to love him. I cannot control my heart, but I could my voice, and never since that day have I spoken his name. I gave him up—not that I would not have gladly married, knowing what he was—because you desired it—because I saw either your heart must break or mine. I let mine go to please you, and have suffered uncomplainingly, and will so suffer until the end; but I *must* see him once again. It will be a pleasure to him to see me once again in his dying hour, and I *must* go. If you love me," continued she, pleadingly, as her father made a gesture of dissent, "let us go. You see he is dying—begs you from the brink of the grave. Let me go, only to say good bye to him, and then, perhaps," concluded she, pressing her hand upon her heart, "I shall be better here."

Her father had not the heart to make any objection, and the next day they started for Philadelphia. They despatched a note to Clarence, saying they had arrived, which Emily received, and after opening it, went to gently break its contents to her brother.

"You must prepare yourself for visitors, Clary," said she, "no doubt some of our friends will call to-day, the weather is so very delightful."

"Do you know who is coming?" he inquired.

"Yes, dear," she answered, seating herself beside him, "I have received a note stating that a particular friend will call to-day—one that you desire to see."

"Ah!" he exclaimed, "it is little Birdie, is it not?"

"Yes," she replied, "they have arrived in town, and will be here to-day."

"Did not I tell you so?" said he, triumphantly. "I knew she would come. I knew it," continued he, joyfully. "Let me get up—I am strong enough—she is come—O! she has come."

Clarence insisted on being dressed with extraordinary care. His long fierce-looking beard was trimmed carefully, and he looked much better than he had done for weeks; he was wonderfully stronger, walked across the room, and chatted over his breakfast with unusual animation.

At noon they came, and were shown into the drawing-room, where Emily received them. Mr. Bates bowed politely, and expressed a hope that Mr. Garie was better. Emily held out her hand to little Birdie, who clasped it in both her own, and said, inquiringly "You are his sister?"

"Yes," answered Emily. "You, I should have known from Clarence's description—you are his little Birdie?"

She did not reply—her lip quivered, and she pressed Emily's hand and kissed her. "He is impatient to see you," resumed Emily, "and if you are so disposed, we will go up immediately."

"I will remain here," observed Mr. Bates, "unless Mr. Garie particularly desires to see me. My daughter will accompany you."

Emily took the hand of little Birdie in her own, and they walked together up the stairway. "You must not be frightened at his appearance," she remarked, tearfully, "he is greatly changed."

Little Birdie only shook her head—her heart seemed too full for speech—and she stepped on a little faster, keeping her hand pressed on her breast all the while.

When they reached the door, Emily was about to open it, but her companion stopped her, by saying: "Wait a moment—stop! How my heart beats—it almost suffocates me." They paused for a few moments to permit little Birdie to recover from her agitation, then throwing open the door they advanced into the room.

"Clarence!" said his sister. He did not answer; he was looking down into the garden. She approached nearer, and gently laying her hand on his shoulder, said, "Here is your little Birdie, Clarence." He neither moved nor spoke.

"Clarence!" cried she, louder. No answer. She touched his face—it was warm. "He's fainted!" exclaimed she; and, ringing the bell violently, she screamed for help. Her husband and the nurse rushed into the room; then came Aunt Ada and Mr. Bates. They bathed his temples, held strong salts to his nostrils—still he did not revive. Finally, the nurse opened his bosom and placed her hand upon his heart. *It was still—quite still:* CLARENCE WAS DEAD!

At first they could not believe it. "Let me speak to him," exclaimed little Birdie, distractedly; "he will hear my voice, and answer. Clarence! Clarence!" she cried. All in vain—all in vain. Clarence was dead!

They gently bore her away. That dull, cold look came back again upon her face, and left it never more in life. She walked about mournfully for a few years, pressing her hand upon her heart; and then passed away to join her lover, where distinctions in race or colour are unknown, and where the prejudices of earth cannot mar their happiness.

Our tale is now soon finished. They buried Clarence beside his parents; coloured people followed him to his last home, and wept over his grave. Of all the many whites that he had known, Aunt Ada and Mr. Balch were the only ones that mingled their tears with those who listened to the solemn words of Father Banks, "Ashes to ashes, dust to dust."

We, too, Clarence, cast a tear upon thy tomb—poor victim of prejudice to thy colour! and deem thee better off resting upon thy cold pillow of earth, than battling with that malignant sentiment that persecuted thee, and has crushed energy, hope, and life from many stronger hearts.

★★★

Aunt Ada Bell remained for a short time with Emily, and then returned to Sudbury, where, during the remainder of her life, she never omitted an opportunity of doing a kindness to a coloured person; and when the increasing liberality of sentiment opened a way for the admission of coloured pupils to the famous schools of Sudbury, they could always procure board at her house, and Aunt Ada was a friend and mother to them.

Walters and dear old Ess reared a fine family; and the brown baby and her sister took numberless premiums[1] at school, to the infinite delight of their parents. They also had a boy, whom they named "Charlie;" he inherited his uncle's passionate fondness for marbles, which fondness, it has been ascertained, is fostered by his uncle, who, 'tis said, furnishes the sinews of war[2] when there is a dearth in the treasury of Master Walters.

Kinch and Caddy were finally united, after various difficulties raised by the latter, who found it almost impossible to procure a house in such a state of order as would warrant her entering upon the blissful state of matrimony. When it was all over, Kinch professed to his acquaintances generally to be living in a perfect state of bliss; but he privately intimated to Charlie that if Caddy would permit him to come in at the front door, and not condemn him to go through the alley, whenever there happened to be a shower—and would let him smoke where he liked—he would be much more contented. When last heard from they had a little Caddy, the very image of its mother—a wonderful little girl, who, instead of buying candy and cake with her sixpences, as other

---

1 Prizes.
2 Traditional phrase for the money and equipment needed to wage war.

children did, gravely invested them in miniature wash-boards and dust-brushes, and was saving up her money to purchase a tiny stove with a full set of cooking utensils. Caddy declares her a child worth having.

Charles and Emily took a voyage to Europe for the health of the latter, and returned after a two years' tour to settle permanently in his native city. They were unremitting in their attention to father and mother Ellis, who lived to good old age, surrounded by their children and grandchildren.

THE END.

Appendix A: Contemporary Reviews

1. From *The Observer* (London), 21 September 1857: 7

The author of this pretty and exceedingly interesting story about slavery in republican America is a young man of "colour," and is a native of Philadelphia. Few writers have begun their career under better auspices. His work is preceded by prefatory eulogies from the pens of two great celebrities—Mrs. Harriet B. Stowe, and Lord Brougham.[1] The noble and truly learned lord wrote his through fear that the distinguished authoress of *Uncle Tom's Cabin* might be prevented, through a severe domestic affliction under which she labored, from fulfilling a promise which she had made to the author of writing a preface for him. Returning quiet of mind has enabled her to keep her word. The author, we think judiciously, presents to the reader both compositions. Mrs. Stowe, as quoted in Lord Brougham's preface, says: "There are points in the book of which I think very highly. The style is simple and unambitious—the characters, most of them faithfully drawn from real life, are quite fresh, and the incident, which is also much of it facti [*sic*], is often deeply interesting. I shall do what I can with the preface. I would not do as much unless I thought the book of worth *in itself*. It shows what I have long wanted to show—what the *free people of colour do attain*, and what they can do in spite of all social obstacles." By "people of colour" is meant not only the pure negro, but every person in whose veins can be traced, however remote, the slightest drop of African blood. We really think it is superfluous to give fresh instances of what great things "people of colour" can do. Why, Josephine, first Empress of the French, was a person of colour,[2] so is Alexandre Dumas,[3] so is the great and good Mrs. Seacole;[4] one

---

1 See above, p. 39.

2 Joséphine de Beauharnais (1763–1814), first wife of Napoleon Bonaparte (1769–1821), was born on a plantation in Martinique. Though her ancestry is somewhat unclear, her Caribbean origins suggested to many Europeans that she was a person of color.

3 Celebrated French novelist (1802–70) whose works include *The Three Musketeers* (serialized 1844), and *The Count of Monte Cristo* (serialized 1844–45). His father was born in St. Domingue (now Haiti) to an enslaved black woman.

4 Mary Seacole (1805–81) was a Jamaican-born mixed-race woman who distinguished herself as a nurse for the British Army in the Crimean War (1853–56). Her autobiography, *Wonderful Adventures of Mrs. Seacole in Many Lands*, first appeared in 1857.

of our best actors, "The African Roscius,"[1] is a veritable black; and there are thousands of instances which prove the high intellect of the negro race. Mrs. Stowe, in the first introduction of her notice to this book, asks, "Are the race at present held as slaves capable of freedom, self-government, and progress?" For our own part, we have not the slightest doubt of it. The negro has every right to exclaim with Shylock, "Hath not the Jew (negro) eyes?" &c.[2] The Jews even in this country were once treated as slaves, as being beyond the pale of society, and what are they now? Why, excellent citizens, and worthy of freedom. So would be the negro race if treated properly. We really believe there are European nations less worthy of freedom than they ...

2. From the *Literary Gazette* (London), 26 September 1857: 917–19

The flourish of an "Introductory Preface" on the title-page of this work may be appropriately described by the venerable adage of "much cry and little wool."[3] The wool in this case is very small indeed. We have a few lines headed "From Lord Brougham," who evidently never read the book, to inform us that Mrs. Stowe intended to write a preface, but was prevented from doing so by a domestic affliction; and this apology for the absence of the preface is followed, or, strange to say, preceded, by the preface itself! It appears that Lord Brougham furnished the apology in July, and Mrs. Stowe supplied the preface in August, and Mr. Frank Webb, desirous of garnishing his volume with such illustrious names, "deemed it best," as he tells us in a note, to retain both. The preface, spread over a page and a half, is of no conceivable value except to enable the author of the story to put Mrs. Stowe's name on his title page. It tells us nothing that Mr. Webb could not have told with much better effect himself, beyond the fact that Mrs. Stowe considers the narrative true to the life it depicts, and thinks that, being the production of a young man of colour, it will help to solve the question as to the capability of the negro race for the cultivation of freedom, self-government, and progress. Of the fidelity of the story to the peculiar classes of American society it undertakes to

---

1 The American actor Ira Aldridge (1807–67), who moved to the UK in the 1820s; he played many prominent parts on the British stage, including the title roles of Shakespeare's *Othello*, *Richard III*, and *King Lear*. His nickname is taken from the most celebrated actor of ancient Rome, Quintus Roscius Gallus (126–62 BCE), who was born a slave.

2 From Shakespeare, *The Merchant of Venice*, 3.1.

3 Idiomatic expression indicating that the praise of something does not match its value.

portray, Mrs. Stowe is a competent judge; but when she draws a general conclusion from a particular and exceedingly exceptionable fact, we must take leave to set aside her authority. This is the kind of reasoning, willfully perverse if not stupidly ignorant, that has done so much mischief, in and out of America, to the cause of emancipation. Mr. Webb is a very remarkable specimen of a free coloured man, born and reared in the flourishing city of Philadelphia. He has written a book, in some respects a clever book, and certainly, considering its origin and its subject, a curious book. The case is singular, almost as singular as that of Touissant [*sic*] L'Ouverture; and if it prove anything at all in reference to the race of free negroes in the northern States, it proves that, whatever capacity they may possess, literature is not one of the channels in which it works.

...

Of this story it may be said that, inferior to "Uncle Tom" in interest of character and constructive skill, it conveys a more just and practical moral. It is different from all other slave stories in the ground it occupies, and the lesson it enforces. Other slave stories are addressed to the evils of American slavery; this story is addressed to the most monstrous and glaring evil of American liberty. Other writers have depicted the vices of the slave states; Mr. Webb, with greater reason, and more likelihood of success, exposes the crying vice of the free states. Books like "Uncle Tom," striking at an institution in which large rights of property are involved, and the social arrangements of whole communities are bound up, cannot, in the nature of things, reflect satisfactorily the complicated aspects of the subject, or conduct the judgment of the reader to sound conclusions. All that they can do is to express a sentiment which, however noble and admirable in the abstract, may, nevertheless, lead to mischievous results when applied to existing circumstances in an irresponsible form. On the other hand, the treatment of the coloured population in the free states is precisely one of those questions which come legitimately within the province of the novelist, because it is purely a question of usage and opinion. Here the writer of fiction may fairly hope to accomplish an actual good. He is dealing with elements which are constantly undergoing modifications from the action of reason, and the direct influence of advancing civilization and if he possess literary power equal to the demands of his theme, he cannot fail to make an impression upon the society whose failings he rebukes.

The effect Mr. Webb's book will produce in America must depend chiefly upon the fidelity of its pictures; in England, upon the merit of its treatment. The pictures upon the main are, no doubt, faithful, and the inconsistent cruelty of the abolitionists towards the mixed people who are settled amongst them is rendered sufficiently revolting to awaken indignation. All this is exhibited with literal truthfulness, and made to look still more hideous in comparison with slavery itself, which the writer generally represents in a favourable light. But the portraiture will appear to English readers at once feeble and extravagant. The characters, oppressed with trivial details, and borne down by tedious conversations, become terribly dull and wearisome; while the necessity of attracting attention to the social condition of the coloured race has led the author insensibly to invest them with attributes which in Europe are found only in the most intellectual and refined classes. The family of the Ellises supply an example. They subsist by their industry, the mother and daughters as needlewomen, and the father as a carpenter. Yet these people have their "family physician," who, when one of the children requires to have his arm set after a fall, calls in another physician "for a consultation"; and while the boy is lying under the effects of the operation, "the knocker is tied up and the windows are darkened." But these are merely the external signs of coloured gentility. The manners and conversation of these people suggest still more curious points for study. Sometimes, indeed, they are coarse and rude enough, but when occasion serves they can be as "elegant" and sentimental as any of the exquisite ladies or powdered beaux of the old Sir Charles Grandison school.[1] This way of describing the emancipated coloured race may probably be referred to the fact that they are here described by one of themselves. To the writer all this finery of language and behaviour opens a kind of intellectual holiday, in which his people put on their bravest airs and gaudiest tinsel.

...

Traits like these are not unimportant in such a work. They distinctly mark its origin, and testify to its authenticity; and they constitute a prominent part of its claim upon the attention of the English reader. The dramatic power displayed in the story is not so vivid or intense as that of "Uncle Tom," and the delineation of character is not so subtle. But it is truer in all essential particulars to the instincts of African blood, and the habits of the mixed African race; and taking into account the circumstances under which it was produced, it is a much more remarkable book.

---

1   *The History of Sir Charles Grandison* (1753), a British novel by Samuel Richardson (1689–1761), follows the morally upstanding and well-bred title character through a series of genteel crises of the heart.

3. From *The Morning Post* (London), 6 October 1857: 7

With objects in view similar to those which led to the production of "Uncle Tom," "The Garies and their Friends" lacks originality, natural pathos, and elastic vigour of that popular effusion. But, as the main incidents profess to be founded upon fact, and as the style in which they are conveyed is simple, unaffected, and interesting, we do not doubt but that the work will find a large class of admiring readers, although it scarcely deserves the laudatory prefaces by Mrs. H. B. Stowe and Lord Brougham, which usher it before the public. "Uncle Tom" has already painfully awakened English sympathies on behalf of the slave race in America, and more appeals to our feelings on precisely the same model may not unlikely prove tiresome and have an opposite effect to that intended.

...

Everywhere the negro and half-caste characters are placed in a favourable light, and in some instances the pictures are so charming, both as regards bodily and mental qualifications, that one might suppose the object of the author to be to prove the superiority of the coloured population over their white-faced brethren.

4. *The Standard* (London), 7 October 1857: 3

We have read this book with much attention, and are at a loss to imagine why the author has allowed his work to be ushered into the world under the patronage of Mrs. Harriet Beecher Stowe. The few feeble remarks which that lady has strung together, and dignified by the name of "Preface," add nothing to the value of Mr. Webb's production, nor to the interest of the story. It is not because Mrs. Stowe has written a clever book that she is to constitute herself the dry nurse, or, if we may be allowed the expression, the Lady Macaenas,[1] of literary aspirants. Mr. Webb might have brought this work fearlessly before the British public and trusted to its own merits for success, without the aid of Mrs. Stowe's name. We hail "The Garies" as a production of great promise in itself, and not less as the production of a member of an oppressed race, which has been inconsiderately thought incapable of exercising the higher intellectual powers; Mr. Webb's work will

---

1 Gaius Maecenas was a Roman statesman and supporter of the arts during the first century BCE. He was particularly famous as the patron of the poets Horace and Virgil. By the nineteenth century, his name had become familiar shorthand for any artistic benefactor.

dispel that weak and unworthy notion. This story, written by one of a coloured race, not at all inferior in liveliness or vigour to the majority of our works of fiction, will show, better than any logic or declamation can show, the falsity of supposing that the coloured race are inferior in natural powers, or less susceptible of the influences of education, than their white brethren.

The scene of the story is laid in the free states of America, which are inhabited to a great extent by free men of colour and emancipated slaves, many of whom by their own industry have attained to a position of comfort and independence. Their struggles, perseverance, and persecutions are detailed with a pathos and simplicity that win our sympathy and command our respect. The author introduces us to the coloured race under an aspect of social life; we trace them through daily scenes of toil and trouble, failure and success; we see the home of industry, thrift, and peace, made desolate by oppression and cruelty—the spirit crushed—the brave heart broken by dastardly and unrelenting persecution. Mr. Webb depicts the race to which he belongs as insulted, wronged, and persecuted; struggling, it is true, to obtain social rights, with a sense and conviction of deserving them; robbed of those rights as soon as won, but ever soaring upwards; cast down, but not conquered, by the unjust prejudice of narrow-minded and illiterate "whites." There is nothing in these pages to thrill us with horror, yet our souls are filled with indignation at the wrongs, and we are taught to sympathise with the sufferings, of the oppressed. The story is full of interest, the plot well developed, and the incidents natural and plentiful. Mr. Walters is a perfect type of "God's image carved in ebony." Clarence Garie is naturally and touchingly portrayed; the small portion of African blood that runs through his veins is the one drop of gall that embitters his whole life; and like the author, whose creation he is, we cannot choose but drop a tear above his grave. The characters of Caddy Ellis and Kinch would not have disgraced the pen of our inimitable Dickens; in fact, each personage that figures in the book is skillfully delineated and plays his part perfectly to the end. Mr. Routledge[1] has done wisely in bringing this work forward. We conscientiously recommend it to the public, and trust that it will gain the popularity it deserves, and win a respect for that race which, in its representative, Mr. Webb, shows that it can touch, command, and deserve our sympathies. A few more works like Mr. Webb's will do more for the cause of true freedom than the most eloquent apologies which can be urged in its defence by those who,

---

1 George Routledge (1812–88) was the publisher of *The Garies and Their Friends*. For more on the relationship between Routledge and Webb, see the Introduction, p. 21.

though they feel strongly for the wrongs of the oppressed, have not one drop of coloured blood in their veins.

5. From *The Daily News* (London), 9 October 1857: 2

[This review was reprinted in *Frederick Douglass' Paper* (Rochester, NY) on 4 December 1857. It was the only review of Webb's novel to appear in any American newspaper in the nineteenth century.]

This is a book which will be read with much interest and curiosity, not merely on account of its intrinsic merits—although they are rather above than below the average—but from the gratifying fact, which is vouched upon the highest authority, that it is the veritable production of a coloured man, and gives, in the main, a faithful picture of coloured society in the United States. It is but repeating a trite truism to say that the subject is one of the deepest interest everywhere, and nowhere more than in this country, where, to our honour be it said, the elevation of the sons of Ham[1] to a level with the rest of the human family has been a great nation-stirring question now for almost a century. We have preached for it, fought for it, toiled for it, paid for it, and it is only a fair instalment of the reward of our labours when we thus see one of the persecuted people able, as in the book before us, to take up the pen and paint their manners in vivid and pleasing colours, and to struggle against their wrongs and oppressions with a weapon which never yet failed the just cause, even when wielded by a feeble hand. He has evidently been a careful reader of Dickens and Thackeray,[2] his book being full of reminiscences of both, and as imitators generally are most faithful in copying defects, he sometimes runs the sentimentality of the former to death, that being the point in which, in our judgment, our prose Shakespeare is sometimes a little prolix and dilute. A boy's letter, obviously suggested by the reading of "Vanity Fair,"[3] is more successful, and is adapted to a new writer, and in new circumstances, with considerable skill and effect. Mr. Webb must not be offended if we thus freely handle his

---

1   Nineteenth-century term for black Africans and people of black African descent: see above, p. 48, note 1.

2   Charles Dickens (1812–70) and William Thackeray (1811–63) were two of the leading British novelists of the Victorian period.

3   Title of Thackeray's masterpiece (serialized 1847–48), which traced the social ambitions of its protagonist Becky Sharp. *The Garies* features several letters written by boys. It is possible that the reviewer is thinking of Kinch's letter to Charlie (p. 263): its guilelessness and enthusiasm recall both Amelia Sedley's and Rawdon Crawley's correspondence in *Vanity Fair*.

coup d'essai,[1] because to do so is at once to give it brevet rank[2] amongst works which are considered worthy of criticism; and we freely acknowledge that it would be on the whole, good and pleasant reading, coming from any one. How much greater, then, must be its merit, as the production of one whose father would perhaps have been tarred and feathered if he had dared to take a pen in his hand, or even to learn his alphabet? As to the question which Mrs. Stowe, who introduces the book in a short preface, says it elucidates, it is one which we have never thought of asking. Our intercourse with the East has enriched our language with one delightfully expressive monosyllable, and that we shall apply to the interrogatory—are the negroes capable of freedom, self-government, and progress? To affect a doubt upon this matter is simply "bosh."[3] Whoever heard of a dominant race that would admit of the presence of the governing faculty in those whom they oppressed? And our cousins on the other side of the Atlantic are only following out the old rule of might against right, in gravely asserting, as one of their excuses for slavery, that their slaves are radically unfit for freedom. The ethnologists have long since scattered such nonsense to the winds. As well might we assert that there was an organic difference of structure between the Suffolk Punch and the high-mettled winner of the Derby,[4] as that the sable son of the torrid zone was not as capable of improvement, both physical and intellectual, as his pale-faced brother of the more northern latitudes. Climate, diet, and culture make all the difference, as we may see even here at home, where, barring the colour, there is as much apparent difference between the wretched pariah of St. Giles's and the pampered pet of St. James's as between the haughtiest planter of Louisiana and his much-contemned bondsman.[5] If Mr. Webb therefore has

1 Trial run; experiment.
2 A military term, suggesting a temporary elevation in rank that happens outside typical promotional procedures—often forced by extenuating circumstances on the battlefield.
3 Foolishness, nonsense. The *OED* notes that it is derived from a Turkish word meaning empty or worthless.
4 The Suffolk Punch is a kind of heavy draft horse, best suited to steady pulling. The contrast that the reviewer draws here is between the slow, docile working animal and the fast, high-strung creature that runs derby-races: they may have been selectively bred for different characteristics over the generations, but both are manifestly horses.
5 St. Giles's and St. James's were London neighborhoods with very different populations in the mid-nineteenth century. St. Giles's was one of the UK's most notorious "Rookeries"—a dense slum that concentrated crime, poverty, and material decay. St. James's, on the other hand, was home to the wealthy and the aristocratic.

taken up his pen merely to prove that a negro or a mulatto is capable of writing a tolerable work of fiction, he might have saved himself the trouble, as far as we were concerned; but if he has turned author in order to give us some true idea of the inner life of his race, he has done good service to the cause of humanity and progress, and deserves all encouragement at the hands of the critics and the public. We are willing to take the latter as having been his main object, and therefore follow with a lively interest the thread of his story.

Mr. Garie is a southern planter, who, having taken as his mistress a beautiful mulatto slave, becomes so deeply enamoured of her as to determine upon making her his wife. As this is impossible in his native state, where the law makes all such unions illegal, he removes to Philadelphia, in the hope that he will obtain sympathy and support amongst the eloquent abolitionists of that city. He finds, however, that between preaching and practice there is an awful chasm, and that the very people whose speeches in favour of negro emancipation fill all the papers are the first to order his wife and children out of the railway cars, and to call "Nigger" after them as they walk along the streets. He has for his next-door neighbor an unprincipled lawyer—astonishing is the antipathy which novelists, white and black, have for the lawyers— and the latter, in order that he may become the planter's heir, stirs up a pro-slavery riot, which, with its fatal results, is thus described.

...

Mrs. Stowe vouches for the substantial truth of the above harrowing description [of the death of Emily Garie], but for the honour of human nature it is also gratifying to learn that the violence of the pro-slavery mobs has much abated since the time of the Garies, and that now the coloured people may live unmolested, although still despised and kept apart, in the chief cities of the Union. The death of Mr. Garie and his wife leave their orphan children the prominent figures in the narrative; the boy to die ultimately of a broken heart because he had endeavoured to conceal his taint from his betrothed and was discovered; the girl to marry amongst her own people, and to live happily as the reward of choosing a true instead of a false position. The lighter portions of the work have considerable merit. There is a coloured boy, named Kinch, who is quite a black diamond, and a thrifty housewife, Caddy, who wields a never quiet carpet broom with immense effect. Manners, dress, and dialogue are handled and discriminated with a fair amount of skill....

6. From the *Athenaeum* (London), 24 October 1857: 1320

[This is a dual review of *The Garies* and *Mabel Vaughn*, a novel by Maria Susanna Cummins (1827–66). We have omitted the discussion of Cummins.]

These two American novels are characteristic of the middle class of American literature—the strong faculty of imitation not yet developing any latent powers of originality. Both works come before the English public under the auspices of literary sponsors. The Preface to "The Garies" is written by Mrs. Beecher Stowe, with a few words from Lord Brougham, written when it was feared that the lady might not be able to fulfil her intention. Mrs. Gaskell[1] has stood godmother to "Mabel Vaughn"; but none of these friends seem to know exactly what to say or do in their position. The various Prefaces are curiosities of good intentions under embarrassing circumstances. Mrs. Gaskell avoids committing herself to the merits of her adopted book, but is expansive about the pleasant intercourse and interchange of novels which goes on so constantly between the two countries—the pleasant American tales which have been written and are now being written—and manages as skillfully as the completest of "complete letter writers" to fill nearly four pages of print with generalities, and begs us to believe the "profound consideration" with which she remains the obedient—Author of the Preface!

As to Lord Brougham, he abstains from saying anything about the book he leads forward by the hand:—he only sympathizes with Mrs. Beecher Stowe on her "severe domestic affliction," and states what he has reason to believe is *her* opinion on Mr. Webb's book, as stated "in a letter to a friend." All he ventures upon in the shape of an original wish in his own person is, to hope that "Mr. Webb's book" may meet with all the success its own merits can obtain for it—a cautious aspiration, so prudently framed that Jove himself could find nothing "to disperse in empty air." Clearly enough, these literary sponsors have no faith in their own office, and little enough in the capability of their *protégés* to run alone. We agree with them in thinking that to put good names as a guarantee to second-rate books is not a pleasant position for the owners of the said names, although it may give an emphasis to the advertisements. The publishers are the only parties who take anything by the device.

...

---

1   Elizabeth Gaskell (1810–65) was a popular and prolific British novelist, biographer, and short-story writer. Her major works include *Cranford* (1851), *North and South* (1855), and *Wives and Daughters* (1865).

"The Garies and their Friends" is, we are told by Mrs. Beecher Stowe, in *her* Preface, written by a young, free man of colour; and it has an interest of its own, as introducing the English reader to a peculiar class of society little known amongst us—the class of free coloured people, who seem to form a society amongst themselves, and to have attained to wealth, mental cultivation, and social importance. Most of them have an admixture of European blood in them; so that the question intended to be at once raised and answered by this work—whether slaves are capable of self-government—is not fairly stated. There is no doubt that the mixture of race gives to the original slave stock capabilities for civilization and moral qualities of self-control which render them capable of achieving freedom and undertaking all its responsibilities, which in their original state they were *not,*—and, when the majority are capable of being free, they will no more remain slaves than the Britons, whose "Britannia rules the waves";[1] but *till then* all the amiable intentions in the world will not make them free or give them the souls of freemen.

The intense abhorrence of the Free States for their coloured brethren is an antipathy stronger than institutions. It is in vain that philosophical American parents give their children black dolls to give them juvenile and pleasant associations; black remains black, unpleasant to white. We may read a story that shall give us intense sorrow and sympathy with negroes; but the negro speciality is always kept out of sight; and Uncle Tom himself—the type and model of chivalrous and faithful slaves—would not have excited the enthusiasm in bodily reality that he does in Mrs. Stowe's description of him. For the rest, taken as a tale of a pariah and oppressed class, "The Garies and their Friends" is interesting, and well written.

---

1 From a patriotic poem written by James Thomson (c. 1700–48) in 1740. The refrain in each stanza is "Rule, Britannia, rule the waves; / Britons never will be slaves." The poem was set to music by Thomas Arne (1710–78).

Appendix B: Law, Culture, and the Color Line

1. From William Goodell, *The American Slave Code in Theory and Practice: Its Distinctive Features Shown by Its Statutes, Judicial Decisions, and Illustrative Facts* (New York: American and Foreign Anti-Slavery Society, 1853), 89, 105–07

[Goodell's *American Slave Code* serves as a partisan compendium of writing about the "legal relation" of slavery in the antebellum United States. In the spirit of helping abolitionists understand the arguments they would have to refute, it includes "the testimony of slaveholders themselves, in their own language, set forth in the most solemn and authenticated form, the public testimony of their legislative acts and judicial decisions, made for the very purpose of defining and enforcing that relation" of master and slave (19).]

From Chapter VI: SLAVES CAN POSSESS NOTHING

MAN was created proprietor of the earth, with dominion over the beasts of the field. The humanity of the slave is denied, by denying to him any share in this original right of human nature of capability of its exercise. He is "not ranked among sentient beings, but among things." A chattel cannot be the owner of a chattel. The slave "can possess nothing nor acquire any things but what must belong to his master." ([Louisiana] Civil Code, Art. 35.) They "cannot take by purchase or descent."

"Slaves have no legal rights in things, real or personal; but whatever they may acquire, belongs, *in point of law*, to their masters." (Stroud, [*A Sketch of the Laws Relating to Slavery*], pp. 25, 45.)

"Slaves can make no contract." (Ib. 25, 61.)

"Slaves are incapable of inheriting or transmitting property." (Civil Code, Art. 945.)

From Chapter VII: SLAVES CANNOT MARRY

MEN may forget or disregard the rules of logic in their reasonings about slavery, but the genius that presides over American slavery never forgets or disregards them. From its well-defined principle of human chattelhood it never departs, for a single moment. If any thing founded on falsehood might be called a science, we might add the system of American slavery to the list of the strict sciences. From a single fundamental axiom, all the parts of the system are logically and scientifically educed. And no man fully understands the system, who does not study it in the light of that axiom.

The slave has no rights. Of course he, or she, cannot have the rights of a husband, a wife. The slave is a chattel, and chattels do not marry. "The slave is not ranked among sentient beings, but among things," and things are not married.

"Slaves are not people, in the eye of the law. They have no legal personality." So said Mr. Wise.[1] So, by their votes, said the Federal Congress. But none except "people" and "persons" ever marry.

"The slave is one who is in the power of a master *to whom he belongs*." How, then, can the slave marry?

"The legal relation of master and slave," with all the vestal robes of its spotless innocency, and saintly Biblical paternity, has *never, in this country*, been held to be compatible with marriage. So early as in colonial times, when parish ministers, all over New-England, owned slaves, it was held by learned civilians, in good old Connecticut, that when a slave master, though inadvertently, gave verbal license to a female slave *to marry*, the license made her free. Being married, she was not a slave, and the husband bore off his prize in triumph, before her master!

The same doctrine has always been held (though differently enunciated) at the South. Slave mothers there are licensed by their masters to be "breeders," not wives, and thus they are retained as slaves.

...

"It is clear that slaves have no legal capacity to assent to any contract. With the consent of their master they may marry, and their *moral* power to agree to such a contract or connection cannot be doubted; but *while in a state of slavery* it cannot produce any *civil effect*, because slaves are deprived of all civil rights. Emancipation gives to the slave his civil rights, and a contract of marriage, legal and valid by the consent of the master, and moral assent of the slave, *from the moment of freedom*, ALTHOUGH DORMANT DURING SLAVERY, produces all the effects which result from such contract among free persons." (Opinion of Judge Matthews, case of Girod *vs.* Lewis, May Term, 1819; 6 Martin's "Louisiana Reports," p. 559. Wheeler's "Law of Slavery," p. 199.)

---

1   Henry A. Wise, US Representative from Virginia (1833–44). Wise made the claim in response to Representative John Quincy Adams's repeated attempts to force Congress to take action on abolitionist petitions instead of tabling them.

2. From George M. Stroud, *A Sketch of the Laws Relating to Slavery in the Several States of the United States of America: With Some Alterations and Considerable Additions*, 2nd ed. (1827; Philadelphia: Henry Longstreth, 1856), 2–4

[First published in Philadelphia in 1827, Stroud's book is a compendium of the laws associated with slavery, enumerated state by state. Stroud (1795–1875) presents this collection as an objective record of the statutes governing the slave system, but his explanations of their practical effects on black American lives reveal his abolitionist beliefs. In the section included here, Stroud discusses the laws that held that individuals born to enslaved mothers are legally themselves also enslaved.]

This maxim of the civil law, the genuine and *degrading* principle of slavery, inasmuch as it places the slave upon a level with *brute* animals, prevails universally among the slave-holding states. The law of South Carolina may be quoted as follows:—"All negroes, *Indians*, (free Indians in amity with this government, and negroes, mulattoes[1] and mestizos,[2] who are *now* free, excepted,) mulattoes or mestizos who are or shall hereafter be in this province, and all their issue and offspring born, shall be and they are hereby declared to be and remain forever hereafter absolute slaves, and shall *follow the condition of the mother*." *Act of* 1740, 2 *Brevard's Digest*, 229; similar in Georgia, *Prince's Digest*, 446, (Act of 1770;) and in Mississippi, *Revised Code of Mississippi*, of 1823, *page* 369; and see 1 *Rev. Code of Virgin.*, (of 1819,) *page* 421; 2 *Litt.* and *Swi.* 1149–50, *Civ. Code of Louisiana, art.* 183. By this law, any person whose *maternal* ancestor, even in the *remotest* degree of distance from him or her, can be shown to have been a negro, or an Indian, or a mulatto, or a mestizo, not free at the date of the law, although the *paternal* ancestor at each successive generation may have been a *white free man*, is declared to be the subject of perpetual slavery. This is a measure of cruelty and avarice which, to the reproach of our republics, there is much reason to believe has no precedent in any other civilized country. "In Jamaica, the condition (of slavery) *ceases* by *express law* to attach upon the issue, at the *fourth* degree of distance from a negro ancestor. In other islands, (British West Indies,) the *written* law is silent on this head; but by established custom, the quadroons or mestizos (so they call the second and third degrees) are

---

1 A term used to denote people of mixed-race ancestry; usually refers to people born of one white and one black parent.
2 Spanish-derived term for people of mixed white and indigenous ancestry.

rarely seen in a state of slavery." *Stephen's Slavery of the British West India Colonies delineated*, 27; *Edward's West Indies, book* 4, *chap.* 1. And, as in the Spanish and Portuguese colonies, slavery is in all respects much milder than in those of the British, it is fairly inferrible that a regulation equally favourable to freedom, by custom, if not by express law, prevails there also. Of the French colonies and of the Dutch, I have not such information as will authorize an opinion which may deserve much reliance; yet in the *Code Noir* it is certain many provisions may be indicated, of a much more humane character than can be found in the codes of our slave-holding states, on kindred topics.

3. **From John F. Denny, *An Essay on the Political Grade of the Free Colored Population, Under the Constitution of the United States, and the Constitution of Pennsylvania, in Three Parts* (Chambersburg, PA: Printed by Hickok and Blood, 1836), 37, 57–58**

[Published in multiple editions beginning in 1834, John F. Denny's *Enquiry* argues that free black Americans are a threat to white society. He worries about the "intermixture of a black and servile caste" and calls free black people "an internal and irreclaimable enemy." Anticipating Chief Justice Roger Taney's majority opinion for the US Supreme Court in the Dred Scott case twenty years later (see Appendix B4), Denny insists, "it is by no means clear that" a black person "is recognized as a citizen by the Constitution of the United States."]

From their first introduction into this country, and until they spread over the whole continent, the negro race were reduced to slavery, by the white population, on account, not of their foreign nativity or descent, but of their *colour* and moral degradation; and as these traits of inferiority were in no degree diminished by their state of bondage, nothing short of *express legislation* could, at the establishment of the government, have so effectually vanquished the antipathy of the dominant race towards them, as to admit of their enjoying the political and civil privileges of the State. Indeed, the experience of the nation has proved that *legislation itself*, seconded as it has been by the arm of charity and benevolence, is inadequate to raise even the most eminent of the coloured ranks to a footing of equality with the whites.

...

The situation of the coloured race in the United States is deeply unfortunate, and addresses a thrilling appeal to the sympathies and kindness of their superiors [*sic*] in fortune, holding them in different degrees of subjection. But that situation, deplorable as it is, must, we are persuaded, ever continue to be, under the present government of these States, one of civil and political inferiority. Should the competent expounders of the laws chance to decide that the free negro is entitled to the privileges of citizenship, *cui bono*[1] the decision? the law of popular sentiment—always transcendent in a republic [*sic*]— would speedily reverse it in practice. The distinction of the two races is a *natural* one, converted by accidental causes to the prejudice of the black: *artificial* rules may disaffirm, but they can never obliterate it. We consider of no account supposed physical and moral differences that unfold themselves only to the vision of a sectional philosophy; but the *colour* of the African, although not debasing in itself, has become, by circumstances, irremediable at this day, here, a badge of servitude, and must forever, we believe, prevent any general amalgamation of the races. This is, indeed, a very important subject, wholly distinct from the one examined in the preceding pages, and not likely to be ever settled by abstract discussion. It pervades the cherished affections of the breast—entwines itself with our habits of life and education,—and, by the very force of its moral impression, irresistably [*sic*] sways the judgement. Indeed, we cannot reason upon it: no sooner is it broached than *feeling*, consecrated and quickened by the tenderest relations, usurps the power of decision and retains it indignant and unmoved.

So revolting is the idea of merging the distinction between the white and coloured population, in a *social union*, that even the ardent abolitionist deprecates it; yet the propriety of emancipating the slaves, and admitting them, when free, to *political* and *civil* rights, is earnestly insisted on.[2] We have no feeling towards the coloured class that is not blended with a lively sense of humanity and justice; but we have a strong conviction that if the constitution could be so amended as to admit of their advancement to the rights and privileges of the white community, the favour would, in due time, be followed by as close an intimacy between the two classes, as wealth, good morals, and education now produce between the different circles of society. We have already examples, sufficiently numerous, of low bred profligates forcing alliances with females who are the pride and ornament of the communities in which they move: These are among the evils incident to the structure of the best regulated social state. Still, however, the affianced parties are of the same race and colour, and their personal dishonor may be forgotten in the merit of their descendants. But when a union of the two races results from the limited intercourse already

---

1 Latin, "to whose profit?"; who benefits from this decision?

2 [Denny's note:] Jay's Inquiry, p. 148.

permitted between them by the custom of society, and the mark of disgrace becomes transmissible, what do we find in the walk or character of its innocent bearer to sooth the sorrow which the event occasioned, or represent the birth and standing of those whom the misfortune has overtaken? We regret to see such repulsive notions of equality espoused by discerning minds in this country. They may well be fitted to effect the purposes of foreign incendiaries, whose aim is to unsettle the principles of our social order; or to reign in the meridian of Hayti, where they are habitually realized among a mixed and licentious population; but they have nothing germane to the habitudes of the American people, either in thought, feeling, or action, and we trust, never can obtain a permanent foot-hold upon their soil. Judging from the present state of opinion in this country, there is but little ground for reasonable anxiety. It is not probable that the requisite number of States will ever concur in an amendment of the constitution that threatens the nation with such odious consequences; and such of the individual States as may choose to encounter the evil from motives of humanity or policy, will be apt to furnish an example sufficiently monitory to deter the remainder from its imitation.

4. **From Benjamin C. Howard, *A Report of the Decision of the Supreme Court of the United States, and the Opinions of the Judges thereof, in the Case of Dred Scott versus John F.A. Sandford. December Term, 1856* (New York: D. Appleton & Co., 1857), 403–10**

[*Dred Scott v. Sandford* was a landmark legal decision in which the US Supreme Court ruled that descendants of slaves had no claim to the rights and privileges of US citizenship. The plaintiff, Dred Scott (1795–1858), was born into slavery in Missouri but had lived with his master, John Sanford (1806–57),[1] for some years in the free state of Illinois. When they returned to Missouri, Scott sued for his freedom on the grounds that he and his family had become free by virtue of living in a state where slavery was prohibited by act of Congress. His master disagreed. The Court's opinion, written by Chief Justice Roger Taney (1777–1864), held that both legal precedent and common sense showed that black people were naturally and permanently subject to white rule, and that they were incapable of assuming the civic responsibilities of democracy. Scott, therefore, had no standing to bring such a case; his petition was denied and his case dismissed. Of

---

1   Due to a clerical error, Sanford's name was recorded as Sandford in official court records.

the nine justices on the Court, seven agreed with Taney. One of the
two dissenting justices, Benjamin Robbins Curtis (1809–74), resigned
as a result of the decision.]

The question is simply this: Can a negro, whose ancestors were
imported into this country, and sold as slaves, become a member of
the political community formed and brought into existence by the
Constitution of the United States, and as such become entitled to all
the rights, and privileges, and immunities, guarantied by that instrument to the citizen? One of which rights is the privilege of suing in a
court of the United States in the cases specified in the Constitution.

...

The words "people of the United States" and "citizens" are synony-
mous terms, and mean the same thing. They both describe the political body who, according to our republican institutions, form the sovereignty, and who hold the power and conduct the Government
through their representatives. They are what we familiarly call the
"sovereign people," and every citizen is one of this people, and a constituent member of this sovereignty. The question before us is, whether
the class of persons described in the plea in abatement compose a
portion of this people, and are constituent members of this sovereignty? We think they are not, and that they are not included, and were
not intended to be included, under the word "citizens" in the Constitution, and can therefore claim none of the rights and privileges which
that instrument provides for and secures to citizens of the United
States. On the contrary, they were at that time [i.e., during the draft-
ing of the Constitution] considered as a subordinate and inferior class
of beings, who had been subjugated by the dominant race, and,
whether emancipated or not, yet remained subject to their authority,
and had no rights or privileges but such as those who held the power
and the Government might choose to grant them.

...

[Black people] had for more than a century before [1776] been
regarded as beings of an inferior order, and altogether unfit to associate with the white race, either in social or political relations; and so far
inferior, that they had no rights which the white man was bound to
respect; and that the negro might justly and lawfully be reduced to
slavery for his benefit. He was bought and sold, and treated as an ordinary article of merchandise and traffic, whenever a profit could be

made by it. This opinion was at that time fixed and universal in the civilized portion of the white race. It was regarded as an axiom in morals as well as in politics, which no one thought of disputing, or supposed to be open to dispute; and men in every grade and position in society daily and habitually acted upon it in their private pursuits, as well as in matters of public concern, without doubting for a moment the correctness of this opinion.

...

[In colonial laws] ... a perpetual and impassable barrier was intended to be erected between the white race and the one which they had reduced to slavery, and governed as subjects with absolute and despotic power, and which they looked upon as so far below them in the scale of created beings, that intermarriages between white persons and negroes or mulattoes were regarded as unnatural and immoral, and punished as crimes, not only in the parties, but in the person who joined them in marriage. And no distinction in this respect was made between the free negro or mulatto and the slave, but this stigma, of the deepest degradation, was fixed upon the whole race.

...

The general words [of the opening of the Declaration of Independence, i.e.: "that all men are created equal"] would seem to embrace the whole human family, and if they were used in a similar instrument at this day would be so understood. But it is too clear for dispute, that the enslaved African race were not intended to be included, and formed no part of the people who framed and adopted this declaration; for if the language, as understood in that day, would embrace them, the conduct of the distinguished men who framed the Declaration of Independence would have been utterly and flagrantly inconsistent with the principles they asserted; and instead of the sympathy of mankind, to which they so confidently appealed, they would have deserved and received universal rebuke and reprobation.

Yet the men who framed this declaration were great men—high in literary acquirements—high in their sense of honor, and incapable of asserting principles inconsistent with those on which they were acting. They perfectly understood the meaning of the language they used, and how it would be understood by others; and they knew that it would not in any part of the civilized world be supposed to embrace the negro race, which, by common consent, had been excluded from civilized Governments and the family of nations, and doomed to slavery.

They spoke and acted according to the then established doctrines and principles, and in the ordinary language of the day, and no one misunderstood them. The unhappy black race were separated from the white by indelible marks, and laws long before established, and were never thought of or spoken of except as property....

5. From Frederick Douglass, *The Dred Scott Decision* (1857)

[A former slave and a popular writer and orator, Frederick Douglass (1818–95) was appalled, as many Americans were, by the outcome of *Dred Scott v. Sandford*. Although he was outraged, Douglass was also hopeful that the decision had finally laid bare for public scrutiny the moral and philosophical evils at the heart of slavery. "[M]y hopes were never brighter than now," wrote Douglass, further explaining that the "National Conscience" would not allow the Supreme Court's decision to stand for long. This selection is taken from the pamphlet *Two Speeches; One on West India Emancipation, Delivered at Canandaigua, Aug. 4th, and the Other on the Dred Scott Decision, Delivered in New York, on the Occasion of the Anniversary of the American Abolition Society, May, 1857* (Rochester, NY: C.P. Dewey, 1857).]

This infamous decision of the Slaveholding wing of the Supreme Court maintains that slaves are within the contemplation of the Constitution of the United States, property; that slaves are property in the same sense that horses, sheep, and swine are property; that the old doctrine that slavery is a creature of local law is false; that the right of the slaveholder to his slave does not depend upon the local law, but is secured wherever the Constitution of the United States extends; that Congress has no right to prohibit slavery anywhere; that slavery may go in safety anywhere under the star-spangled banner; that colored persons of African descent have no rights that white men are bound to respect; that colored men of African descent are not and cannot be citizens of the United States.

You will readily ask me how I am affected by this devilish decision—this judicial incarnation of wolfishness? My answer is, and no thanks to the slaveholding wing of the Supreme Court, my hopes were never brighter than now.

I have no fear that the National Conscience will be put to sleep by such an open, glaring, and scandalous tissue of lies as that decision is, and has been, over and over, shown to be.

The Supreme Court of the United States is not the only power in this world. It is very great, but the Supreme Court of the Almighty is greater. Judge Taney can do many things, but he cannot perform impossibilities. He cannot bale out the ocean, annihilate this firm old earth, or pluck the silvery star of liberty from our Northern sky. He may decide, and decide again; but he cannot reverse the decision of the Most High. He cannot change the essential nature of things—making evil good, and good, evil.

Happily for the whole human family, their rights have been defined, declared, and decided in a court higher than the Supreme Court. "There is a law," says Brougham,[1] "above all the enactments of human codes, and by that law, unchangeable and eternal, man cannot hold property in man."

Your fathers have said that man's right to liberty is self-evident. There is no need of argument to make it clear. The voices of nature, of conscience, of reason, and of revelation, proclaim it as the right of all rights, the foundation of all trust, and of all responsibility. Man was born with it. It was his before he comprehended it. The *deed* conveying it to him is written in the centre of his soul, and is recorded in Heaven. The sun in the sky is not more palpable to the sight than man's right to liberty is to the moral vision. To decide against this right in the person of Dred Scott, or the humblest and most whip-scarred bondman in the land, is to decide against God. It is an open rebellion against God's government. It is an attempt to undo what God [has] done, to blot out the broad distinction instituted by the *Allwise* between men and things, and to change the image and superscription of the everliving God into a speechless piece of merchandise.

Such a decision cannot stand. God will be true though every man be a liar. We can appeal from this hell-black judgment of the Supreme Court, to the court of common sense and common humanity. We can appeal from man to God. If there is no justice on earth, there is yet justice in heaven. You may close your Supreme Court against the black man's cry for justice, but you cannot, thank God, close against him the ear of a sympathising world, nor shut up the Court of Heaven. All that is merciful and just, on earth and in Heaven, will execrate and despise this edict of Taney.

---

1   See p. 39, note 1.

6. Edward Williams Clay, *Life in Philadelphia*, Plate IV (Philadelphia: S. Hart, 1829)

[Edward Williams Clay (1799–1857) was a Philadelphia artist and engraver famous for the creation of his *Life in Philadelphia* series of aquatint engravings (1828–30). Many of Clay's fourteen plates ridiculed Philadelphia's lower-class and black residents, reserving particular scorn for characters manifesting an interest in social mobility. The text of this plate reads, "'How you find yourself dis hot weader Miss Chloe?' / 'Pretty well I tank you Mr. Cesar only I / aspire too much!'"]

Courtesy American Antiquarian Society.

Appendix C: Black Philadelphia in the Antebellum Era

1. Map of Philadelphia (1848), from *Philadelphia Described to the Stranger and Citizen* (Philadelphia: Peter Thomson, 1848)

[This 1848 map of Philadelphia shows the city's districts. Many black families lived in Moyamensing and Southwark on the south side and Kensington and Spring Garden on the north side of the city.]

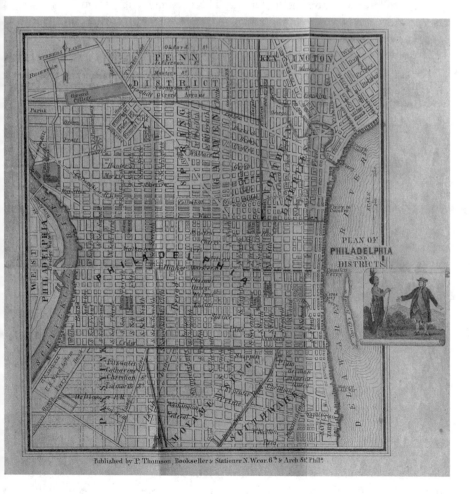

Courtesy American Antiquarian Society.

2. From *A Statistical Inquiry into the Condition of the People of Colour, of the City and Districts of Philadelphia* (Philadelphia: Kite and Walton, 1849), 5

[This volume records the results of a census of black Philadelphians undertaken by the Society of Friends in 1847. The table included here shows individuals listed by gender, age, and neighborhood.]

IT being thought desirable to obtain an accurate account of the number and condition of the coloured population of the city and districts of Philadelphia, means were taken in the autumn of 1847, and the following winter, to obtain it. Three competent persons were employed to take the enumeration, and to make inquiry into the occupations, means of livelihood, estates, and general condition of the people of colour. It is believed that the results which have been obtained are, in the main, to be depended upon; and they furnish information which will be found useful to those who take an interest in the welfare of this people. The following table exhibits the population as thus ascertained.

	Males.	Fem's.	Total.	under 5.	5 to 15.	15 to 50.	above 50.
City of Philadelphia	3772	5304	9076	1209	1642	5205	1020
per cent.	41.56	58.44	100.	13.3	18.1	57.3	11.3
Spring Garden	359	476	853	119	169	441	108
per cent.	42.09	57.91	100.	14.	19.8	51.7	12.5
N. Lib. and Kensington	608	677	1285	245	277	682	81
per cent.	47.31	52.69	100.	19.	21.6	53.1	6.3
Southwark	512	605	1117	198	230	579	110
per cent.	45.83	54.17	100.	17.8	20.6	52.	9.7
Moyamensing	1491	1900	3391	523	649	1975	244
per cent.	44.	56.	100.	15.4	19.1	58.2	7.2
West Philadelphia	154	184	338	76	86	153	23
per cent.	45.56	54.44	100.	22.5	25.4	45.2	6.8
Total	6896	9146	16042	2370	3033	9035	1586
per cent.	42.99	57.01	100.	14.7	18.9	56.3	9.9

3. From Robert Purvis, *Appeal of Forty Thousand Citizens, Threatened with Disenfranchisement, to the People of Pennsylvania* (Philadelphia: Merrihew and Gunn, 1838), 1–4

[Robert Purvis's *Appeal of Forty Thousand Citizens* argues against the passage of a law in Pennsylvania repealing black male suffrage. Pennsylvania had permitted black men to vote for decades, but in the 1830s, afraid of growing unrest in southern slave states, some state legislators wanted to limit black political rights. They were successful in passing the law; black men did not gain the right to vote again in Pennsylvania until the US ratified the Fifteenth Amendment in 1870. Purvis (1810–98) was one of the wealthiest black Philadelphians. He was born in Charleston, South Carolina, to a free mixed-race mother and a white English father. Upon his father's death in 1826, Purvis and his brothers inherited a considerable income. As an adult, Purvis chose to identify with the black community of Philadelphia. He married Harriet Davy Forten (1810–75), an activist and writer, and daughter of wealthy Philadelphia businessman James Forten (1766–1842). Together they worked tirelessly on abolitionist, anti-segregation, and suffrage causes.]

FELLOW CITIZENS:—We appeal to you from the decision of the "Reform Convention," which has stripped us of a right peaceably enjoyed during forty-seven years under the Constitution of this commonwealth. We honor Pennsylvania and her noble institutions too much to part with our birthright, as her free citizens, without a struggle. To all her citizens the right of suffrage is valuable in proportion as she is free; but surely there are none who can so ill afford to spare it as ourselves.

Was it the intention of the people of this commonwealth that the Convention to which the Constitution was committed for revision and amendment, should tear up and cast away its first principles? Was it made the business of the Convention to deny "that all men are born equally free," by making political rights depend upon the skin in which a man is born? Or to divide what our fathers bled to unite, to wit, TAXATION and REPRESENTATION? We will not allow ourselves for one moment to suppose that the majority of the people of Pennsylvania are not too respectful of the rights and too liberal towards the feelings of others, as well as too much enlightened to their own interests, to deprive of the right of suffrage a single individual who may safely be trusted with it. And we cannot believe that you have found among those who bear the burdens of taxation any who have proved, by their abuse of the right, that it is not safe in their hands. This is a question, fellow citizens, in which we plead *your* cause as well as our own. It is the safeguard of the strongest that he lives under a government which is obliged to respect the voice of the weakest. When you have taken from an individual his right to vote, you have made the government, in regard to him, a mere despotism to all.—To your women and children, their inability to vote at the polls may be no evil, because they are united by consanguinity and affection with those who can do it. To foreigners and paupers the want of the right may be tolerable, because a little time or labor will make it theirs. They are candidates for the privilege, and hence substantially enjoy its benefits. But when a distinct class of the community, already sufficiently the objects of prejudice, are wholly, and for ever, disenfranchised and excluded, to the remotest posterity, from the possibility of a voice in regard to the laws under which they are to live—it is the same thing as if their abode were transferred to the dominions of the Russian Autocrat, or of the Grand Turk. They have lost their check upon oppression, their wherewith to buy friends, their panoply of manhood; in short, they are thrown upon the mercy of a despotic majority. Like every other despot, this despot majority, will believe in the mildness of its own sway; but who will the more willingly submit to it for that?

To us our right under the Constitution has been more precious, and our deprivation of it will be the more grievous, because our expatriation has come to be a darling project with many of our fellow citizens. Our abhorrence of a scheme which comes to us in the guise of Christian benevolence, and asks us to suffer ourselves to be transplanted to a distant and barbarous land, *because we are a "nuisance" in this*, is not more deep and thorough than it is reasonable. We love our native country, much as it has wronged us; and in the peaceable exercise of our inalienable rights, we will cling to it. The immortal Franklin, and his fellow laborers in the cause of humanity, have bound us to our homes here with chains of gratitude. We are PENNSYLVANIANS, and we hope to see the day when Pennsylvania will have reason to be proud of us, as we believe she has now none to be ashamed. Will you starve our patriotism? Will you cast our hearts out of the treasury of the commonwealth? Do you count our enmity better than our friendship?

4. From Joseph Willson, *Sketches of the Higher Classes of Colored Society in Philadelphia. By a Southerner* (Philadelphia: Merrihew and Thompson, 1841), 13–20

[Joseph Willson (1817–95) was a black southerner who moved to Philadelphia in 1833. His *Sketches of the Higher Classes of Colored Society in Philadelphia* describes the economic stratification among black Philadelphians and advises his wealthy black readers about how they should use their status to help the city's black working class. Contrary to many contemporary accounts of northern black life that flattened community dynamics in the interest of expressing racial solidarity, Willson depicted a complex society of people with a diverse set of skills and experiences. Reprinted as *The Elite of Our People: Joseph Willson's Sketches of the Black Upper-Class Life in Antebellum Philadelphia* (University Park: Pennsylvania State UP, 2000).]

The prejudiced reader, I feel well assured, will smile at the designation "higher classes of colored society." The public—or at least the great body, who have not been at the pains to make an examination—have long been accustomed to regard the people of color as one consolidated mass, all huddled together, without any particular or general distinctions, social or otherwise. The sight of one colored man with them, whatever may be his apparent condition, (provided it is any thing but genteel!) is the sight of a community; and the errors and crimes of one is [*sic*] adjudged as the criterion of character of the whole body. But the first of these considerations is far from being correct; the latter, too openly palpable to command a moment's attention. Compared in condition, means, and abilities, there are as broad social distinctions to be found here, as among any other class of society; aye, and, it may be added with as much justice, too;—for what are all human distinctions worth, founded otherwise than in virtue? True, it is readily admitted, they have not, to any great extent, the customary grounds which have always obtained, for marking their lines of separation with distinctness; but this is the fault of circumstances—the offspring of existencies [*sic*] which they had no agency in producing— and which they have never been able to surmount.

Taking the whole body of the colored population in the city of Philadelphia, they present in a gradual, moderate, and limited ration, almost every grade of character, wealth, and—I think it not too much to add—of education. They are to be seen in ease, comfort and the enjoyment of all the social blessings of this life; and, in contrast with this, they are to be found in the lowest depths of human degradation, misery, and want. They are also presented in the intermediate stages— sober, honest, industrious and respectable—claiming neither "poverty nor riches," yet maintaining by their pursuits, their families in comparative ease and comfort, oppressed neither with the cares of the rich, nor assailed by the deprivation and suffering of the indigent. The same in these respects that may be said of any other class of people, may, with the utmost regard to truth, be said of them.

They have their churches, school-houses, institutions of benevolence, and others for the promotion of literature; and if I cannot include scientific pursuits, it is because the avenues leading to and upholding these, have been closed against them. There are likewise among them, those who are successfully pursuing various branches of the mechanic arts; tradesmen and dealers of various descriptions, artists, clergymen, and other professional gentleman; and, last of all, though not the least, men of fortune and gentlemen of leisure.

Their churches embrace nearly all the Christian denominations, excepting the papal, and those which may be considered *doubtful*, as I am not aware that there is any Universalists'[1] society among them. Whether this arises from a determination to keep on the sure side here, and enjoy the benefit of others' doubts, if realized, hereafter, it has never occurred to me, till now, to inquire! The Methodists are by far the most numerous, and next to these, in numerical order, may be named the Presbyterians, Baptists and Episcopalians. There is in existence, I believe, a Unitarian society; but their house of worship, for the want of competent support, has, for some time past, been relinquished.

Mutual Relief Societies[2] are numerous. There are a larger number of these than of any other description, in the colored community. They are generally well sustained, to the great advantage of those who compose them. There are also one or more others, strictly devoted to objects of outdoors benevolence. The last mentioned are chiefly composed of females.

I pass by here the several literary associations, proposing to make them a distinct subject in another place.

In addition to the public, or common schools supported by the commonwealth—for the continuance, and prosperity of which, much interest and solicitude has of late been manifested—there are also three or four private schools, male and female, conducted by colored teachers. The great facilities afforded by the first mentioned of these, has had the effect greatly to decrease the numbers in the private schools; nevertheless, the latter class still present a favorable condition—particularly the female—from the superior excellence of their government, and attention to the general deportment of the pupils.

In addition to this brief random glance at some of the more prominent features which distinguish colored society at large, the annexed statistical account is added for the convenience of those who desire accuracy on the subject. It is gleaned from a statement "showing the progress and present state of the colored population," compiled by the "Board of Managers of the American Moral Reform Society," and published in their first annual report, which latter was kindly furnished me, by the chairman of said Board, Mr. John P. Burr. Though

---

1 I.e., Christian Universalist.
2 Charitable organizations.

the statement referred to, bears [a] date as far back as 1837, yet it is presumable that no very remarkable changes, in most instances, have occurred since then; and as there has been no later enumeration in this wise, it is adopted, leaving the reader to form his own judgment in regard to more recent advancements.

For the City and County of Philadelphia, is given as the

Number of Churches	15
" Clergymen	34
" Day-schools	21
" Teachers	6
" Sabbath schools	17
" S. School Teachers	125
" Literary Societies	3*
" Debating [Societies]	3
" Mutual Relief or Benevolent [Societies]	64
" Moral Reform [Societies]	1
" Temperance [Societies]	4
" Lyceums[1]	1+

* There has been some change in the character of one of these.[2]
+ Since formed.

In the same tabular view, the number of mechanics for this city, are set down at 78; and real estate owned, and taxes, rents, &c., paid, at $850,000. In what manner this eight hundred and fifty thousand dollars is proportioned among the population, rising nineteen thousand inhabitants, it is difficult to determine; although it appears to be undoubtedly true, that but a small number are actual free-holders, when compared with the whole body.

5. Letter from Harriet Beecher Stowe to Lady Hatherton, 24 May 1856 (Harriet Beecher Stowe Papers, Clifton Waller Barrett Library of American Literature, Albert and Shirley Small Special Collections Library, University of Virginia)

[In this letter, Harriet Beecher Stowe introduces Frank and Mary Webb to Margaret Percy, Lady Hatherton (c. 1825–97), a British abolitionist. The Webbs toured the UK in 1856–57, with Mary giving dramatic readings in halls and parlors from London to Glasgow. These

---

1 Lecture organizations.
2 I.e., a change in the membership or pursuits of one of Philadelphia's black literary societies. See McHenry for more on these organizations.

performances often included a rendition of *The Christian Slave*, a dramatic version of *Uncle Tom's Cabin* that Stowe adapted for Mary in 1855.]

Boston May 24 '56
    Lady Hatherton

Dear Madam

This will introduce to all my friends, Mr. & Mrs. Webb, in whose success in your country I am greatly interested.

Mrs. Webb is the daughter of a fugitive slave who secured her liberty by heroic effort before her birth. She was born in New Bedford, New England, and was subsequently sent to Cuba, where she passed the earlier years of her life in a convent. Having been endowed with an extraordinary genius for education she was induced to try the profession of a dramatic Reader and her success in this line is attested by hundreds of notices written by some of the most competent critics in this country. Her success has been so great that even Pro-Slavery Lyceums have broken through the prejudices of colour so far as to solicit her assistance in their courses. The season for readings having terminated in this country, she is induced to try success in England. Her reading of Uncle Tom's Cabin—which I dramatized expressly for her—has been pronounced unequaled.

Mr. Webb also is a gentleman of talent and cultivation, and any assistance in kindness you may render them will be well bestowed as her success will benefit the Antislavery Cause by showing the talent which lies concealed in the race which she represents. And I take the greatest interest in their success both from personal friendship and for this reason. I feel the deepest interest in her success.

Every new development of a talent or a prowess in this much depressed people is a new argument for us & helps the struggle in the right direction.

From my knowledge of your interest in every good work I feel a confidence that you will if possible extend your patronage to these people, and I am sure that you cannot but be both surprised and gratified should you hear her.

Very truly yours,
H.B. Stowe

Mr. Longfellow[1] has been much pleased with Mrs. Webb's reading of his new poem — Hiawatha.

---

1 Henry Wadsworth Longfellow (1807–82), American poet.

Appendix D: Racism in Philadelphia

1. From "The Philadelphia Riots," the *Philadelphia U. S. Gazette* (2 August 1842); reprinted in *The Liberator* 12.32 (12 August 1842): 126

[Accounts of the riots in Philadelphia in the 1830s and 1840s filled local and national newspapers. These stories were of particular interest to black Americans and abolitionists, many of whom were the direct targets of this violence. The account below describes the disruption of a peaceful public assembly and the murderous crowd actions that followed—a pattern of escalating violence all too common in the antebellum city.]

THE PHILADELPHIA RIOTS.

From the Philadelphia U. S. Gazette of Aug. 2.

Riot and Bloodshed.

Yesterday morning there were arrangements for a procession by the colored people attached to an association called the "Moyamensing Temperance Society."

In Shippen, between Fifth and Sixth streets, a disturbance arose, how caused we could not ascertain, but understood that it was the result of some interference with the procession by boys or lads. This led to further violence, and a disturbance was caused, which called for the interference of the police. Several arrests were made, and the violators of the peace were conveyed to the Mayor's office. The Mayor proceeded at once to increase his establishment, by swearing a large number of police men, and sending them, with proper badges, to the place of disturbance. Meantime the rioters were assaulting the houses of the blacks in the vicinity of Lombard street, between Fifth and Eighth, where are numerous small alleys and courts, and in which a vast number of colored people reside. Their windows were beaten in, doors knocked to pieces, and other injuries committed.

About half-past four o'clock, one or two blacks rushed from a small house in a place called Bradford's alley, a court extending west from Seventh street, parallel with, and north of, St. Mary's street, and discharged a gun at a crowd of boys. One was so severely injured, that it was stated that he was dead. Another we saw, with his leg considerably injured.

This act brought a considerable number of persons together, and a rush was made upon the house into which the blacks retreated. One charged with being concerned in the act, was seized and dragged out, and a violent blow given him, which cut open his head. Colonel McCahen seized hold of the wretched man, and with the aid of one or two other persons, bore him off from his assailants.

Another of the number was, we understand, beaten so that his recovery is doubtful.

The third fled into the upper room of the house, where he was beset by a number of men, who broke open the windows, and split down one or two doors. The black attempted to escape by the roof, but no sooner did he show his head above the scuttle,[1] than he was pelted with brickbats.[2] Meantime several persons attempted to save him from the vengeance of the persons who were pursuing him so hotly. Fortunately, Mr. Herman Yerkes, one of the city police, arrived, and though informed that the man was armed, proceeded into the chamber and took him. In bringing him into the court, a man struck him with a large piece of board, and others attempted a rescue. Yerkes held on to the man, and ordered that his assailant should be arrested. Another person took the other side of the man, and they proceeded towards Seventh-street. Here the crowd was perfectly dense, and seemed determined to take vengeance on the black. Yerkes pushed forward, though certainly suffering very much, as he could scarcely fail of receiving a portion of the blows intended for the prisoner; and his able assistant must also have shared in the evils.

They crossed Washington square; but the mob headed them at the north-east gate, and beat the black most awfully. Thousands and thousands were assembled. How many were participant with crimes, we could not tell. Assistance was procured, and the man was taken to the police office; but so shockingly beaten, we should think that he could scarcely survive. The state of excitement is fearful in the lower part of the city. But the acts of violence to which we have referred, are all that we had heard of at 5 o'clock, P. M.

The names of those arrested and committed up to six o'clock last evening, are Jacob Keyser, held to $2000 bail for a further hearing, and committed for want of it. Edward Kerrick, $2000 bail; committed. Samuel Montgomery, Samuel Luskey, and Joseph Hamilton, each $1000 bail; committed. Francis P. Henry, Edward Stuart, and Eliza Stewart; committed. Henry Johnson, $2500 bail, and John Johnson, $4000 bail, both committed.

---

1 A metal container used to store coal.

2 Pieces of brick used as weapons.

About six o'clock, a colored boy and man, the first named Henry Van Brancle, and the latter, Anthony Harvey, were brought in. They were the negroes mentioned above, taken in Bradford's alley. A brass pistol, with a barrel from six to eight inches long, was found in the possession of the boy. It was heavily loaded and capped.

One colored man, called George, was brought to the police office with a terrible swelling on the forehead, and his head fractured above his forehead, so much so as to endanger his life. He was likewise severely beaten on the body.

Another negro, named Fullman, was brought into the police office with his eye horribly cut, from a blow which he had received in the melee.

Both this man and the one named George received their injuries while endeavoring to protect some of their comrades.

At a quarter past six o'clock, an attack was made on two houses on Lombard between Seventh and Eighth-streets. In one there were no inmates, but the windows and furniture were destroyed. In the other there were several persons, old and young, who were driven out and unmercifully beaten by those in front. The active participators in both cases obtained entrance by the rear.

Great numbers of colored people crowded the ferry boats during the latter part of the day, seeking safety on the other side of the Delaware.

After the above was written, the work of destruction commenced. At a late hour last evening, we understand that upwards of twenty rioters had been arrested and brought before the Mayor.

We know not how to express our feelings at this outrage, this destruction of life, this waste of property, this outrage upon the city's propriety.

We trust, that as some of the rioters can be identified, that the utmost severity of the law will be administered to them.

2. From *History of Pennsylvania Hall, Which Was Destroyed by a Mob, on the 17th of May, 1838* (Philadelphia: Merrihew and Gunn, 1838), 137

[Pennsylvania Hall was dedicated on 14 May 1838 and burned to the ground three days later in an anti-abolitionist attack. Likely compiled by Quaker activist Samuel Webb, *History of Pennsylvania Hall* collates speeches and letters that illustrate the building's brief use as a space to discuss radical causes—including abolition and women's suffrage—as well as its destruction.]

The first indications of a disorderly spirit manifested in or about the building, were on the evening of the First day of the Dedication, during an address on Temperance; a pane of glass was broken by a stone or other missile being thrown against one of the windows. On the morning of the 16th,—the time specified in the placards,—there were seen from twenty to fifty persons prowling about the doors, examining the gas-pipes, and talking in an "incendiary" manner to groups which they collected around them in the street. Some of them ventured to hiss during the discussion that morning, showing that the spirit of misrule was becoming more rampant. These incendiaries, or recruits from the party, continued to hang about the Hall throughout the day, at times crowding into the Anti-Slavery Office, and creating an excitement by their violent and abusive language.

The evening meeting of this day was the one addressed by William Lloyd Garrison,[1] Angelina E.G. Weld,[2] and others,—the audience numbering more than three thousand persons. In the account of the proceedings of that meeting, we have already stated that there was great disturbance. Many of the windows were broken and the congregation were annoyed by the constant yelling and hooting of the mob.

---

1   White American abolitionist author, orator, and reformer (1805–79) most famous as the founder and editor of the antislavery newspaper *The Liberator*.

2   White American abolitionist, suffragist, and social reformer (1805–79). She was born to a wealthy, slave-holding family in Charleston, South Carolina, and moved north to Philadelphia because of her antislavery beliefs.

3. John Sartain, *The Burning of Pennsylvania Hall.* **From** *History of Pennsylvania Hall, Which Was Destroyed by a Mob, on the 17th of May, 1838* **(Philadelphia: Merrihew and Gunn, 1838)**

[Included in the *History of Pennsylvania Hall* (1838), the official publication sponsored by the Hall's association of supporters, this mezzotint shows the burning of the building after an attack by an anti-abolitionist mob. Sartain sketched the image while witnessing the building's destruction. It was widely reproduced and circulated in abolitionist circles, not only as a mezzotint, but also as a steel engraving. Courtesy American Antiquarian Society.]

Works Cited and Select Bibliography

Bell, Bernard W. *The Afro-American Novel and Its Tradition*. Amherst: U of Massachusetts P, 1987.

Borgstrom, Michael. *Minority Reports: Identity and Social Knowledge in Nineteenth-Century American Literature*. New York: Palgrave Macmillan, 2010.

Bruce, Dickson D., Jr. *The Origins of African American Literature, 1680–1865*. Charlottesville: UP of Virginia, 2001.

Chakkalakal, Tess. *Novel Bondage: Slavery, Marriage, and Freedom in Nineteenth-Century America*. Champaign: U of Illinois P, 2011.

Clark, Susan F. "Solo Black Performance before the Civil War: Mrs. Stowe, Mrs. Webb, and *The Christian Slave*." *New Theater Quarterly* 13.52 (1997): 339–48.

Claybaugh, Amanda. *The Novel of Purpose: Literature and Social Reform in the Anglo-American World*. Ithaca, NY: Cornell UP, 2006.

Clymer, Jeffory A. *Family Money: Property, Race, and Literature in the Nineteenth Century*. New York: Oxford UP, 2012.

Crockett, Rosemary F. "Frank J. Webb: The Shift to Color Discrimination." *The Black Columbiad: Defining Moments in African American Literature and Culture*. Ed. Werner Sollors and Maria Diedrich. Cambridge, MA: Harvard UP, 1994. 112–22.

———. *"The Garies and Their Friends*: A Study of Frank J. Webb and His Novel." PhD diss., Harvard University, 1998.

Davis, Arthur P. *"The Garies and Their Friends*: A Neglected Pioneer Novel." *CLA Journal* 13.1 (1969): 27–34.

DeVries, James H. "The Tradition of the Sentimental Novel in *The Garies and Their Friends*." *CLA Journal* 17.2 (1973): 241–49.

Duane, Anna Mae. "Remaking Black Motherhood in Frank J. Webb's *The Garies and Their Friends*." *African American Review* 38.2 (2004): 201–12.

duCille, Ann. *The Coupling Convention: Sex, Text, and Tradition in Black Women's Fiction*. New York: Oxford UP, 1993.

Engle, Anna. "Depictions of the Irish in Frank Webb's *The Garies and Their Friends* and Frances E.W. Harper's *Trial and Triumph*." *MELUS* 26.1 (2001): 151–71.

Ernest, John. "Still Life, with Bones: A Response to Samuel Otter." *American Literary History* 20.4 (2008): 753–65.

Farmer, John S., and W.E. Henley. *Slang and Its Analogues Past and Present*. 7 vols. London: Harrison and Sons, 1896.

Gardner, Eric. "Frank J. Webb." *American National Biography (Supplement 2)*. Ed. Mark C. Carnes. New York: Oxford UP, 2005. 588–89.

——. "'A Gentleman of Superior Cultivation and Refinement': Recovering the Biography of Frank J. Webb." *African American Review* 35 (2001): 297–308.

——. "'A Nobler End': Mary Webb and the Victorian Platform." *Nineteenth-Century Prose* 29.1 (2002): 103–16.

Goldenberg, David. *The Curse of Ham: Race and Slavery in Early Judaism, Christianity, and Islam*. Princeton, NJ: Princeton UP, 2005.

Golemba, Henry. "*The Garies and Their Friends* Contextualized within African American Slave Narratives." *Lives Out of Letters: Essays on American Literary Biography and Documentation, in Honor of Robert N. Hudspeth*. Ed. Robert D. Habich. Teaneck, NJ: Fairleigh Dickinson UP, 2004. 114–42.

Greenberg, Kenneth S. "The Nose, the Lie, and the Duel in the Antebellum South." *American Historical Review* 95.1 (February 1990): 57–74.

Jackson, Blyden. *A History of Afro-American Literature*. Baton Rouge: Louisiana State UP, 1989.

Kinney, James. *Amalgamation! Race, Sex, and Rhetoric in the Nineteenth-Century American Novel*. Westport, CT: Greenwood, 1985.

Knadler, Stephen. "Traumatized Racial Performativity: Passing in Nineteenth-Century African-American Testimonies." *Cultural Critique* 55 (2003): 63–100.

Kohl, Natasha. "Frank Webb's *The Garies and Their Friends* and the Struggle over Black Education in the Antebellum North." *MELUS* 38.4 (2013): 76–102.

Korobkin, Laura. "Avoiding 'Aunt Tomasina': Charles Dickens Responds to Black American Reader Mary Webb." *English Literary History* 82.1 (2015): 115–40.

Lang, Amy Schrager. *The Syntax of Class: Writing Inequality in Nineteenth-Century America*. Princeton, NJ: Princeton UP, 2003.

Lapsansky, Emma Jones. "Friends, Wives, and Strivings: Networks and Community Values among Nineteenth-Century Philadelphia Afroamerican Elites." *Pennsylvania Magazine of History and Biography* 108.1 (1984): 3–24.

Lapsansky, Philip S. "Afro-Americana: Frank J. Webb and His Friends." *The Annual Report of the Library Company of Philadelphia for the Year 1990*. Philadelphia: Library Company of Philadelphia, 1990: 27–38.

Lemire, Elise. *"Miscegenation": Making Race in America*. Philadelphia: U of Pennsylvania P, 2002.

Levine, Robert S. "Disturbing Boundaries: Temperance, Black Elevation, and Violence in Frank J. Webb's *The Garies and Their
Friends.*" *Prospects* 19 (1994): 349–74.

Maillard, Mary. "'Faithfully Drawn from Real Life': Autobiographi-
cal Elements in Frank J. Webb's *The Garies and Their Friends.*" *The
Pennsylvania Magazine of History and Biography* 137.3 (2013):
261–300.

McHenry, Elizabeth. *Forgotten Readers: Recovering the Lost History
of African American Literary Societies.* Durham, NC: Duke UP,
2002.

Nash, Gary. *Forging Freedom: The Formation of Philadelphia's Black
Community, 1720–1840.* Cambridge, MA: Harvard UP, 1991.

Nowatzki, Robert. "Blurring the Color Line: Black Freedom,
Passing, Abolitionism, and Irish Ethnicity in Frank J. Webb's *The
Garies and Their Friends.*" *Studies in American Fiction* 33.1 (2005):
29–58.

Nyong'o, Tavia. *The Amalgamation Waltz: Race, Performance, and the
Ruses of Memory.* Minneapolis: U of Minnesota P, 2009.

Otter, Samuel. *Philadelphia Stories: America's Literature of Race and
Freedom.* New York: Oxford UP, 2010.

Peterson, Carla L. "Capitalism, Black (Under)development, and the
Production of the African-American Novel in the 1850s." *Postcolo-
nial Theory and the United States: Race, Ethnicity, and Literature.* Ed.
Amritjit Singh and Peter Schmidt. Oxford: U of Mississippi P,
2000. 176–95.

Rael, Patrick. *Black Identity and Black Protest in the Antebellum North.*
Chapel Hill: U of North Carolina P, 2002.

Reid-Pharr, Robert. *Conjugal Union: The Body, the House, and the
Black American.* New York: Oxford UP, 1999.

——. Introduction. *The Garies and Their Friends.* By Frank J. Webb.
1857. Baltimore: Johns Hopkins UP, 1997. vii–xviii.

Sollors, Werner. *Neither Black nor White yet Both: Thematic Explo-
rations of Interracial Literature.* New York: Oxford UP, 1997.

Stockton, Elizabeth. "The Property of Blackness: The Legal Fiction
of Frank J. Webb's *The Garies and Their Friends.*" *African American
Review* 43.2–3 (2009): 473–86.

Webb, Frank J. "Biographical Sketch." *The Christian Slave: A Drama,
Founded on a Portion of Uncle Tom's Cabin. Dramatized by Harriet
Beecher Stowe, expressly for the Readings of Mrs. Mary E. Webb.
Arranged, with a short biographical sketch of the reader, by F.J. Webb.*
London: Sampson, Low, Son, and Co., 1856.

——. *Fiction, Essays, and Poetry.* Ed. Werner Sollors. New Milford,
CT: Toby P, 2004.

———. *The Garies and Their Friends*. Introduction by Arthur P. Davis. New York: Arno P, 1969.

———. *The Garies and Their Friends*. Introduction by Robert Reid-Pharr. Baltimore: Johns Hopkins UP, 1997.

Whiting, Bartlett Jere. *Early American Proverbs and Proverbial Phrases*. Cambridge, MA: Belknap P of Harvard UP, 1977.

Winch, Julie. *A Gentleman of Color: The Life of James Forten*. New York: Oxford UP, 2002.

———. Introduction to *The Elite of Our People: Joseph Willson's Sketches of Black Upper-Class Life in Antebellum Philadelphia*. Ed. Julie Winch. University Park: Pennsylvania State UP, 2000. 1–73.

———. *Philadelphia's Black Elite: Activism, Accommodation, and the Struggle for Autonomy, 1787–1848*. Philadelphia: Temple UP, 1988.